# Starline

## Warriors of the Elector Book 1

### Featuring bonus novella

# The Star of Ishtar

ISBN Print - 978-0-9954182-0-2

# Contents

# Acknowledgements

As an author, it's always difficult to know where to begin thanking those involved in the production of any book. However, it is only with the assistance of others that any author can complete a book, let alone a series. I'm no different. Without all those who were there, this series would remain in my mind only.

Thank you also to my wonderful team of Sassie who ensured that the internal contents were perfect and Willsin who listened when I said no I don't like that photo. Without his forebearance, the cover wouldn't be perfect.

Thank you to JL who read the original manuscript and Tracey the worlds most super Beta Reader!

My family who have learned that when I say I'm writing mostly know to keep out of the way - yes and Super Pup, Cocoa Bean and Galilee too.

Lastly, to you, my readers. I wouldn't have this many titles without you being there to enjoy them. Thank you!

Imogene

# STARLINE

# Prologue

**D**uvall McCord stepped out of line as the parade was dismissed, inwardly wincing as his new boots rubbed his feet and his new uniform scratched his neck. He looked at his family, considering and measuring. He'd worked hard to attain the grades needed to be able to enter the academy, but it was all he'd ever wanted and dreamed of. To travel the stars and eventually captain his own ship. Now there he was on the cusp. Even as a fosterling, his room had been decorated with the ships he one day wanted to command, and at the age of twenty-three he was finally on the way.

His father, Captain Gentry, who had given up the chance of a plum command to keep his family happy, was always in the back of his mind. He now captained inter-galaxy runs for the Admiralty. He'd even given up his Star Destroyer for his wife's peace of mind. Duvall promised himself he'd never do that.

He belonged somewhere out there, among the biggest, the boldest, and the best.

His little sister, Meredith, bounced up and down, squeaking excitedly, and his parents smiled. He felt their genuine fondness for him, their foster son. They were proud of his many achievements, and if there were doubts in their minds, they were never spoken of.

Duvall was driven, almost obsessive in his desire to become the best of the best. That was why, now at the end of his time in the academy, he had been nominated as Best of his Class. The Top Graduate. The one his peers looked up to. The question had been asked and answered: was he good enough? His answer was always an unequivocal "yes." His family, peers, and instructors saw the drive and accepted it for what it was—an integral part of who he was.

His mentor, Captain Gustav Elphin, had requested that he serve aboard the Star of Ishtar, and had taken a great personal interest in this cadet.

It was acknowledged he would be on the fast-track to the stars. And, as Elphin told him again and again, emotional entanglements grounded a man; a piece of advice Duvall took seriously, so he had been careful in his social encounters. Always keeping a light touch with his lovers. Love 'em and leave 'em was his motto. He refused to let anything get in the way of his achievements and the desire to captain his own ship.

If privately his parents had any doubts about his lack of emotional ties to the women he was seen with, they kept them to themselves. No doubt they believed that one day a woman would change his mind and the attitude he had worked so hard to foster. For now, he accepted their belief that he knew what he wanted and had the drive to achieve it.

War was finally over and there was time to settle down. Long days of peace stretched out before them. The uneasy truce between the Earth Empire and the Ru'Edan, while new and tenuous, meant that there were opportunities diplomatically for the right kind of man and woman.

The rogue Admiral of the Ru'Edan Empire, Crick Sur Banden, might still be on the loose, but there was a belief that soon he would be brought to ground and that a true peace might be the outcome. Well, that was the opinion of the hopeful in the Empire anyway. The Empire held its collective breath as the newest graduates of the Earth Empire Academy marched out. They hoped to reap the benefits of those who came before.

Crick Sur Banden, crouched low, on the balls of his feet, hoping that once he got into the craft, he could escape to Sienna V, where a base had been set up during the struggle. The cold, miserable planet on the edges of the Ru'Edan Empire was far enough away that it was rarely considered a haven for anyone. His lips curled with derision for the current ruling Senate. Oh, they may think that calling a cease-fire would allow them to rest and recover, but he knew that this struggle could not end so swiftly. Not at all, if he had anything to say about it.

He darted through the open doorway as soon as the corridor cleared. During the celebrations, he'd arranged for his most trusted supporters to prepare the shuttle. Freedom was in sight, and not looking back, he lunged in. The door shut behind him, and making his way swiftly to the bridge, he bellowed, "Ascend now!"

In the chaos of celebrations only one controller was on duty in the Space Control Center, and he didn't even notice one small shuttle make its way out of the atmosphere until it was too late. Abruptly, the craft disappeared from view.

# Chapter 1

**M**aybe it's time for a romantic interlude between George and Eliza, Mellissa mused as she headed to the door of her little bookstore, where she sold both new and used books.

The day had been long and the weather continued steamy so she'd kept an eye on the door, ensuring the air-conditioner worked optimally. Mellissa pushed her hair out of her eyes and stretched slightly left and right to relieve the kink in her sides from hauling titles in and out of the shop. Her left hand raised in farewell to her assistant, Jemma, who was heading out for a hot date.

"Have a good night," she called out as Jem swaggered out the door, wriggling her bum in the skin-tight jeans she'd just about poured on, teamed with a glittery top that worked really well with the black hair that swung across her back.

Mellissa watched her totter and wiggle around the corner in the stilettos that made her look much taller and older than she really was, and she sighed. Jemma was looking for a connection so hard that Mellissa worried she'd never find a man who accepted her for herself.

She shrugged. "Not much I can do about that right now." She closed the door with a jingle of the bell and snapped the lock shut. Summer hadn't waned yet and she felt as limp as lettuce. She snorted to herself silently. "Oh Mel, that's really poetic."

She continued shutting the shop down for the weekend, watching as the blind dropped over the door with a clunk. That would ensure her privacy, she thought as she headed toward the back and the cooler office she loved.

A quick stop in the small staff bathroom—little more than a glorified toilet with space for changing and a shower—

and she was ready to work. A glance in the mirror showed a moderately passable female, with a trim figure, hazel eyes, and mousy brown hair against white skin.

She grimaced at her wide mouth, wishing as always for cupid's bow lips like Jem's. Mellissa had always found it hard to be thankful for what she had. She'd been called nondescript by some, but accepted that her brains and work ethic would get her forward in life, so she had worked religiously since she was sixteen. She'd told herself time and again that wasting time outside, running and athletics weren't her strong point.

Whatever DNA inhabited her system it must be okay, because even though she didn't actively exercise, she didn't seem to run to fat, just lacked the toned appeal of other women. Not that she was unhealthy, far from it, but she had other fish to fry and a future to build.

"Where the hell did those pitying thoughts come from, Mel? Hmm. I think a session of George and Eliza will do me wonders."

Glancing at her white linen camisole top and black pants, she grimaced. The outfit wasn't exactly high fashion, and after a full day, not as fresh as it could be, but she too had a date.

She pushed the bag of Jem's discarded clothes to one side. "Well, you obviously had other plans for tonight." She just hoped Jemma remembered to be safe. Given that she'd chosen to leave her work clothes behind, it was obvious Jemma wasn't intending to go home tonight, otherwise she would have stashed them in her backpack and taken it with her.

She moved into her office. Truly a haven, she mused as she eased into the squeaky, squishy office chair she had splurged on last year when she finally made the decision that she wanted to write a book. Not just any book, but a romance novel. Her lips curved upward as she booted up her ancient computer, listening to the chug and churn as it groaned into life. That would be her next treat, she reassured herself. Soon. She'd promised herself that she would invest in a new machine—which she had already picked out—once she reached the halfway point in the book.

The monitor blinked and the room filled with music as she logged into her remote server. Stretching again, she set the clock for ten PM—her self-imposed limit for working nights. Thankfully, living in the apartment upstairs from the shop, she didn't have to worry about a commute, and she allowed herself time to run through the chapter she'd worked on last night.

"George leaned forward in his seat as Eliza moved the throttle toward the point of lifting the machine into the sky," she read aloud. "Oh please, George's actions should be more interesting than that," she grumped audibly to herself and slowly immersed herself in the theory of how a space captain, and maybe someday, wannabe-lover, would move while teaching his young, sexy protégée how to go about moving a space freighter into the sky.

Slowly the words came, spilling out like a river flowing from her mind to the paper via the keyboard.

✪ ✪ ✪ ✪ ✪

"What do you mean the handbook is missing from the secure records, sir? No one else had access except the crew of the *Elector*, your personal staff, and the designers and builders."

Duvall McCord ran his hand through his hair. Tension screamed in the tense fingers that scraped along his scalp. "I thought everyone had top-level access and as such had been thoroughly screened before being awarded a position in this project?"

"We don't know at this stage how this could have happened, Captain McCord. However, I fear the worst, which means it could be an infiltrator. The thing is, we just don't know. I have security checking the vidscreen records as we speak, and we're running full scans of the crew and staff backgrounds again, including deep-level family screening. There has to be more to this. We just don't know what that is though." Admiral Gustav Elphin sounded weary, and Duvall could almost hear the disgust in his mentor's voice as he leaned forward in his chair.

"Sir, do we even have any inkling where it might have gone?" Duvall tensed as he waited for an answer.

"Not really, Duvall." In the viewer he looked exhausted and worried. "I need you to keep eyes open on this one. If there is an infiltrator, he or she could be aboard the *Elector*. If that's the case, we don't know exactly what has been passed on or how it was done. All I can tell you is we need to catch them quickly. I don't need to remind you this is a *need to know* case though."

Duvall shifted uncomfortably in his chair. The concept of an infiltrator, a mole aboard his command, sat wrong. "Aye, sir, will do." His eyes narrowed with frustration.

"Duval…be careful. Crick Sur Banden is obsessed with you at the moment. You made the list when you rescued Elara from his people, and with your latest mission…" Gustav shook his head. "According to our intel, that inflamed the situation. It wouldn't surprise me if he is involved in the disappearance of the handbook." His voice tapered off to a thoughtful silence, then a sound suspiciously like the clearing of a throat. After a further short silence, indicating he was viewing something on his screen, he continued brusquely once again. "That's all I can tell you at the moment. Elphin out." The communication abruptly cut out, leaving Duvall with more questions than answers.

Duvall gazed thoughtfully through the screen separating him from outer space and contemplated what steps he would need to take next. The handbook carried the schematics for the *Elector*, which was enough of a concern, but was that everything regarding this mission? It was also fitted with the technology to allow for time travel. If whoever had the book knew this, then they could replicate it.

Not only did that put the past in jeopardy, but what he knew may never come to pass or even exist. Until he had further information, or arrived in the time he was authorized to travel to, he would continue to investigate the loss of the handbook.

His mind turned to the ship itself. The *Elector*. He grinned. Damn, what a bird she was, the first of her class. The prototype stealth ship would allow them to maybe claw their way to the front of the battle and perhaps finally bring the last threats to peace in the galaxy to justice.

Slowly, he spun his chair back to the front of his desk and rose to his full height. Time to begin investigating what had happened. Not trusting his second-in-command would be tricky, particularly given Grayson had been with him almost from the beginning. It was the price of leadership though, and he would need to start by taking another look at the records of his men. He strode through the door, which shut automatically behind him, and headed for the bridge.

✪ ✪ ✪ ✪ ✪

The buzz of the alarm cut through Mellissa's concentration. Thoroughly lost in the exploits of George and Eliza, the clock reminded her to go up and make dinner and perhaps head straight to bed. Slowly stretching, she reached out to save her work, then rose, stiff from her hours in front of the computer. Mellissa inwardly celebrated the progress made: another couple of thousand words written. The writing made for slow work, but her characters sizzled each time they came in contact. *Excellent.*

She made her way through the door, turned left and headed for a hidden staircase, then continued upstairs. Her stomach growled, and she thought, something easy and cool perhaps. As she reached her small living room, Mellissa walked over the rough bare floorboards and passed the metal utility chairs on her way to the kitchen. *Maybe a basic salad will do.*

Reaching the refrigerator, she grabbed a ready-made salad and poured a glass of cold white wine. She had just sat down on an old stool at the eatery when she heard a thud. *Hmm, probably another book drop-off.* She didn't really pay any attention as she munched and crunched her salad and continued plotting the evolution of the book.

She could get George and Eliza together quickly or… She discarded idea after idea. "Okay, so maybe it's time for me to try something else." Mellissa considered her options for the evening. "I'm thinking a quick shower and bed sounds just about right. Tomorrow's Saturday, so I get a whole day to work on my book." She grinned. "Who knows, maybe George and Eliza will see some closer action."

With the meal finished, she discarded the disposable plate and padded in the direction of the bedroom while tossing possible scenarios of seduction over in her head.

"Sir, you have an encoded message incoming from Admiralty," Engineer Corbin Jard stated. A young officer, new to Duvall's team, he looked up expectantly at his captain. His pretty-boy face showed eagerness, and he looked ready to jump up and grab something, anything his captain commanded. Jard had joined the crew just as the ship prepared to make its maiden journey. A big step up for someone so junior who had, until recently, served on the *Star of Ishtar* under the command of Elphin, before his promotion to Admiral.

"I'll take it in my office, Jard," Duvall said, striding through the automatic doors and heading to his office.

The crew of the *Elector* carefully trained for multi-tasking, and given the relatively small size of the crew and the status of a stealth ship, if one officer sustained injury, someone else could continue their role. While they'd all been newly transferred, Duvall felt satisfaction in the way they'd integrated.

Hopefully this information would take them to the handbook they sought, something to give them a break in the ongoing hunt for Crick Sur Banden. Duvall's neck itched, and while he didn't consider himself superstitious, he never neglected to listen to what his senses told him. Right now they screamed that he needed a lead, and quickly.

Once in his office, he locked the door and opened the secure link. "McCord here."

"Duvall, I have a lead, or something, for you." The earnest voice of Warrant Officer Meredith Gentry came over the line. As much as he looked forward to hearing from his sister, she wasn't the person he was expecting to hear from.

Meredith continued her work safely tucked away on Aenna. *Didn't she?*

"I don't have a lot of time," she hurried on. "I think someone knows I suspect something. I rigged the handbook with a tracking device. The code is—" He could hear the sound of voices behind her. "Quickly, it's V-four-two-two-J-five-three. That will allow you to access the feed," she said as he jotted down the tracking device's code. He could hear her taking quick breaths. "It moved through the gate outside Eris on code L-X-five-four-three-G-H-four." He knew that code. He had just generated one giving a similar time path.

"Meredith, are you in a safe location?" he demanded forcefully.

Another hitched breath echoed. He gripped his table and leaned forward, not that he could do anything. The sounds faltered from thousands of miles away.

"Meredith?" His sister was in danger, and here he listened on a ship so far away. *Barsha!* He should have protected her.

"Duvall, you need to access frequency…" She rattled off the information he would need to follow the device as he tapped into his unit. "Oh God! They're here—" Abruptly, the line went dead.

"Meredith? *Meredith?*"

Quickly accessing the Admiralty, he demanded a connection to WO Meredith Gentry. A voice informed him that Gentry could not be raised and asked if someone else could help with his query. His demands to talk to the Admiral met with a similar fate.

Frustration welled upward, nearly choking him as he disconnected. He knew he couldn't go back and couldn't think who else he could contact. He had to maintain a chain of silence while investigating the handbook's loss. But what if the Admiralty had been breached? Never had any other thoughts shaken him so much.

His heart thudded as he sat back down. Could more than a single infiltrator exist? He hoped not, but the itching at his neck grew in intensity, and he feared the worst. Tapping the information Meredith had given him into his desk screen, he started toward tracking the handbook, thankful for the foresight of officers such as his sister.

The blip of the machine echoed through the room, and an answer bounced back to him. A heading he would never have guessed. Toward the Time Port and back in time. If he couldn't help Meredith, he could at least work toward retrieving the item she had risked so much to track. It wasn't nearly enough, but it would have to do. For now anyway.

He hailed the bridge. "Full speed toward the Time Port," he instructed, just in time to see the blip disappear.

✪ ✪ ✪ ✪ ✪

Saturday morning greeted Mellissa as she woke up and bounced out of bed. Quickly dressing and grabbing breakfast, she made her way downstairs. "Nothing to do today but help George and Eliza."

She loved what she did. Owning a bookstore allowed her the freedom to indulge in her favorite vice—a good book—and allowed her fertile mind to feed. Yes indeed, nothing could be more perfect. Of course, Jem had hounded her to go on a date with the brother or something of her latest boyfriend, but in Mellissa's experience, a good book made up for the lack of a man.

As she rounded the corner, she spied a package wrapped in paper on the mat by the back door, just below the slot. "Hmm, so that was another book in the slot."

Bending down, she scooped up the package and opened it to find a tablet device inside. The item was small and hard, more like a PDA, she thought, shaking her head. Maybe somebody had accidentally dropped the wrong thing in the slot.

Well, no doubt they would come back for it. So many people would just deposit a book through the slot—though they usually used the flap at the front, instead of heading around the back where the mail slipped through—because they didn't want a credit on a new book. It always amazed her, but sometimes the most interesting titles came her way like this.

Slipping it in the crook of her arm, she headed toward her office. Another day of happy writing awaited, and she couldn't get started soon enough. She placed the package in the pile behind her desk, planning to take a closer look at it later. Maybe she could find an identifier on it so she could track its owner, she thought absently.

She pulled her mind back to the task she looked forward to starting on: the antics of her George and Eliza.

✪ ✪ ✪ ✪ ✪

The pounding on the door pulled Mellissa from her thoughts as it echoed through the building. It interrupted her thinking, but given it had continued for a while, she just couldn't ignore it any longer.

She rose from her chair, and making her way toward the front of the store, she muttered under her breath, "It's Saturday, people." Couldn't they see the shop was closed? Opening the blind on the door, she peered out to see a man on the step. "We're closed!" she called.

He looked at her and made a move to open the door. "We are closed," she repeated.

She heard the man mutter, "You have something…"

She lost the gist of what he said as she got a good look at the muscular man with black hair and piercing green eyes standing on the stoop. *God, he looks so sexy!*

"Can you let me in?" she finally heard.

"What? Oh, sorry," she said, quickly unlocking the door and opening it a crack. "Now what did you say?"

"You have something that belongs to me," said the impossibly sexy man.

She wondered if he would think she was nuts if she asked to take a photo of him. He looked just like what she thought George would. She grinned to herself. *Sure, girl. Jem would ask something like that.* She blinked away the thought and focused on the man in front of her.

"Ummm, I don't think so," Mellissa said, making to close the door.

"A pad…" And the memory twigged.

"Oh, right," she said, sliding away from the door just enough to let him in, then re- securing the locks. "We're closed on Saturdays, so you're lucky I was here."

Motioning for him to follow her, she made her way to the back of the store. She stopped at the doorway and watched him look around.

"Please take a seat," Mellissa offered, gesturing to a chair sitting in front of her desk. Casting around, she looked for the package. "I'm sorry, what did you say your name was? Mr…"

"McCord, Duvall McCord," the gorgeous stranger intoned. His gaze roamed over her, and she had the most uncomfortable feeling he liked what he saw, because his eyes twinkled and the smile on his lips grew wider.

Mellissa chastised herself, because she looked so very ordinary. She certainly wasn't the sort of girl who would appeal to a buff and sexy male like this. He had that totally alpha look about him, she thought. Then she embarrassed herself by blushing at her thoughts, and felt the heat of the red tide rising on her cheeks.

Spying the package on a small table just behind her desk, she stretched for it, when suddenly a loud crash and whine came from the back of the building, and before she could blink,

McCord reached into his pocket and pulled out some sort of device. A red light on it blinked and his face took on a harsh cast.

"Get down!" he shouted, leaning over her, covering her body with his. He grabbed her hand and the package together. "Two for transport *now*!" he shouted, and the world turned black.

# Chapter 2

Sound. Lights. Slowly, consciousness reasserted itself. Melissa felt a pillow beneath her head and the softness of a mattress underneath her body. Even with her eyes closed, she couldn't place the surroundings; it didn't feel like her comfortable little bed above the shop. Her eyes opened to white walls and bright lights that stung them. She blinked once, twice, then again.

Memories filtered slowly. A man! Her office! Where was she? More importantly, where was he? She started to rise, but a thick band lay over her chest, restraining her. Agitation and panic bloomed in her chest, smothering her, and her breath caught. This didn't feel right. Had he trapped her? What had happened? She tried to free her hands, and a beeping started fast and furious.

Footsteps sounded just beyond her view, measured, light. Then a face surrounded by a halo of red hair caught her attention. She saw deep scarring, and fear bloomed again, stronger than before, choking her in a cloud of sour and oily emotions. Where was she?

"Ahh, you're awake. Don't be afraid. My name is Elara, and I'm just going to give you a quick check over." The voice slipped over her like silk. She got the impression that the modulated tones were those of a highly educated woman.

She looked at the woman with scarring on her face and neck. She didn't know this woman or what had happened to her, and her fear grew. Was this what she had to look forward to? Fright choked her, and she struggled again to free herself.

The woman who had called herself Elara reached out a hand. More scars. Mellissa's eyes rose to the woman's. The gaze that met hers was watchful and wary, and the fight-or-flight reaction pumped in Mellissa's veins.

"Apologies, we didn't wish to startle you." The hand lightly touched a switch, and the band over her chest retracted. The mechanical heartbeat sound stopped. "Please be easy. You're safe now." The woman smiled, uncertainty clear in her eyes.

"Where am I?" Mellissa demanded, surprised by the weakness she heard. She winced— not at all the way it should have come out, and not as strong and self-assured as she would have liked.

"You're aboard the *Elector*. Captain McCord brought you here to keep you safe." The woman smiled again. "I'm ST Elara Sudonne. Uh, I believe you would call me a medic. Now, how are you feeling? You may have a headache as your endorphin levels are higher than usual, as is your adrenaline, but no more than should be expected."

*Elector*? ST? Huh, what did they hope to gain? This was a rather elaborate setup, and the whole mess made no sense.

Mellissa stared at the woman, mesmerized by the patterns on her face and hands. She realized quickly that she was staring. She could hear Mother Superior telling her *don't be rude*. She lowered her head. "My name is Mellissa. But where is the *Elector*, and why am I on a ship?"

Elara's face crinkled. "Ah, it is not a ship as you know them, but a stealth ship—well, you see, it's the latest generation starship," she informed Mellissa, who gaped at her.

This woman must think her simple. *Starship? So funny... not!*

"But that is not the only thing that concerns you, is it? The scars worry you too."

She removed a small device from her pocket. Mellissa started, but Elara put her hand out.

"Nothing to worry about. I just need to check to make sure everything is well. All of this is just a precaution to make sure you're okay," she said, waving the device up and down.

"I was taken prisoner by the Ru'Edan when I was younger. They are an alien humanoid species we have been at war with. They wanted to…" Elara hesitated briefly. "…experiment on a human, and I was their chosen guinea pig. McCord, the captain, and my partner, Grayson, found me. Brought me back, but not before what you see here," she said, waving to herself.

"Right, and I'm Professor Xavier of the X-Men!" Mellissa leaned toward the woman, hoping she'd cave and give her the information she needed to get out of there. "Who are you, and where in hell am I? Oh, and don't start with the spaceship hocus-pocus rubbish. We all know that the limit of current space exploration is only to the moon." Anger rose once more. What did they think she was? An idiot?

Leaning over and holding out a hand, Elara helped Mellissa to rise. Unsteady, and once again surprised, Mellissa accepted the help grudgingly. Looking down, she saw the clothes she had thrown on earlier, with nothing out of place. Thank God, she thought, inwardly cataloging aches and pains in her body, but none betrayed any form of physical abuse that she could pinpoint. She looked into the woman's eyes, this Elara.

"I understand that this seems hard to believe, but everything you've been told is fact. No lies." The woman paused for a heartbeat. "Come on, you must be hungry, and McCord will need to know that you're well and truly recovered. The first time we transmit can have all sorts of effects, so we like to keep observation for a good eight or so hours afterward, and you haven't been here that long." She motioned for Mellissa to follow her. "If you will follow me up to the mess hall, I'll do my best to explain what has happened." Elara continued slowly. Mellissa followed her into a larger room then toward a hidden doorway. "Let's grab something to eat, and I can answer some of your questions." The woman showed her the way to some steps.

Mellissa's stomach rumbled with hunger, and now she showed more than a little interest in her surroundings. She might find a way out of there, so she decided to go along with the woman. But she started getting an uncomfortable feeling that the woman believed her own words or that this was an elaborate hoax. The rattle of metal steps and decking made her wary though. She had no answers to either who would play such an elaborate joke or why.

Reaching the top of the stairs, they walked along a small hall and into a large but sparsely furnished room with booth-style seats. Not welcoming or comfortable, but serviceable. The walls sported the usual gunship gray she had read of in many books about naval ships, but the ports that held her attention: the black inky sky outside, and stars. Whoever had put this ruse together had planned it well.

A small unit winked and blinked with bright colors in the wall on what looked like a palm screen. Elara stepped up to it and put her hand on the screen, saying firmly, "Tea, black, and nut mix."

A plate appeared, drawn up from an aperture below, with a packet of nuts. Beside the plate, a steaming cup of tea appeared in an aperture that slid open. *Holy moly!* Now that intrigued her. She had never seen anything like this before. Maybe she should investigate more? There was some serious technology here, and while she really didn't keep abreast of that sort of thing, this no doubt would have inspired discussion with the techies that came in to buy those sorts of books from her. And she had seen a lot of those sorts of books while undertaking her own research.

Elara turned back to Mellissa. "What appeals to you? There is a list above of what is available at this point in the day," she said, inclining her head.

Options including soup, light sandwiches, and some berry sweets seemed logical for snacks. Mellissa shook her head, but her stomach rumbled, giving her away.

Elara grinned at her. "Come on, just tell it what you want."

"Umm, can I get a coffee and chicken sandwich?" Mellissa asked.

"Sure, just place your palm on the pad and make your selection," said Elara.

Moving forward, she placed her palm against the cool plate, but suddenly a voice said, "Unknown print—access denied."

Mellissa jumped back, startled.

"Stupid machine!" Elara groused. "I didn't think that you wouldn't register with the palm scanner."

And not for the first time since waking, the Alice in Wonderland effect hit Mellissa. "This sort of thing doesn't happen often," Elara told her over a shoulder. "Not too many come onto the ship that don't have active prints. Here, take this and find somewhere to sit, and I'll get your coffee and sandwich." Turning back to the machine, Elara placed her palm against the plate and ordered.

Mellissa slowly made her way toward a seat and sat down. She had a sinking feeling that nothing would ever be the same again.

The beeping on the bridge alerted Duvall to a possible breach in the mess hall. *Breach?* He quickly rose and double-timed it up the stairs only to stop in the doorway where he saw his SurgiTech Elara sitting with the pretty woman he had rescued from the bookstore.

*Eshra be damned.* There he was on a need-to-know mission, and he'd picked up a human woman from a different time. "What was I thinking?" He smiled humorlessly. Well, he would have to make the best of it; she couldn't go back. Such a risk outweighed any possible benefits, and he had to get back to the Admiralty. *I'll need to consider how to work this into my report.*

He strode forward, his large black boots eating up the distance toward the seat, and on reaching it, he noticed surprise and fear on the woman's face. A very pretty woman, beautiful, but not stunning, he thought, cataloguing the lean body, pale skin, and brown hair.

Her lips were slightly too large and wide, but surprisingly full. Her hazel eyes were ringed with long eyelashes. A feeling of something akin to interest surprised him. For a minute, he allowed it to bloom, then tamped the unusual feelings down. He'd experienced interest before and not acted; this time couldn't be any different, he reminded himself.

"Captain Duvall McCord, ma'am," he introduced, then looked away to see Elara watching him. "That looks like a damn good idea," he said, and he trod over to the dispenser to make a selection.

Steaming coffee and nuts would tide him over while he found out what the woman knew, if anything, though he had a feeling this could take time. With the items in hand, he headed back to the women and sat next to Elara.

"I suppose you have some questions?" he queried, looking expectantly into the eyes of the woman—Mellissa, he thought she had said her name. Funny, he hadn't noted the smooth, oval shape of her face, somehow soft and feminine with a hint of strength in the nose and around the eyes.

"Why am I here?" she demanded boldly.

Her hands gripped the cup, and he noticed no communal marking on her skin. The most common marking in vogue was three teardrops inside the wrist to represent the contract of Life, Commitment, and Love. His knowledge of historical mating customs was slim though, so he made a mental note to question this later. His tension released somewhat. No one else would need transporting if she was indeed unpaired. At least he hoped so. A feeling of relief that he wasn't going to investigate rose in him.

"Elara, if you are finished, I'll clear away." It wasn't a suggestion or query, but more of a soft order.

Elara immediately excused herself, saying, "I'll be in the medical station should you need me."

He watched as Elara moved toward the entrance and disappeared around the corner. He needed her out of the way so he could concentrate on his soft interrogation.

"The package you were in possession of contained classified information. The noise you heard before we transmitted was the start of a Ru'Edan attack force trying to retrieve it." He looked at her intently; her face betrayed no trace of a connection with any of the information. Perhaps a hint of fear and distrust, but it disappeared quickly. "Once they have your DNA signature, they will keep after you until they can retrieve either the package or the information as to where it has gone from you. You saw what they did to Elara. If you look like that when they're finished with you, you'd be lucky." The blunt words hit home, and he watched her eyes widen in comprehension and fear.

"Who or what are these Roo-E-Dan you lot keep on about?" she asked up front. He shifted in his chair, not wanting to share a lot of information with her.

"Many, many years ago, humans formed an alliance. Earth was becoming politically unstable. Some believed it was a direct result of overcrowding. For years the shuttle program had been delayed and the focus of inquiries after a slew of accidents. Once the first successful relaunch, it was determined that a push needed to be made to populate other planets. Scientists worked around the clock, seeking alternatives."

Duvall paused and glanced down at his coffee. Taking a sip, he let that information sink in before starting again.

"In order to travel further, humans needed to improve their spacecraft. It became a priority. Within twenty years, man was at the point of colonizing the first planet. One success led to another, and we became not just more adept, but also more capable of long voyage travel. I suppose you would call it a form of scientific evolution."

She watched his eyes as he explained what he knew, and he could see the disbelief in her face.

"Anyway, once humans finally got beyond the boundaries of our galaxy, we found many habitable planets and also other species. The alliances we formed outside our solar system and galaxy with these species improved our technology, which gave us the drive to move beyond the area of space we knew. The alliance had been working quite well until we met the Ru'Edan some…oh, I don't know, hundred or so years ago. They believed we were going to invade their pre-determined spatial boundaries. They didn't want us in their space. We needed more planets. As a result, we've been at war with them now for at least eighty of those years. In the last fifteen, we have operated in a state of diplomatic truce."

He looked at her now, watching him. He could see the skepticism on her face.

"However, during this time, both sides have sought out the leader of the Ru'Edan rogues. Their leader, Crick Sur Banden—" He watched her eyes closely, looking for a flicker of recognition, anything at all. "—has managed to elude capture. He's working behind the scenes to derail the process that is currently in place, attacking our ships and seeking ways to disrupt our Empire. Any expansion throughout the areas which we have pinpointed as having possible habitable planets has been halted until we can find him."

She watched him. Disbelieving. *Barsha!* He may need to prove that his assertions were real. Frustration made him want to grab her and haul her off to the bridge and show her the reality of the inky blackness of space. *Damn!* He would never have thought that working with those from the past could be such a nightmare. Thank *Eshra* so few ships used this technology. Imagine more disbelieving types having to hear about their advances? He couldn't suppress the small shudder that shook his body.

"Look, I don't know what you think you are doing, or who is playing this joke, but I just want to go home. Let me go now, and I won't tell the police. I'll keep it to myself." She sat forward in the seat, leaning on the table, hands clenched and eyes narrowed. He could see her uncertainty in the pallor of her skin and the tiny drops of sweat that beaded her upper lip.

"You think I'm kidding?" He grabbed her arm and

dragged her to the port. "Do you really think this is a joke?" he demanded of her. "See that asteroid?" He pointed to one, which seemed so far away. "Do you really think that is made up? What about the Earth then?" He pointed to a distant sphere that was rotating slowly, the distance making it look like a tiny ball. Getting smaller. He knew she could see it clearly now, as she swallowed. "Do you think that is made up? Tell me then, how did we do it? How did we get you here without anyone seeing us?" he asked, his words as hard and stormy as her eyes when she looked at him.

He dragged her back to her seat. The fear in her face startled him. His face wrinkled in disgust at himself. He'd really mucked this up so far.

"I want to go home," she whispered from lips that trembled.

"You can't." He said the words with a steely voice. He felt his face harden, the muscles ticking in anger and exasperation. "We'll be moving out of this zone shortly, and you're coming with us. You have seen too much, and the Ru'Edan will be searching for you. Whether I want it or not, you're stuck here. I suggest you accept your new reality."

He rose and indicated with his hand that she should accompany him. He collected cups and plates, glanced at the half-eaten sandwich on her plate, and looked toward her. She blushed, the tinge of pink coloring her pale skin. He dropped the plates on the side of the dispenser and depressed a button. They disappeared.

They took slow steps back to the front of the room, down the stairs, and through a door that opened into a sort of corridor with what looked like cubicles and, at the end, a small room. The door whispered open, and he stepped inside to one side and waited for her to join him.

There is much to do, he told himself, and no time to sugar-coat it for her. Deep down, he thought of comforting her, but he ruthlessly shoved those thoughts aside.

✪ ✪ ✪ ✪ ✪

His face betrayed an emotion; for a moment Mellissa thought she saw pity, but in an instant it was gone.

She stopped in the doorway briefly and looked around. It looked like a set off one of the sci-fi programs she watched. A single seat sat in the middle of the bridge, and a bank of seats circled around it, two more situated in the front at the bottom of a number of steps, all gray with black seating. There was some sort of computer screen in front of each seat and a large window- looking thing, rather like a windscreen in a car. It's eerie, she thought, stumbling forward.

"Captain, we are ready to go to jump."

She noticed an increase in the vibration beneath her feet as soon as the young man sitting in one of the front seats made the comment. She closed her eyes briefly and waited.

"Prepare for jump speed. Find a station and buckle in," a disembodied voice announced. Once more, she jumped.

She jerked toward the seat Captain McCord motioned to, and she cast around looking for buckles, noting that the seats felt better than those on a plane. They conformed to the body. A set of large hands came to the rescue. She heard him sigh as he fastened the belts, strapping them over both shoulders and across her lap. Then he sat and buckled himself in.

A large desk-like feature sat between them with, apparently, an intercom system, since he pressed a button and said, "Captain McCord. Go to jump."

The ship seemed to buck, then a sensation of pressure from everywhere surprised her. For an instant, a strong emotion passed over his face. Pity? Then it was gone, controlled in the cold face that she watched intently.

"No! I want to go home," she wailed, but something told her it was too late.

Mellissa sat looking at the captain. She could see his eyes scanning her, taking everything in. Why didn't he understand? She wanted to go home. And if he thought she hadn't realized he was fishing for information before...well, that was his problem. She had read in her research books about types of questioning techniques, knew what he was attempting to do. She knew nothing about any of the people or places he had mentioned.

Her choices had been stripped from her, and she felt sick. She had done the victim thing once before and had promised herself never again. Not after all those years in the orphanage, where she'd had no control of her own destiny. Now, years later, there she was again in the same boat. She straightened her back. *No way!* I will have some control over my life, she promised herself.

She started pulling at the buckles, but his commanding voice told her to wait. Anger, despair, and fear roiled in the pit of her stomach as she worked to make sense of what she was experiencing. She looked up and saw pity his eyes.

She had so many questions to ask, but the main one included *why*? Why her? She had played by the rules she'd learned in the orphanage. She considered herself a contributing and upstanding member of society, so how could this possibly happen to her? She sniffled. *Don't whine. Get out there and accept the trials you're given.* The voice of Mother Superior rang in her head again. The woman had loathed shows of strong emotion, and no doubt this would count as such.

"Where are we going?" Mellissa asked, traces of her tears evident in the husky question.

But she would be damned if she would give in to the tears. She turned her eyes on him.

"Back to where I came from. Earth Empire Admiralty on Aenna."

"Aenna? Where's that?"

"It's really a glorified asteroid, located between Mars and Jupiter," he said, relaxing into his seat. "Admiralty has its strategic offices there, but first we have to get to the Time Port outside the solar system, just beyond Eris."

"Time Port?" She leaned forward. "What is a Time Port, and why do we have to get there first, and where in hell is Eris?"

She dragged her eyes away from his and looked around. The gunmetal gray that met her eyes again teamed with sensitive lighting. Black streaked with slashing lights filled the ports. He sighed and huffed out a breath, and she could tell that dealing with her frustrated him to no end. Once more she questioned the sanity of what he had said, and what she had seen.

Quickly undoing the buckles with fumbling fingers, she rose and hurried to the window, looking out. Nothing made sense though. Nothing looked even remotely like anything she could see on Earth or anywhere else. This so had to be a nightmare, she told herself, hoping it would settle the nerves that floated around her brain, buzzing anxiously.

Okay, she could go along with this; after all, she would wake up back in her office after her fertile imagination had given her fodder for her book. *Right?* But what if this was really happening? A click sounded, then a hand settled on her shoulder, breaking her reverie.

Warm, heavy, and somehow reassuring, that hand gently turned her back toward the most magnificent man she had ever laid eyes on. Duvall McCord. Captain of the stealth ship *Elector*. His eyes mesmerized her.

"It'll be all right," he said. "We'll make this right for you, but you can't go back." He looked at her, and she felt a charge of something—some kind of new emotion, *desire*—flash through her system.

Then she stopped, the internal commentary jarring her. *Yeah, like some mouse like me could ever interest a man like this. Look at those shoulders, abs, and arms, not to mention that face. Yeah. As if.* She mentally shook herself. Obviously, I need some male companionship, or at least a frontal lobotomy, she thought, snorting again.

"Thanks." She glanced away, her mind settling back to the bigger issue. He said she couldn't go home. "Nothing can make this right for me," Mellissa explained, slowly shaking her head. "If I can't go back, what can I do?" A bitter laugh erupted from her. "The me that I am will no longer exist." The sensation of being lost in a warp settled within her mind.

"I'm going to call my second, Grayson, in to get you started on the identification process. The sooner that's done, the sooner you can begin the integration process. There'll be some learning ahead, but maybe we can learn some things from you too. Let yourself get acclimated first. I'm sure there will be an occupation suitable for you, and your skills will be evident." The vibration of his voice soothed her.

She allowed him to usher her back to the seat.

He quickly called on Grayson—Ah, the disembodied voice from before, she concluded on hearing his acknowledgment—then, explaining he had duties to see to, he headed to the door, stopping just before it closed to say, "I know this seems tough, but there really is a lot riding on this mission. I just don't have choices either."

Then he acknowledged a tall, Nordic man who slipped in through the door before he left.

"Alice, welcome to Wonderland," she said aloud.

# Chapter 3

Lying on a bunk in a room—cabin, she reminded herself—she considered what had happened to her since the morning. Nothing in her wildest dreams could have prepared her for what had occurred.

"This is a dream," she assured herself. "Nothing more than the figment of my overactive imagination. I'll wake up and find none of this happened." If only she could truly believe that, but the things she had seen since waking in what had looked like a medical suite told her otherwise. How could a perfectly ordinary morning lead to such an overwhelming change in her life?

She stared sightlessly at the military-grade gray room. In fact, everything seemed gray- colored. Dull. Bland. If this was a future reality, why not discover a new shade of military gray? she wondered with sour humor, then mentally corrected herself for the negative thought.

Rolling onto her side, she pulled up the sheets and blankets and settled in for an uncomfortable sleep when a klaxon alarm surprised her. "Holy… What the hell is happening?"

Scrambling out of the bunk, pulling on her shirt and jeans, and slipping into the slippers she had arrived in as quickly as she could, she opened the door to see a handful of crewmen running down the corridor. One grabbed her by the arm and pushed her, thrusting her roughly back into her cabin. "You need to remain here, out of the way." He said no more as the door whispered shut, and she stood alone.

A voice called through the noise, "Emergency lockdown procedure commencing."

She tottered over to the bed and collapsed. Feeling quite

useless, she gripped the side of the bed, feeling ill.

An interminable period followed, though probably only a quarter of an hour or so. The wail of the klaxon finally ceased. She sagged on the bed, breathing heavily. She hadn't realized that her muscles were so tense until she relaxed them. A brief bout of dizziness followed, and following tried and true methods of dealing with it, she leaned forward, taking controlled breaths. The room remained in silence.

"Maybe I should wait here? At least until Captain McCord tells me it's okay." The echoing words calmed her fears a little.

She stayed in the cabin, listening for the thud of boots on the decking, but she heard nothing. After a while had passed, she lay down and drifted into a restless sleep.

A noise woke her, and she sat up groggily. Her eyes opened, and there he stood. Impressive. Her warrior captain. *Whoa there! Where in God's name did that come from?*

"Are you okay?" he asked simply, helping her to rise from the bed. His face showed nothing, but in his eyes she could just detect a hint of concern. His hand felt soft on her arm.

"What happened? One minute everything was fine, and the next we have sirens and running crew? Was it something with the ship?" She had a momentary panic that it would stop dead in space and they would all die. Claustrophobia such as she had never experienced washed over her.

"No and yes. Someone tampered with a setting in engineering. Thankfully, we were able to deal with it swiftly," he assured her. "But I think whoever did it knows that while we have both you and the information we retrieved, we are a danger to them. I'm going to move you to my cabin for the duration of the journey as a precaution."

She looked at him, disbelieving. *What? No way.* Mellissa wasn't prepared to question why she felt so strongly, she just reacted.

✪ ✪ ✪ ✪ ✪

As Duvall watched Mellissa he realized that she could be dangerous to his sanity. The need to protect this woman overshadowed the anger he'd felt over someone tampering with his ship. Nothing in his experience had ever prepared him for this. He forced his mind back to the current situation.

"Nope, no way. Isn't going to happen." Her retort came swiftly.

Duvall looked at the woman. She couldn't be serious? By *Eshra*'s sake. He certainly didn't look forward to sharing his cabin with the woman that was turning him into a walking bundle of mixed feelings. His temper was frayed, and he couldn't concentrate on his job. All he wanted to do was grab her and hold on tight. *Kiss her.* The situation was deeper than anyone could see on the surface, and he told himself to get his head into the game. She was the key somehow to the whole plan, he knew, and no way would he jeopardize everything by letting his emotions run rampant. Or his physical attraction either.

Her cheeks flushed pink against a pale face. Her eyes appeared shadowed, and he could detect the weariness about her. Her shoulders drooped and her lush lips etched downward. The urge to touch her rose, but he suppressed it. He wasn't sure how in *Eshra*'s name he would keep his hands off her. Ever since he'd met her, his overwhelming desire had been to kiss her senseless. It was beyond him how one woman had turned him inside out. Since their meeting, he'd been telling his brain to slow down and think through the situation.

"I don't have the manpower to ensure your safety, so you'll move to the captain's cabin until such time as we get to the Admiralty. Or until we find out who is looking for you. It'll take us another two days to reach the Time Port, another day to get through, and one more to our destination. Four ship days at worst, barring anything unforeseen." He hoped his voice soothed her.

"But what about you? Where will you sleep?"

"In my ready room—just off the cabin." And boy, wouldn't that be comfortable? The couch was barely wide enough for two to sit side by side. But when needs must, he thought to himself. "I can be with you in an instant, and you'll be safer there than anywhere else on the *Elector*."

Without any further arguments, he pulled her along swiftly toward his cabin and the start of what he quietly considered would be his own private hell.

Mellissa once more fought for sleep, this time in Captain McCord's cabin. The musky scent of his body rising from the sheets and pillow surrounded her. It seemed to pull her in ways she couldn't imagine, make her wish for things she couldn't have. Namely the sexy captain who had pulled her into an intrigue she couldn't possibly conceive. To top things off, parts of her body throbbed insistently, and the thrumming of the engines exacerbated it.

"Urgh." She dragged the pillow close and hugged it.

Tossing and turning only made her mind more jumbled as it reeled from thinking about the man, from the top of his black hair to the bottom of his booted feet and every buff inch between. His essence intoxicated her, surrounded her as effectively as if he held her in his arms, and her body started to heat. The thought of him made her tremble, not with fear though. No. With anticipation.

Visions of him and her together and naked, danced in her head. Her breasts tightened at the thought of it, and she wondered how long she could go without embarrassing both of them with unrequited lust.

"Those are foolish thoughts." She cocked her head to the side, hoping he hadn't heard her whisper.

What would he look like naked, entwined within the sheets of this very bed? Her insides melted and every sense worked overtime. She wanted him. That wasn't such a surprise. But how would she cope with a rejection from him? Probably not very well, she reflected with brutal honesty. She wasn't hardwired for any real kind of commitment. Dammit, not even her parents had thought they should keep her around! Best to keep it to herself, she decided with a hard nod.

However, the thoughts kept her awake for hours before she drifted into a fitful slumber.

In his ready room, Duvall kept looking toward the doorway, wondering if she slept. The couch was uncomfortable. "Damned short and lumpy thing." He kept thinking about the bed that lay beyond and the woman who filled it. He rolled slightly and groaned in discomfort.

He should concentrate on his work. His comm desk kept beeping to let him know updates on the crisis continued coming in from his people. There was so much to achieve, but his body reminded him that the woman who lay just beyond that door teased his senses. For all the wrong reasons.

He focused on the incident in the engine room. This time, they'd come out okay. He was thankful it hadn't been worse. That someone would tamper with the environ station had surprised him, and he'd concluded they'd used that as a ruse so they could attempt to send a message through one of the comm channels. They'd only caught the tail end and hadn't managed to glean anything more than that there was someone aboard the *Elector* with the know-how to disrupt their plans.

He turned again on the uncomfortable couch. Funny, he had never realized how short it really was. The blanket slipped a little, and he reached to retrieve it. "*Barsha!*" Discomfort took its toll on his temper.

His mission gnawed at him. He had many souls under his watch, each one his responsibility. Something he took seriously. Someone on his ship didn't think that was so important. They wanted to be a hero—for the wrong side.

Once more, he contemplated who had the opportunity to undermine the ship. Several came to mind. He flicked mentally through the crew with both the motive and the opportunity.

To top it off, the woman in the other room, Mellissa, was interfering with his thoughts.

Repeatedly. She was sleeping in his bed. Alone.

He wanted to join her. Badly. Rarely did he feel this need to be with a woman. To hold her. He needed to keep working so he wouldn't make a mistake, but he also knew he needed to rest, to be fresh so he was on target.

*Go into that room*, whispered his body. With a grunt, Duvall gave up on any chance of rest. He rose and went to his desk. It had worked in the past; it would work again. He had always walked away from women without a backward glance.

"Entanglements bind a man to Earth," he reminded himself, listening once more to the words his mentor had taught him. But this time, no matter how hard he worked, the hunger didn't go away. This time he wanted more, and that was dangerous. "Work is the answer."

Focusing on his role had always overcome any fascination with a female. He just needed to work at it harder. Turning back to his comm desk, Duvall started scanning the information filtering through. Maybe once it was done, he could consider moving forward and seeing if there was more to this feeling that kept nipping at him, whispered the voice inside his mind.

Duvall answered another hail and continued toward his investigation, all the time reminding himself that entanglements grounded a man. For tonight, it would be enough. It had to be.

Mellissa woke slowly. "Where am I?"

Memories rushed back, and for a moment she wondered if it were a dream or the result of her overactive imagination. Waking there in that cabin told her it was real and something she needed to accept. Not only did the situation seem real, she needed to make it work for her.

Stretching relieved the last of the fogginess in her brain, and she slowly crawled out of the bed. At the end lay a gray uniform, socks, and boots.

"Great. More gray." She grimaced while she slipped out of the t-shirt she had worn to bed with her panties. She dragged on the bra she had washed the night before, pulling on the clothes she had found.

When she looked in the mirror, her first thought pulled her up short. How much more anonymous could she look? She grimaced, finger-combing her hair. Once done, she shrugged. That was as good as it would get.

Today she would begin learning about the changes that had taken place from her time to the one she was moving to. "God, I hope there's real coffee in the future." The smell pervaded the air. Was that real coffee? She sniffed again. The coffee the day before was watery and thin. There was nothing thin about this aroma though.

Following it, she found her way to McCord's office. She refused to call him Duvall. That seemed way too intimate for her peace of mind. Far too personal and intense. The distance might become a necessary tool if she was going to keep her head straight around him. He already intoxicated her and made her want things that she couldn't have. Things she could only dream of.

There on his desk sat a steaming cup. "I heard you up and around," he growled.

His facial growth, dark stubble on his chin, made him look somehow harder yet sexier. *I really need to rein in my libido if I'm going to get anywhere.* With that thought in mind, she reached out, grabbing her drink. Her fingers brushed his, and warmth quickly spread up her arm. She saw him look at her, and her body wanted to melt in reaction to the look in his eyes.

Sipping cautiously on the beverage, she noted the brown liquid in the cup and tasted no sugar. Clearly he'd watched her order it in the mess. The coffee was perfect. Like him, smooth and full-bodied. Stop it, she told herself as she took a chair at his desk opposite him.

"So what do I need to do today?" she asked.

"Now that we've started to gather the information for your identification, we need you to start accessing the teaching program. You've got a lot to learn before we can let you loose on the world. We'll also be drilling you in safety procedures for the ship so you know how to react under a range of circumstances. Lastly, if there's time , we'll be putting you in the hands of the security officers to teach you basic combat skills."

He didn't look overly happy with that concept. Actually, he looked really cross, perched on the edge of his seat with rings around his eyes and a hard set to his mouth.

"In the event of a breach or security breakdown, you need to know how to protect yourself," he continued harshly. "But you will be safe with me. I won't let anything happen to you," he finished, the words sounding almost like a mantra.

God, she hoped that proved true. Slowly, she was coming to the realization that he'd only told her the honest truth. The reality of interstellar travel excited her as much as it scared her.

Eyes sore and weary from watching information on the changes and major events since her own time had passed, Mellissa reached out and turned off the screen. "Amazing." So much had occurred, and to think, she had a chance to be part of it. She shook her head. "Who would have thought so many changes could take place?" Disquiet filled her as she considered how she'd learn it all.

She slumped in her seat inside the cramped cubicle of a security officer, aware that it protected her from prying eyes. So many wonders! Interstellar travel—a huge technological leap there alone, she thought, and the change in the governmental systems.

Meeting new species, forming alliances, and colonizing other planets. "Inter-species marriages or communing." She formed the words with a smile. How amazing was that? In her time, they still carried on talkfests about the feasibility of some day considering travel to the stars. It was still a talking point after centuries. "No more talking about it. It's all happened."

She grinned. And there she was, Mellissa Davis, in space and traveling toward a future she couldn't possibly have imagined.

"George and Eliza would love this," she muttered to herself.

"Who are George and Eliza?" McCord peered at her, making her jump at the sound of his voice. She had missed the thud of boots on the flooring during her musings.

Mellissa gulped, wishing the floor would open and engulf her. How could she explain without him thinking less of her, not to mention her characters? George, a rough, tough space captain, and his protégée and maybe sometime lover, Eliza. Was it really something you could just blurt out? "Umm, they're characters in a book," she said.

"A book? Of course, they were still huge in your time. In ours, only the rich have them. The rest have bookpads." He smiled. "Who was it by? I might be able to access a copy for you."

Her discomfort deepened. "Umm, I was writing it." Her cheeks grew rosy.

"Really? Wow. What kind of book is it?"

He looked at her, and she felt sure his interest seemed genuine, but she cringed at the thought of telling him it was a romance. After all, wasn't it maiden aunts who wrote that sort of stuff, let alone read it? Uh-oh, she knew what to expect, she thought to herself.

"Umm, it was a sci-fi romance."

"You know, some of the most enduring titles from your time are romances. Fancy that, an author." He grinned, and she could feel the air clear a little. She still felt embarrassed, but not as much as she had.

"Well, I'm only working on my first one."

His gaze warmed her, but the silence stretched. She needed to say something to fill it.

"Yeah, in my time, romance writers are sort of...well, you know, the bottom of the pack. We're gaining ground though. We actually have associations dedicated to reading romance."

Then she grimaced, screwing up her face with embarrassment. *What must he think of me? I'm some kind of old spinster?* But wasn't that what she was on the road to becoming? That insidious little voice in the back of her head chimed in.

He stared at her, and a stray thought pierced her. *If only George could be half as sexy as Duvall McCord. God, Mellissa. He's a real rough-and-tumble captain and not some figment of my imagination.*

"Well, there is definitely a career waiting for you as a writer of romance." He grinned. "Come on. I'll grab you a coffee, and you can give me the lowdown on your characters. What were their names? George and Eliza?"

She hopped up quickly and followed him toward the mess hall. Really, it seemed funny how quickly she had settled into ship life, she mused.

"So, do you believe in romance yourself?" he asked, and he seemed just as surprised as she did by the question.

"Romance? Yes, absolutely." Her enthusiastic answer surprised him. It radiated clearly on his face, the way it screwed up slightly. "That's why I own a bookstore and am writing a novel."

"Hmm, yes, but did you live alone?" His query zeroed in on a spot she didn't really like to explore. "I mean, is there a man in your life?"

His gaze settled on her again. She hoped, in fact had prayed, that there was more to the question. *Stop imagining possibilities!* Her libido was far too busy looking for the possibility of a relationship that didn't and couldn't exist.

"Not really. I mean, my man is really George at the moment. It's kind of hard to explain." She floundered a little, looking for the right words. "The way I grew up, in an orphanage, I never really got to see how families worked together, and I guess it kind of made it harder for me to work out what it looked like, so I guess…"

He looked at her strangely. "Orphanage? I was a fosterling. The Gentrys fostered me. They're great." His face softened. "Really good people. The Gentrys gave me a fabulous sister, Meredith. It must have been hard with no one in your corner." His hand gently grasped her chin and raised it until her eyes looked into his. "Really hard for you though…" The words dropped to a trailing whisper as he leaned toward her by the doorway to the mess.

Her eyes fluttered closed as the distance between them melted away. She knew he was going to kiss her. Knew it probably wasn't a good or even wise decision, but she needed to find out if he tasted as good as he looked.

"Captain, Miss Davis," Elara called, interrupting the moment. "I see you think it's time for coffee too. Wonderful!" Then she looked again, the expression on her face making it clear that she realized she had walked in on something. Elara seemed to mutter to herself and headed for the mess hall door.

The moment broken, they looked at each other. A wry grin on his face softened the years and hardness from his features somehow. He turned, motioning her toward the door and the coffee that lay within. It didn't make her feel any better though. She had nearly made a mistake. A big one. Hadn't she?

Duvall was seated on the bridge when Mellissa walked in. His awareness of her came instantly. Since the near interlude outside the mess hall, the vision of her lips—firm, pink, and ready—had dogged his waking hours.

Her body made him burn at night, and he hadn't slept a wink. In the days since she had joined them on the *Elector*, he'd walked a fine line. If truth be told, he wanted to feel her body beneath him, but that wasn't all he yearned for. The fact that he wanted more was sobering. His constant need to be around her and hunger to hold her messed with his thought patterns.

No matter how intrigued he was by her, he wouldn't give in. He remembered his foster mother, always looking out for his father. She'd hated his job, and no doubt Mellissa would feel the same. He couldn't do that to her, because it would be unconscionable.

His attention split once more. "Concentrate on the job, Duvall." Moving through the slipstream at the Time Port was of the greatest importance, as was getting back to the Admiralty with the handbook they had retrieved from Mellissa's office. Thank *Eshra* for the tracking device Meredith had fitted to it.

Like a siren to his blood, though, Mellissa called to him She made her way to the seat he indicated, and once more, the voice sounded over the speakers. "Boys and girls, strap in. Slipstream horizon in ten minutes."

His second-in-command, Grayson, grinned at him like a big schoolboy. Grayson had commented on his preoccupation with Miss Davis earlier. He'd obviously noticed, and he knew Elara had too. Grayson and Elara had been with him for years, and he knew he could only keep the comments at bay for a short while. Elara sat in another of the viewing seats on the bridge. She used her position as SurgiTech to ensure she was on the bridge for these events. Inwardly, he grinned. That had been a perfect pairing, the SurgiTech and his second. Their Communing had taken place long ago and like any happy couple, because it worked for them, they hoped others would find love and a lasting relationship.

*At least I don't have to worry about Grayson making a play for Mellissa.* Once more, thoughts of her intruded, ones that smacked of possession. *Barsha!*

He barked out an order to cover his discomfort, and

everyone scurried to their seats in preparation for maneuvering through the Time Port. This had to be right. He focused on it completely, looking forward to see the Portal Gate looming.

✪ ✪ ✪ ✪ ✪

Mellissa noticed a large gate looming in the darkness. "How could anyone miss something this large?" It was inconceivable that scientists hadn't yet discovered it. She snickered, realizing how silly her comment was. It was hidden behind Eris, the newest of the planets named in her solar system, so maybe it was hidden from the telescopes?

Her mind struggled to accept this first view of a future she now inhabited while excitement flowed in her veins. She sat forward in her seat. They were all going home, and there was a palpable emotion flowing in the air on the bridge while the increased chatter since she entered this hallowed zone indicated the depths of their pleasure.

Since joining the *Elector*, she had harbored some residual doubts that it was a hoax, with talk of Time Ports, slipstreams, and colonization of the stars. This time she could see it for herself.

Twin emotions of excitement and apprehension warred within her. "What if I can't make a living or fit in?" The murmur was lost in the hubbub. Doubts filled her mind. *What if they use me as a sort of human display from the past? Can I trust Duvall and his crew to help me integrate?*

The rumble of the engines told her that the time for the introspection had passed. Her new future loomed large, and she would need to embrace the challenge even while she feared the unknown.

Grayson Myatt, the good-looking blond man, quite Nordic in looks with clear blue eyes, perfect skin, and a trim figure, counted down, his voice echoing over the speakers. She knew Elara was connected to him, not married, though there was some formalization of the relationship. She didn't want to pry though. While she admired his good looks, he just couldn't compare to Duvall.

"What are you thinking?" she muttered and shook her head. She needed to concentrate on the Time Port and looked forward to seeing and entering the slipstream. What would this slipstream look like? Would it be dark, or lights flashing in the air around them? What else could she imagine? Oh, how she wished for her manuscript to use her experiences to write a better book.

She patted about for the notepad she usually kept on her. "Damn. I left it on my desk." She raised her shoulders in a shrug. Why bother? Anything she wrote now was pure fantasy and she had real life to look forward to.

"Approaching Time Port," the young male officer at the front of the bridge called.

She pulled out of her thoughts and looked. It just looked like a metal ring with glyphs on it, floating in the middle of space. It didn't even seem remotely flashy to her gaze. How could they possibly use this to access the slipstream?

"Calling a full halt. Captain, do we have a green light for go?"

She looked at Duvall. He looked not only handsome but in control. A series of rapid-fire questions moved between him and the crew before he finally stated, "Green for go."

The engines began humming beneath her feet, and the deck vibrated harder than she had ever experienced before. All of a sudden, the ship moved forward toward the Port, swiftly gathering speed, and finally they were through it. A feeling of disorientation overtook her as they slammed through the time barrier. Now the starlight appeared as strands of color trailing past the ship. This was the slipstream.

# Chapter 4

Since entering the slipstream over an hour before, Mellissa had watched, mesmerized.

Duvall could see it in her face, the way she gazed through the center screen. She told him that the concept of time travel had been something that scientists in her time discussed and aimed at, but the actual reality amazed her.

He knew she must find it mind-blowing watching the blurred lights racing by and knowing that she was seeing star trails. The first time he saw them, he'd felt small and insignificant, and yet amazingly gifted with an experience so rare. Knowing that humans had finally made the final leap from fantasy to fact awed her. It was clear in the way she studied everything. While her fingers curled in the arms of her seat she gazed with wide eyes at the movements around her.

She turned her head, and he read surprise in her eyes. Surprise to see Duvall watching her. "What?"

"I'm watching you. Your reactions are so clear. I've seen this now many times." His hand waved toward the viewing screen. "But it's like the first, seeing it through your eyes."

He grinned at her. *Wait until she sees hyper drive. All those new worlds to explore.* The opportunities to watch her loomed endlessly and the fascination that gnawed at him kicked up another full notch.

Once more though, he thrust those siren-like thoughts aside. The struggle to remind himself that Mellissa wasn't for the likes of him took more energy every time he had to shove it away. She was soft and gentle. Untrained for the dangerous and hard life he led. No woman like her could possibly want it.

She turned her head again. He saw her mood change

from anticipation to agitation.

Why did he feel so drawn to her reactions, and more to her?

She stood suddenly. "I'm going to grab a coffee. Can I get you something?" She inclined her head toward him.

"I'll come with you," he said, rising from his seat

She followed him to the stairs leading to the mess hall. They moved up the winding stairs, nearly halfway there when a loud thud and a scream raised the alarm. Smoke started filtering through the halls, oily, thick, and dense. For an instant, they stood still, grappling with what could be happening.

"What the…" Horror churned in his gut. Just what had happened? Duvall increased his speed as he took the steps two at a time now.

He needed to get Mellissa to a safety point and find out. His thinking sharpened. The nearest possible location for him to send her was the mess. Duvall's mind already began weighing possibilities and contingency plans as he dragged her up the last steps. She'd be safe at the meet point while he investigated and ensured the safety of the crew and the *Elector*.

At the door to the mess, he turned to her. "Stay out of the way, in here. Follow any instructions."

Then with a whirl he turned in the direction the smoke wafted from. *Engineering*. He focused on the gray mass of smoke, eyes narrowing before he entered it.

The cloud curled from the plant access way on the third deck. He skimmed around quickly, scanning for anyone in sight. No one. Grabbing his weapon in his right hand, he slipped against the wall nearest the door, then ducked his head in quickly to see what he could find. No one could see him through the billowing smoke. But he couldn't see anyone either. *Barsha*!

There was no reason for a fault with the ship, so in his mind, the only other reason was a saboteur. The itching at the base of his skull indicated just that, while his mind added that he'd have little time to find them if that was the case. With careful touches, he ran his hands along the smooth walls, finding the doorway he sought.

Slipping through the door, he found another small alcove to his right and used it to crouch and look around. He felt his face grow hard as he called up the layout from his memory.

This wasn't the first incursion and caustic fury assailed him. The person carrying out these attacks had to be apprehended quickly before they could seriously damage the *Elector*. The last thing they needed was for the engines to go offline in the middle of the slipstream.

In the case of irreparable damage to the ship, they could remain lost in the slipstream— irretrievable. He knew the stats. Ninety point seven percent of all ships with serious engine failures in the slipstream disappeared. Hell, he'd seen the echoes of those ghost ships with his own eyes.

The knowledge burned his gut. The *Elector* carried enough food and oxygen for up to two weeks, depending where the damage had occurred, but after that… With a shake of his head, he washed off the negative thoughts. They needed to find whatever was smoking and fix it. Stars knew, anything more serious would mean certain death.

His hands gripped the butt of his gun, wrapping around the sturdy stock. "I'll kill them before I let the people under my command die."

He knew the saboteur could be any one on his crew. They were a mix of old and new hands. Most of the crew were handpicked by himself. The Admiralty had instructed him to build a crew with excellent training and experience, and for the most part he'd achieved that. He'd also agreed to trialing a system of exchanging alliance members within the ships, members of other species placed to foster a greater appreciation and sense of camaraderie.

He needed to find whoever didn't belong. Quickly. He hoped that it was one of the newer hands. Not that he wanted an infiltrator, but the concept of someone who had served with him for years turning them over to the Ru'Edan made his stomach churn and bile rise in his throat. No, he needed to find out what happened.

Pulling his thoughts back, he concentrated on staying quiet, moving silently along the metal grating toward the core of the energy matrix that fueled the ship. The gray smoke hung eerily in the air. He moved onward and slipped on something on the ground, falling heavily and losing the weapon in the billowing smoke. It clattered to the ground, and he silently cursed. He found the wall and used it to rise slowly, his gaze flicking from side to side.

Why was engineering empty? Had they all evacuated, or was it for some other reason? What should have been a hub of activity lay eerily silent. The only sound he heard was that of his labored breathing.

Moving on and gaining space, he scanned the matrix, and a wash of relief rolled through him. From here, it looked undamaged. He shifted a little and saw the reason for the smoke and alarm. A commdesk was burning, the tiny flames on the console feeding the black, oily smoke. He coughed, the cloud around him filling his lungs.

A lurch forward and he spied a pair of feet. "*Barsha!*" He crouched down, his eyes streaming as he took in the sight before him. A body.

It was clear the crewman was deceased from the large laser hole in the center of the man's forehead. Dark red blood, black in the dirty light, oozed along the decking.

The fury he'd contained nearly spilled over, and he clenched his fist. "I'll get you, and I'll crush you for this." No one attacked his own, and even more to the point, not on his own ship.

He made a lightning fast decision. Until he could work out the identity of the infiltrator, he only wanted his most trusted crewmembers involved in the investigation. Besides, he didn't want dozens of crewmembers in the way and potentially losing any small amount of evidence that might exist.

On top of the crewmember lay a small piece of card. He moved forward and crouched over the body. Carefully, Duvall lifted the card to see three words printed on it. *Her turn next.* He pocketed the item. It would need further investigation.

Nothing I can do for him, he thought grimly. He made a mental note to prepare a letter for the family. Max Lingstrom had a wife and a child at home. Duvall couldn't do anything to bring the young chief engineer back, but he would tell his family about his conscientious efforts aboard the *Elector*.

For now, though, his thoughts focused on how to save the ship, and save the crew. His mind continued to churn over the note. Her turn next… Who was the *she*? Mellissa? Meredith? He exhaled and the swirl of smoke whirled before his aching eyes. If only he'd been able to make contact with his sister. He'd tried so many times.

He reached for his commbadge. "Grayson and Elara? I need you in the engineering section immediately," he said, his voice grim.

The immediate answers of "On my way" from both filtered into the silent room.

He waited silently, casting his gaze around. But the perpetrator was long gone.

His heart thudded for a moment as he heard noises. The clank of boots on the deck told him more than one person had entered the room. With his laser pistol somewhere on the ground, out of view, he could be a sitting duck, and it sat badly with him.

He rose, carefully shuffling around the body while he searched for a possible weapon. Duvall's hands touched a long, cylindrical item, and when he leaned in to investigate, he smiled, realizing it was an extinguisher.

He grabbed it, hefting the weight in both his hands. "Who's there?" he demanded. He would need this to put out the fire once he determined if whoever had entered the room was friendly.

"Duvall, what in the stars name happened?" Grayson's voice.

He released his grip on the extinguisher, letting it drop to one hand, feeling the pull of its weight. He took a shallow breath as he looked at both of these trusted officers. On their faces lay shock when they took in the scene with the dead crewman.

Elara handed him a breathing mask, and he gratefully put it on. Each new breath relieved the burning sensation in his chest.

"We need to extinguish the fire. Elara, cover us."

She took position, her eyes hard as he pulled the cover off the extinguisher and depressed the nozzle. Foamy spray pumped toward the commdesk, covering it, and it soon smothered the fire.

Elara dropped her stance and moved to the crewmember. Her fingers pressed against the side of his throat, and he knew she was checking for a pulse. With a sigh she closed his eyes which gazed blindly upward.

"We need to clear the air," Grayson's voice ground out, and Duvall nodded.

"And the site needs investigation. Gray…" The band around his chest eased a little. "This has got to be kept on the quiet. Whoever is doing this isn't going to stop."

"I'll handle it, Duvall."

Duvall watched as Grayson called for air-cleaners, which were swiftly dragged in, and Elara removed the body to the SurgiTech suite. The temperature in the room dropped to close to normal.

Finally, as the room emptied, he lowered himself to the floor, waiting for Grayson and Elara to join him. Their faces were grimy and betrayed a bone-deep exhaustion.

"As you've guessed, we have a problem," he informed them. "It is my belief that we have an infiltrator aboard." His bald announcement shocked in its simplicity. "Elara, I need you to find out what happened to the engineering crew. Specifically, why it was empty and if there are any further casualties…or fatalities." He looked hard at her. "If you find even a sniff of something, I want to know. At this point, we'll keep this among ourselves and Chowd."

Security Officer Chowd had silently joined them and he

loomed behind Grayson.

"Take Chowd with you. From now on, we have to ensure everyone moving around the decks has a shadow. No one goes anywhere alone."

The words hung grim in the silence. Never before had it been necessary to use those methods aboard any ship he'd served on. Once this was settled, he'd be damned if it ever happened again.

"I'm going to retrieve Mellissa. I want both of you in my office as soon as possible. We need a strategy, and we need one fast." With that, he stood, then turned on his heel, leaving his trusted officers to attend to the cleanup.

✪   ✪   ✪   ✪   ✪

While Duvall had disappeared into engineering, the alarms kept blaring. Grayson and Elara had double-timed it out toward the smoke on his hail, and other members of the crew, disturbed, kept looking in the direction of the smoke. No one spoke a word, but the threat of alarm continued clear in the atmosphere of the room.

Mellissa's stomach churned. Was this it? Was her time up? She refused to admit that the thought terrified her. *Falling apart now is not an option.*

She wanted, needed to do something, but in this completely foreign environment she didn't have a clue as to what. So she waited, hands clasped, watching the crew in the mess hall. Time passed slowly as she feared what might happen to Duvall. What if someone had done something to the ship, maybe to lure him in?

Wild thoughts swirled and her stomach clenched as visions of him facing danger pounded into her head. Maybe he was injured or dead. She pushed those thoughts away. "Come on, Mel. This isn't helpful," she whispered. Her imagination had always worked quickly, overactive.

A dozen times she started to get up, but everything he and the security officers had told her filtered through her brain. *If you don't know what to do and don't have a role, stay out of the way until you are needed.* They didn't need her making a nuisance of herself.

It seemed like a lifetime until Duvall strode back, his gray uniform looking dirty with grimy streaks on his arms and back. His face sooty with trickles of sweat trailing down his face. His eyes looked tired and worn.

She moved to him, faltered for an instant, then the need to hold him raced over her. Just to walk over and hold him. To feel his body warm and alive against hers. To see him unharmed. It took a lot of reminding herself that not only would that be inappropriate, but also probably unwanted. She jammed her hands in the uniform's pockets.

She watched as he looked at her. He gave a nod, as if he understood her emotions. Then drawing himself up, he turned to address his crew. "We have a situation in engineering. I'll need everyone at their active stations, but before you leave, from this point…" He paused, looking around the room at each crewmember's face. "No one." He stopped to emphasize the point. "No one is to be on duty or to travel the ship alone. We are at alpha alert from this point. Any queries or comments, take them up with Security Officer Chowd. You're to ensure that you're adequately armed with weapons appropriate to your positions."

For an instant, he stopped and looked at her again. This time she saw something in his eyes—a fleeting glance full of hurt and sadness.

"Today we lost a good officer. Engineer Max Lingstrom gave his life in his duty to the Empire, to his crewmates, and to his ship. His loss will be mourned but never forgotten." He turned away. "Now, dismissed to stations." He said no more. He didn't need to. She watched the crew file past, questioning looks sent their way, but she ignored them.

✪ ✪ ✪ ✪ ✪

"*Barsha*!" The word erupted from Duvall's lips.

Mellissa looked up at him expectantly. Their eyes met, and suddenly, as if his life depended on it, he crushed her to him. His head speared down, and his eyes watched hers as their lips finally met, holding her close, his need clawing at him.

Warm, supple, and reassuring gave way to heat. His mouth opened over hers.

Compelling. Driving her to open for him.

His tongue launched into her satiny mouth. She moaned. Her exotic, spicy taste invaded his senses. She felt heated and pliant.

Pulling his mouth away, he lifted his head and touched his forehead to hers briefly. Looking at her, he saw her desire, banked but present in her gaze. He knew it mirrored his, felt it in her quickened heartbeat and harsh, panting breaths.

"Not now. We don't have the luxury at the moment, but soon. I want you." He looked at her, his eyes seeing through her to her desire. He wanted this woman with an intensity that shocked him to the core. "I want you. No interruptions. Think about it." He paused and looked at her to make sure she got the message.

*To hell with my mantra. I will have her.* This wonderfully warm and vital woman. He wouldn't and couldn't give her any promises, he reminded himself. But maybe for a time, they could enjoy the passion they shared.

"For now we have jobs to do. An infiltrator to find and a crewmember to farewell."

He held her hand in his, savoring her warmth for an instant. Then he turned with her and headed toward the door.

His tasks needed completing, and he had no time to waste. Coffee would wait. They would wait. But the time would come.

In a dim and dark room, far beyond prying eyes, a message formed. One that informed Crick Sur Banden of his people's failure and McCord's arrival with the woman. He wouldn't send the missive yet—couldn't until they cleared the slipstream—but soon. He would get them and the handbook. Then he would be a hero.

Crick Sur Banden had promised him his own ship, and a senior position in his new order. All he had to do was keep the others busy so they wouldn't stumble across the plans for Earth's history. He grinned. Once they arrived in the time they headed toward, he could collect the handbook and personally hand it to Crick Sur Banden. Then they would know. Then they would see his commitment to the new order.

He made plans to try again. This time, another would perish. He would get that bookpad though, and he'd deal with the woman. Nothing could stop him, and he'd prove to Duvall McCord, once and for all, that he was the better man.

The thrill of anticipation melted away. Duvall McCord had nearly caught him, so he needed to be more careful in the future.

He looked over the tiny communicator in his hands. That message had been a piece of genius. His plans to kill the woman would keep them all running in circles while he did his own job.

His task completed for the moment, he opened the door and moved toward the desk overloaded with work. He needed to blend in with them for a little longer. But oh, he would show them all. They would know and recognize his genius in time.

Grayson paced, Elara looked grave, and Duval just felt tired and more than slightly frustrated with the latest turn of events. The crew had been informed of the security status. No one worked or moved around the ship alone, not under any circumstances. Those few he trusted implicitly—and there could only be a limited number—he had taken into confidence.

He saw Mellissa looking at the hurt and anger in their eyes. He knew she felt helpless. But there wasn't much she could do for the moment. He'd already learned that she hated feeling useless.

Duvall's Chief Security Officer, Chowd, was the last to join them for the security briefing. As the tall, thin man took his place at the table Duvall's blood boiled. They had an infiltrator. He felt a betrayal of immense proportions. He would deal with the issue swiftly and efficiently, but the fire of anger still burned him.

One exemplary officer was dead, and the group he trusted was now pared down to the five he knew almost as well as himself.

"Please take a seat." He waited as the others lowered themselves into their chairs.

Mellissa bit her lip, her hands clenched together, and he acknowledged that his need to protect her and keep her close made no sense. But he'd long ago learned to trust his intuition, and right now it screamed she needed protection.

Chowd frowned. "Where is the senior comm officer and the engineer?"

He'd expected that question. "The comm officer is only on his first tour in this post. He lacks experience." It was a weak answer, but the best he could give for the moment. "As to the engineer..." His shrug drew all eyes. "I don't know him. Until I'm sure of his allegiance, I believe it's best to keep our information among us."

Elara opened her mouth, and he knew she was about to argue the point. He shook his head and she subsided.

"We have an infiltrator. The problem is, with so many crewmembers from different backgrounds, so many we've not personally served with, it's impeding our ability to investigate."

He took a moment to balance his thoughts. "We've encouraged multi-tasking and taken on those from outside our own... Dammit, it could be anyone."

Duvall considered carefully the need to use the skills and abilities of those he trusted, the crewmembers who would follow his instructions implicitly and ensure tasks were carried out without query. They needed a quick resolution to this issue. This time the damage sustained was minimal and repairable. Next time, though, they could have trouble. Thank *Eshra* the matrix remained intact. If that had been damaged...

No need to consider what could have gone wrong; enough had happened now. Focus on the facts, he reminded himself as he pulled himself up to his full height. Time to begin investigating.

He could see Mellissa watching their faces, saw the movements that indicated their knowledge and their willingness to follow any order, including that of *shoot to kill*. He had no question that they would follow this through to the bitter end.

She got up and reached for a glass of water. No one had time to clean up between the alarm and this meeting. The air still full of stale smoke, wafting from clothes worn in a stressful situation. The scent of sweat also filled the air, astringent. The jerky movements told him that she neared the end of her emotional tether.

"We need to bait a trap before we reach the Admiralty. Mellissa, I don't want to ask this, but I need you to agree to be the bait."

She looked shocked at his suggestion. He threw the piece of card he had picked up onto the table.

"I found this there," he stated baldly. "I don't care who it is, but they are baiting us."

His stomach churned at this necessity, but something had to happen. They had to find some way to flush out the one willing to let his crew, his people, die. The one who had made this threat.

Chowd and Grayson both investigated the card  Chowd

pulled out a palm-sized unit, checked the note with it, and passed it to Duvall again, without a word.

Duvall waited for Mellissa to glance in his direction. "I need to invent a situation where I have to leave you alone. I won't be far, and you will be safe. But I need you to understand that there is still an element of danger." He knew what he was asking her to do, could see in her face the second that it occurred to her. Duvall hoped she understood his frustration.

Banked feelings bloomed when she straightened her back and said the one word that changed everything. "Yes."

He looked at her. She needed to understand the danger she agreed to place herself in. His shoulders ached from fighting the tension. She looked around the room, and he could see that she knew everyone there was watching her, counting on her.

Never before had he felt so powerless, but they needed to know who posed a danger to them before they struck again. Next time they might succeed in either killing her or killing them all. Neither option would happen if they pre-empted the move successfully.

Mellissa's lips quivered as she spoke. "I know you need this finished, so what do I need to do?"

He relaxed slightly. "I need to leave you alone and attend to an emergency, something we can cook up." He turned to Chowd. "How long do you need to set this up?"

Chowd considered the request. "At least another six to seven hours. But in the interests of not putting them on their guard, I think it's something we need to leave at least another day or even two. We need them to think they got away with it." Looking at Grayson, he asked, "Can you arrange for the incident?"

Grayson thought for a moment before nodding. "Yes, I believe that we can make it look like the incident that previously compromised the enviro drives. We've been having intermittent issues, so that can be made to look believable, with only myself and Chowd to set it up."

Chowd scanned Mellissa up and down. "I can arrange for

a guard I trust to be stationed in the crawl space over the cabin. I have one in mind, and I would trust him with my life. We can also place one in the captain's cabin if she is within the ready room, which I believe would be most easily defensible." He looked at Duvall as he said that. "While I would normally suggest a Grade A secura-shield too, we only have one on board, and I would prefer to keep it as an emergency backup precaution."

Duvall stiffened. "What do you mean?" he demanded, feeling agitated.

"We had not finished accessing security supplies when the order came to ship out. I left you a message." The discomfort was clear in his short answer. He shifted. "We had minimal time at Aenna to complete the provisioning once the initial order came through that we had a mission. They only had the one, and the Admiralty experienced some supplier issues. They had more shipping within a short period of time. We missed the shuttle by thirteen hours."

Duvall considered the situation. What else hadn't been fully provisioned? Concern grew and he made a mental note to contact Admiralty when this mission was done. Sending them out without adequate security provisioning at this stage was something he didn't want to contemplate. Together with the interception of the transmissions Meredith had contacted him about, he began to wonder just how deep this deceit went.

He had so many issues to contend with. Meredith, his sister, in danger, a possible infiltrator aboard the *Elector*, and a woman driving him crazy, not to mention flying an ill-provisioned ship hurtling through the slipstream and time. The Empire was always in danger, and yet here he sat until they either got to the gate or hunted out the infiltrator aboard the vessel.

Admiralty's whole diplomatic solution had just imploded, he mused to himself. When he finally got back to Admiralty, his report to Elphin wouldn't pull any punches. His face tightened further.

"Captain, may I suggest we all get a good night's sleep and finish the planning process tomorrow when we're fresh? That would also allow time to consider all the aspects and perhaps gather further information," Elara suggested in a sympathetic voice. "We're all tired and not thinking clearly. As the resident SurgiTech, I recommend a minimum of four hours sleep. Six would be better of course." She looked at Duvall, and he knew she spoke the truth. Grayson chose well, he thought.

"The voice of reason, as always, Elara. We'll meet back here at 0700 hours. Dismissed."

The crew rose and filed out of the room.

$$\bigstar \quad \bigstar \quad \bigstar \quad \bigstar \quad \bigstar$$

Mellissa hovered against the wall furthest from the door as it closed after the retreating crewmembers. She couldn't sit any longer. Her agitation during the discussions had played through her mind, increasing her uncertainty. Duvall had asked her for help; she feared the task he'd asked her to complete.

Breathing deeply helped marginally, but her stomach still turned knots as she faced Duvall. On his face, she read the weariness and desire. *Hungry* was the only word that came to mind when she saw his face, stripped of the mask of civilized behavior, and she could see the instincts of a predator on show. It didn't shock her. Instead, she felt herself drawn deeper into his web.

"We should eat." That was all he said, but his eyes invited something so much more.

So clear. So green. So fathomless.

He turned toward his commdesk and ordered a meal, requesting that it be sent to his office. He spun around and she shivered in reaction to the promise she saw in his eyes. She knew the instant he saw it. The involuntary movement of her body must have signaled. His face tightened further as his eyes burned with passion. Her body heated in anticipation. Time to take a chance. Life was fleeting, and dammit, if she was going to die soon, she wanted to taste him at least once, and by heaven, she knew he wanted her too.

She smiled. In the midst of such danger, a moment had come. Theirs. She decided to grab it with both hands.

Dinner arrived and proved both an interesting and excruciating affair. How could salad have such overtones? She would certainly never look at it in the same way again. Each mouthful filled with expectation while their gazes caught. Unspoken promises passed between them. The experience became foreplay. Each swallow of drink, every taste enhanced her desire. He seduced her without touch and burned her from the inside out.

By the time the cooling sorbet came, she squirmed in her chair. The discussion was sparse; neither able to break the mood. Ahead of them lay only promise.

As he spooned the sorbet to his mouth, hers dried. His tongue flicked out, and he licked the small ice crystals. Inside her belly the fire erupted, stronger and brighter than ever before. His eyes smoked in their intensity, and his gaze glittered with knowledge.

Extending a hand, he asked her without words.

Mellissa answered in the curving of her lips.

They rose together, moving away from the table and toward each other. He reached a hand to her. Touched her face softly. Framed it and moved in to kiss her lips. Each action controlled. Just like a predator, she thought.

When their lips touched, she exploded. Their lips opened, and tongues tangled. His mouth was dark, his taste spicy. One hand rose to the back of her head; the other went around her. Her hands, neither still nor hesitant, rose to his shoulders, gripping him close.

Their bodies melded to each other. His mouth slipped from her mouth, across her jaw to her neck. She moaned her pleasure, her head thrown back and her eyes closed.

She savored the warmth of his mouth on her flesh. Her hands roamed over his chest, feeling the tensile strength beneath her fingers. She pulled at his shirt, wanting to touch his flesh.

Wanting him as much as he wanted her. She tugged with motions jerky as her hunger matched his.

His hands had moved to her waist, slipping under her shirt and roaming over her skin, the torture so exquisite. Tongues of fire followed in the wake of his fingers. She wanted him to touch her everywhere. Her breasts tightened.

She leaned back. Slowly, oh so slowly, he found the buttons on her shirt, slipping them through the holes. She felt the sense of release ripple through her body as each in turn exposed more skin. Her white bra molded to her breasts, peaked nipples clearly outlined. She watched as he stared, taking in their lush bounty.

"So beautiful," he murmured. His hand slid from her collarbone to cup her breasts through the cotton as they ached for his touch.

"I want to see you," she said, the throaty voice unrecognizable.

His hands left her breasts, brushed fingers away as he gripped his shirt. A single sharp action and buttons flew through the air as the cotton thread gave under the onslaught. Densely-packed, muscular skin bared to her sight. She hissed out her pleasure through clenched teeth.

He reached for her, holding her shoulders and pulling her close. Once more, their mouths mated. This time the press of his flesh to hers ignited a fire. She gasped.

He pulled her toward his cabin. Beyond lay a dimness. A bed, soft and welcoming. They reached it and fell together over the edge. Once more, he pulled her close.

"By *Eshra*! You are truly beautiful," he muttered against her mouth.

She opened hers and scorched him with lips and tongue. Duvall rolled her onto her back, releasing her mouth slowly, nipping at her skin, little nibble bites across her jawline that made her shudder. Her hands held on to his shoulders, almost mindless now, gripping and squeezing in demand.

*Oh God!* She wanted this man. Yearned to feel the power

of his body against hers, within hers, moving and soothing the fire that licked at her nerves.

Duvall pulled her up and reached behind to unfasten the clasp of her bra. He looked into her eyes, and the intensity in his gaze branded her. She took her opportunity and laved his skin, everywhere she could reach. The saltiness of his body enticed as the scent of arousal grew around them.

She brushed soft fingertips over his nipples. The small, brown discs reacted by peaking with each touch. Now came his turn to moan.

Her bra fell away, and finally her breasts were exposed to him, not small, but lush and pink tipped. He sighed and his eyes glinted. Her breasts had grown so very tight, the pink tips hard and aching, ready for the touch of his mouth. She watched his gaze narrow as he leaned toward one, opened his mouth, and drew the tip in.

The pleasure exploded as his tongue rubbed while he sucked. His hands didn't stop, slid over her back and down and around her waist to the button of her pants. She panted as he unfastened it, slipping the material down her legs.

She moved eager hands down his front too, needing to feel him and touch his length, so hard and yet silken, the soft skin with an iron hardness she knew lay just beyond the fabric. He pushed her panties to one side so he could find her core. She was wet. Hot and eager for him. Mellissa allowed her hips to move. Inviting. Tempting. Calling.

He rubbed his hands over the hair he found. Explored. Touched. Opened.

He found the small nub and touched it. Rubbed it.

She bucked. "Oh God!" she moaned, burning and writhing under his touch.

He drove two fingers into her sheath while she writhed, mindless with need. Her body gripping powerfully as she panted.

"I want you," he growled.

She tore at his pants, pulled on them, needing him, every delicious inch.

With a bark of laugher he pulled away and she mewled the loss. Duvall stood to remove what clothing he had left. Mellissa got a brief view of his nakedness before he tore her panties down her legs and flung them over his shoulder.

Reaching for her again, he covered her, and she tugged at him, loving the feeling of bare skin against skin. She grabbed his erection, finally feeling the glorious length of him in her hands, so tight and powerful, and he grunted as she traced her fingers over him. Her hands quested, found the base, and tested his weight. "So big."

He groaned and moved above her as she felt her way back to the tip, touching and exploring him. A droplet of moisture seeped out, coating the slit of his cock, and she smiled a feline smile of satisfaction. He was as wild for her as she was for him.

His fingers slid within her core and moved. Pleasure coiled deep in her belly while her breath fled. The sensual friction continued, and she shifted, undulating beneath him.

The longer he teased, the more urgent her desire, and Mellissa was sure she'd explode if he didn't fill her soon. She hooked her legs around him in demand.

"Yes." His grunt was all she needed as he positioned himself at her entrance. Duvall gave one push and joined their bodies.

She nearly came as the pressure of his entering surprised her, filled her. Made her whole.

They moved. He rubbed against her. She moaned as he gasped.

Hands gripped. Bodies grew slick with sweat. Faster and faster, they moved together. Harder. Demanding. The thrust and parry continued until finally she came apart in his arms, her body milking his before finally releasing.

So glorious.

He followed with one more thrust, clinging tight as the sound of heavy breathing filled the air. Duvall released himself within her, the feel of him jetting amazed her. They held on as their heartbeats slowed.

Duvall rested while Mellissa slept. He held her in his arms, dazed by the pleasure. Never had he experienced anything like that before, the pressure building or the primal need to brand and hold. To claim her.

"How can I follow through with tomorrow?" His mutter broke the silence, but another question rose. How could he not?

Inhaling her scent, he nestled her against his heart, feeling her softness. It was sobering to realize that whatever emotion it was that had taken up residence inside him could cause him to question his actions. She wasn't a warrior. She was soft and womanly.

Duvall had heard her talk of the orphanage where she'd grown up, of the hardships, but she wasn't hard because of it. Unlike him.

Over the years, Duvall allowed the Admiralty to mold him into a fighter and a protector, yet there he was, asking her to take risks. He'd have to stand back and hope their side of the ledger was stronger.

"What's wrong with me?"

She stirred in her sleep, and he pulled her closer, glad she wasn't awake to hear his fears. He shoved them firmly back into the box in his head, along with the other confusing emotion. The one labeled *commitment and entanglement*. But it was a long time before sleep came.

Awareness fluttered through Mellissa's brain as she slowly woke. He held her close in his arms, and she felt loved and protected. Things had moved fast, almost too fast, and there was no permanence implied. The feelings that coursed through her swirled around in her mind. Talk about jumping feet first into something. Not that she regretted it. The most amazing passion had surprised her.

In his arms, she'd experienced something she'd never felt before. Sure, sex had been satisfying, but she felt as if this promised so much more. The thought brought her up short. *He didn't promise anything, Mel.*

Even as she told herself that her heart ached at the thought of giving him up. But she wouldn't hold him if it didn't work out. She wasn't cruel. After all, she'd done well by herself up until now. She could do it again.

A tear leaked from the corner of her eye, and she dashed it away. Her heart argued that after an encounter like that, just maybe, she might find more to this than just lust.

Turning in his arms, she snuggled closer. He woke, turned, and smiled softly. Her heart nearly stopped, and she reached over to touch his face. He dipped his head down and captured her lips.

This time, the loving was soft, hands sliding over skin and soft sighs. And when they finally became one, the emotions filled her.

They slept again, holding tight to the other through the night.

# Chapter 5

**B**ing! *Bing!* Mellissa's pleasant dreams of a broad-shouldered Duvall holding his body to hers shattered in an instant.

Her eyes snapped open and shock ricocheted. Naked. With her. Holding her. Loving her. Hang on. She was…he was… The memories of the night came back. Mellissa blushed.

They had made love several times throughout the night, napping in between. What a lover, she thought, then squirmed. *God!* Her face heated as she remembered exactly what they had done—and how many times. His loving both voracious but also tender, Duvall had ensured that whatever they did, they were both fully invested—and boy, did she feel! Something she had certainly never experienced before. She rolled over, startled to see his eyes open, watching her.

"Good morning." Duvall rolled toward her, his mouth descending for a quick, passionate encounter with her mouth. The kiss scorched her.

He seemed regretful as he rose. "We need to dress and be ready. It's nearly 0600, and there's a meeting in my ready room in an hour. I need to check in with the bridge first." His eyes rested on her for a moment longer, then, regretfully, she thought, he turned away.

Unashamed of his nudity, he wandered around picking up his scattered clothing. She could appreciate that body, she thought. He was all long, lean flanks and miles of smooth skin. Duvall's body was muscular and warm. Mellissa grinned to herself as her gaze ate up the view. Never before would she have ever described herself as a sexual being. He'd brought that out in her. He'd held that body close to hers all night. Just remembering, she could feel herself get hot all over again.

"Uh, my clothes?"

The wolfish grin he gave her stole the oxygen from her lungs, and he gestured to the floor where her panties and bra lay strewn. Getting up, she reached for her clothes and quickly threw them on.

"Hurry up, and I'll grab us both a coffee." Mellissa needed a minute or two to get her mind on the task before any crewmembers arrived in the ready room, and to perk her mind up. *What if they can tell?* Embarrassment clawed at her. With a shake of the head, Mellissa reminded herself that she needed to work out her role in the skirmish ahead. Sure, her part was simple—be the bait—but inattention could bring the whole mess down in a heap.

Within the hour, they both waited in his office, strong coffees in hand, watching as the others entered the room. Duvall sat with Grayson, talking about the night just past, inquiring if there were issues with the ship, and the things she supposed that a stealth ship captain needed to know at the beginning of his shift. She watched his face and hands. His body. She could tell that he was confident in his role and that his crew obviously respected him.

Elara cast her a long, measuring look that said *I know what happened*, and Mellissa privately acknowledged that while she felt a little discomforted that the other woman somehow knew, she wasn't embarrassed.

She almost asked what had changed about her. Had she acquired some kind of glow? Were there whisker burns on her face? She slumped in the chair as she mulled over how this strange woman, who didn't really know her, had worked it out. When she took another deep gulp of coffee, Mellissa choked, her concentration still centered on the disturbing thought.

Elara's eyes glinted with amusement. "It's okay. No one else has worked it out."

"But…" Mellissa shook her head, not sure she wanted to know.

Duvall cleared his throat after the briefing with Grayson

had concluded just as Chowd entered the office, then the three rehashed the briefing from the night before. Elara's statement had been correct as the rest had allowed them to refresh their batteries.

They sat in the same chairs they had yesterday, ready to discuss the strategy. Mellissa listened intently but found it hard to follow, many of the terms they used beyond her understanding. She felt at a disadvantage but knew she had an opportunity not just with the upcoming skirmish, but with this new future, to do something amazing. *To belong.*

"We need to ensure that whoever is behind these attacks doesn't work out this is a ruse," Chowd said. "They need to be off-balance so we can get the maximum benefit from this little show." Grayson looked at Duvall expectantly. "I suggest waiting until tomorrow morning. One of us calls a minor emergency. Something believable but not highly technical. Given we don't know who is the infiltrator, they could be in any section, including engineering, security, or even on the bridge, so it has to be something that we can create and fix without assistance. The only section we can be sure of is medical." He glanced quickly at Elara.

"Suggestions?" requested Duvall, who had got up and paced close to Mellissa.

Both Chowd and Grayson shot assessing glances in her direction, and she reminded herself it would be unlikely that they guessed what had happened. Yet, from their questioning expressions, it seemed unlikely that this was the usual behavior from their captain.

Chowd ran his fingers through his hair. "I can rig a minor glitch to the environs system. A small tweak would ensure one section has a buildup within a valve. It's fairly simple to engineer something along those lines. It's not unexpected in a new vessel on her first major voyage to have these kinds of glitches, and especially after yesterday and all the smoke." He stopped for a moment as if examining a thought, then resumed talking again. "I would require at least moderate input from the captain and

Grayson, which means they wouldn't be on the bridge."

Grunts of approval came from the men around the table.

"There would be a secondary requirement for the security detail." Chowd stopped and shook his head, his brow furrowed. "I can arrange a mix-up in the security detail, that way it will seem as if everyone's bumbling around, unsure of who's on safety patrol."

"I don't think that would work," Elara piped in. "What about a test that's required by the SurgiTech, taking the security officer away for a minimal period? During this time, Mellissa could be within the cabin unattended or the office undertaking further training. Those are both believable scenarios."

The men looked at her, evaluating and weighing, and slowly, one by one, they nodded agreement.

"We'd still need the security patrol." Chowd leaned forward, and Elara nodded.

"We would need to assure Mellissa's protection," Duvall spoke sharply.

Once everyone had agreed, the officers assembled dipped their heads, and all seemed engrossed in other things, notes or handscreens. She sighed and looked in Duvall's direction. He frowned, clearly surprised they'd caught on. Elara had told her they hadn't, but it seemed as if his actions right now, his bald direction to them, had tipped them off.

She wanted to tell him that it was his possessive reaction that had affirmed their suspicions. Mellissa decided it was best to keep that to herself.

"I believe an officer in the crawl space, another in your cabin, and a tracer disc inside Mellissa's clothing would allow us to monitor her at all times," reassured Chowd.

"What time would we need to begin this?" Mellissa asked, suddenly feeling a little scared.

She looked at Duvall, seeking his assurance. The reality of the gravity of the situation hit once more and rocked her. She knew, no matter what protective actions they took, it could still go wrong. And this thing with Duvall, so new and precious, could be lost with one false step. His face appeared tight, and yet he reassured her with a sharp nod. She breathed again.

"Around 1000 hours would be believable."

Duvall moved back to his seat. "No. Tonight. We need this done quickly. The longer it drags, the more damage that can be done."

Chowd pursed his lips. "I could argue your decision."

Duvall gave a tight smile. "You could, but you won't."

"Of course, Captain."

"Just get on with it."

Elara snickered as Duvall spoke, and Mellissa could barely restrain the headshake.

"We don't want it to look like it is set up, and first thing in the day would smell like the set up it will actually be. We need to go about the day as usual, briefings and so on. Act in the way the crew are used to." Chowd nodded to himself as if carrying on an internal conversation. "By doing this, we can lull the saboteur into thinking everything is back to normal."

Elara nodded. "Even this meeting has been covered by the usual post-mortem reporting, so there can be no questions raised."

A chorus of grunts met her words. When Elara glanced in Mellissa's direction, she was frowning again.

"Since Elara is here, this fiction raises no questions among the crew." Chowd's gaze returned to his handscreen and he tapped something in.

"Captain, I believe that this all sounds quite plausible," stated Grayson from his seat. "But we need to take them alive. Who knows what information we will glean if we have the opportunity to interrogate them? They may even know the location of Crick Sur Banden and we'll be able to complete our mission before returning to the Admiralty."

Mellissa questioned the choice she'd made to agree to this plan. It was crazy. Insane. She didn't want to be here, yet she'd agreed. Now the reality impinged—she was to act as bait. Although her fears left her pulse racing, she wouldn't go back on her word. "How will we ensure everyone is in place?" Mellissa asked.

"Simple. Any planning must be done now, then there's no excuse for further contact. We have a fail-safe word or action, but any other contact needs to be either social after our shifts, or purely *Elector* related. No one will question the social side as we all served on the Ishtar together," Grayson assured her. "Above all though, whatever is said, we have to remain in character. Go about our daily tasks."

"We need a time plan, Captain. I would suggest we aim for 1830 hours. After the shift change so there will be few in this area as we place our key personnel." Chowd spoke quietly, his words pulling them back to the body of the plan. "I can have the support crew in place in the crawl space by 1800 hours. The security detail will be in place at about the same time. That way they can dribble in and be in place well before the time we are planning to run the ruse. I can have them booked into the holodeck for a training session."

The others gathered around the table nodded.

"I will personally handpick the security crew and place them. Most have been with me long enough that I'm sure of their loyalties, and I'll set duties to keep the others busy and away from this location." Chowd seemed comfortable with his decisions and laid down his handscreen. "Once they're in place, we need to maintain radio silence," he reminded them quietly.

"Good. Make sure everything is ready, Chowd. This absolutely must go to plan. I want the final rundown tonight by 1500 hours, maybe over a coffee here in my ready room. If you must contact me, secured channels only. Dismissed."

They all stood together, and without much more than a murmured word, trailed out, the only exception being Elara. She placed a hand on Mellissa's shoulder, giving it a brief squeeze and shooting a questioning look over to Duvall before she too left.

Mellissa could see Duvall's worry. Could read it in the way his eyes moved and the tense set of his jaw. She wondered whether setting the trap or their situation made him most uncomfortable.

She took a chance and stepped toward him. "Duvall? I haven't asked for a commitment, and you haven't offered one." Her lips quivered and she wondered if she'd done the right thing.

*You can do this.* But even thinking it hurt. However, if this was a problem, she needed to set his mind at rest, not make him feel trapped. Take the pleasure he offered and let it last her for as long as it would.

"And I know you will do everything you can to ensure my safety. I trust you." She smiled quickly before turning toward the desk screen and sitting down in preparation for logging into the sessions she needed to take.

Her chest hurt. There was more at stake than her feelings over what could be a brief fling. He remained quiet, and she told herself it was the right step, to reassure him she wasn't some kind of clinging female. With great effort, Mellissa forced her mind away from this relationship that wasn't and focused on the mission. A wondering *why* was nagging at her. Why her? What made them choose her as a target?

She looked up and saw Duvall watching her, his face closed as if he were trying to hold in something. A frisson of emotion arced through the air between them. Deep and dark. She shivered.

Finally, Duvall excused himself. "I'm needed on the bridge." He hailed the security officer as he left.

Mellissa sat alone at the conference table and dropped her head into her hands. "How the hell am I going to get through this?"

There wasn't an answer. Only the sound of the door chime, heralding the arrival of the female officer.

Mellissa spent the day familiarizing herself with the

technological advances that had happened since her time.

"There's no use in trying to find work until I understand where it all came from."

Sharia, her security officer, gave a laugh. "I can't understand how you got by without commbadges and using currency."

"Money." Her correction had Sharia nodding.

"I could never remember that in Ancient History."

Mellissa winced at Sharia's words before returning to the vidscreen and the documentary she was watching. Perhaps that was where her future lay? Teaching others about her past. Maybe in a university or museum. The moment of excitement passed when Mellissa considered that she'd be something of an antique.

"I wonder what work might be available for me once we reach the Admiralty?" Mellissa said.

Sharia glanced in her direction. "It will depend on what useful skills you have."

Clearly, Mellissa needed some kind of plan for the end of the journey. Her brief time aboard the *Elector* had whetted her appetite for interstellar travel. She knew her skills were neither innovative or of the new time she would inhabit, but she felt sure that she could learn quickly and become useful. Adaptability was a skill she had in spades.

Besides which, everyone important to her would be gone. She worried about the effects this would have on those left behind, especially Jemma. They'd held together since their time in the orphanage. The thought that she'd be gone and Jemma never know what happened… She closed her eyes and took a deep, calming breath before returning to her work.

Perhaps the Admiralty needed a researcher? Someone with knowledge of her time? The question kept her busy for some time, formulating a plan of attack.

A thought bloomed. Maybe Duvall needed someone with her skills to ferret out information here on the *Elector*? She filed that away as something she could consider and discuss down the track.

Mind you, it seemed that Duvall was laboring under the tense cloud as well. He had spoken about his concern that no transmission had arrived from the Admiralty, and he'd been white-lipped while worrying about his sister, WO Gentry.

He explained the bouncing of transmissions through the slipstream when she queried him, further adding to her store of knowledge and surprising her that they'd found a way to communicate through time. There'd been more than just a thread of frustration and anger in his tone as he informed her that this kind of radio silence wasn't unusual.

His explanation that her family had fostered him and their relationship was familial had washed away the traces of jealousy she felt when first hearing of Meredith. It didn't soothe his concerns that he hadn't he heard from Admiral Elphin, his long-time mentor.

When he dipped his head into the alcove she shot a smile in his direction. "I just wanted to check in and see how things are progressing."

"They're going great, Duvall. I think I'm mastering the commdesk and the vidscreen, see?" She swiveled the screen so he could see. Then she sobered and leaned toward him. "Any news?"

Surely by now he'd have some kind of communication with Admiralty, but the frown chased those thoughts away and she knew he'd understood her question.

"Nothing. It's silent." He sighed. "I don't know. Maybe it's because it's my sister, and maybe it's not. It's not uncommon for them to keep radio silence." He shrugged, and for a moment she had to fight down the urge to comfort him.

"It'll be fine. I'm sure of it."

"Yeah. Look, I better let you get back to work. I'll just…" He turned and walked away while she watched.

"You like him?" Sharia spoke softly, and she stilled.

"Yeah. I do."

✪ ✪ ✪ ✪ ✪

Duvall brooded through the day. He knew that his feelings were now firmly tangled.

He'd crossed his own line, putting the needs of Mellissa before those of the Admiralty, the crew, and the *Elector*. There had to be some way to break his dependence on her touch and smiles.

The first step, he felt, was to find a way to keep a distance. When she moved into his office to start her data input, he excused himself and worked from the bridge for most of the day.

He knew if anyone, friends included, privately thought him a coward, they would never say so to his face. Inwardly, he agreed with them. Sometimes, though, the coward's way was the only way forward, so he remained diligent, reading reports, making decisions, and overseeing his officers on the bridge. By lunch he was almost climbing the walls.

"Are you going to call her?" Chowd towered over him, and Duvall grimaced.

"No." He wanted to. Heavens knew, just hearing her voice would likely give him a surge of adrenaline.

"You want to." Chowd dropped down into the seat beside him. "This is the first time I've seen you knotted up by a woman."

Duvall shook his head, hoping Chowd would stand up and walk away. He didn't. "Look, I really don't want to…"

Chowd sighed and rose. "Well, should you change your mind, you know how to find me. The shift is taking a break. I'm heading to my office to sort out paperwork." But even after Chowd left, he mulled over the question.

A million times he reached to contact her, but every time he drew back.

Later in the day Elara brought him coffee. He accepted the hot mug with a smile.

"Where's Mellissa?" The glint in her eyes betrayed her interest.

"I'm not sure. Maybe on the holodeck or in my office."

He refused to be drawn, that yes, he knew exactly where she was. He didn't need to ping her locator.

In his mind's eye rose a picture of Mellissa, her face sheened with sweat, her eyes glowing. The lump in his throat grew bigger, as did another region of his anatomy.

He cleared his throat. "Why?"

"I want to be sure she's adhering to a nutritionally efficacious diet." The grin betrayed her teasing words.

"I had Chowd organize her food. He delivered it to her at 1300 hours."

"You could just—"

"No, Elara. Don't. Just, don't."

For a moment she looked downcast before her ready grin returned. "Fine. Not now. But soon you're going to have to consider what you're doing. She needs to know too." With a nod that told him she'd expressed what she came to say, Elara moved away. But it left him with plenty to think about.

Duvall told himself that he didn't need to know her whereabouts and that what he felt was a simple and uncomplicated attraction, and no doubt in time he would actually believe it. It did not change the fact that he worried about her, wanted to be with her to the exclusion of his responsibilities. That alone contradicted everything he believed and practiced in the years of his career with the Admiralty. He wouldn't compromise his crew and his ship for one woman.

Better to keep a distance between them in whichever way worked. Deep down, he knew he lied to himself.

The day passed quickly as Mellissa stayed busy. At 1700 hours Duvall contacted her to tell her preparations for dinner had stalled.

She knew exactly what that meant. The plan they had meant to put into play tonight was postponed. Mellissa drew a heavy sigh of relief. One more day before she had to face whoever their enemy was.

Duvall joined her at the end of the day for the final meal in the mess. The room was a hub of activity when she arrived with Elara, Sharia having finished her shift hours earlier.

"Does everyone eat here?" Mellissa asked.

Elara gave her a questioning look. "What do you mean?"

"Well, from what I've read, the senior staff of the services usually have a different dining room."

Elara's laugh tinkled through the air. "On some of the ships we practice that tradition still, but because of the size of the ship, it was considered and discarded. We need every available bit of space for reinforcement and... Well, the hull plating is thicker than average, meaning we have to be more frugal with the layout."

"Oh." Now Mellissa understood.

Elara encouraged her to join the line, and she made her choices. They'd barely settled into their seats when Grayson and Duvall joined them. Grayson stole a quick kiss from Elara and Mellissa looked away.

"He likes you." Elara spoke quietly once the two men left to join the line.

"I..." What could she say? She liked him too? That he was excellent in bed? Instead, she grabbed a celery stick and started chewing on it.

"If you need someone to talk to, I'm here. I'm his friend, but I can be yours too." Elara reached out a scarred hand and placed it on hers, which rested on the table. "Remember that."

Tears threatened as her eyes burned, but she managed to keep them at bay, while a warm glow bloomed in her chest. "Thanks. I appreciate that."

The men returned and any kind of personal conversation ceased.

Mellissa anticipated the night to come, but Duvall surprised her wishing to spend the night quietly. He showed her his collection of movies from past eras, pointing out that he had some, which were by comparison old, but new to her. He suggested she pick through his collection. Then he left her to view them by herself, excusing himself on the grounds that he had work to complete.

She sighed inwardly and watched two of the movies, enjoying what the future generations thought was a representation of her time. Watching them trying to use money was hilarious, and she couldn't help laughing out loud.

Mellissa ached at the distance Duvall tried to put between them. She knew what she wanted and understood he needed to feel in charge. She even remembered Jemma's most useful piece of advice. *Men like to feel invincible. When they get moody and quiet, leave them be.* The memory felt like cold comfort as she looked out the window as she rose from the lounge in his ready room. Each time she looked in his direction during the movies, he'd had his head bent over his desk, and in the end she simply gave up, yawning and stretching.

"I'm going to bed." The emotions she'd been containing exhausted her. She'd participated in physical training sessions, and emotionally she was battered by things she'd learned and experienced.

Her need to share everything with him grew stronger with each passing minute. Mellissa was also aware that her personal defenses were weak right now. The drag of the reality and unknown, of what she would face the next day, swamped her.

In silence, she crept out of the room toward his cabin, grabbed her nightclothes, and changed in the ablution room before padding softly toward the bed.

"Lights out." She lay there listening to the room beyond. She wanted to call out to him but restrained herself.

"Moonlight display?" the computerized voice queried.

"Engage," she answered.

Moonlight filled the room, and the soothing patterns eventually lulled her to sleep.

✪ ✪ ✪ ✪ ✪

Duvall told himself to stay away as he heard Mellissa head for the cabin. The sounds of her pattering around in preparation for sleep called like a siren, but he firmly ignored them. "Don't be foolish. Ignore it." But no amount of muttering and reminders helped as he worked his way through reports with only half his mind engaged.

He worked until his eyes burned and weariness dragged him down. When the time came to retire, he found he couldn't stay away. It was beyond his ability to ignore her.

Even as he rose and headed for the cabin, he called himself a million types of fool. Yet, staying away and ignoring her felt wrong. He moved into the room silently, and the moonlight captured her image, making her skin glow. The last thread of resistance snapped when he caught sight of her, sleeping in his bed, by moonlight.

"Damned foolish instincts." Duvall stripped off his clothes, letting them fall into a pool at the side of the bed, while he watched the rise and fall of her chest.

He climbed into the bed beside her and gently lifted her into his arms. She roused, drowsy eyes opening to his, not hiding any of the longing he could see in her eyes. He gave in, both of them needing the reassurance of intimacy and touch.

"Duvall?"

The whispered words echoed, and he smiled. "Yeah, I'm here. Now let's get these clothes off you."

She shivered a little but slid off her bottoms as he toyed with the top. When she stopped, he drew the material over her head. This time, the loving evolved, soft and slow. He traced her body as she moved with him; she held him close while he adored her. Hands gripped, bodies sheened and strained, and finally the stars were within their reach. They found them together.

When they woke in the morning, they still lay wrapped in each other's arms.

Sitting at Duvall's commdesk, Mellissa busily scanned through information he'd arranged for her to view today.

"I hope I can concentrate." She shook her head, clearing the memories of the loving the night before.

"That good, huh?" Sharia winked, and for a moment Mellissa wanted to duck beneath the wood desktop.

"I…uh…"

"It's okay. Captain McCord is a great guy and a hero." Shock ricocheted through her. "Hero?"

"Yeah. He and Grayson are the ones who found Elara. They've tracked down quite a few who've been taken prisoner by Crick Sur Banden. That's why he's been promoted so quickly. There aren't many in their thirties who have command of a ship like this."

Mellissa absorbed the shock. But it made sense. She'd seen just how comfortable he was in the position and the way his people respected him. It also explained why the *Elector* had been targeted and his mission.

That brought her mind back to the situation, and that she was waiting to bait and hopefully unmask the infiltrator. *Dear God! Let it be over quickly.* Nerves, like butterflies, took wing inside her belly, flickering and fluttering anxiously. *Don't let me make a mess of this.*

She desperately needed to contribute to this crew who had welcomed her as one of their own. They'd all helped her immeasurably, and she felt some enduring friendships would grow from the experience, especially with Elara and Sharia. During her brief time aboard the *Elector* the women had bolstered her mentally during the meetings and chance encounters. The women exuded warmth and understanding, which Mellissa badly needed.

Duvall strode into the office, and she rose. He shook his head, and she wandered to the coffee pot and poured a cup. Her hands trembled as she lifted it to her mouth. Nearly time, screamed her mind. The butterflies became great big bats, whirling inside her stomach, and she put the cup down with a clatter.

The chime of the comm interrupted her musings. "Captain McCord, please meet me in SurgiTech. We have a situation that requires your attention."

Duvall cast Mellissa a look that said *stay safe*, then he left without a word, striding forcefully through the door, his long gait eating at the space until finally he looked back briefly. He only uttered grimly, "Security Officer Cooper will be here with you." Then he turned and moved through the doorway, out of sight. His eyes had burned her with intensity.

Now came the time, she thought as the door slid quietly shut behind him. She was on her own except for Sharia, soon to be called away on some bogus errand. Her last visible barrier of safety, she mused.

Not more than five minutes later, Sharia Cooper received a request from Elara to come to the sickbay, and she instructed Mellissa to "lock the door after me and only allow myself and the captain in."

She watched her leave the cabin and took a deep breath to steady herself, arms wrapped around her middle defensively. Her stomach clenched with nerves, and she made an effort to appear relaxed and settled. Not an easy thing to do though.

Mellissa touched the ankle holster that Duvall had pressed on her earlier in the day, containing a small laser pistol. "Dammit all." She dragged the tiny laser out and clutched the small weapon in her lap. It was hidden on her lap under the desk. She wouldn't use it unless she had to, but it became a safety blanket, she told herself. Sharia had taught her how to use it during the sessions they'd passed on the holodeck, but she wasn't confident.

Mellissa made herself scan the information on the screen before her as if she didn't have a care in the world, but nothing made it through the fog as she sat there. Waiting.

She worked hard to appear engrossed. She wasn't very

good at acting and squirmed with nerves in the seat while waiting for the traitor to arrive, her body shaking. Chimes sounded, then the door shushed open. The engineer, Corbin Jard, entered the room, his hip canting against the edge of the wall. He looked friendly, yet in his eyes, she detected a wary perception.

"Miss Davis, what a pleasure, and just the person I needed to talk to."

She held herself still, the tiny laser wobbling in her lap. The moment they had planned for had come, and she'd be damned if her actions jeopardized the planning with an ill-conceived deed or action.

Mellissa smiled. "Officer Jard, what can I do for you? As you can see, the captain isn't here. I think he got called to the SurgiTech. Would you like me to buzz him?" She kept her voice even and friendly, as if nothing untoward was taking place.

He looked around, and she had the impression he was assessing her. "No. It makes no matter whether he's here or not."

His eyes took on a frigid hardness, which left her quaking inwardly. His pale blue eyes and sandy hair made him look so very ordinary, and yet she knew that made him far more dangerous. Her mind told her he made the perfect infiltrator.

He slipped a hand into his pocket and tugged out a snub-nosed weapon. She gulped, knowing this could be the end. Slowly, he raised his weapon.

Mellissa's fingers slid a little on her own, clutched in one hand.

"What…what are you doing?" Mellissa had to play for time. They wanted to take the infiltrator—Jard—alive if possible.

Her free hand toyed with the mat, finding a small, hidden communicator. Using her nail, she pressed the tiny button so Duvall would hear everything. Just as they'd agreed. Jard had information they needed, information that could break open the web of deceit.

"Why are you…" Her voice trailed off.

"Poor Mellissa Davis. Plucked from your own time, only to become a martyr for the cause." He spoke quietly as he shoved away from the wall and advanced in her direction. "Don't you think I would make a great captain? Sadly, as much as I think you'd look great on my arm, it's already too late, isn't it? You've taken up with McCord."

She shook her head forcefully, not trusting her voice.

"Oh, don't lie. I've seen those looks you give him." He sneered, and she shook in her seat as his vitriol filled the air around her. "Well, all I need to do is take a few minutes while he's busy. Then in one moment, you're gone and he's lost. Couldn't have planned it better myself, could I?" He laughed, the sound strident, as if he wasn't quite in his right mind.

She rose with care, lifting out of the seat. "You don't mean that. I haven't done anything to you." She slid her hand behind her back, hoping he wouldn't catch sight of the tiny silver pistol.

"It really doesn't matter anymore. Now come on, Miss Davis, how about you make this easy?"

She took a deep breath, expanding her lungs. "Why? Why would you do this?" she asked, her voice breathless with fear.

"Why not? I've been promised my own ship. A crew who will be loyal to me. I've watched Duvall for years. It all came so easily to him, while I've had to work. But now I'm on the winning side. Just ask Crick Sur Banden." His voice threaded with hate, betraying the depths of rage he held for Duvall. "While the women threw themselves at Duvall, he turned them away, leaving what was left for the rest of us. The more he turned away from them, the more he got them." He leaned in. "He knew people before he even started at the academy, which meant he got the mentorship of the Admiral, and let's not forget the position of captain of the *Elector*."

He looked at her, his eyes glittering with a madness she hoped never to see again.

"Crick Sur Banden himself offered me a place in his regime when he finally defeats them Admiralty. He wants Duvall, and I'm happy to give him to my master. I can get even with Duvall, set the Admiralty into a spin, and do it all in one go. First, I got the handbook, and now I get the woman." Jard smiled broadly once more. "I can't wait to see what opportunity comes next." His voice rose on the final words.

He started forward, once more raising the gun that had dipped down during his rant. She moved in the split second that he depressed the trigger, dropping as she had been instructed. The whining shot whizzed over the top of the chair where she had sat just minutes before. A sound split the air again, this time aimed at the center of the desk, but she moved just in time, rolling over the floor.

He lunged and prepared to fire again, and just when she knew he would shoot, a different low whine came from the doorway of Duvall's cabin.

A security officer had soundlessly moved from the cabin to the ready room and fired on Jard, but the engineer caught sight of the officer and ducked, evading the shot.

She panted breathlessly, fright pushing her to protect herself. She crawled to the meager safety afforded by the meeting table. Peering over the tabletop she could see his face, surprise and hatred warring on his features. This time Mellissa and the security officer both managed shots, Mellissa's making contact with the desk as Jard once more attempted to duck, but the security officer's aim was true, connecting with Jard's body as he grunted.

Jard's body was mid-swing, and momentum continued, turning him as he pressed the trigger, his gaze locked on her. This time she could see her face mirrored in his eyes, knowing the pistol was automatically acquiring a target.

Aim and fire, she thought, as a whine split through the air. Jard moved backward toward the desk, the acrid smell of burned flesh filling her nostrils. He fell, his body thudding against the desk and hanging there for a split second. A final whine split the air as the officer squeezed out one more shot. It connected with center of Jard's chest.

His face, cleared of shock, assumed the blank mask of

death. Jard's corpse slid, and the sound of the body thudding as he hit the deck echoed.

Mellissa could hardly breathe. Her stomach heaved, wanting to empty her breakfast, but she controlled it firmly. Jard was clearly dead, the immediate threat neutralized.

○ ○ ○ ○ ○

Duvall waited for the signal from the security officer while listening to Jard's diatribe. He ran after the quick bleep shrieked. His pulse thrummed as his legs pumped, eating up the metal decking.

Would he make it? Visions of Mellissa lying on the floor, bleeding out, haunted him as he panted, his body moving faster than ever before. Duvall reached the door and pulled it open, but for a moment he was sure it was empty. He moved toward his ready room and heard the whine of lasers, his heart stuttering in his chest.

He pushed past the security officer at the door, then stopped in his tracks. One look at Jard on the floor and his face tightened, not just with distaste but also the shock of betrayal. He swiftly headed for Mellissa across the room, where she sat huddled on the floor, pale and shaking. He reached for her. "Are you hurt?" he demanded, his voice rough with emotion.

She shook her head wordlessly, and he lifted her into his arms. She held onto his arms as he hurried to remove her from the room. Once safely within the cabin she looked at him, her face pale. "I did what I had to."

"I know, honey." Holding her close, he damned himself and the need to use her, unable to conceive why it had felt so wrong. He rocked her, soaking up the warmth of her body, and she lay in his arms. Silent. Soundless. That tightened the knot in his chest further.

*What have we done?* He'd never felt so frightened in his life as he had when he'd had to leave the cabin and Mellissa.

He'd known the risk was high, but had made every attempt to protect her. It had been enough to protect her body, but what had it done to her soul? Yet that damned card had ensured she remained in the middle, whether he wanted it or not.

"God, I nearly didn't make it to SurgiTech. I worried the whole time," he told her gruffly. "I don't think I could have coped with you being hurt." He kissed her hard, holding her body tight against his, his lips seeking reassurance that she was unharmed. They both knew this emotion exposed only the tip of the iceberg where their feelings were concerned.

She pulled away, and he growled.

"Not now, Duvall. We need to work out what he knew." Her voice was husky and forced.

He felt her pain, but wasn't sure how to help her. Of course, he knew she was right. He needed to find out what Jard had been up to. They knew why Jard had betrayed them, but it didn't make sense. When had he had the opportunity to meet with Crick Sur Banden?

He thrust the questions aside. Finding answers to the questions at this point was Chowd's role. He trusted him with his own life and that of this fragile woman lying in his arms. He and his command crew would find out everything there was to know.

He watched as Chowd gave orders to his people who came and went, some checking the body, while others were sent to search Jard's cabin. Chowd started making lists of known associates. The security officers wasted no time looking for clues and answers.

Engrossed in what was occurring, Duvall was surprised when Mellissa roused, shifted in his arms, then pulled away. "You have work to do," she said, her voice hoarse.

He couldn't deny her statement, but he was unsure if he should leave. When she pushed against him, and uttered a firm "go," he stood and spoke firmly. "You'll rest here." He didn't wait for her acceptance, just strode out to his ready room. Now he would join with his crew to get the answers.

Chowd stood sentinel at the door, directing his men. "What do you plan to do next?" Duvall asked.

"I've got men checking Jard's office and his private compartment. If they find so much as a notation on a piece of paper, they'll let me know. He has to have communications equipment, though I doubt we'll find any more than a go-between at the end of the comm." Chowd's words reinforced his own thinking.

"We have to have this cleared away before we reach the Admiralty."

"I would agree with that, Duvall. But I don't know that we're going to have all the answers you want."

Duvall dragged a shaky hand through his hair. "No. But whatever we have is going to be a step in the right direction."

Duvall's fury banked while they worked to piece together the known facts and made him short with the crewmembers. In no time, Jard's remains were removed from the office, Elara taking control of the corpse with her customary efficiency.

"We'll take him to the morgue," she said, her words soft while she cast an eye over Duvall. "How's Mellissa coping?"

"She's..." He shrugged. She'd remained in the cabin, her face chalky white, and she'd refused any offers of anything.

"I'll go check her over if you'd like?"

He nodded. There wasn't much else he could do for her right now. Tension wrapped around him as Elara disappeared inside the cabin and time passed at a creep. When she finally reappeared, he sucked in a breath. "Is she okay?"

"She'll be fine. I've prescribed a shower and something to eat. She'll join me up in SurgiTech later." She left him then.

Chowd was ushering his people out of the room, and Duvall brooded. There were so many questions. How to deal with the body, and questioning the trustworthiness of his crew felt like bitter blows. His anger at Crick Sur Banden rose like a fire in his throat.

He checked the incoming reports, and Chowd took the seat opposite him. Ready to share the information recovered from Jard's cabin.

"He had accessed a range of Admiralty records, and his personnel file showed anomalies that hadn't really seemed so out of place before. Placement on destroyers, nothing out of the ordinary there of course, but some of the dirtside placements included Rubicon VII," Chowd told him.

Duvall scanned the placement records as they talked. "Rubicon VII is a training outpost."

"One of the most taxing we have. There is a lot of dissent there." Chowd relaxed back into the seat. "Most of the men sent there face war-like situations."

"Even so, how did he meet with Crick Sur Banden? We have no intelligence of his being there."

"He's not going to tell us where he's likely to visit." The bitter words slipped from Chowd's mouth.

"No. So what came next?"

"He was given his choice of placements. He asked for the *Star of Ishtar* then, under Elphin, and from there jumped straight to the *Elector*. I'd extrapolate that he bided his time, knowing the perfect opportunity would come up. I would suggest that all his following placements were at Crick Sur Banden's request."

Duvall ached to lay his hands on the rogue leader. "Do you have his service records? What's in the personal folder?"

Chowd handed it over, and Duvall flicked through the pages of the hard copy. He exhaled with a whistle having found a notation in his final months aboard the *Star of Ishtar*—an extended leave.

"That was when we were finalizing the placements. I remember, distinctly, that he was unavailable until just prior to launch. I nearly replaced him, but Elphin himself had crewed with him. Told me he was a great engineer and just what the *Elector* needed." Duvall smothered a curse.

"He only arrived the day before, the only other time I'd met him was when he came aboard to receive his orders and uniform. That would coincide with the disappearance of the handbook."

"*Barsha*!" Given the duration of his leave, it was certainly long enough to get rid of the stolen book.

Chowd shifted in his seat, it squeaked a little, and Duvall shot him a searching look. "Duvall, there will need to be changes in the security screening in the Admiralty."

He agreed, grimly making a mental note to add it to his written report for Elphin.

Once they had the mess cleaned up and the members of the team debriefed, Duvall returned to the bridge as the approach chimes sounded throughout the ship. As the ship entered the approach to the gate that would take them out of the slipstream, Duvall mused that so much had happened in a short period. From there came the approach to Aenna.

Mellissa trailed behind him as he made his way to the bridge. He'd watched her and itched to grab her in his arms.

He'd forced her to grab a quick meal in the mess hall, and Elara had indicated that she was steady enough. His reluctance to have her out of his sight remained a concern, but she'd handed herself so well and coupled with her lack of combat training, he felt dealing with the aftermath might require some coping strategies. He made a note to discuss that with Elara.

Duvall motioned to her to take one of the vacant security spots nearby, watching as she let herself sink into the seat just as he did the same. He flicked the commbutton. "Boys and girls, time to leave the slipstream. Find your allocated places and strap in. We have no idea what we're going to find waiting on the other side."

They both agreed that on a ship the size of the *Elector* no secrets such as that of the Corbin Jard situation could be hidden. So he'd briefed the entire crew earlier, ensuring they understood exactly what was at stake.

Mellissa felt like a fraud, sitting beside Duvall on the bridge. His people worked efficiently so that when the chimes rang through the air, there was no sense of panic.

"Shielding set to maximum, Captain."

"Preparing report for transmission."

The voices called out to Duvall, and he acknowledged each and every one.

*Admiralty.* The very word imprinted itself on her brain. Would they see her as a liability or an asset? What future could there be for her in this new time?

Would they allow her to stay, or would they send her back to her time? Or worse still, send her to somewhere far from Duvall? The thought of the last two options made her shake.

On one hand, this relationship, if she could call it that, was new and untested. He hadn't promised her anything, yet the care he'd shown after Jard—she shied away from the memory of his body and knowing she'd shot him—told her he felt something. If she were honest with herself, she wanted a chance at building something long term with Duvall, but the knowledge she was leaving everything and everyone she knew behind filled her with despair.

"God, I'm a mess."

Duvall shot a look in her direction. "Just… Just talking to myself."

Closing her eyes didn't make her feel any better. Mellissa knew their short time together didn't make for a stable grounding for a relationship, but oh how she wanted the chance to build one, to consider what might come of their time together and whether it would be a long-term thing or just a short-term fling. Either way, she felt committed to making it work. *But is he?* Her chest ached, as did her mind. *I've got nothing to gain by running this around in my head constantly.*

She nervously looked around the bridge. Everyone seemed to know what to do, and even Elara, as the ST, had a spot and strapped in.

A large patch of black loomed before the ship, and she gripped the sides of her seat. A jolt, thud, and whine of the drives of the ship seemed to change pitch. The flowing star trails stopped, and once more she looked upon twinkling stars through the screen ahead. Slipstream behind them, an enormous gate loomed. Slowly, almost gracefully, the *Elector* sailed through it.

"Welcome to my time." Duvall had turned and watched her. He smiled suddenly, seeming more at ease, she thought. "Comms, any unfriendlies?" He turned toward his main comm officer, a young, blond man at the console.

The comm officer turned briefly and looked at Duvall. "None on the first sweep, Captain. However, I'll run a secondary sweep using the radar transmission in case there is the potential for cloaked bogies." He turned, and his fingers flew across the starpad station situated next to his desk screen. He cocked his head to one side briefly, as though listening through headphones, shook his head, and this time, when he looked at Duvall, he smiled. "No bogies out there, sir."

"Grayson? We need to make time to Admiralty. Better take us to maximum running speed. Gaines? Keep an eye peeled for unfriendlies. I'd hate for things to get any more interesting." He grunted.

A ripple of nervous laughter split the air.

"Elara, take Mellissa to the ST station and start running her through the systems. Show her the basic medical devices, just in case you need an assistant." He turned and looked at her before turning back to his desk screen. "Chowd, go with them. I need you to do a quick assessment of the ST facilities anyway."

No time like now to prepare for the worst-case situation, she thought, watching him turn back to his station. Not that he had any expectations of interception this far into Empire space. She could read his body language now. His body had lost some of the aura of concern, the tension of earlier washed away. But given what had already happened on this mission, somewhere deep inside, she wondered if he also dismissed her.

She shook herself and quickly re-evaluated what he had done. She realized that his sending her to the SurgiTech suite was a way of giving her a place aboard the crew. Not only did he ensure she felt like she had a role, but he wouldn't take any chances with her safety. They both knew there was potential for further threat on the ship, though neither admitted it. She worried that he had left himself vulnerable, but then she reconciled herself. Other security officers worked on the bridge. And he had a job to do. Best to let him get on and do it. She rose and followed Elara.

# Chapter 6

**M**ellissa wandered around the SurgiTech and marveled at the changes in technology that brought about the array of tools that could heal so many things. She entered a tiny cubicle, carrying the equipment Elara had handed her.

The first time she'd been in this room, she'd woken on the bed over by the wall. The slim bar, currently retracted into the wall, was smooth and metallic in color, she knew from experience. Elara watched her from the doorway as she cast her gaze around the room with interest.

"What are these?" Mellissa gestured toward long, cylindrical devices that were stored on a shelf by the doorway.

"Those are applicators. I think they're similar to what you called syringes? We use them to deliver a dose of whatever. Most of our medications can be absorbed through the skin."

"So different to our time. I hate getting needles."

Elara laughed. "Then you're admirably suited to our time, I'd think."

The next room looked more like a traditional ward. Four beds held position against the walls with a larger one in the center. "That doesn't look very comfortable!" It reminded her of a photocopier top.

"It's a holobed. We use it for diagnostic purposes, so it doesn't need to be comfortable. Just unobstructed."

The last medical room in the suite was a mini intensive care unit. It contained two beds. "How do you manage by yourself? I mean, you've got seven beds total. That's a lot of bodies to cope with by yourself."

"Most of the crew have a modicum of medical experience. If it were necessary, I could request assistance through Gray.

But mostly, the injuries I deal with are able to be repaired quickly. You're still thinking with a twenty-first century view of medicine." She dragged Mellissa into her office. "Even the common cold and cancer no longer require long-term treatments. We've come a long way, Mellissa."

"But what about the scarring on your arms and face?" The words slipped out before she could recall them.

Elara smiled. "Well," she answered good-naturedly, "just like in your time, the sooner they are treated, the better the outcome. In my case, a considerable amount of time passed before I was rescued. They look a lot better than when Grayson found me. Now? They're just a part of who I am and my experiences."

Deep down, Mellissa thought that perhaps they still held Elara to a past she hated. She saw the bleakness that filled Elara's eyes for a second, and she mentally kicked herself for causing Elara pain.

"So, how did Grayson and Duvall know where to find you?" Mellissa knew that she probably shouldn't open that can of worms, but she had an inkling Elara needed to talk about it, remembering that brief flash.

"More by luck than design." Elara's face screwed up, her green eyes crinkling. "The guards got hungry and one went out to get food and forgot to lock the door. Grayson and Duvall patrolled the area and they had continued looking for me because my family knew Duvall's foster family and they asked for his help. Neighbors had lodged complaints about weird noises coming from the warehouse where I and others were being held. They hadn't been able to get in previously because the doors were locked, so Duvall and Grayson followed it up, and while they were watching one of the guards left. They crept in and found me with the other guard. Pretty simple really," Elara said.

"So, Grayson stayed with me while Duvall called for a SurgiTeam, and I guess it all happened from there. I was sixteen at the time. I joined the EEA—" She grinned at Mellissa's lost expression. "The Earth Empire Academy. That was at eighteen, and I entered SurgiTech training then. In time, when Grayson and I caught up, he found out what I was doing, and it kind of went from there. I could say it was fate, but I'll let you in on a secret. I had always kept tabs on him, and we became friends who hung out together, because…well, because I wanted to thank him, and of course I thought he was something sweet. But the rest is a story for another day." She grinned at that.

"I applied to be on the *Star of Ishtar* when there was an opening for a SurgiTech so I would be on the same ship as my friends Duvall and Grayson. When we were finally deployed together, things happened. Mind you, I had to help it along somewhat." She smiled. "Duvall is great too," she added coyly, whipping a quick look at Mellissa then turning back to her diagnostic instruments.

"Yeah, he is," answered Mellissa. "The best."

Elara turned around. "You know, Duvall isn't really quick to trust, yet he somehow seems quite different with you. I don't know. Maybe it's not my place to say anything, but if your feelings aren't deep, please be honest with him." She looked at Mellissa with a piercing gaze, then her face softened. "But that's not really the case with you, is it? You have feelings for him?" She smiled at Mellissa, who stared, before she continued, "I hope it works out for you two. He is so much more…I don't know, human? Relaxed? Comfortable, even? With you. I'd like to see him happy and settled. Well, as settled as he can be." She chuckled.

Motioning toward a machine, she changed the subject.

"Come on, let me show you how a bone regen works." She picked up a tiny box with straps extruding. Its lights flashed, and Elara continued to show Mellissa the marvels of the time.

On the bridge, Grayson handled a range of day-to-day matters while Duvall worked through the background files they had downloaded on Corbin Jard. Nothing really stuck out as to why he would turn traitor, just the information they had already gleaned.

No single opportunity existed for an engineer to meet with one of the Ru'Edan except on Rubicon VII, as Jard had according to his dossier. It worried him that at some point an officer with whom he served had turned his back on his race and people and aligned with some of the worst sort of murderers. How did the opportunity arise? The question plagued Duvall

He slipped through the list of postings in case there was more to this situation. The *Crede* under Vosman, the *Explorer*, and even the *Inflector*. All Star Cruisers, but not in senior posts. The *Meritorious* and the *Bountiful*. Hang on. Didn't the *Bountiful* carry some diplomats from the Ru'Edan? He quickly keyed in the dates; briefly, his spirits rose. Maybe he had blown the situation out of proportion. The answer came back.

No. No match. "*Barsha!*" he muttered under his breath.

"Captain? We are on approach to Aenna. Ground Control is requesting our commsig." The routine of planetary docking intruded on his thoughts.

"Thanks." He tabbed the mic. "All stations to position. Entering Aenna space in three minutes. Find your seats and buckle in."

He'd given Elara instructions to bring Mellissa to the bridge as they prepared for the approach. He knew she'd enjoy the view.

Meanwhile, he had some communicating to do. He tabbed the secondary mic. "Aenna Ground Control, this is Captain Duvall McCord of the *Elector*. Requesting final approach to Admiralty." He waited for the response.

"Aenna GC, *Elector*. You are cleared for approach. Hangar A33-Z2. Commence your approach. Approximate entry in five minutes from my mark. Aenna GC out."

The bridge became a hive of activity as his people filed in, taking their places. The low hum of the engines, the buzzing of communicators, and the flashing of lights as information streamed through the viewscreen settled him briefly with their familiarity. Everything and everyone worked at their tasks. Updates on every aspect of the ship and preparations flicked to his desk screen.

He knew the instant Mellissa had arrived on the bridge, making her way to the seat she had filled earlier, strapping in and preparing for the entry to Aenna. Her gaze briefly flicked to his, and she gifted him a small, private smile before her gaze moved once more to the large screen at the front of the bridge.

Aenna rose on the viewscreen, light gray with domes filled with light, a pillar of darker gray rising in the black sky, and beyond it a field of smaller gray objects. They moved closer and closer, thrusters employed to keep them on a true approach. The ship moved and swayed around other items as it made its way toward the hulking asteroid-sized planet they aimed for. He concentrated on the approach, watching the information still scrolling on the screen.

His people were well trained and the approach smooth. The largest gray structure they headed for came into view, rimmed with lights. He tensed briefly then relaxed his muscles; watching the ship maneuver into dock always affected him. The ship slowed as it moved into the hulking structure getting lower and lower toward the ground.

When the ship finally entered the hangar and landed, the hangar doors closed behind them, the vision from the rear of the ship filling the viewscreen. He once more tabbed the mic. "Well done. Complete the shut-down sequence and await further orders. Captain out."

A tinny voice filled the air. "Welcome back to Aenna, *Elector*. Please ensure any flight crew not required within the base remain on ship. Captain, please alert us when you are ready to disembark. You'll need to move through the hangar to the end entrance and make your presence known to the staff before proceeding to your meetings. Ground Control out."

"Ahh, the voice of bureaucracy." He smiled.

Of course, landing at Aenna wouldn't be complete

without signing the appropriate paperwork. His eyes swept over the bridge. Time to get the ball rolling.

He unclipped his safety belt and took a few steps to Mellissa. "Come on. Let's go find the Admiral. Grayson and Sudonne are with me."

The four turned through the doorway together. She knew Duvall had completed his mission, and he required her with him for the reporting. He'd earlier pointed out that ensuring the Admiralty took note of her assistance would work in her favor.

She could only hope that now the Admiral made an order for her placement aboard the *Elector*. She watched Duvall, wondering if he was about to request another security officer based on the information that had been uncovered, but he obviously thought differently about it.

Mellissa felt a frisson of something close to anticipation tinged with fear. What would the Admiral say, and would they allow her to stay with Duvall? The fear swirled inside her. *All I need is courage. This is a time for new beginnings.*

Their footsteps clanked as they made their way along the corridors of the *Elector*.

They went to the rear of the ship, and the ramp descended with a groan while they waited. They exited the ship into the large hanger, and she couldn't help but gape at the sights before her. Great big walls of gray metal rose from a concrete base, and large lights beat down upon them, making it heated after the cooler atmosphere within the *Elector*. Beyond, near the walls, what looked like glass barriers rose from floor to ceiling, and workers swarmed in and out of these areas.

"This is huge." She could tell the scaffolding around the shed also served a second purpose—to hold crane-like structures and lighting.

Bodies seemed to swarm over the *Elector*, which rose like

a great bird within the hanger. They worked without speaking, the only sounds the creak and groan of metals and equipment. The *Elector* itself sat in the giant hanger, black and sleek with only simple writing in white on the side that she could see, the occasional light shining on its gleaming hull.

"How… When…" She hadn't grasped its size from within, but now it rose like a great creature from the dark. The wings tapered toward the rear, and a range of what looked like portholes dotted the sides of the beast.

Mellissa felt a sort of communion with this ship. This ship had now become her home, and she feared that this might be the last time she saw it.

"The Admiralty moved here about two hundred years ago. The location was chosen because it could be easily defended. It's a bit hard to get to." Elara chuckled.

Sweat trickled down Mellissa's back, the collar of the gray uniform itched, and she had to swallow the urge to hide, to run, or at least hold Duvall's hand. She gained strength from his proximity, and her gaze roamed over the view from the back. His starched uniform glittered with silver pips on the shoulder. Silver on dark gray. The way the uniform molded to his body made her mouth go dry, and she itched to touch him once more, but this wasn't the place and certainly not the time.

Elara walked beside her while Grayson strode along beside his captain. Mellissa tried to maintain an air of nonchalance, but it was difficult under the circumstances.

They reached the end of the hangar and Duvall opened the door. "Come on in." He smiled, and her insides turned cartwheels.

Then she stepped through the doorway and into another world.

Hidden from view, another planned.

"Oh yes. The time is coming. You, McCord, will suffer as you should have before. Indeed. This time, though, I will make it painful for you. You will suffer an anguish such as you have never known." The man watched Duvall McCord and his second-in-command leave the ship, duly noting the women accompanying him and the deference McCord paid to the one beside him in particular.

Oh, what joy to make him suffer. She looked like his weak spot, and maybe she'd be the next avenue he attempted. He rubbed his hands together gleefully. Once Duvall McCord was out of the way, then he could move on to the next target. His plan was underway.

Of course, Duvall thought his problems solved finding Jard, but far from it. It would take time for his chance to come, and he grinned at the thought. The best opportunities required time to build. He would set his plan in motion; he couldn't guess when the opportunity would rise though. Jard had failed; he had his ways of knowing these things. He had deducted that immediately when they started unloading the bodies from the hold, one covered with the flag of the Empire, the other in an unmarked casket. A dead giveaway. He snorted at his own joke.

But patience was imperative if he hoped to be successful. Crick Sur Banden promised him a place in the new order, perhaps even his own ship, but he needed to wait for the chance. He stood and moved to the rear, helping to carry the bodies from the ship, smiling as he concealed his thoughts.

Duvall watched Mellissa. To date she had met every challenge thrown at her with grace. He watched her back straighten there in the hanger; he had held her in the aftermath of the attempt on the *Elector*. He had held her in his arms and experienced the passion she shared. His emotions jumped from humbled to confused and back again.

From all accounts, this problem with the Empire loomed much bigger than anyone had expected. The records of transmissions off the ship had borne that out.

"If only we knew where the communications led," Duvall said.

"We'll find that out. Chowd will get to the bottom of that." Grayson's words were an attempt to soothe his ragged emotions.

They had to get to the bottom of it and quickly, otherwise others would be hurt, or the Empire and Admiralty compromised. Not on my watch, he vowed.

Behind him, Mellissa marched over the plascrete flooring in the hanger. He turned back once, and she frowned. She looked both frail and yet strong in the gray Admiralty ship suit he had found for her. The uniform didn't really fit her, but that was a small thing. He'd arrange for that to be attended to here. Then she'd be far more comfortable and relaxed. A feeling rather close to possession jerked through his system, shocking him to the core.

*Since when do I do possession?* This woman's a keeper and you're not, he reminded himself. Long-term wasn't in his plan, and now he certainly couldn't start thinking about commitment to a woman; his commitment to the Admiralty had to come first. He struggled to remember that with her curvy body so close to his.

"Grayson, I need to find my sister's office, and we'll need to meet with the Admiral. I transmitted the report to him, so by the time we arrive he'll have the basic facts. For today, I think we should stick together. At least until we sort out the lay of the land." He looked at his second, who nodded a quick agreement.

"I agree. Both Mellissa and Elara should stay with us," he said, his response terse and to the point. Grayson looked back at Elara and Mellissa as though quietly ordering them to follow his instruction. Elara quickly touched his arm in assent then dropped it.

He knew she had wondered about Elara and Grayson's

relationship and had asked on the ship during the time in the slipstream. His brief explanation of the system of Communing had come as a revelation. Marriage as a formalized partnership had been discarded among all but the very religious or rich. Society had accepted Communing, an alternative, with no barriers. It allowed for monogamous and committed relationships between members of the same and different genders, races, and species.

She was a strange mix for someone with a firm Catholic upbringing. He'd seen the documentaries on the old religious beliefs and was also aware she'd been raised in an orphanage. No doubt she'd experienced a very strict interpretation of their beliefs.

They'd discussed the concept of marriage and the exchange of rings over dinner one night, and he'd made the case that the removal of a ring seemed easier than the removal of the markings etched into their skin. For that reason, he explained, society now preferred the marking ceremony. It was odd, talking to someone with direct experience of times he'd learned about in history. He shook his head, trying to get it back on track. Thoughts of her disturbed his concentration.

They reached the door, a large frosted-glass-looking affair that slid open when Duvall raised his palm to the scanner. Then they entered the room beyond.

The door slid open to a world away from the hangar.

Soft, muted colors of gray and blue met her eyes. Carpeting, lush and thick, continued as they entered into what felt like a corporate office. Several young women in matching blue uniforms looked up at their entry; some saluted, but they all came to attention at Duvall's entry. One of the women simpered as she looked at him. Mellissa mentally dismissed the woman, all legs, blond hair, and blue eyes. Big boobs. Nothing to hold his attention, she snorted inwardly.

Duvall strode over to a large reception desk. "Duvall McCord and members of my crew. We're here to meet with Admiral Elphin."

"Oh, let me alert his office." The woman smiled and simpered while touching a key on the screen before her, and Mellissa's gut churned. "He's free and would like you to proceed. Do you need me to guide you?" There was a determinedly hopeful gleam in the woman's eyes. It was on the tip of Mellissa's tongue to say no, but Duvall beat her to it.

"We're fine." Taking Mellissa by the hand, he led them down a long corridor toward an office.

The atmosphere within the offices felt hushed and unhurried, yet conveyed an air of determination. No decorations adorned the walls, just a number of blue doors, each with a palm screen beside them and a discreet silver nameplate. They moved toward the far door without pause. Mellissa wanted to crane her head and take in the scene, but they were hurried along.

"So apart from the fact that you need to check in with your Admiral, why are we here? Why not just leave me on board?"

Duvall stopped, and she nearly cannoned into him. "I need to report, and we need the Admiral's help in integrating you into society, which is why you're here. There are also a few other housekeeping matters that need to be dealt with, and I need to see my sister."

"Okay." She wasn't sure if she was satisfied, but the door slid open to a secondary waiting area, this one even more intimidating than she had expected.

The heavy wood door acted as a physical barrier, and two more women waited beyond it. It was clear they held rank. They looked up as the crewmembers from the *Elector* entered. The first woman smiled at Duvall, and Mellissa had to restrain the tiny bite of frustration that rose within her. Once the woman looked in her direction and noted the proprietorial way Duvall ushered her forward, her smile became a grin. Mellissa took another look at the woman. She was the quintessential willowy woman, with blue-black hair. One of the ones that always got the guy because of her brains, she thought sourly.

The second woman looked at him warmly and remained sitting, tapping a comm, and though she was slightly older she also flirted subtly as she tapped a button beside a flat screen. Quickly addressing the person on the other side, she explained, "McCord, Myatt, and Sudonne are here. There is another person with them." She smiled into the comm.

"Send them in," boomed the voice through the device.

The tall woman—Francesca, her badge told Mellissa—gestured to a retracting wall, which Mellissa hadn't noticed previously. The door opened, and they went through the doorway to see the man behind the desk waiting. He rose as they entered, extending his hand toward Duvall.

She wondered if the man could tell she and Duvall had some kind of relationship. After all, he had brought her along with the other two to the briefing. She met the man's intense stare once he'd greeted the others, pushing aside her roiling thoughts. Like he would really give a damn. But she felt as if he was sizing her up.

"Mellissa, this is Admiral Elphin. Mellissa Davis."

He nodded acknowledgment at her brief, "Sir."

The Admiral motioned that they should each take a seat, then Mellissa watched the Admiral while Duvall briefly outlined the situation. Finding the handbook within her shop, the necessity to transmit her to the *Elector*, and their speedy removal from the area before detection was laid out for the Admiral. Duvall explained the attack in the slipstream by Jard and the short transmission from Gentry, the Admiral's face growing darker with each fact.

"To answer your questions, I haven't answered your hails, as there are concerns around some intel. You sent through a report indicating possible breach in security. I noted your concerns, Duvall, but I felt complete radio silence on this matter would be best. You remembered what I had always drummed into you—right from the academy."

Duvall looked at him, his features schooled, but she could see the whiteness around his mouth that betrayed his anger and frustration, both of which he was working to control. His hands gripped the arms of his seat, the knuckles white.

"You mean radio silence is best when there are any doubts concerning security. Yes, sir, I do," Duvall intoned. It sounded rote to Mellissa's ears.

"Yes, Duvall, exactly that. Now on to the other matters you raised." He glanced at notes on his desk. "Ah yes, WO Gentry. She came to me immediately. It seems someone certainly tried to get into her office, but she had caught on and had an escape plan in place. She found her way to my office and waylaid me. I arranged for a priority shuttle to Earth at the first opportunity and put our best security officers I could spare to protect her. Currently, she is in Bundaberg, with your mother, under heavy guard. She also encountered some weird transmissions, she tried to alert you to when she narrowly evaded capture. The infiltrators here managed to get into her office as she escaped. I can't tell you how as I don't know, just that she is safe and uninjured. What I do know I'm keeping safe up here." He tapped the side of his head with a blunt finger. "I am concerned that your report indicates this goes much deeper than we thought. There's at least one potential mole here in the Admiralty, one aboard your ship. We don't have a damn clue as to how many others at this time."

Duvall's lips tensed further and Mellissa was tempted to reach out and take his hand. "We did attempt to take Jard alive."

"Oh, I realize that, Duvall. As a result, I'm calling in all my operatives in the Diplomatic Corps to ascertain what they know. There is one, I think, who may shed a little more light on this, but…well, to be honest, I haven't raised her yet. She's been in deep cover for a long time. Until now she's always been reliable, and this close call with Gentry….well…"

His voice trailed off as he spread his hands wide above the desk.

"She isn't answering my queries. I can't do anything right now to extract her, and that angers me. I don't have a competent crew to access. Anything I do in pulling personnel may tip their hand to whom I have on the inside, and as a result, their contacts. If she's not in trouble, I can't compromise her, in case she has found a way into their organization, and I cannot jeopardize this mission. The last I heard she was on the brink of a major breakthrough. I certainly hope that's correct."

"Admiral, I can understand your situation. I believe that we may be able to pull a lead through WO Gentry, but we would need your support to raise a mission." Grayson sat forward in his chair as he spoke. "I believe that they are aware that Jard is dead, but I would expect his contacts will attempt to access his records and-or effects as they could potentially hold secrets we have not yet discovered. We think that's similar to the reason Meredith became a target as well." Grayson indicated himself and Duvall. "We need access to Jard's apartment on Earth. Further, we believe Miss Davis may also have seen or heard something that makes her a target now, though at this point we don't know what it could be. That would account for the attempt on the *Elector*." He flicked a look at Duvall.

Duvall's face tightened upon this assessment, and even the Admiral noticed it. "Son, is there something else you need to tell me?" His brows rose with the query. A small smile played at the corner of his mouth.

"Mellissa is an innocent bystander in this whole mess. I removed her from the situation in order to minimize the possibility of further casualties. She didn't know anything about the handbook, and it's my intention to keep her safe."

Mellissa sat upright in her seat, a smile playing over her lips. *Yes! He wants to keep me aboard the Elector.* Elation swept through her.

Duvall turned toward her, his eyes sorrowful, and fear pierced her. "I think it best to put her under your protection, Admiral, until such time as we can get to the bottom." He all but spat the words out.

Now she sat, still as stone, her heart taking on the likeness of a rock, heavy in her chest.

*No!* She wanted to scream and rage, but there'd be no benefit in that. Besides, she'd promised not to hang around if he decided he was done with her. It seemed more than obvious their time had already passed, and she'd missed the signs.

"Duvall, if I could ensure her safety I would, but we've already experienced one breach here. I believe the best place for her now is aboard the *Elector* with you." Elphin rubbed a hand over his face. "You need to rendezvous with your sister and find out what information she has. In the interests of her safety I bundled her out of here as fast as I could without gaining a lot of background about the information she's acquired."

He looked defeated for the briefest moment, and Mellissa had the impression that it was an uncommon emotion for the man. In the blink of an eye, whatever she'd seen on his face was gone, and he straightened up.

"My priority is to investigate and find whoever had the temerity to attack my people on my own ground. I need you to go to Earth and get the information and put it to work for us. I'll arrange sealed orders for you within the hour. You'll also need to finalize some documentation for Miss Davis. See my Executive Officer for that. In the meantime, arrange a restock of the ship as required, and access whatever crew and armaments you believe you'll need. I won't compromise on this mission, Duvall. We have to get to the bottom quickly before this spreads and we face a bigger issue." He stopped and looked at Duvall. "And McCord? This is N-T-K. Inform your crew of whatever you believe they need to know, but keep it brief."

He looked over at Elara.

"Sudonne, I have made arrangements for you to access whatever equipment you require for the SurgiTech suite. I'm aware your provisioning was incomplete when you left." His gaze returned to Duvall. "McCord, I've sent the Commissary aboard to ensure you're fully stocked with food, water, and any items that were unavailable at the time of the initial provision run. I can't spare any further security staff at this time, but we have taken steps to replace your engineer. I have already arranged for a list of available crewmembers for your perusal. All are immediately available, and I believe at least one on the list will fit your criteria." The Admiral almost smirked at the final comment at Duvall. "And for *Eshra*'s sake, take care. I may need you again, Duvall, before you leave Aenna. Be available." He nodded their dismissal.

"Yes, sir." Duvall was tense and marched toward the door, only stopping once it opened.

"I believe Chowd would appreciate some of your time too." On that strange comment he left the office and headed to the desk in the anteroom.

Mellissa followed him, dejected and hurt. When she looked back at the Admiral, he surprised her with a tiny smile before his door closed on her

Within the hour, all members of the crew had arrived back on the *Elector*. Duvall's anger spiked at the rigmarole he'd been through. In front of him was the choice of a new engineer. "I hope there's someone suitable on the list."

Grayson shot him a grin. "You have four options, but I think I know which one you'll take." He slid a sheet of paper in front of Duvall.

Looking down, he scanned the names, and some of the tension melted away. "Yes. Raven." Of the four possibilities, there was one he not only trusted, but had also served with before. "Grayson, contact personnel and get CE Raven Fraser here pronto."

Grayson accepted the sheet of paper back. "Thought you'd feel the same. It says here, if we can make immediate contact, we can pick him up at the space station when we dock there on our way to Earth."

Grayson exited his office and Duvall sighed. As always there was a backlog of paperwork to transmit, including the final file transfer for Lingstrom. He contacted his widow through the vidscreen and hated the stoicism with which she accepted his condolences. While he was with the Admiral and completing the necessary clearances and paperwork the equipment and stocks were being loaded at double-time. He wondered where Mellissa was and was surprised when a new name entered his list of active personnel.

Mellissa Davis. Junior Research Assistant. An inquiry flashed that she was to be allocated a cabin and the necessary uniform allowances. He grimaced. During their brief meeting with Elphin he'd seen the way she paled when he'd mentioned leaving her with Elphin. It bothered him that she didn't understand it was for her safety.

He growled and turned back to the piles of paperwork. The chimes on the door sounded again and again as his crew entered, made reports, deposited documentation or relieved him of some.

The last minute checks ensured that they'd only need to make one more stop on their way to the new mission, but as each time another new person entered, and none were Mellissa, his temper frayed a little more.

Ten minutes before they were due to depart he'd settled himself into the captain's sling on the bridge. His gaze settled on the chair he now considered as hers. Empty.

Duvall opened the communications channel and hailed Elara. "Is Mellissa with you?"

"Yes, she is. We're about to make our way down to the bridge. Do you want—"

He damned himself for foolish behavior. "No. I'm just checking on her safety."

Of course, he was fairly sure Elara wasn't in the least bit convinced, when moments later she ushered Mellissa to the seats. Even as Mellissa took her spot, he could see that she was determined to give her full attention to the movements of the *Elector*. With a sigh he gave the command to engage engines.

The *Elector* withdrew from the hangar, her movements

slow and pendulous as she crept like an enormous dragon from its lair. The whole time the maneuver was underway, Duvall was aware of Mellissa's scrutiny.

Duvall backed the ship away from the hanger, his hands on the controls. Mellissa knew his skills were the result of hours of training, but the minute movements of the large ship still amazed her.

During the short stay at Aenna, Duvall had arranged for a low-level clearance of documents and access to schooling programs so she could continue to study and become acquainted with the current time. It had become clear that she'd remain on the *Elector* for some considerable period of time.

Duvall had also taken the liberty of having all her items, the few she had, moved into his cabin. She wasn't quite sure how she felt about that given he'd tried to offload her at Aenna. Did he want her? Didn't he? It was more than a little confusing. Her fingers curled into the padding on the arm of the seat.

The sounds and movement on the bridge increased, rousing her from her reverie. The by- play between Duvall and his crew was respectful as he called orders and they responded efficiently. Meanwhile, Mellissa watched his face and those of his crew as they interacted with each other. It was clear the crew respected him in the way they responded to their captain. Each member of the crew had a role to play, but for the first time, she had a clear idea of what her own role would be. Soon, she would commence her role as the *Elector*'s junior researcher. For now, she had to be content, Mellissa reminded herself.

"Aenna GC, *Elector* here. We have completed pre-ascent check and request clearance." His voice soothed her even as a frisson of excitement raced through her body.

"*Elector*, this is Aenna GC. Clearance to go is granted."

The gravitational forces pushed her back into the seat as

they shot out into the dark, inky sky.

"I'm pleased I won't be experiencing that too often," Mellissa muttered.

Elara glanced at her and smiled. "You'd be surprised. But the first few times are always the hardest."

Her stomach tightened as did her chest. She took one deep breath after another, panting slightly. No one else seemed to be bothered and she frowned, feeling like a failure. Finally, the forces released her and she filled her lungs.

Duvall opened the comms channel to address the crew. "We are en route to the space station. I will be heading for Earth with some of the senior crew. In my absence Chowd will be acting captain. Any issues, take them up with your direct supervisor. On our return we will be picking up our new chief engineer. Once we leave, I will update the crew with the mission specifics. Captain out."

Duvall had already informed them of the circuitous route they'd be traveling, and she heard the hum of the thrusters even as ripples of vibration tickled her feet. The sensation energized her. A quick glance at Duvall told her he was watching her with an intentness that was overwhelming.

"What?" she asked.

"We will need to slingshot back toward Earth once we clear the asteroid field," he informed her, and he quickly gave the navigator the command to plot a course to Earth. "It will take us a day and a half ship time to arrive at the space station. Meanwhile, Sudonne and Grayson, my office 1500 hours." He stood, motioning for Mellissa to follow him as he left the bridge.

Earth was only thirty-six hours away.

# Chapter 7

**D**uvall ushered Mellissa down the stairs quickly.

He'd fought it, but the urgency within him kept building. Did she feel it too?

Her gaze was distrusting, but unable to help himself, he turned her from the bridge. Spinning her in his direction, he kissed her just beyond the doorway. Whatever she did now, he'd tasted her once more and hungered.

"Duvall?" Her gaze slid over his face. "You tried to get rid of me. You told the Admiral…"

He growled. "Only because I wanted to protect you. But the whole time I felt like I was slicing off a part of myself."

Dammit, he'd hurt her. Without intending to. His swiped a careful hand over her hair, pushing a stray strand behind her ear.

"I would have come back for you." He leaned in, his lips touching hers. He'd wanted soft and gentle, but the hunger roared, taking control.

He'd prepared himself to let her go. Hell, he'd steeled himself for it. Told himself he didn't mind saying goodbye and that it would only be for a time. But when the Admiral refused his request, the bubble of hope in his chest had erupted, warming him through. She was his now. His responsibility, he'd told himself, hoping to stave off the emotions. It was a weak argument.

Now, here she was, vibrant and wanting him. In the midst of such upheaval, she was prepared to take a chance on what could only be a short-term liaison. Yet something, an indefinable quality in her smile, called to him, made him want what he had always refused himself, and this time he couldn't deny it.

Their feet tapped on the metal planking as they hurried down the stairs and angled toward his office. Feeling a heat rising within him, he swiftly pressed his palm to the plate, and the door slid silently open. The need burned in his gut to touch her again. Once could never be enough.

They stepped inside, and in a whirl of movement, he grabbed her as he gave the command, "Door lock—unlock only on my voice print."

He pushed her to the wall. The passion he knew she'd see on his face was also in hers. His body met hers, so soft and yielding. He pressed in. The warmth of his breath mingled with hers. She opened her mouth, ready for his. The shock of soft lips touching his, her tongue invading his mouth was electric. His hands grasped her body, hauling her closer.

She moaned low in her throat. The passion of her heat burned him, shaking his existence.

He needed it just like he needed air to breathe. Her hands came up, grabbed his head, holding him closer to her, gripping him. Her body arched into his, and *Barsha*, he still wanted more.

"Mellissa!" His hands shifted to the top of her suit, grappling with buttons.

Caught up in the fever of lust, he nonetheless recognized that she shook as much as he did. With shaking hands she clutched at him. He hurried to burrow under her clothing to touch the skin below. The need to hold her and love her made him clumsy as he peeled away clothing without his usual practiced movements.

He lifted his head. "I need to touch you." He pulled her away from the wall and tugged her toward the middle of the room, all the while working on unfastening the closures of her suit.

Her face suffused with color as she panted, her breathing fast and broken. He itched to grab her, but let her hands have free rein for an instant before brushing them aside. He ripped off his suit, letting it drop to the floor, then dispensed with what remained of hers. She stood in her underwear before him. His hands gentled on her, slipping below the band of her panties, and she mewled her pleasure. They shared a carnal kiss, full of molten desire, tongues tangling together.

He worked his other hand into her bra. She grabbed his shoulders, and he felt the bite of fingernails digging into his muscles. She moaned as his finger found her center. Warm, wet, and enticing. He slid a finger inside her, slowly moving in and out, ratcheting up the desire that scorched him.

Mellissa dropped her hands to his briefs, burrowing beneath, and he shuddered. She grabbed his buttocks tightly and molded them with soft movements. He groaned into her mouth.

Savagely, he lifted his mouth, sought her eyes, and said, "I am going to have all of you. I need to feel you. I need to be inside you. Now." With a quick jerk, he tore her panties off her, then had her bra sailing over a shoulder.

One quick push had his underwear down his legs, freeing him from the constraining cloth. His chest shuddered as he stepped back, glorying in the sight before him. She was hot and naked. Ready for him as her skin glowed and her breasts moved in time with her heaving breaths. Her eyes glittered, and her lips were swollen from his kisses.

He jerked her back into his arms, angling her toward the cabin door. They tottered tightly wound around each as they made their way through the doorway, then he pushed her down onto the bed.

He could feel the shock of her skin against his, and it sent ripples of sensation down his body. Opening his mouth over her breast, topped with a pink bud, so tight and erect, he sucked the luscious berry into his mouth and laved it with his tongue. He suckled at her breast while she grabbed his head with her hands, urging him closer still.

His fingers danced within her, pushing her closer and closer to the brink, while she grew wetter and tighter. *Hotter.* She squirmed and writhed in pleasure.

Letting go of her breast, he slid his mouth down her body. His tongue and lips skated over her lush skin, down her belly and past the silken curls. Toward her core. His tongue touched the soft folds hidden under the curls that lay there. He pulled his hand free and spread her legs while the other slipped beneath her bottom, arching her up toward the most intimate kiss of all. She opened to his mouth as he set his tongue to her, long strokes that left her jerking beneath his ministrations.

His tongue invaded, and his free hand roamed, stroking and touching. Her cries were incoherent as she gasped and moaned. Her hips undulated. He murmured broken words against her skin, eager to push her further. She gripped the sheets, head thrashing as he invaded her totally, finding the sensitive nub and flicking it with the tip of his tongue. Finally, he lifted his head. She grabbed his shoulders, pulling him up.

He came up to meet her mouth as she touched him, circled him with her hand, stroking and pleasuring, while tasting herself on his tongue. He groaned as her hands worked up and down. Her hard nipples brushed against his chest, creating a pleasure-pain spiraling through him. His heart raced, and his chest heaved as the pleasure exploded inside his body.

Duvall grabbed her hand, and once more putting his hand below her bottom, he raised her. With a speed that was almost brutal, he plunged straight into her, straining. Her legs circled his hips, holding on. She moved; he groaned. The feel of her enveloping him as she threw her head back in pleasure and the scent of her skin invaded his senses. He craved the feel and touch of her. Her hands gripped his hips, urging him harder and faster. Mouths still fused, he pushed and she met his thrusts, until finally the pleasure exploded in him. He felt her exquisite muscles milking him as she orgasmed beneath him, and he met her, emptying himself within her. Holding on. Holding tight.

Gradually, as their breathing slowed, their bodies disentangled until only their arms encircled each other. They lay like that, while they came to terms with the explosive encounter, each lost in their own thoughts.

Duvall let his breathing return to normal, lying there, holding this woman. The one who set his world alight like the trail of stars he traveled. Inside him, thoughts and feelings fought their way out. The need to love her, keep her with him, railed against his refusal to see what they could have.

He lay on his side, eyes closed, unable to sleep. He'd laid there for what felt like hours. *Barsha!* He couldn't keep his hands off Mellissa. The tension had built since they'd been in the Admiral's office. It made no sense. He didn't want to leave her behind. It had felt so wrong.

He needed to ensure her safety, and he knew that was best achieved aboard the *Elector*. Once Gustav said she would be safest with him, he'd reacted instinctively. He had felt elation and relief that she would remain with him. That too was counterpoint to what he'd worked to achieve. His emotions were best further away from her. The constant see-saw of head versus—he didn't want to acknowledge *heart*—was draining and confusing. How could he want her there with him, in his arms and bed, when he knew it was against everything he worked for? Hadn't he always agreed that relationships grounded a man?

He had never before experienced this bipolar range of highs and lows. Previously, his mantra of "love 'em and leave 'em" worked perfectly. He could find nothing simple about his feelings for this woman though. He wanted…what? Exactly what did he want? Forever? Hearts and flowers? White picket fences? Children? He shied away from that thought.

He knew he wanted her. He couldn't doubt that. The feeling ran like a fever in his blood. He heated just at the thought of her, and when she met him passion for passion, he exploded like an incendiary device. Her passion ran as strong as his. This woman was there with him, but what exactly did that mean for him and the future?

He groaned in his mind. What a mess he continued to make of this…whatever it was. He refused to call it a relationship, that would give it some substantial footing.

His gaze shot to Mellissa. Her eyes were closed as if she were asleep. A wave of tenderness flooded him, and he reached out, but tugged his hand back before touching her. He— Duvall McCord, one of the fastest-promoted captains in history—was in the middle of a mission that could affect the entire Empire, and all he could think of was getting this woman, this bundle of arousing flesh, into his arms and his bed.

Duvall rolled off the bed and headed to the other room. *Barsha!* Less than ten minutes and Elara and Grayson would arrive in the office for a briefing. He lifted shaking fingers to his forehead. He grabbed their clothes and headed back to the cabin, pulling his clothes from the tangle as he went. He stopped at the cabin door and watched as she looked at him.

"Mellissa, we can't do this. I need to concentrate on what I'm doing. That means this cannot continue. You and me? It's great, but I have a commitment to my crew, to the Admiralty, and the Empire. I don't have time for a relationship." The words cut through the air around them.

The minute he spoke, he wanted to call the words back. Her face paled and lines appeared at the side of her lips. He had to stop the ties from forming, and if that meant hurting her now, then he would do it. But damn, it felt as if the tendrils had already found their way to his heart and he'd just smashed them. His thoughts fractured.

He closed his eyes, blocking out the look of hurt he knew she felt. Hiding from his own emotions wasn't adult, but it was all he could do right now as his heart squeezed.

Behind closed eyelids, he hid, listening to the sound of her rising and dressing. No words. Nothing.

A chasm had opened in the time from their explosive encounter to now. He didn't like it. Not one bit. But what else could he do? In the back of his mind though, in the deepest darkest recesses, something told him that once damaged, this fragile bond might not be repairable.

Duvall had shattered her heart without a thought or understanding of just what he'd done.

He'd retreated in the most hurtful way anyone could have conceived. He turned his back and dressed silently as she gathered herself.

"Mellissa, I..." He glanced in her direction as they entered his office, but she willed herself to stay quiet and calm, hiding the scream that rose in her mind.

*How could he say that?* Her heart bled like someone had cut her with a knife. The pain seized her and squeezed until she wanted to cry out with it. Something inside her broke, and her eyes burned with unshed tears, but she wouldn't give in here.

She would go alone into the world once more. She had gone into this knowing he had promised nothing. They might physically stay on the same ship together until the mission concluded, but she knew how to remain strong. She would not let him see how his actions gutted her.

She firmed her shoulders and looked him in the eye. "I think it would be best if I had my own cabin again." She congratulated herself, pleased her voice sounded so calm. "I know this was good while we waited to see what would happen, but you need your space and so do I. I'll move my things out today." She almost sounded like she meant it, which was fine to her thinking. That well of determination she had built up over the years once more came to her rescue.

He looked at her. There wasn't a trace of her tender lover left, and she hardened her emotions. "No." His eyes grew cold like ice on a frozen river.

Her temper rose, but she checked it. After all, they were both under enormous pressure. He had a mission, a very important one, and she understood that. The fate of millions might hang on it. He had a family whose safety was in question.

Biting her lip, she thought over her words. Maybe she needed to phrase it in a way that he didn't feel that she threatened either his authority or emotions? She told herself his rejection wouldn't smash the small well of confidence she had left.

"Duvall, after what you have just said, it's the only thing I can do. At least allow me my dignity and space." Her tone was just right, she told herself. Level, capable, and not clinging. She would have laughed at herself if her heart weren't breaking into tiny little pieces in her chest. The ache grew every second, larger and heavier. She worried that it would suffocate her.

"No. You'll stay here with me. I can sleep in here until this mission is finished. We don't know if there is any other threat aboard. We won't discuss this again." As he turned, the pinging of chimes sounded. "Identify," he snapped out.

Mellissa gritted her teeth. They certainly hadn't concluded the discussion, she promised herself.

"ST Sudonne and Commander Myatt," the computerized voice droned.

"Door unlock and open," he growled.

Mellissa tucked away the need to discuss this again with him at a later time. He was busy, so perhaps if she just did it, he wouldn't object so strongly. After all, once she'd moved out, he'd surely see the sense in her actions. Yes, she believed that would work best.

She headed for the end seat, thinking that some space would help. She could concentrate better. Elara's glance as they entered the room asked questions Mellissa didn't want to answer, so she looked away. Elara must have caught a whiff of the distress in the air, because the frown she aimed at Duvall was tight. Mellissa dropped her head and studied the desk screen that rose out of the table, hoping that if she concentrated on the information on it, she could ignore the burn in her eyes.

"Mellissa, Captain." Elara acknowledged both as she seated herself. Elara cast a quick look at Grayson, and it was clear he was as confused as Elara.

Mellissa realized that she and Duvall had only left the bridge a short time ago, and no doubt Elara and Grayson wondered what had happened in so little time. Quickly cutting off that thought, Mellissa smiled at them, but she knew Elara had seen the sadness in her eyes and no doubt noticed that she refused to look directly at Duvall.

"Captain, based on the information contained in the mission report, I believe there's a possibility that WO Gentry has intercepted transmissions that could point to another infiltrator in the Admiralty. Some of the notes she passed to the Admiral before being escorted to Earth indicate that she's only been aware of this for an limited period of time. One thing she did pinpoint was the use of time travel using the slipstream technology."

Duvall gave a sharp grunt at the news and tapped quickly at the desk screen. He was obviously reading the reports. Mellissa sat waiting quietly. His mouth tightened further, and when his head rose, he looked directly at her.

"Somehow, you were not just an accident. Based on the limited intelligence we have, I believe that you were chosen to receive the handbook . We need to find out why." He turned back to Grayson. "How much sooner can we squeeze the travel time to Earth?" he demanded.

"I think we can cut it to a little over twenty-six hours to the portal, but that will mean tightening the slingshot and using max speeds. The engines have not yet run at this speed in the inner solar system, and Raven hasn't even joined the crew yet. I'm not sure that would be overly wise given the situation."

Duvall's brows drew closer together with concern. "You don't believe we can do that?"

"I can understand your concern, Duvall, but we need to get there in one piece to be of any use."

"It won't be an issue. Once Raven comes on board, he'll get this bird flying optimally." Grayson opened his mouth, but Duvall held up a hand, stopping him. "However, I will take your suggestion under advisement."

Chowd entered the room. "I believe that an infiltrator may have already tipped off their associates that we are heading for Gentry." Everyone in the room looked up at him.

"We need to get there before they reach her. Elara, I

need you to make sure we're ready for anything, especially if we encounter the Ru'Edan once she's on board." He closed his eyes.

"Sir, the Admiral already indicated—"

"This is my sister, and given we already know there are issues with security, we need her here. Where she's going to be safest. If we're away on the mission and things happen, we won't be able to get back here. Besides, we could use her knowledge of cyphers." He chose his words for maximum impact and was rewarded with their nods of agreement.

"Grayson, we need a full briefing of security, and an engineering briefing for Raven once he arrives—you see to that. Chowd can relay any information. I've already made contact, and he will come aboard while we're on Earth."

He heaved himself up to stand by the table.

"Elara, Grayson, we have to get Meredith out. As quickly and safely as possible. We need the information she's managed to cobble together. It's vital to our mission. We won't jeopardize the momentum we've built up. She got the information, we can interpret it while in transit. We're the first line of defense. Whatever happens next, the Empire must be our first priority."

*And that pretty much makes my position clear, doesn't it?*

He stood up and strode out of the office, leaving them sitting at the table, each engrossed in their own thoughts.

✪ ✪ ✪ ✪ ✪

Mellissa wandered out of the mess hall, wondering what she should do next. She hadn't heard from Duvall since he had walked out of the office, and she was pissed. The coffee she'd consumed wired her further.

Okay, so no one had promised a happily ever after, but whatever had occurred to him after that session of sex in his cabin had destroyed any chance of an ongoing relationship. Well, too bad. She'd stewed all afternoon, and frankly, if he couldn't at least give her the common courtesy of dealing with the situation like an adult, then he could go jump in a lake somewhere. Or asteroid field. Or whatever. *And if he thinks I'll hang around for sex on tap anytime he's feeling horny, he's got another thing coming!*

Her feet took her to Duvall's cabin, and as she looked at the door, the answer came to her. She entered the cabin and stomped over to the wardrobe. With vicious swipes, Mellissa scooped up the meager wardrobe she'd assembled. The toiletries.

Stomping down the hall didn't make her feel better, but at least she didn't run into anyone. "'Cause that would be just my luck." Muttering to herself, she initiated the palm swipe on the door of the cabin she'd been assigned.

She dumped her clothes on the bed and glanced at the door. *Start as you mean to go on.* She wouldn't give up everything just because one man thought he knew best about how to use her body.

With economical movements, she folded every piece of clothing and thrust them into the wardrobe. "Now what?" Her voice echoed in the near empty room. She heaved a sigh. She could go back to the mess hall, but she might run into him. "No way. Not now."

The mad was melting away, leaving her feeling lost and alone again. *Stay busy, find something to occupy your mind.* She could start on George and Eliza's story again. "But it won't make any sense." The words sounded stupid even to her ears. This was her opportunity to make it better. Maybe she should start from the beginning again anyway.

The comms throughout the ship blared. "Captain required on the bridge."

It was a sign, so she hurried out of her cabin and headed for the mess. Her mood was still sour as she reached the dispenser, grabbing a quick soup and sandwich with a glass of milk, and made her way to a table. She didn't know anyone well enough to sit with a group, so she chose a seat by itself and made short work of her dinner. Once done, she returned her plates and cup and headed back to the cabin.

Deciding on a quick shower, she hurried through her ablutions. Pulling on a coverall, she headed for the table in the corner and engaged the desk screen before she called up a new file to the screen. She could start the story again.

She moved quickly toward the door and closed it. "How do I lock this thing?" she demanded of the computer.

"Lock engaged," the ship's computer replied, and she breathed deeply. Grayson had instructed security to ensure she had access to the most basic of programs within the system so she could work, make notes, or continue her education. But none of those seemed appropriate somehow.

"Well, George and Eliza, how would you like a change of scene?" She settled in, and within no time, the story reasserted itself.

This time, she could see the cockpit, the characters, and though she would not admit it, even to herself, George had an uncanny resemblance to Duvall McCord. The book once more opened to her, so much clearer than she had ever seen before, and she knew starting again and fresh had made it so much better. All her earlier incarnations seemed like faded versions now that she had seen and experienced the future. She'd realized she needed to begin it all again, to take advantage of what she now knew.

Working at an almost feverish pace, she tapped away until a pinging interrupted. The security system locater flashed onscreen. Pressing the locator button on the screen, she saw the flashing name. *Duvall*. She wavered for a minute, considered not answering, but cowardice hadn't ever been her strong point.

She engaged the audio. "Yes, Captain? Can I help you?" she answered with a calm and distant tone.

"Where are you?" he demanded. He sounded mighty upset. Well, too bad. So was she.

"I'm in my cabin working. Is there something I can do for you?" Her fingers jittered over the screen, betraying her agitation.

"Get yourself back to my cabin now," he growled.

She could almost see him in her mind. Angry. Oh yes, no doubt about that. His face tight, those magnificent lips thinned and white. His fingers stabbing through his hair in agitation. He probably stood next to his desk. She'd noticed he hated to sit when he was annoyed.

"No. We went through this earlier. You need your space, and I need mine. Now if you don't mind, I'm about to retire for the night." She quickly toggled the comm to off. "Desk screen, save and disengage program." She scurried toward the empty bed as she gave the commands and crawled between the cold sheets. "Lights off," she commanded.

As she lay in the dark the only thing that came to her mind were those thoughts that she was alone again. *He doesn't want you. Nobody ever wanted you.* That insidious little voice again whispered in her ear. She slowly gave way to her emotions. Tears leaked from burning eyes, and sobs erupted. It took a long time until they ceased. Then she lay there, eyes hurting in the dark and her heart trampled, but she didn't sleep.

In his office, Duvall paced. He raged inwardly about women who didn't follow simple instructions. He told himself he didn't need her. None of the emotions he had experienced with her were more than wishful thinking on his part. When Grayson pinged him through the system, he growled orders. He brooded.

But the cabin and work area remained empty, his bed cold and uninviting. When the door chimes started, he rose, thinking it was her, but to his dismay he found Elara at the door.

"What are you doing here?" he groused.

Elara took one look at him, quickly scanned the room, and sighed. Entering, she sat down at the table. "What did you do?" she asked quietly.

He looked at her, and she looked back expectantly, silently waiting.

The words tumbled out. His fears that Mellissa's needs and safety were becoming his focus over and above the mission, something he had fought so hard for years, were hard to swallow. He knew she would play a vital part in the mission, but he fought the connection because he had always followed the teachings of Elphin—that connections grounded you. How, in his blindness, he'd hurt Mellissa. The truths he spoke sliced at him, but he forced them out in a rushed wave. Elara listened without comment until he got to the end.

"And she moved into another cabin. Left me!" The petulance in his voice surprised him. But then, what else did he expect? His mind questioned his hot and cold reactions, and he knew it was his see-sawing emotions which had damaged the budding relationship and his equilibrium. The one he relied on to captain his ship effectively.

"Duvall, you know that at some point, you need to either make a commitment or let something go. Can you do that? Are you able to watch her walk away?"

He stilled. Letting her go wasn't an option, so he needed to find a way to balance a relationship with his command.

"No!" came his response, urgent and unequivocal.

She looked straight at him and said simply, "Then you need to go get her and tell her what you just told me. But be mindful, if you make that commitment, it is yours forever. If you break it, it's damaged and gone. Never to be regained. There can't be any half-measures where the heart is involved."

He closed his eyes as pain shot through his system. Had he damaged it irreparably? He opened his eyes and looked at her. "When did you get so wise?" he questioned quietly.

"When I met Grayson." Elara stood and placed a soft, quick kiss on his cheek, then turned, palmed the door, and walked out without looking back.

He sat in his office, once again alone. Brooding. Elara had asked the one question he had tried avoiding overall. Could he let Mellissa go? He'd answered no and that was the truth. Now, he had to find some way to marry the conditioning with his emotions. When he'd left the academy, he swore to himself that emotional entanglements would ground him, just as Elphin had said. Now he looked back, considering how many of his peers had been able to both achieve a lasting relationship and continue to move up the ranks.

In the emptiness of his cabin he attempted to decipher exactly how he felt about Mellissa and how he could make a relationship work. "If she'll have me after today."

Things would need to change, he acknowledged, but could he make it right? Was there some way to keep Mellissa safe and by his side, while keeping his promises to the Empire? Scary questions, he acknowledged privately, but the answers frightened him even more. If he didn't take the chance, he would lose something that didn't come along more than once in a lifetime.

Duvall scrubbed his hands through his hair, head aching as he contemplated the mess he'd made. He sat in the darkness, aware of loneliness, and nursed his Arturian wine.

# Chapter 8

**M**ellissa dressed slowly, grimacing at her face in the mirror. She'd slept restlessly the night before, and her rumpled appearance reflected that. At least the choices of clothing limited her dissatisfaction. She had either a blue research services uniform, several nondescript gray shipwear uniforms, or blue dress uniform. "Such an exotic range of clothing."

With a final twist, she fastened her hair back and left the cabin, heading in the direction of the mess hall. As she started to enter, a hand shot out and grabbed her arm. Swinging around quickly, Mellissa came face to face with Duvall.

His eyes were unusually shadowed and red-rimmed, while dark growth fringed the edges of his jaw. He looked strung out, as if he'd had little sleep. His hands raked through his hair, radiating tension and frustration.

She looked at him mutely. What did he expect of her now? First he trampled her heart, and now he wanted more?

"Mellissa, I need to talk to you." His voice was rough as he continued, "Please come and sit with me while we eat, then we can find a quiet spot to talk."

She didn't know how she felt about that. He'd hurt her, and now he wanted to talk? She opened her mouth and closed it again. If she spoke… A pang echoed in her chest as she peered closely at him. For the first time, he looked lost and unsure.

"Okay, let's talk." She followed him into the mess hall.

They joined the line and grabbed a coffee and roll then found a spot to sit. The silence, far from the companionable quiet she had come to appreciate with him, stretched uncomfortably as tension zinged through the air.

Overnight she'd concluded that her behavior had skated

on the edges of childishness. And while his behavior had been lacking, as the good Mother Superior had always said, *two wrongs don't make a right*.

She fidgeted in her seat, unable to eat her roll. Mellissa picked at it, small crumbs falling to the basic white plate, as her stomach roiled in sympathy with her feelings. The longer the silence grew, the less certain became her stomach. It rattled around, and the queasiness grew.

After a couple of minutes of pulling their rolls apart and pretending like they were eating, she stood. "Look, uhh, let's just forget it."

"No. We'll get rid of these and go to my ready room. To talk."

She scanned his face, looking for a hint of what he was thinking, but her head ached so she gave up. "Sure."

After dumping the plates on the side, they headed back to the room, and by the time they arrived, the silence had grown unbearable and thick. They kept a careful and respectful distance from each other as she slumped into the chair she had filled yesterday afternoon at the opposite end of the table.

"Mellissa, I was wrong. I should have told you what was bothering me. I'm not used to feeling any sort of..." He seemed to fish for the words. "...connection in my relationships. I'm sorry." He looked uncomfortable and somber. "I can't make you any promises. I won't make promises I can't keep. I can say that I never intended to hurt you. What we have...well, I don't really know how to describe it." He paused, looked at her. "I don't want it to end, but I can't promise you forever. I belong to the Admiralty. I took an oath when I became an officer. It's one I hold sacred. I have a mission, and millions of people rely on me doing my job and keeping them safe." His eyes beseeched her to understand. "I won't lie to you, I can promise you that."

Her heart lurched in her chest. She wanted to wipe the pain from his face, but protecting herself was part of her makeup.

Duvall sighed. "I missed you last night, and I really want you to move back into the cabin with me. I am sorry." He stopped. She guessed he waited for her response.

"I don't know what to say to you, Duvall." She wanted to believe him, to ride the high again, but could she? Should she take the chance he could break her heart again? "I mean, we had a terrific interlude, then you shut me out. Just like that, and yes, that hurt me. Either you want me or you don't. But the hot and cold…well, I just can't do them." Mellissa sucked in a breath. How she wanted that connection back, but she was scared. "You need to work out what you want. Short term? Well, I could move back, but what if you change your mind again?"

He flinched as she spoke.

"You say you won't lie to me, but it could be a lie by omission. You didn't want the kick of intimacy? I can understand that." She stopped and took a deep breath. "Take up again? I don't know that I can do that without some sort of commitment on your part."

He started at that, shocked.

Mellissa looked at him, her eyes glistening with tears. She screwed up her courage. Her voice thickened. "Commitment doesn't necessarily mean forever, but we do need ground rules. I have to ask though—do you want me? Not just sexually, but everything I am?" She waited, cringing when she heard the words erupt from her mouth.

"*Barsha!* Yes!" he answered, fists clenched tight against his body, his face strained.

She took a step forward, hopeful. Then she stopped. "Then we need some sort of understanding. If either of us thinks it's time to end it, then it's done upfront. We tell each other honestly and clearly. No silences and no just letting the relationship fade away. When it's done, from either side, we both let go. Do you agree?" she demanded. Her heart had lightened from the dead weight she had experienced since the night before.

He nodded his agreement. He made to hold her. She stepped back though, knowing that more had to be said first.

"I keep my own cabin so if things end, I have somewhere, a bolt hole to… A place to retreat to."

He looked ready to argue.

"It's non-negotiable. I need it, and so do you. Then we both have equal footing in the relationship. Right?"

He didn't seem to like that. Duvall's lips had tightened at her demands. He opened his mouth again, and she raised a hand.

"I have next to nothing. I've left my entire life behind, so I need to have something to ground me. I need this. I have to have a place for me and my peace of mind."

He looked upset but eventually nodded.

"But if you need your space, you need to tell me. Be clear. This will only work if we both know what our roles are. What the expectations of this…thing…" She waved her hand at both of them. "…is." She crossed the space between them and slowly reached up. When her eyes were level with his, she said, "I want you too. I want this to work. Just as I know you do."

She closed the gap and softly pressed her lips to his. Her eyes closed briefly, but before he could grab her, she moved away. He looked disappointed, but they had much to do and little time.

She turned toward the door. "I'm going to grab some of my things and bring them back. Not everything though. I'll only be gone a few minutes. While I'm out, think about what useful things I can do. I need a place in this crew if I'm staying on. I know I'm supposed to be placed as a junior researcher, but I need something worthwhile to do now." She left him standing watching her, knowing he would continue to think about what she had done, what she had demanded.

She made the trip to her cabin slowly, thinking long and hard about her agreement to move back into his cabin. Passion on tap…oh yes, that certainly was a motivator, but commitment beyond the mission? No, she couldn't rely on that, so whatever happened, she needed to prepare herself for the eventuality that this relationship would end.

Mellissa stopped dead in the hallway, taking a moment to be honest with herself. Perhaps she should have just refused, but truthfully, she could no more refuse than she could do without air.

"No, the best way is forward," she muttered, clenching her fists against the tiny kick of pain. "I need to prepare now for the end of this relationship."

She strode down the corridor, her mind running a million miles an hour. She'd need to find what usable skills that she had and shore up her position in this time. Build a new life, one that let her experience everything she could. She wasn't totally satisfied, but having reached some point of stability in her life plan, Mellissa clung onto it.

At her cabin, she palmed the door. She glanced around the small, cramped cabin. Yes, perhaps it was cold and impersonal, but it was all hers. If things ended sooner rather than later, at least she had things here ready.

She grabbed only the essentials, a couple of changes of clothes and some toiletries. Depositing the items in the bag she had carried down yesterday, she swiftly made her way back to Duvall's cabin, listening to the clank of her feet on the floor as she went. She had raised her hand to the palm scanner when it opened, and she looked inside.

"I had your imprint added to the door, so you can come and go at will."

He looked at her, and she melted right back to the beginning. Yes, right now she was sure she'd made the right decision.

"Do you…" He cleared his throat. "Can I help you with that?" He gestured to the bag, and she shook her head.

After she had put her clothing back in the drawers she had used previously, he grabbed her hand and led her to the bridge. Back in the chair that had become hers, she reclined as the seat molded to her body. "Holy mother of…" The whisper escaped as she marveled at the view. Earth, the green-blue planet, rose in front of her on the screen. "It's an awesome view, isn't it?"

She glanced at Duvall, who watched her. "Yeah. It really is."

Twirling into view and getting larger by the minute,

floated a spaceport. Large and glowing, it seemed to jut out at angles, with spires and rings, blazing lights and small ships darting around. The large and small ships appeared connected to it, moving back and forth like bees at a hive.

It looked long enough, it seemed that the space freighters and passenger cruisers she had learned about had docked four and five alongside each other. Other massive gray starships, destroyers she guessed from the education programs, floated in orbit around it, waiting or protecting, she could only guess.

She'd marveled at the international space station on the television in her own time, but this structure far outweighed anything she'd ever imagined. She was gazing at a piece of engineering magnificence.

"How long has that been there?" she asked.

"The port? Oh, that one is about thirty years old, but it's almost ready for refurbing again. The military section gets worked on every five to ten years." He pointed to the far side of the port. "That's where we'll dock the *Elector*." They inched closer to the structure.

Truly, it left her awed at how small it seemed from space, yet so imposing. The sight of it she could use in her novel, and her fingers itched for a notebook to record what she could see.

Then she realized Duvall once more watched her.

"Once we've docked, a shuttle will be waiting to take us dirtside," he said. He turned then, back to the job at hand.

Navigation requested an update on heading, and Duvall hailed the station. "Earth Station to *Elector*. Present credentials and stand by."

His fingers tapped on the molded arm of his seat.

"Earth Station to *Elector*, proceed to berth alpha-one-one-three. We are transmitting bearing to navigational units."

The officer in charge of navigation gave a curt nod, letting them know he'd received the information. Mellissa's gaze returned to Duvall, fascinated with the unhurried way he dealt with the intricacies involved.

"*Elector* to Earth Station. Bearing received, correcting

course now."

Within minutes, the process was completed. Chowd had explained they'd used both thrusters and space tugs in order to dock in position against the stark gray, walled structure.

They docked with an almost imperceptible bump and a slight rise as she connected to her berth. The squark of communications announced that they could now leave the ship, but Mellissa sat marveling for a little longer, lost in the immensity of the action. Finally, she looked up and saw Duvall standing beside her, watching her. He motioned for her to walk with him.

They walked to the rear of the ship and into the port, where the small bag Duvall had arranged for them sat on the floor. "We have a bit of a walk to meet our shuttle, but once on board, it's a quick trip down." He gripped her hand tightly, his fingers slipping between hers as Grayson, Elara, and Chowd flanked them.

The five made their way through the terminal and toward the military shuttle lounge, and she looked out every port. She watched, goggle-eyed, as the population passed them. Creatures of other species moved along the walkways. She gaped, even though she didn't want to. The sights defied even her imagination as blue and yellow creatures, mainly humanoid in looks, paid them no attention on their way to their own destinations. A gray, shaggy creature with some sort of air-driven device passed them, calling out as the machine chugged along.

Duvall kept hold of her hand and guided her forward to the lounge. Unsurprisingly, she noted the lounge was decorated with grays and nothing to alleviate the dull color. On arrival, they quickly and efficiently moved onto an empty shuttle that sat waiting.

"No one else?" Chowd raised an eyebrow.

"It was specifically held for us. A secured shuttle." Duvall ushered Mellissa forward.

"You can have the port seat," said Duvall with laughter in his voice. He'd obviously taken notice of the craning she'd done as they had made their way to the shuttle.

Finding seats, they sat down, and Duvall checked her belts then his own. An announcement of imminent departure sounded through the empty shuttle, and a clank echoed as the door shut, then it moved away from the station, maneuvering in the direction of the planet. From her seat, it looked as if it were rapidly growing. She grinned, comfortable with the travel until they hit the atmosphere. The portal beside her showed the red-yellow haze during the entry procedure, and she reared away.

"We're safe in here. The shields can withstand greater temperatures than that." Duvall placed a reassuring hand on her shoulder.

She wasn't game to even exhale heavily until the glare of heat dissipated and they drew closer to the ground.

The shuttle sliced through the air traffic quickly, and she thought about the early days of space travel—the days she knew of—and marveled at the advances once more. She took hold of Duvall's hand again for comfort as the ground neared. The speed with which they traveled amazed her as they descended through the fluffy, white clouds.

The dirt of the Earth rose up swiftly, and she watched as the shuttle leveled out and prepared for landing. The journey was brief, as Duvall had said. "How long?"

"That was about forty-five minutes."

"And where exactly are we?" She peered out the window, sure she recognized some of the landmarks, though they looked distinctly older than she remembered.

"Welcome to the Brisbane Space Port."

"Really? Uh…" She had recognized the city, although she'd rarely ventured into the center. "Why Brisbane?"

"For two reasons. First, because my family lives in Bundaberg, one of the outer suburbs. Jard lived in inner Brisbane in one of the high-tops." He didn't say any more, but the look on her face told her that now was not the time to inquire further.

Duvall tugged her harness off. She hadn't realized he'd also removed his own. He helped her up and toward the now open door. Chowd slipped in front, an imposing and protective presence. A tunnel connected them to the terminal. At the end they made their way along a corridor and out where a series of massive tables waited. Heavily armed guards stood behind the staff, who hovered.

"Military customs," Chowd said quietly as Duvall moved forward to hand over a small disk. It was checked, and they were waved through swiftly.

Chowd explained that, given the number of humanoids moving throughout the galaxy, the military services had undertaken a portion of customs for their own personnel. She nodded, dazed by the constant stream of facts.

Beyond the doors, transport waited at the curb. She wiped a hand over the back of her neck, noting the slick sheen coating her hands as a result of the sweltering January heat. Trickles wound their way down her back and under her hair.

Around the terminal buildings rose like monoliths toward the sky, and small vehicles, ground and air, moved around them, rising vertically into the air before smoothly accelerating in the direction of their destinations.

They stopped beside a drab brown vehicle. A small bubble of mirth escaped from her mouth.

"What's so funny" Duvall asked, looking genuinely puzzled.

"In all the time that's elapsed, the military still have ugly vehicles!"

They all found this quite funny and laughed, except Chowd, who frowned.

The young security officer hovering nearby saluted as he handed over the power keys for the vehicle. It looked like a small, flat disk and she made a mental note to ask Duvall about that later. The vehicle itself was comfortably appointed, and Mellissa wondered about getting a license for one of these as she climbed into the car. Something else to learn, she thought.

Duvall pulled out a set of light shades from his pocket and slid them over his eyes. "Hold on now!"

The vehicle punched its way into the sky. Mellissa had a moment of panic and grabbed the edge of the seat until it leveled out and she grew more comfortable.

"Where exactly are we going?" she inquired once her stomach settled sufficiently.

"We have a stop to make at Jard's apartment first. Not too far away. Then on to Bundaberg."

She settled into the vehicle and looked around as they zipped over the city. Many of the buildings looked old, with crumbled facades, but the river snaked its way around the bend, just as she remembered.

They banked and headed to the heart of the built-up area, the skyscrapers disappearing into the clouds. Many bore the marks of long-term habitation, stains on white stucco. Interspersed here and there, newer buildings nudged into the skyline. It was clear the city had increased its density. Vehicles whizzed around them. Bodies below moved like dots around the mazes of buildings, going about their daily activities.

After a short while, they reached a single building, blue with glass paneling, cold-looking but relatively new given the sparkle and shine. She looked at Duvall.

"This is where Jard lived. We're paying a short visit to his apartment. The security officers know to await us. Military takes precedence over any other local militia or police, so no one has had access until we got here. Chowd and I are going to look for evidence of his involvement. Hopefully we can also find out who his connection was. You're going to have to come along, as Grayson will also be required."

The vehicle docked in a parking area at the top of the building. It looked like any other car park she'd ever seen, except with entry only reachable by flying car. They found a location to leave the vehicle and, in formation, made their way to the door.

An officer stood waiting. They flashed identification, and the young man saluted. "Sir, no one has had access to the premises since we were informed by the Admiralty. My partner is waiting at the entrance as per the Admiral's orders."

He led the way to a bank of elevators. They waited for the doors to open and stepped inside. The officer pressed the panel, and the elevator moved, the motion smooth and soundless. She watched the numbers on the screen descend until they reached level twenty-seven. The doors slid open, and Chowd inserted himself in the doorway, quickly checking left and right. He motioned for them to join him in the hallway, and they moved forward together.

"When we get to the door, do what you're told. Do not enter until I know it's safe." Duvall looked at her. "Promise?"

Mellissa nodded her agreement and waited for him to show her where she should stand. He and Chowd remained at the front as the security officer and Elara flanked her. Grayson followed Chowd and Duvall as they inserted the security disk the officer had handed them.

Chowd held up a small box, which she had seen him use before. "Clear here." He looked to Duvall. "They should be clear to enter, but it would be best if they waited in this room."

Duvall indicated that they should enter the apartment and gave the command for one member of the security team to take position outside while they searched. Mellissa waited in the door as Chowd entered each room slowly, using his box to check for unexpected surprises.

"Clear here."

"So that means we can come in?" Mellissa clung to the doorway.

"Not yet. We need to check in case there is anything that could lead us to his contact." Chowd glanced in her direction. "But you can sit down while we work."

Peering around, she saw a modular chair and considered sitting, but discarded that option, thinking it looked uncomfortable. She waited as Grayson, Elara, Duvall, and Chowd began sifting and sorting through items, peering under oddments and using hand screens to take photos of the rooms. They opened drawers and cupboards in their search. The rooms were spartan with some shelving and photos, but other than that, no personal items were on display. The furniture was modular, with a cheap look that denoted this was somewhere he didn't live so much as slept in.

Finally Duvall made his way back into the room where she waited. "Anything?" she asked.

"No. We've checked behind every door and under the furniture. Hell, Chowd even ran a scanner over the bed and lounge. We found layers of dust, but all that proves is he's not into housekeeping." He shared a small smile, but it didn't lift her spirits much.

"Are you sure there isn't anything here?" The words had barely crossed her lips when Grayson called to Duvall and Chowd. She followed as they moved into the tiny kitchen where Grayson held up a small disk.

"This was hidden in the cooler box. I nearly missed it because he'd hidden it in an ice water cube. Looks like our boy attempted trying to keep his information cold." Grayson ran warm water to dissolve the cube then pulled a box from his pocket. She frowned at what Chowd informed her was a safe box. He dropped the disk into it and turned to search again.

With nothing else much to do she stood, hip against the doorjamb. "Since there's nothing here I can help now, right?"

Duvall and Chowd looked at each other.

"Yeah, sure. Work in here only though." He indicated to the lounge room, and Mellissa started looking at the photos that set on the otherwise bare shelving.

She trailed her fingers along them, picking them up and looking in wonder at the moving images. As she did so, she caught her finger on a sharp edge poking from the back of one.

"Oww." Mellissa inspected her finger, but there was no blood. She turned the photo and saw something sitting with an edge protruding from the frame. "Duvall, have you got a minute?"

He poked his head around the door. "What? Have you found something?"

"I really don't know. But with all your technology

available, why would you have something sharp sitting at the back of a photo?" She held up the frame for his inspection.

He grabbed it and inspected it. He jiggled it, and a holoimage emitter fell out, showing Corbin Jard and another man. She didn't recognize the face, though it fascinated her, with the gray tinge to the skin and yellow eyes. She heard Chowd growl "Crick Sur Banden", and her eyes widened.

"Oh my God," she breathed.

He turned the image emitter over. A series of numbers and letters were inscribed on the back.

"And there's the evidence that he knew Crick Sur Banden." He shook his head.

"Something so simple, yet damning." He turned away, slipping the image into another safe box.

They worked for another hour retrieving data from desk screens and removing disks and handheld communicators.

Duvall made audible notes on the palm screen he held. "Evidence of his involvement with Crick Sur Banden and the plots he was involved in." Carefully, they loaded the evidence into a small box to take with them.

They silently relocked the doors when they had finished.

The tone of the group remained somber as they trooped out the front door, the formation back in force with Mellissa in the middle. They stepped into the elevator, ready for the swift ascent to the top of the building.

They reached the vehicle, and Chowd pulled out his box once more, raised his hand, and Grayson and Duvall's heads snapped up. Duvall grabbed Mellissa by the arm firmly and forcibly propelled her away from the vehicle. She looked at a startled Elara, also grabbed by Grayson.

"What's going on? Duvall?"

"Stay with Grayson and Elara. Whatever they ask you to do, do it." He looked at her, his eyes glittering in the subdued light. Only once she nodded did he move away. She watched him retreat, her heart thudding in her mouth.

He joined Chowd, and the two of them conferred before

Chowd got down on the ground and moved underneath the vehicle. Duvall searched the top. She couldn't make out what they said but could clearly see them searching the vehicle. She felt chilled by the time Chowd slipped out from underneath, holding up a safe box. Grayson stepped between the car and the two women, shielding them.

"Elara? What's going on?" Her voice croaked.

"I don't know. Just wait and see."

Her insides turned somersaults as she waited. What if something happened to Duvall?

She buried her fears as best she could and waited while they talked. Chowd handed the box to Duvall, who opened it, looked inside, and handed it back with disgust. Whatever it was, Duvall seemed clearly unimpressed.

Slowly, they turned, and Duvall make his way toward her. He took long, powerful strides as he dragged his hands through his short, black hair. God, how she loved to watch him walk.

Then she dragged her thoughts back to the gravity of the situation at hand. "What did you find?" Grayson asked, beating her to the query.

"A planted photo. Crick Sur Banden holding an image of Meredith in his hands. I think it's a fairly clear warning that she is also on the hit list. We need to get to her before he does. Come on."

Mellissa knew there was much more than the information he had given, but she could see he was in no mood to share any more.

They piled into the vehicle. Chowd had professed that no further threats existed, and Mellissa wanted to believe him, but her stomach flip-flopped as they took off. Duvall grasped her hand.

"How…" Her mind screamed that someone must have accessed the vehicle, here in the parking lot. That meant… "Duvall—"

"Not now, Mellissa. When we get to our next location."

"But that's—"

Elara touched her hand before she could finish the sentence and shook her head. Mellissa understood. They could have planted a listening device. Fear crept up her spine, a chilly finger leaving her shivering.

"I wouldn't ask you to get into a vehicle I wasn't sure was safe."

Their eyes held and clung for a moment, then he let the vehicle drop into the traffic below. He turned the vehicle north, and soon they had left the main population area behind.

Duvall seemed as comfortable here as he had on the ship, and she wondered if this was his old stomping ground. She felt lost. She was a city girl who ran a bookstore and read romance but never really expected any kind of adventure to happen to her. She sat back in the seat and watched the sparsely populated areas pass by her. Along the trip, he mentioned areas of interest, and she looked around. His commentary included the green-treed paddocks he called farmlets.

"This area has been used as farming land for hundreds of years, and not much changes quickly here. Probably the thing you would find different is some of the animals that are now farmed. Some farms still have cows, but others carry other meat-giving animals too. The lobred, which is the size of an elephant but very docile, making it a great animal on a small allotment. It has a moist, red meat, which tastes spectacular. Then there's the wallamprat, which is about the size of a chicken. It's a delicacy, as the meat is green and flakey. Of course the local meats are still harvested, such as wallaby and even kangaroo as they have a low fat content."

Some of the animals she knew of, and had even tasted, but others... The green meat one didn't really appeal at all.

"We've also imported a lot of the domesticated animals from other planets, and they've become dietary staples because of their nutritional value."

She must have made a gagging sound as he looked at her as she wrinkled her nose in distaste. "I'm not sure I could manage some of the ones you've mentioned."

He gave a bark of laughter and turned back to the road with a smile.

# Chapter 9

The sun was setting as they arrived in the small city, the vehicle turning onto a street and heading toward an older house. Mellissa could see a range of vehicles parked in front. Most were similar in size and shape to the one they traveled in. Once they parked, Duvall climbed out and hurried to open her door. Chowd was last to alight, and followed behind the two men who managed to keep Mellissa and Elara in the center.

Just beyond the first vehicle, she caught sight of a security officer. He stopped them, demanding their identification, which he then confirmed.

"Please head inside, Captain. Your family was wondering when you'd arrive. I apologize for delaying you, sir."

Duvall flashed a tight smile. "It's okay. You did exactly what you were supposed to." Mellissa admired the way he reinforced his words with a careful pat on the young man's arm. He'd make a great mentor, she thought.

A large fence ensured the privacy of the house beyond, and the officer opened it with a flourish, waving the crew through, then Duvall lead them through a dense jungle of green shrubbery.

"This must be nice in summer." Mellissa gazed about.

"Yeah, it is."

They went up a set of creaking wooden steps to the front door, and before Duvall had time to knock, the door opened to a fearsome screech. "Duvall! You're here. Come in, come in and bring your friends."

The older woman who met them at the door had shining blue eyes. She was perhaps in her sixties, though her hair was only slightly grayed. Her rounded body was hidden within the voluminous folds of her dress, floral and brightly colored, which was covered with a large white apron.

She seemed so excited to see Duvall, wrapping her arms around him before kissing him on both cheeks. For a moment, Mellissa hung back.

"I hoped you'd arrive today. I baked all your favorites, just in case. It has been too long since you came home to see your mother, young man."

She ushered him in the door then turned to greet Elara and Grayson by name. Each received the same treatment of hugs and kisses.

Then Duvall turned and gestured to Mellissa. "Mum, this is Mellissa."

She looked at Mellissa then Duvall. A smile grew, and her eyes twinkled. "Welcome home, Mellissa. Welcome. My name is Kathryn, and that's what you'll call me. That or Mum."

Then she too was enveloped in a hug, warm and tight, the kind she had never before experienced. After that, she dimly realized Chowd was being introduced as well. Amid laughter and chatter, they all trooped into a kitchen that looked like some kind of cooking explosion had taken place.

Dishes covered the sides, lying everywhere in a discarded manner, wooden spoons sat in dishes, while batter dripped. A sniff of the air told her that whatever was cooking, it smelled amazing. The wafting smells of homemade bread and roasting meats, possibly lamb and chicken, made her mouth water.

Mellissa's stomach rumbled, and she grabbed it in dismay and embarrassment. Everyone chuckled, and no one louder than Duvall's mother. It wasn't a laugh to embarrass though, and Mellissa found herself joining in.

"Sit down." Duvall's mother pinned him with a mock stare. "You're obviously doing what you normally do, ignoring everyone else's need to rest and eat," she scolded him, wagging a wooden spoon at him. "Mellissa, dear, has he fed you today?" she asked kindly. Mellissa responded that they had eaten, but his mother's eyes narrowed. "Obviously not for some time. Here, grab a cake and I'll make coffee." She moved like lightning around the kitchen, all the while calling loudly, "Meredith! Meredith!"

A small face, ringed with black hair ending in waves, popped around the corner. "Duvall!" she squeaked. "You came!" A little dynamo, judging by the way she zoomed into the room in old holey jeans and light blouse, catapulted into his arms. Mellissa sat back dismayed when Duvall turned to meet the black-haired woman who had launched herself at him

"Mellissa, meet my kid sister, Meredith Gentry. Aka Bouncer."

Meredith raised her head, and violet eyes in porcelain skin and pink bow lips looked back at her. A grin split her face. She was utterly gorgeous.

She winked at Mellissa. "Hi, Mellissa. Welcome to the mad house. Hey there, Elara, Gray." She looked at Chowd, who gave her a brief nod. A tinge of red crept over the young woman's face. "I know you. Chowd, right?" She held out a hand and he reciprocated, though Chowd didn't look very comfortable.

Mellissa knew Chowd was a man of few words, yet he said even less than usual as he watched Meredith, the crest of red creeping over her cheeks as he watched her greeting the others who had arrived.

"Mum, we need to talk to Meredith, and we don't have much time. We can only stay tonight, and it's something we can't share. Can you leave the kitchen to us for a while?"

Kathryn's eyes grew wide, but she firmed her lips. "If it has to do with your sister—"

"It's okay, Mum. I've been expecting Duvall. Look, you go and we'll wash up while we talk, okay?" Meredith wheedled, and for a moment Mellissa was sure Kathryn would refuse.

"Fine. Just make sure everything goes back where it belongs." There was a touch of asperity to her words, but she quickly left them to it.

Elara and Grayson jumped up, clearly used to the lack of ceremony in this household, and before Mellissa could blink, they had the sink full of sudsy water and tea towels in hand as Meredith settled herself into a seat opposite Chowd and Duvall.

Mellissa hopped up and grabbed the tea towel from Grayson. "Since you obviously know your way around this kitchen, I'll dry the dishes and you can put them away."

They worked quickly and companionably, both Elara and Mellissa looking to give Chowd and Duvall the freedom to talk with Meredith. While he helped in the kitchen, Grayson asked the occasional question for clarification on matters. Mellissa tried hard not to pay attention, but a name mentioned caught her ear, and she listened quietly.

"Crick Sur Banden. I've heard that name before.. just can't place it." Mellissa thought for a moment. "Wasn't that the name of the man in…" She fished for the right words. "That was the alien in the photos from earlier, wasn't it? And the name the Admiral used."

Both men nodded, watching her intently.

"Oh, for heaven's sake. I've already told you I have no idea who he is, or even seen him in real life." She looked at Duvall, willing him to accept what she said.

He watched her carefully, as if searching for something, before slowly nodding. She wanted to growl at his lack of trust.

She wasn't aware that Elara had detected her hurt, until the woman was beside her. "Don't mind them. After all the years we've been fighting the Ru'Edan, Duvall probably has lost the most at their hands. Be patient with him."

Elara's soft words soothed the ache in her chest a little. "Yeah. I know what you're saying."

Another soothing rub on the arm and Elara moved back to the sink.

Duvall and Chowd spent the next ten minutes in deep conversation with Meredith about what she had seen and heard in the transmission room while Mellissa, Elara, and Grayson zipped around the kitchen putting it to rights. As the last bowl went into the cupboard, she heard Duvall tell Meredith to prepare her things for an early-morning departure.

Meredith rose and circled the table, dropping a quick kiss on Duvall's cheek before heading back out the door she had come in through. She turned quickly and said, "Don't forget dinner is early here, and Mum will want free rein soon. You'd better clear out or be prepared to help cook." She chuckled as she left the room.

✪ ✪ ✪ ✪ ✪

"Well, it seems there was more to you being chosen, Mellissa. Come and sit down and I'll fill you in."

She looked at Duvall questioningly.

He motioned to the chair beside him and looked at Grayson and Elara. "You'd better hear this too," he told them, and they settled back into their seats.

"Mellissa, do you know a Jem?" Mellissa jumped quickly in surprise.

"We know Crick Sur Banden is involved, just not how. This has his fingerprints all over it." He looked back at her. "You said you'd heard that name before?"

"Just from you and the Admiral. Previous to that, no."

"What about a Jem?" he asked again.

"Yes, she's my assistant. Why?" She leaned forward. "Did she have something to do with this?" She tapped a foot agitatedly. "She's a good girl. A bit flighty and young, but I can't see her getting into something dodgy."

He looked at her worriedly. "No, she was the mark, apparently. They knew she worked in a bookstore and had been in contact with a messenger. Someone called Andurs. Does that ring a bell?" he asked.

"God, yes! That's her current boyfriend. She met him in the store about…I don't know…five or six weeks ago? He had been a sort of semi-regular until then. Then suddenly he kind of pursued her in earnest. He brought her flowers and popped in almost every day. Oh God! Is she in danger?" Mellissa's voice rose, and her fear radiated. "We have to help her. Can we?"

She looked around. Duvall reached out and placed a hand on hers. Grayson and Chowd shared a long and meaningful glance.

"She is in danger, isn't she? We have to go back and find Andurs and find out what they plan by going back in time. Then we can help Jemma at the same time."

"Just so long as..."

The bubble of worry in the pit of her stomach pitched and wobbled.

"We have to go back. But, Mellissa, she's not the primary objective. Finding the contact is. We'll do what we can for your friend." He cleared his throat, and her stomach dropped. "Just so long as it doesn't jeopardize the mission."

The words exploded in her brain. The words *just so long as it doesn't jeopardize the mission* in particular. She nodded, but knew he had suspicions when his eyes narrowed at her quick acceptance.

Duvall, Grayson, and Elara opened up during dinner, sharing anecdotes from their early days together, making for a lively meal. Duvall made comments about their karaoke singing abilities, comparing notes about their adventures throughout the galaxies, and Kathryn shared many stories from both Duvall's and Meredith's childhoods, ensuring the atmosphere remained buoyant.

Duvall's mother, a cook of some local renown, had made a magnificent rack of lamb and chicken with local vegetables, which she declared Duvall's favorites, followed by crème caramel that melted in the mouth. Mellissa marveled that with the hundreds of years that had passed simple foods remained a staple dinner.

At the end of the meal, the group sat back, relaxing in

their chairs with deep glasses of wine sourced from throughout the galaxy. Mellissa watched the by-play between those at the table, feeling welcomed and part of the tight-knit group. Even Chowd had unbent and seemed to enjoy the mutual respect and genuine affection of the group.

The family was clearly close, even though Duvall had been fostered by the Gentrys after his parents death during a Ru'Edan raid on the planet where his father was a scientist. She learned that Meredith had been only weeks old when Duvall had come to live with them. Duvall had followed his foster father in the Admiralty, and in quick succession, so had Meredith.

"So there I was, in the parking lot, three boys surrounding my vehicle, and the next thing I know…" Meredith loosed a tinkling giggle. "…here comes Duvall doing the big brother thing. He single-handedly scared all of them off. Oh, it was so funny, because the look on his face!"

"Yeah, well, how was I supposed to know they weren't intimidating you?" His gruff voice carried traces of annoyance, and the intriguing thought of Duvall on a white horse charging to the rescue had Mellissa snorting into her wine.

"You weren't. Anyway, not long after that, I received notification of my acceptance into the academy. But I've always known, no matter where I was, Duvall would be in my corner." She hugged him hard, and he screwed up his face with embarrassment.

"Why did you join?" Mellissa couldn't stop herself from asking, and Meredith gave her a smile.

"Well, my Dad gave everything for the Admiralty. And would have continued, except Mum really struggled on her own. Then I had Duvall and later Gray and Elara as guides. I was lucky, too, that the Admiral encouraged me to learn the languages and comp systems. It seemed like I had everything and I needed to give something back."

Meredith shrugged and Mellissa mulled over what she'd said.

"Of course, unlike Duvall, who was top of his class all

the way through and requested flight school, my path was more cerebral." Meredith laughed as Duvall snorted. "Okay! So I know you remember when I wanted to join flight training. My instructor used to duck each time he saw me coming."

"Yeah, he was terrified you might actually sneak through and get to fly a shuttle." Duvall grinned. "The only thing she could do with them was bring them down...in a fireball. Eventually, he took you aside and told you not to try any further."

"I'm so pleased he did. Cryptology isn't exactly the most exciting aspect of what the Admiralty does, but I do it very well."

Mellissa must have silently broadcast that she didn't understand what cryptology was, because Meredith glanced at her and chuckled.

"It's the science of making and breaking codes." Meredith smiled. "I actually did my thesis on the codes of Crick Sur Banden. He has an intriguing use of coding systems that, I don't know, just appealed to me. I'm now the highest-rated currently serving officer with the Admiralty that works totally with the codes of Sur Banden." She shrugged it off, but Duvall was obviously very proud of her achievements, boasting about her being named head of her class and securing a plum position on Aenna.

After the meal, Meredith, Kathryn, and Chowd excused themselves and headed to their rooms. Duvall and Mellissa, with Grayson and Elara, moved into the garden and under the light of twinkling stars. Knowing that in the morning they would have to leave to save the world was sobering. They sat on old wood seats in a paved garden, so far removed from the world they inhabited daily. The scent of exotic flowers filled the air and their senses. Nothing could remove the fact that these people, quietly soaking up the night, were warriors. Perhaps warriors with metal birds, but nonetheless they knew the dangers and accepted them.

Earlier, Kathryn had taken Mellissa aside to let her know that her presence was welcome and that as a friend of Duvall she always had an open door. Especially given that Duvall had put her bag into what she could tell was definitely his room, she understood also that Kathryn's words meant if something grew between herself and Duvall, there would be no familial dissent.

Mellissa felt touched by the warmth of Kathryn's words, and though she knew his mother wanted to know more, she hadn't pressed. Besides, what could she say? They were enjoying the passion that ran rampant without a commitment. This may be the future, but no mother would want to know that her son had formed a relationship with a woman for sex without commitments, would she?

They retired late to his room, lined with spacemen of all shapes and sizes, ships and models of planets and starships hanging from the ceiling. They entered the room silently, hand in hand.

When they stopped at the edge of the bed together, her gaze questioned him, and he opened his arms. Mellissa stepped up to him and into his arms. They stood quietly for a moment with her head against his chest. The skylight from the top of the room let in the shining moonlight.

Without a word, they moved apart. He reverently removed her clothing piece by piece and kissed every inch bared slowly to his gaze. His face glowed in the moonlight. Then Duvall stood, looking at her. Mellissa reached for him, but he lightly stepped away.

"Duvall, I want you. I want to feel your skin against mine," she said, her purr throaty and her hands seeking.

He moved in, shucking his clothes, then stood, letting her look her fill. He shined in the moonlight, a perfect male specimen, and she drew in an unsteady breath. He reached down as she reached up. Their bodies touched as her nipples, now hard, scraped across his chest. His erection pushed at her belly. Lips met and clung in drugging kisses that pulled at her senses. Mouths and tongues danced. He pulled away long enough to find the erogenous zone on her neck. He licked and kissed her until she writhed in his arms, both his and her hands quietly seeking.

"Duvall?"

He slid a finger inside her hot, moist core, and she moaned. She grabbed his erection in her hand, running her thumb over the end, finding it soft and responsive. It jerked under her fingers. His finger withdrew and circled around the aroused flesh, just barely touching. She moved her hand up and down his engorged length. He threw his head back, the muscles in his neck corded as he hissed between clenched teeth. Melissa smiled, watching his reaction. Then she gasped as he slipped a finger back into her, hastening the rhythm of his hands in and out and in and out. Smooth. Intensity flaring in their eyes, she burned beneath his hands.

She tensed, and he swooped in to grab her, pull her down on the bed with him, and his mouth touched hers. His tongue speared into her mouth, mimicking the movement of his fingers. She moaned again, and he pulled his hands free.

"*Barsha!* I love the feel of you, to touch you. To fill you," he said, his voice guttural and low with need.

She opened her legs, and he crawled between them. His eyes were slits of fire, his face hard with need. Her heart was racing, and the need on his face nearly tipped her over the edge.

She grabbed his shoulders. "Now! I want you inside me now!" Mellissa demanded as quietly as she could. "Oh, God! Duvall! Please!" Her voice splintered.

His hands grasped hers and held them away from her body, his smile wicked. He once more opened his mouth over her neck. Mouth wide, he sucked lightly, then ran his tongue over the site he had just loved. He lifted away from her, hooded eyes glinting in the starlight. His gaze dropped to her breasts. He moved slowly, rubbing his hands over her breasts, weighing and measuring. Adoring. Her hands grasped the cotton sheets beneath her body.

His lips softly touched one perfect, peaked nipple, opened and lightly blew, torturing them. Then he opened his mouth over the peak and licked, sucked hard, and when she felt she couldn't hang on, he stopped, changed sides, and blew, then sucked the other. The pressure mounted and grew as she writhed beneath him. Slowly, he pulled his leg up between hers, which were now open for him, and rubbed against her intimately. Up and down while her body tried to contain the wildly escalating throes of pleasure. She nearly bolted off the bed.

Mellissa reached for him, but he laughed and continued the torture, finding the valley between her breasts and licking his way to her navel. He investigated it with his mouth until it became too much for both of them. He moved down her body, and continued to her core, which burned for his touch.

She grabbed his shoulders and tried to pull him up. Once more he refused. He found her heat, the one he'd stirred to a raging fire. One quick lick excited her further, and she gasped and bucked as he repeated the action. She writhed below his hands and mouth, feeling the mounting pressure of ecstasy.

He moved back and gazed down at her. She knew her body flushed rosy with exertion and sheened with sweat in the starlight. She bucked up, kissing him hard on the mouth, her taste on his tongue, then pushed him back toward the sheets, her mouth now the arouser, her tongue taking control.

"God, I love what you do to me," she murmured, even as she dropped tiny, nibbling kisses at the corner of his mouth.

With a moan, she waited for just a brief minute before continuing down the side of his jaw. At his Adam's apple, she gave a flick of her tongue and he arched. He tried to grab her, but she danced away from his hands.

Making her way down his body, she nuzzled his nipples. So beautiful, she thought, inhaling his scent, spicy and exotic. She laved her way down his torso toward his erection jutting proudly from his body. Her mouth opened once more and slowly settled on the head of his penis. Softly, she suckled at him, and he jerked beneath her.

He tried to hold her still with a guttural, "Wait!"

She paused, looked up at his face, and watched as he fought for control, her heart beating a rapid tattoo in her chest. He held still, his breathing ragged, body tightly clenched, and eyes squeezed shut. With her mouth still closed over him, she teased, licking the tip of her tongue over his head.

Then slowly, oh so slowly, she let her lips move up and down his aroused length, gently pulling with her mouth as she sought to push him closer to the edge, faster and faster until his firm hands grasped her, halting her.

His chest was heaving as he grabbed her, pulling her up his body. He flipped her over so she was lying on the bed, then moved between her thighs. He slid his hand over her where she was damp and aroused. He rubbed again, and she almost came, shuddering with the sensations.

Sensing they were both at the end of their endurance, she guided his cock to her body, and he plunged quick and deep. She cried out, but he captured her cry with his mouth. She held on desperately, both pounding and pumping each other in their search for ecstasy. Tongues danced, and both gasped incoherently as they moved, her short fingernails digging deep into his flesh.

He demanded more, pumping faster, their bodies damp with sweat as they exerted themselves in the most intimate of ways. She rose to his need, winding tighter and higher head thrown back, until finally with one more powerful, flexing pump they exploded, holding on to each other, both lost in the awe of a passion so strong that it blocked out the world.

That night, after Mellissa's mind finally cleared of the amazing, passionate experience, she lay in Duvall's arms, restless and agitated. Could she let this be the end of the adventure and go back to the life she knew? Would he leave her behind when the time came to come back to this time if she had to save Jem? He didn't seem inclined to leave her, she acknowledged to herself.

Their lovemaking, so slow and unhurried at the beginning, had turned hot, the resulting explosion cataclysmic, but she knew in his mind the mission came first, no matter how bright their passion might flare. She needed to keep reminding herself his duty to the Admiralty came first—if she thought anything else, she was a fool—but each encounter made it harder to remember that fact.

A voice at the back of her mind said that maybe, just possibly, this type of passion could only come from love. God, she hoped so. She was realistic enough to know that it might not; he had made no promises about a forever. She also had a duty to look after Jem. It was up to her to put both herself and Jem first before the Admiralty. Did she think she was strong enough to do what had to happen? The thought made her uncomfortable as she slipped into an uneasy sleep.

$$\bigstar \quad \bigstar \quad \bigstar \quad \bigstar \quad \bigstar$$

While Mellissa dressed, Duvall wandered out to the garden where his mother sat looking at the sky.

"You know, each time you go, it still feels like the first time," she said, her voice soft and sad. "I remember when you first went to the academy. Standing in the kitchen in your blue uniform. Such a long time ago, yet now here you are. Your sister is so excited she is finally getting to serve with you." She gave a long, heaving sigh. "Both of you in a dangerous location...I know, you can't tell me where." She looked at him, her blue eyes so deep and glittering with unshed tears. "Just keep yourself and Meredith safe. I don't want to lose the two of you."

"Mum, you know I'll protect Meredith. Neither of us has any intention of checking out of life just yet. Too much to do and see," he joked, trying to raise her spirits. He knew that each time they left she suffered.

His father also served as a captain, though these days he kept to short runs between the planets of the solar system. He had requested the run after the last attack of the Ru'Edan on Aenna, when Duvall's biological parents died in the firefight that had destroyed their ship. The Admiralty decided Earth needed a specialized, experienced pilot, and his father had taken the posting, knowing his wife suffered greatly after their friends' deaths had left Duvall orphaned.

In the past, Duvall had never understood his father's need to choose a path that limited his options. But since meeting Mellissa, he began to understand. Sometimes you had to look at the needs of the others in your life, and if that meant compromise... Well, you did it because it allowed you to have it all. He'd always seen this as a weakness in his father, but now? He'd had it wrong for so long.

"She's a nice girl." His mother changed the subject, standing up finally and turning to hug her son. "You chose well. But I can sense... She seems strong, but…"

"Yeah, I know. I'm not sure I'm what she deserves. I don't think things have been easy for her. She doesn't talk much about her childhood. And *Eshra* knows, I don't want to hurt her." He looked at his mother, so dear to him and wise. "I have my duty, but I feel torn." He let his mother see the trouble in his eyes. "I mean, how do you know? Then how do you compartmentalize your feelings?" He pulled his hands through his hair. "I just don't know at the moment, Mum."

She patted his hands. "Maybe that's your answer. The fact that you have to question what's always worked for you." She smiled softly at him. "Well, your dad is due home in the next day or so. He'll be sorry he missed you." She diffused the situation as if sensing his discomfort.

Together they walked inside, arm in arm, and she left him with a soft kiss on the cheek, checking all was in readiness for their departure.

He wandered over to the coffee machine and poured a strong cup of coffee, sitting down to wait and to think. To plan.

Even after the restless sleep and thinking she had done the night before, Mellissa felt no closer to any surety about what to do. She shrugged it off though. She needed to prove to herself and to Duvall that she had a place in his life. That way he might allow her to remain. And she had to prove to herself that she had an inner strength.

Once back into the gray ship suit, she took a look at herself in the mirror. The woman looking back seemed tougher, more purposeful. The time had come to show Duvall how strong she could be. To believe in herself. Her hair was fastened back with a band that kept it out of the way, and she looked at it dispassionately and thought, I don't really need all that.

She marched into the kitchen. "Do you have any scissors here?" she asked Duvall.

He looked at her, got up, and reached for a drawer, pulling them out and handing them over. "What are you planning to do with them?"

Without a word, she grabbed her ponytail and snipped it off in a few short cuts above the confining band.

He looked at her, almost horrified. "What did you do that for?"

"Because I wanted it gone," she answered. She flicked the hair, now short, and felt a weight gone. *There, I feel more decisive already.* She handed him the scissors and asked, "Where can I get rid of this?"

He took the long hair without a word and deposited it in a receptacle. He looked concerned and surprised.

Elara and Grayson wandered into the kitchen. They both wore their gray ship suits and looked well-rested. Grayson looked at Mellissa, raising an eyebrow. Elara took one look at her and smiled. "I like it."

Quickly reaching into cupboards, they arranged a hasty breakfast as Meredith, Chowd, and Kathryn joined them. After eating and clearing away, Duvall glanced at his wrist.

"Time to make for the port. Mum, I know you're worried, and I'll take good care of Meredith, but she has a job to do, and

I need to help her get it done right." He grabbed both her hands and looked her in the face. "We have to go." He pulled her into a big bear hug, holding her close. Mellissa knew he was special. Here he was, unashamed of his emotions in front of his peers and friends.

Meredith said goodbye next, a small ship bag at her feet. "Mum, I love you. I'll be back as soon as I can. I promise to stay safe, and I'll watch out for Duvall too." The words were said as if by rote with an impish smile and a hug. Kisses on both cheeks dispensed, she headed over to Duvall, who held the bag they had brought with them.

One by one, the others said their goodbyes.

When Kathryn got to Mellissa, she pulled her into her arms and whispered in her ear, "Don't give up on him. He's a good man, just sometimes loses sight of what is important to him personally. Come back soon." She gave Mellissa a kiss on the cheek before releasing her.

They all trooped back to the vehicle and clambered in. The fit was tight, and Duvall insisted that Mellissa sit in the front with him. Elara, Meredith, and Grayson sat in the middle, Chowd bringing up the rear. The sun now well in the sky, the temperature rose hot and sticky, according to the computer in the vehicle, as they pulled out.

Mellissa glanced back, getting a final view of Kathryn on the stairs watching as they left. How must she feel, Mellissa thought, watching her family leave time and time again? Going to places where no human had traveled, or participating in battles where it was unlikely that the bodies of the deceased would be retrieved.

"Your mother's great." She spoke quietly, hoping to keep the conversation between herself and Duvall.

"Yeah. I got lucky. She's the real anchor in the family. Keeps us together, no matter where we are in time and space."

Mellissa looked back out the window and smiled as he slipped his hand over hers. "She liked you." The warmth of his touch and his words made her feel secure.

"That's nice to know. I liked her too."

The trip was quiet and uneventful. She considered what she had learned the night before, playing the events over in her mind, the comments made during their departure. She wondered what Kathryn had thought of Duvall spending the night with her. Would she see that as a positive? She knew the time had come to look forward though and forcibly pulled her mind from the events of the last thirty-six hours.

Mellissa looked forward to getting back aboard the *Elector*. In a short space of time, the *Elector* had begun to feel like home, just as the cabin she shared with Duvall felt like her own space. Lost in her own world of introspection, she dimly noticed the soft whispers interspersed the silence of the vehicle ride as they sped along the airway.

They pulled into the port in short order and tossed the keys to a different security officer this time. "Sir, I am authorized to hand this to you." He extended a small packet to Duvall, who accepted it silently. Duvall looked inside then swiftly pocketed the item. Mellissa looked at him, and he shook his head.

Duvall grabbed her hand, and the six of them quickly slipped into the impressive building, Duvall at the front with Mellissa, Chowd protecting Meredith and Elara, and Grayson bringing up the rear, their bags slung over their arms as they moved into the secure area. Duvall's body remained tense until they were finally on the shuttle.

The forces of lift off pushed her back into her seat, and she watched, amazed at how far they had already traveled. The sky darkened and clouds obscured the land. She looked forward, and her heart felt a sense of excitement. Soon they arrived at the *Elector*. She gripped Duvall's hand as they exited the shuttle.

Once on board the *Elector*, Duvall pulled the packet from his pocket. "That was the mission disk handed over at the vehicle," he told Chowd, who merely raised his eyebrow.

He handed over a reader, and Duvall inserted it and scanned the contents, making an occasional sound as he read it through.

"We have permission to move through the time gate. Chowd and Grayson, you'll need copies. I'll arrange them."

"What kind of information do you have on the disk?" Mellissa craned her neck to see, and while they made their way to Duvall's cabin he patiently explained how the gate worked, the passwords being good for only one use each way.

"There is also replication information concerning money and maps, not to mention cultural facts concerning the time period. It's everything we need to make it back to your time and not stand out."

She swiped her hair out of her eyes as she considered his words. How many times had she passed people on the street who had come through the slipstream? Duvall had indicated that it was rarely done because of the damage it could potentially cause to the time continuum, but then how could you possibly know?

He gave the reader back to Chowd and gripped her hand. No wonder she loved him, she thought, and started at the revelation. *Dear God!* It was true. *I've fallen in love with Duvall.*

"What's wrong?" he said, quickly looking around the cabin.

"Nothing, really. I just thought about home." Well now, there was the icing on the cake, she thought. She never meant to fall for this man, but obviously her heart had no intention of listening to her head. "Nothing to worry about," she assured him with a small sigh, laying her hand on his arm. She didn't argue with herself, as once the flash of intuition passed, she knew it was the honest truth. It made sense now, the sense of betrayal when he had left the bed the other day.

# Chapter 10

Stepping back onto the metal decks of the *Elector* felt like coming home for Mellissa.

She'd never really felt an affinity for where she lived previously. Growing up in an orphanage, you learned quickly that what was yours also belonged to someone else. When she finally left there at age sixteen, after the State released her from their care, she had worked hard to find a meaning for her life and to give herself a sense of worth.

Life in those days had been tough. She'd lived in a one-room efficiency unit, eking out an existence so she could finish school at night, but even though she wanted a degree, she couldn't afford it. Then fate had smiled as she got a job in a small bookstore.

That work had led to a lifestyle which fostered a sense of who she was. Within months, she showed a knack for knowing what customers wanted, knowing the authors and titles people sought. She took over the ordering process and had become a senior staff member in a few short years.

She had continued to live in the flat, scrimping and saving while dreaming of a future. Then Frank, the bookstore owner, had declared his intention to sell. Mellissa didn't have a lot of capital, but he had offered to loan the deposit to her, knowing that with her drive and determination, the store would continue to grow and flourish.

She'd declined and pushed herself harder, saving for the deposit. Frank held on for an extra twelve months, giving her time to get her finances in order, before declaring he needed to retire as he was sick. Thankfully, it was only a few days later that the bank informed her the loan was approved and she'd delightedly told Frank. She'd followed through with a flurry of packing her life into the meager boxes she had taken with her to the bookstore's unit above the shop.

All of that was gone now. She wondered if there'd be an opportunity for her to gather the things most important to her. While living and working at the shop had made her feel happy, it hadn't dominated her existence.

"Duvall, I have an idea." She touched his arm and he stilled, raising an eyebrow.

"What?"

"Uh, it's probably better that we discuss it later," she said. His eyes smoldered, and she rolled hers. "Nothing like that." His grin had her heart lurching.

They made their way to the bay connected to the *Elector*. As they strode back onto her decking, she heard the hollow sound that made her feel welcome.

Coming down the ramp, she saw a tall, blond-haired man with piercing green eyes. "Who's that?" she asked.

Duvall growled.

"Well, hi there, Duvall." He welcomed them, a smile ready, extending a hand to shake Duvall's. "Who is this lovely lady? And why was I summarily summoned to join your crew?" he asked with an Australian accent. Grinning at Mellissa, he held out his hand, and without giving Duvall a chance to answer, he introduced himself. "Hi, I'm Raven Fraser, the new engineer of the *Elector*."

"Raven, be in my office at 1300 hours. Briefing then." Duvall turned and stomped away, looking thoroughly irritated with this Raven Fraser.

Mellissa extended her hand. "Hi, I'm Mellissa Davis." She looked at him. He seemed nice and friendly, but while he was well-built and extremely good-looking, he didn't have the same zing about him as Duvall.

"Hey, Mellissa, we need to get moving."

Turning her head, she saw Elara standing at the doorway, grinning.

"Raven Fraser, it's been a long time since you've darkened a space dock with us. I see you've met Mellissa." Then looking at Mellissa, she motioned for her to join her on the walk to the bridge. "Duvall will be looking for you on the bridge."

Mellissa turned, and just before she headed away from Raven, she said, "Nice meeting you." She walked toward Elara, the clanking of the deck reassuring.

The women made their way out into the corridor. "Better watch Raven," Elara said with a little laugh. "He likes to think he's a ladies' man, but everyone who knows him well sees right through him." She draped her hand through Mellissa's arm. "Now, before I say anything, forgive me for sticking my nose in, but can I give you some advice?"

Mellissa looked at her before nodding quietly.

"Duvall is a man with focus. Sometimes that focus blinds him to other things. But make no mistake, he's a good man. Just sometimes a bit slow to see what is important to him. Give him a chance to work it out." She glanced at Mellissa with a small smile. "I like you, Mellissa, and I really hope you stick around for the long haul. Duvall needs balance in his life, and that was missing before you came along. I would really love for you to become a permanent fixture here. You and me…boy, we could have some fun." She chuckled. "Is all that fine with you?"

Mellissa laughed lightly. *What an unusual discussion.* She'd never had one even remotely like this, even with Jem, who until now, had always been her closest friend. Given the connection she felt to Elara, though, she smiled. "I know what you mean. And I will certainly do my best to stick in for the long haul."

Elara squeezed her arm with hers, and they continued toward the bridge together, two friends in harmony.

Watching the Earth spin away was surreal for Mellissa,

but she hovered on the bridge for an hour after they left the port.

She frowned then swiped her palm over the door of the office, and it opened wide. Heading in, she noted that Elara and Grayson had arrived before her.

"Where is everyone else?" Mellissa asked.

"Late. Meredith buzzed me, she's sorting out some issues. I don't know where the rest are." Duvall sounded distracted, so she trailed over to the seat and slid into it. Her body dragged with an ache and she sighed.

"Long day, huh? It gets better, eventually." Elara snickered, and Grayson simply shook his head.

Meredith wandered in a few minutes later with Chowd, red-faced, following. Now the only member of the new leadership crew missing was Raven. Duvall looked up, impatience written all over his face while he tapped his fingers on the table. She could tell he wanted to contact him when Raven thudded into the room, looking angry and frustrated.

"Who for *Eshra's* sake was running your engineering before me? *Barsha!* It will take days to iron out the kinks." He sat with a thud, a black look on his face.

"Well, now that we're all here, I can fill everyone in. Raven and Meredith, you're newest on board. Our mission is quite delicate. We believe that Crick Sur Banden has placed infiltrators not just through Admiralty, but also somehow has managed to get some to Earth. In the past." He stopped, waiting for everyone to digest the information. "Meredith—Warrant Officer Gentry—is here to decode messages we believe were sent from someone in Admiralty to Crick Sur Banden, the leader of the Ru'Edan rebels." He nodded toward his sister. "Raven Fraser, replacement engineer. Briefly, our previous engineer, Corbin Jard, was an infiltrator for the Ru'Edan. He got hold of and released the handbook for the *Elector*. We intercepted it before Crick Sur Banden received it through his network."

Raven let out a surprised whistle.

"Mellissa is here as she is both a material witness and also has information of times, places, and people involved. As a civilian she is not to take part in any encounters. However, she will act as consultant on this mission."

Duvall looked at Chowd, who looked happy with the mission details so far.

"Here's what we know." He breathed deep before carrying on. "Crick Sur Banden continues to be a thorn in the side of the Earth Empire. He has had infiltrators placed throughout the Admiralty, and we believe may have found Elphin's plant within the diplomatic corps. We have our own operatives looking for information concerning other places they may have infiltrated. Aboard the *Elector*, we've faced issues while Corbin Jard attempted to endanger our crew and the *Elector*. At a later point, he made an attempt on Mellissa and he was neutralized, but not before we lost a crewmember and Jard himself."

Raven and Meredith's faces were slack with surprise. "But how did he—" Meredith started.

Duvall held his hand up. "In a moment. There's more yet. Raven, Meredith intercepted transmissions from Admiralty to the Ru'Edan which lead us to believe that they are attempting to access the slipstream in order to alter Earth history. We believe the plan is to ensure that the Empire does not evolve as we know it."

Duvall stopped once more, waiting for everyone to absorb the information he'd shared. She could tell that recounting the information that they had managed to cobble together raised his ire.

"Corbin Jard was in a perfect position to cripple our new fleet of stealth ships by passing their specs to operatives. However, we believe this is a much bigger plot than just disabling our ships. We believe Sur Banden knows who were the lynchpins in the formation of the Empire's Senate. Should he stop that from forming, it would leave our defenses weak. It stands to reason he's doing the same with the Ru'Edans." He breathed deeply. "This is a long-term game. Damned risky, but if it pays off, not only do we have an attempt to disrupt the Empire, we also have our latest weapons up for not just minute inspection but also every possible weakness in full view and we are unsure of the ramifications of a changed timeline."

He looked around the table.

"Our mission is to travel back through the slipstream, get the information concerning the infiltrator, and neutralize them before they can wreak havoc on the time period. We also need information on who else is embedded and where." He paused, bringing up images of Mellissa's bookstore and Jem in a holovision pad set up on his table. "This has to work without detection, people. At this point in history, there has been no real extraterrestrial travel bar to the moon. We must not effect that timeline, otherwise it puts pretty much everything we have achieved so far in jeopardy."

Chowd nodded. "I agree, Captain. Miss Davis will act as our historical researcher as she has access to information we do not, including the acceptable social behaviors. We will use her knowledge and contacts to find Andurs Feinstein, who we believe is the conduit to the infiltrator, and hopefully, ultimately to Crick Sur Banden. We believe Miss Davis's bookstore was chosen because of both its geographic location and also because they may have become aware that in the future you would have access to the slipstream technology, making you yet another target for removal."

Mellissa gasped. "No. I mean, how would he know what I'm aware of in the future? I don't even know now, what..." Confusion descended like a fog on her brain.

"Miss Davis...Mellissa, the captain and I have found what we believe is the connection between the books you will write in the future and the plot against the Empire. We think this is the reason you were chosen as the target. You are the key to what happens."

Shock ricocheted. It hadn't occurred to her that something she hadn't even done yet would affect the future. "But... I haven't actually done anything."

Chowd smiled. "Not yet. But your position in the future is important to the continuum. We aren't sure why at this stage.

I'm sure that will all be revealed in the future."

"I haven't even finished writing one book yet," she cried. "And I certainly don't intend to release any secrets through them." She looked around in distress. "I can stop writing if that helps?"

Elara placed her hand on Mellissa's. "I don't think that's what they meant, Mellissa. Is it?" She looked at Duvall. The scarring on Elara's face seemed harsher than ever, giving the woman a dangerous quality. Mellissa guessed it had frightened more than one junior officer into submission when needed. Mellissa gripped Elara's hand, appreciating her support.

"No. In fact, it's important that you do write them. They'll have their place in history, and if you don't complete them, there'll be an element of history missing, not to mention a shift, or anomaly if you will, in the space-time continuum too." Duvall sighed and looked at her again. "We need a researcher aboard the *Elector* capable of understanding both the historical aspects of the travel and able to handle the current technology. We need you to go back to where you came from and act as if nothing has happened. Which in and of itself can be tricky."

Duvall paused for a moment before continuing.

"I've calibrated the settings so that the slipstream returns us to the same time, within about twelve hours, to your store. Chowd and I have both discussed this at length since returning to the *Elector*. I… We believe that we should return you to both your place and time, with the two of us there acting as your guard." He stopped, taking a breath. "We need to get to your friend Jem, find out where and when she is meeting Andurs, and somehow arrange a meeting. From there, we believe it is wisest if we apprehend him. Get him to…if not help us—" He smiled cynically at that comment. "—then at least lead us to his connections and tell us exactly what they are up to."

He looked toward his sister.

"Meanwhile, Meredith will continue to decode the messages moving between the ship, Admiralty, and the Ru'Edan Empire. Particularly those she intercepted. She'll double up with intercepting and decoding any further communiqués while there."

Mellissa's head spun. So much to do and prepare. Was she even up to it? She closed her eyes.

"Are you okay, Mellissa?"

Her head jerked up at Duvall's cautious tone.

"Yeah, it's just… There's a lot to take in."

He nodded. "There is a lot riding on this." His gaze pierced her. "Shall I continue?"

She smiled. "Yes."

"Right. Normally we would expect our comm officer to do this, but because of the status of this mission, this must be contained here. Between us."

Meredith nodded her agreement.

"Meredith will remain on the ship. Grayson will remain here as well and ensure we're not detected and get us out of there quickly if necessary. He'll assume command until my return. Elara, you'll remain on call."

Elara bent her head as she tapped the instructions into her mini-computer. "Yeah."

"Raven, I need you to repair whatever's been done to the *Elector*. We don't have a lot of time, and I need her systems at optimal, including weapons systems. Given Jard was aboard for at least three weeks, we can't rest thinking he just 'tweaked' the engines. I expect full updates."

He looked at his crew, handpicked for this mission. Mellissa was sure there was no team better able to deal with this crisis. She nearly laughed at the horrified expression on Raven's face.

"I'll have a thorough assessment within twenty-four hours." Raven began tapping at the screen in front of him. His face screwed up as his blond hair flicked forward as his fingers flew.

She assessed him quickly, watching his movements. Evidently, Raven could fill the position of engineer easily. The fact that the crew had welcomed him immediately into the fold spoke volumes, not just for what he could do, but also for the man himself.

"Chowd, I need you to ensure the security team is fully briefed and ready for the mission." Duvall looked at Chowd, also busily tapping away on his screen. "We don't have a lot of time to make this happen, and it must be seamless."

"I'll arrange a security briefing for 0800 hours tomorrow. From thereon, all crew will be directed to their roles," Chowd answered, looking at Grayson. It was clear they'd discussed this between themselves as they seemed to know what the other would want.

"Captain, I must state now, I believe I should be the one to accompany Mellissa—"

Duvall interrupted Grayson. She guessed it was standard protocol to ensure the captain remained safely on board.

"No, I'll accompany Mellissa together with Chowd. We will need to be able to take immediate action. Is everyone clear with their roles?" He looked around the table. "Right. Meredith and Mellissa, can you stay back please?"

The implicit dismissal had the rest of the crewmembers rising from their seats.

"Mellissa, when this is done, can you come to the ST suite?" Elara looked at her, and

Mellissa nodded slowly, not sure what the reason was but welcoming a distraction nonetheless.

✪ ✪ ✪ ✪ ✪

Duvall launched straight into business. "Meredith, do you have all the equipment you need to finalize the decoding? I need to know in case we have to detour back to Aenna. Though, frankly, I would prefer not to. The sooner we get into the slipstream, the sooner we get back and clear this mess up."

"The systems and equipment here should do the trick, Duvall. The cabin I have been assigned is fully kitted out, and

Grayson has also cleared one of the security desk screens for my use. I believe I should have some answers by the time we leave slipstream."

"Good." He nodded. "Okay. Well, you'd better get off to your cabin, unpack, and familiarize yourself. Mess at 1900 hours, right?"

"Sure, big brother." The formality now brushed aside, she started sassing him and grinning. "You know you've needed me for the longest time. 'Bout time you get your priorities right." Meredith stood and sashayed toward the door. Palming it, she turned briefly and winked. "Don't let him push you around too much, Mellissa. Give him an inch and he'll take a light year." Chuckling at her joke, she made her way out of the door, the quiet whoosh closing them off from the world.

Mellissa looked at Duvall. "Where do you need me to work, and what do I need to do?" she asked. He stood up and grabbed her.

"This is what I need." Pulling her in closer, he breathed in the scent of her hair. The feel of her body settled him as nothing else had ever done, and the whisper of her breath against his collar soothed his anxiety.

She grabbed him around the waist and snuggled for a minute, and he reveled in the closeness of touch. Then she pulled away. "You have things to do, and so do I," she reminded him. "Now I have a date with Elara, and you have…well, you have stuff to do." She smiled at him, and electricity arced through the air between them.

"When you're done, head down to the bridge. Grayson's setting a unit up for you with full access to all the historical databases and anything else you might require. I need you to run through some information to make sure it's accurate. We also need a detailed floor plan of the bookstore so we can transmit there safely and end up in the right place." He kissed her quick and hard then, letting her go, turned. "I better get onto the bridge." With that, he headed out the door.

# Chapter 11

Elara looked up as Mellissa entered the SurgiTech suite. "Good, now that you're here, we can have a proper chat while I work. Roll up your sleeve please."

Mellissa looked at Elara, completely lost. "What do you mean? Do I need some sort of injection?"

"Not exactly. I just want to be sure you're covered, for your and Duvall's peace of mind. Now don't get upset, but do you have an adequate plan for conception control?"

That hadn't crossed her mind. Always before she had been so careful, remembering to use condoms, so how could she have forgotten? Sure, their encounters had been unplanned, and that alone was out of character for her, but still... She closed her eyes in self-castigation.

While she felt an immediate enchantment at the thought of a child of hers and Duvall, another part of her said it wasn't the time or place. Neither had she considered if any diseases were an issue. *Are there even sexually transmitted diseases in the future?* She felt sick at the thought that her stupidity may have endangered her own health. That, together with the fact that they still hadn't discussed anything long term, gave her pause. She had no intention of having him think she had trapped him. The thoughts whirled through her mind.

"Mellissa?" Elara prompted, pulling her out of her thoughts.

She shook her head. "Oh God, that thought never crossed my mind." How could this have happened? "With everything happening... I never considered that!" In fact, inquiring as to what forms of contraception were available hadn't even occurred to her.

Mellissa strongly believed that the woman should protect herself, and in the few encounters she had enjoyed in the past, she'd always ensured her own safety. Now should have been no different, and given the hot passionate sex they enjoyed, she should have thought about it.

Mellissa tried mentally to work out her cycle, but confusion over the to-ing and fro-ing had her looking at Elara. "Does time travel interrupt a cycle?" She grappled to untangle her thoughts. "And uhh… What about sexually transmitted diseases? Do they still even exist?" The words tumbled out.

"Actually, that's an interesting question regarding cycles. So far we haven't allowed for that, as most of us are on an enforced contraceptive routine during these sorts of missions. As for the diseases, thankfully, you can rest easy there. All known sexually transmitted diseases have been wiped out, and we do require all active adults to submit to regular testing, just to be safe."

Mellissa closed her eyes at Elara's words. One less concern, but she still kicked herself mentally.

"Oh God! How soon can we find out about pregnancy?" Mellissa asked.

"Taking that as a no, you hadn't really thought about it, so we're going to take a sample for testing, and if you have an all clear, we'll begin you on an implantation routine to ensure you remain safe. If that's fine with you?" She looked at Mellissa closely. "Testing and contraception implantation is normal, you know." She grinned. "And the best part of all? It won't hurt one bit."

She grabbed an instrument and showed Mellissa how it would take a quick sample for instant testing.

"So we hold it here, and this button allows me to take a micro-sample via transmission. It only takes a minute or two to check, so we can be totally clear before I start your injections. Are you okay to go ahead with this?" She patted Mellissa on the back, obviously sensing her discomfort with the subject. "If it is positive though, we'll need to think about what happens next.

And you would need to discuss this with Duvall." She looked at Mellissa firmly. "You know that."

Mellissa nodded. Elara turned away to prepare the tools required for the testing. Mellissa watched with her mind in a stir.

The sample was taken quickly and the testing underway in the small pathology unit that Elara kept in the ST suite. Mellissa sat tensely, trying hard to ignore the ramifications of a positive test. A vague image now played in her mind of a little boy with Duvall's eyes, dark curly hair, and the sweet baby-powder smell. While they waited, Elara made coffee for both of them, and Mellissa kept watch on the figures scrolling over the viewscreen of the unit. Damn! Pregnancy hadn't even rated in her mind during the sexy encounters.

"What forms of contraceptive do they use now?" she asked Elara.

"The majority on long range use a contraceptive implant. We fit it below the dermis, and it's a slow release of hormones. They also regulate the cycle, which is handy." Elara gave a short laugh. "The last thing you want to worry about is if your period is going to arrive at some inconvenient time." She sobered. "Most women on short runs also use a variant but with different doses. If you prefer a non-invasive, short-term option, we now use a hypo spray with thirty-day efficacy." The choices rolled on. "There's also a daily application, similar to an inhalant I found a record of, for lung deficiencies in your time. They are effective, and there are very few side effects, but it depends on the user remembering, of course." Elara held one up for Mellissa to see, and she sat forward, inspecting the item.

They were deep in conversation when the machine sounded. Mellissa started, jumping slightly, and beads of sweat suddenly dotted her upper lip. She eyed the pathology machine, fearful of the answer. What if it was positive? How would Duvall react?

Elara looked at her, and Mellissa got the impression she could almost read her mind. "Ready to find out?"

"Not...not really." She quaked and her voice carried a

quiver. Elara reached over to grab her hand briefly.

Mellissa took a deep breath while she steeled herself for whichever answer came. "Okay, then. Let's find out."

*It could be... I could...* Fears whirled while the idea of a baby played on her mind. If it was a yes, she'd tell him. If he didn't want... Well, she'd raise and care for the child herself. Love him or her.

"You know he would make a great father." Mellissa whispered the words to herself, then stopped herself short. *Whoa, I'm sure he would be, in time anyway, just not yet.*

It was more a matter of when the time was right, and that wasn't now. Ahead of them lay traveling into a dangerous situation, not to mention time travel. What effects would that have on a growing fetus? And coupled with the unstable nature of their relationship, she knew, deep down, neither was really ready for a child.

He'd be protective of a child and its mother, she knew that already. But it wouldn't be a matter of choice. For her, there could be no option of getting rid of it—her background had made sure of that. Besides, she believed children were as long term a commitment as it got. Mellissa closed her eyes, mentally kicking herself for not thinking first before jumping into a physical relationship with Duvall.

"Negative." Elara looked at her with the single word.

Mellissa breathed deeply, trying to calm herself. Her fears that it would put too much pressure on their growing relationship were gone, and she felt devastated.

"So how would you feel if it had been positive?"

"It never even crossed my mind, until the possibility was there. Once I knew there was a chance, I wanted it. But now that I know it's not, I feel...empty." Mellissa closed her eyes, a feeling of sadness washing over her. "I mean, all my life I was kind of prepared for being alone, without children and family. Then all of a sudden the opportunity could have been there. It sounds odd, I know, but now it's something I would like. One day. But neither of us is anywhere near ready or settled, and who knows what the future will hold?"

"That's not so unusual, you know. I'm guessing you and Duvall haven't discussed this yet. Is that right?" Elara sat down on the seat opposite her and took her hand.

"No." Mellissa rubbed at her aching eyes. "I know we weren't prepared and that it's better that way, but still…"

"I know. It feels like you've lost something."

Silence stretched and Mellissa dug deep, looking for strength. "We should… Tell me about your suggestion for contraception, please."

Elara scanned her face. "Okay then. There's a few, but for you, I'm thinking a longer term option might be best. Just until things settle down a bit." She grabbed up one and Mellissa saw a cylindrical capsule, about half the length of her fingernail. "This will be good for six months. I strongly suggest that should you choose to let it run out, you discuss the situation first with Duvall. If you choose not to renew the implant, then we can start discussing options and routines and pregnancy." Elara grinned at Mellissa, who still felt like bursting into tears.

Mellissa smiled shakily at her friend. "Yeah, that sounds like the best option."

Elara slipped it inside an applicator and held it against her skin. "This will only take a second or two." She pressed the button. "All done. If you experience any side effects, let me know immediately. Now come on back to my office. I need that coffee."

They finished their drinks, sitting at the desk in the ST suite. She didn't want to talk any further about it and Elara let the conversation lapse.

Just before she left the suite, Elara made one final point. "Mellissa, I don't want to pry, but I know Duvall really well. He's not an open kind of person, and you may have to take that first step yourself. I know it's scary. Relationships are a gamble, and sometimes you need to make sure your dice is loaded before they can get theirs in place. And Duvall isn't a great dice player. But what he will do is keep any commitment he gives to you."

She gave Mellissa a hug and left her to ponder the information.

After the session, Mellissa had a feeling that she needed to take some action toward formalizing the situation with Duvall, but as to what? That still remained a mystery.

They reached the gate to the slipstream without needing to make a stop at Aenna, and it loomed ominously in Mellissa's mind. She watched the crew in action from her seat on the bridge. It was truly a marvel to be able to travel like this, she thought.

"Transmit code." Duvall's face was a study of concentration as he monitored the scrolling information on the screen. An overlay of details whirred before them, slightly obscuring her view.

The data flow stopped briefly while Duvall and Grayson tapped on their desk screens. "Override command beta." Grayson's voice filtered through the silent room.

"Inputting now." The *tap tap* of the keys filled the air. "Override command alpha. Status…accepted." Duvall cleared his throat, and all eyes turned to the viewer.

A single word flashed onto the screen. *Acknowledged.* Duvall typed instructions, his hands flying across his keypad.

"All hands, strap in. We have the go to slipstream." He toggled the mic and gave the command to his crew. He turned to the navigator. "Good to go."

Mellissa was heartened when he winked at her before giving the command to head through the port. When the chimes finally announced the opening of the slipstream, a whine started from the engines. The deck vibrated, but the sound was… harmonious, she thought. Looking around, she noted the rest of the crew strapping in and she followed suit, the heavy canvas sliding over her, and with a clack she secured it within the buckle.

"It wasn't so long ago that you didn't know how to do

that." Elara's voice echoed amusement, and Mellissa smiled with her.

Then there was the gathering force, shoving her back in her seat as the *Elector* roared and finally sped forward, within the gate.

"The engines sound... I don't know. Less forced than before?" She turned toward Elara who grinned.

"Grayson said Raven found some engine issues that needed adjusting. But yes, I think you're right. It sounds better and seems to have more power than before."

"Last time I was here, I didn't even have a rudimentary knowledge of time travel or slipstream technology. It's odd, because that was only days ago, yet I feel like... I don't know. Maybe I feel like I've changed. Now that sounds stupid, doesn't it?"

"Not at all. The person you were when you joined the *Elector* was unaware of the great leaps that have been made, both scientific and social. Now that you're aware, essentially you are a different person."

Mellissa mulled over Elara's words. Turning her attention back to the viewscreen, she watched the information scrolling across. Some of it she understood now, and that filled her with satisfaction. Now through the gates, she slipped her chair back around to marvel at the view from the ports at the side of the bridge. The black of the stream enveloped the ship, and once more, the flying star trails whizzing by caught her attention.

"Well, as much as I could sit here on the bridge for hours, I have work to do. Don't suppose you'll join me in the mess for a coffee?" Elara asked Mellissa.

Before she could rise and accept Elara's invitation, Duvall interrupted. "Stay for a while. I need to evaluate what you understood of our maneuvers." She glanced at Elara.

"That's okay. I should get back to SurgiTech. I have plenty of work to keep me busy there." Then she left them.

Even though the bridge was crowded, it seemed as if they were alone, in their own private world, when Duvall motioned her to take her seat and swiveled his around to face her.

"So, what did you understand?"

She explained her rudimentary knowledge. "You have a two-phase key that activates the slipstream. Once they are keyed in, you wait for a ping, then enter the coordinates, which stretches the stream through the time continuum. After that things get a little hazy."

His eyes widened. "That's pretty good. Of course each gate, or door if you will, has its own set of commands or key. Without the correct one, the gate won't activate. The two-phase passwords are set commands to activate it. Then there is override, and it's good for one return use only. Then we input that continuum log points."

"Wow. Okay, so I remember most of the actual steps."

"Yeah, you did really well." They sat in silence for a moment, then he leaned forward. "What are you..."

"I need to get started running through the data files and making sure everything is fine. Then I need to see Raven about generating the required equipment." Her voice wobbled a little, betraying her nerves. "I really want to get this right."

Duvall slid his hand over hers. "You'll do fine. I better let you go then."

For an instant Mellissa was sure she saw a wisp of regret on his face. "Will you join me later? For lunch?"

He gave a nod and she stood, walking away from the bridge to the small alcove that had been set aside for her use. Settling into the chair, Mellissa logged into the desk screen. A file flashed up at her, and she quickly brought up the information from the messaging system. The first message contained a number of files, which described the social situation of her time. Mellissa opened that one first, quickly losing herself in the descriptions, sometimes amending the information she felt was inaccurate, until she felt a hand on her shoulder. She looked up to find Duvall standing there.

"Ready for a break?" he asked softly. His tall frame towered over her and made her feel protected and cared for. Not emotions she usually attributed to herself.

"Sure. Coffee sounds pretty good right now." She smiled at him.

He leaned down toward her. "I could even suggest something a little more exciting, but unfortunately there's such a lot to do, that it will have to suffice…for now."

The look on his face turned wolfish, and heat coiled low in her belly. He indicated she should stand up.

"Grayson has taken control of the bridge, so at least we can sit and talk in the privacy of my office." He led her toward the stairs. "So, how are our records?" he asked.

"Some of it is really uncannily accurate, then I find something that makes me laugh because it's so wrong. I was reading this information about money and banks. It talks about how banks are multiple repositories for blood, money, and even sperm! Honestly, anyone would think you don't have those in your time." She looked at him.

He seemed confused. "We don't. Is that so wrong?"

His answer stopped her in her tracks. "Yes. No. I mean your understanding is just a bit off." She went on to explain the differences between the three types of banks. "What do you use to purchase things with?"

"We don't buy things using money. You're allocated a credit depending on what you do for the Empire. You can amass credit in order to purchase anything you want."

She looked at him for a moment. "So you budget and effectively bank your credits until you can afford the item you want."

"Sure, we have a budget, but credit shows on our ID accounts. We swipe our wrist IDs, and that's how we acquire items."

"Well, there you go." She grinned up at him. "No wonder you can afford to buy a girl coffee."

"Food items, those of a basic nature, are available as needed. There is no need to utilize your ID. Other items, of a luxury nature, they're the ones you need your ID for."

She let that settle as they moved forward. The door to his office slid open and they stepped inside, then he moved in toward her. Their lips met, and the familiar tingling began as she opened her mouth to allow him access.

She sighed with pleasure when his hands dropped to her bottom, caressing and kneading. He lifted his mouth only to look into her eyes, then allowed his hands to dip down to her mouth and beyond to her neck then back up again. Slowly, sensuously, he traced her cheeks with his lips, little nips here and there as he reached her chin. He flicked the sensitive flesh with the tip of his tongue.

Heat simmered between them as Duvall grazed her neck with his lips. She reached up and tangled her hands in his hair, luxuriating in the thick, rich silk.

Even as Mellissa arched back his hands cupped her breasts, slowly kneading them. Her hands gripped him tighter now, and without conscious thought, she moved her legs slightly to allow him to stand between them as she arched into his kiss and hands. He moaned and lifted his head. The heat in his eyes promised further encounters. *Just not now.*

The coil of desire in her belly gnawed, but they eased away from each other, and he rested his forehead against hers as their heartbeats returned to their normal rhythm. The moment passed.

They stayed like that, neither saying a word for a long moment.

"*Barsha!*" Eventually, he moved away from her. "I can't seem to stay away from you, and yet we have so much to do before we emerge from the slipstream. I didn't bring you in here to ravish you. But it certainly is an added bonus." He smiled at her, seeming more relaxed than before.

The reason for his tension became evident later when he showed her a report from Meredith. Crick Sur Banden had infiltrators throughout the various countries who remained signatories to the United Nations and were using a single human courier. *Andurs Feinstein.*

"We haven't managed to locate any information on him, and I need you to check the historical records. See what there is regarding him, his background, and how he may have come into contact with the Ru'Edan Empire." He stopped and looked at her. "Can you do that? We need the information quickly. Given the nature of this investigation, I need to keep this between us if possible. I need you to do it, but here on my secured system." He indicated his personal desk screen.

She nodded. "Yes, based on what I have been shown, I believe I can find that information, depending on what documentation you have. I may require things such as telephone books and electoral rolls from that timeframe though. Do you think you have access to those?"

He looked mystified. She wondered what other concepts she would raise that would surprise them both.

"I honestly don't know. But if we don't, what other options are available?" he asked.

She knew he was floundering, his knowledge of her time weak. *Well, I finally have something solid to add to the crew. For all their expertise, this is beyond them.*

"Depending on what equipment you have on the ship, I wonder…is it possible to access the internet?" She quickly continued before he even had time to reply. "Stupid question, you probably can't do that using the technology you have available and in slipstream, right? Besides which, it's ancient technology for you and likely none of your machines will even be able to make a connection." She babbled furiously, angry with herself for the ridiculous question about the 'net'.

He looked confused, and she sat behind his desk and tapped a query into the desk screen. Information concerning the internet popped up on the screen. He moved around the desk, behind her, leaning over her shoulder and reading quickly. "Oh, that's what you mean? I had heard about that. Hang on, I can get the comm officer to take a look. He might have an idea how we can hook you into it." He toggled the commswitch and quickly paged the officer.

He arrived, panting a little. "Yes, Captain?"

"Mellissa needs access to some very old technology called the intranet—"

The officer looked confused, and Mellissa took pity on him. "The internet. I need to be able to access some historical documents."

The man smiled. "I have just the thing." He left the office at a quick trot, the thud of his boots quickly dying away, only to return some minutes later with a palm unit in hand. "I've been working on replicating some of the ancient technologies, particularly this. It's called a doogle?"

Mellissa worked hard to keep a straight face. "It's called a dongle."

"Ahh." He smiled sheepishly. "It's a sort of hobby. I thought when we were told we'd be moving through the slipstream, that I might have the opportunity to use it." He handed the palm unit over.

Mellissa picked it up, turned it on, and watched it scan for a connection. None yet, but she was sure it would work. She grinned at the comm officer. "This looks pretty close to what I'm looking for, but unless it can connect…" She fiddled a little more, touching icons on the screen.

The comm officer watched her intently, asking questions that she could thankfully answer.

A few minutes later, she looked up and smiled. "Yes, it's exactly what I need. When we are closer, I'm guessing you should be able to find a way to hook me into a satellite and away we go."

"Just say the word and I'll come down and we can configure it."

Finally, she'd found her place, and it felt right.

Duvall watched the delight in Mellissa's face and felt a

cold emotion, rather like jealousy, sweep through him. Here she was, headed back to her own time. In the short time that had passed, she'd changed and become more…assured?

But during the by-play with the comm officer she'd unbent and become almost playful. It confused him. Was she drawn to the man? Or was this just her true nature finally breaking free of the confines she seemed to tie herself up with?

Hell, he still didn't even know if she wanted to stay. But even if she wanted to remain behind in her time, he couldn't allow that. The danger to everyone involved was too great. She knew far too much, and that threatened everything his people had fought for. He thrust the thought away before the ache in his chest got larger.

"That's one more hurdle cleared away. Now you can check through the records and find Feinstein."

"Well, when we get closer, yes. But I'm going to look through the records you have available, just in case I can pick something up there."

He watched as she started working, flicking through ancient computerized files, just as he'd requested. He stayed for a minute, just taking in the view of her in his space, at home and relaxed. Comfortable.

He turned and left her to it.

# Chapter 12

**M**ellissa sat at the desk screen, contemplating a summary of her time while they traveled through the slipstream.

Taking a break for a coffee, she stood and gazed out the portal. The star trails slid by like long strands of light. 'I've spent a lot of time contemplating since I got here." Her voice echoed in the silent cabin.

The most accurate description of her situation at this point was nervously content with the occasional traumatic experience. She laughed out loud at the whimsy of her thought before giving a sigh and swallowing the rest of the rich brew.

She'd spent hours hunched over the screen researching Andurs for Duvall, but by the end of the day she'd only managed to find partial information using the variety of searches. Andurs Feinstein was an enigma, official records with his details were few and far between. Right now, she didn't have any records of an address or even contacts for him. Without more information, she couldn't hope to find any family or friends.

"If I didn't know better, I'd think he didn't really exist." She racked her memory, trying to remember what Jem had told her about her latest boyfriend.

She stretched tiredly and returned to the computer. They'd finally drawn near enough that she could access the internet with the assistance of the comm officer. She clicked on a newspaper page and a small article caught her eye. She followed the link to a report.

The story detailed the woes of a small bookstore, where the owner had disappeared. The report alluded to something underhanded going on. Mellissa looked at the date. Six weeks from her disappearance. She checked the image and scanned the story again. The bookstore was Readabout Books. Hers!

*The Readabout Store was the scene of an explosion overnight. It is thought that it was a cover-up for a break and enter. Since the owner, Mellissa Davis, has disappeared a range of unusual and disturbing incidents have taken place in the small township's only bookstore. Ms Davis, twenty-eight, was reported missing several weeks earlier, and the police presume that she is deceased.*

The story jolted her, her stomach souring as she scanned the brief report. The journalist stated that her assistant, Jemma Cardnew, had no idea where Mellissa was, and on that basis, police had taped off the building and the bookstore would be demolished as the site was considered unsafe.

A tear trickled down her face, and she dashed it away. Jem, described as devastated in an interview, had been termed a 'person of interest'. Mellissa continued to scan through the paper's archival listings, searching for updates. Hidden in the obituaries, three weeks later, she found a listing. Jemma Cardnew died at the site of the bookstore. An industrial accident. The building had caught fire from one of the gas fittings damaged in the earlier explosion and the basement had collapsed.

Mellissa raised a shaking hand to her mouth. Jem gone? Dead? She sat looking at the obituary, and the floodgates of tears opened.

"What's wrong?" She heard the panic in Duvall's voice and lifted her face to him. She had been so distraught she hadn't even heard him enter the room.

Mellissa struggled to pull herself together and waved a hand toward the report on his screen. He quickly scanned it, his eyes closing briefly only to reopen with a wealth of understanding as he crouched down beside her on his knees. His head now level with hers, he opened his strong arms and enveloped her.

"I'm sorry, baby. So sorry."

His gruff voice washed over her as sobs racked her body, exhausting her. They subsided to a slow hiccup, and he rubbed her back as she quieted. When she stopped, he stood then leaned over to pick her up in his arms.

"I'm sorry for that outburst, Duvall."

"Don't be sorry. Don't ever apologize for feeling. I wouldn't have you any other way." He turned to sit down in the chair with her in his lap, and she buried her head in his shoulder. "I had no idea," he said quietly.

She shook her head. "Jem came from the same home as me. I knew her for years before I left. I suppose she was like a little sister, so when she needed a job, I took her on. She lived with me until she found a place of her own." Mellissa hiccupped, sighed, then resumed. "She won't have anyone except Andurs, and now, well, I don't suppose he counts, does he? Especially if he's using her." Her mind blanked, the emotions wringing her dry.

"Then you found out what happened to her."

"Yes. I left everything to her in my will. She was supposed to at least have something to fall back on," she whispered, leaning into his strength.

He listened to the words, knowing how hard she found the situation. This Jemma meant such a lot to Mellissa. A lump lodged in his throat, and his heart raced. Never before had she cried. Not like this. Such a strong woman, but blow after blow had finally taken their toll.

He'd been working with Chowd and Grayson, and they'd formulated a plan. Maybe there was room to add to it? Give her more than just her own belongings. His chest tightened. He wasn't sure if it was even fair to tell her right now. If he couldn't pull it off and he'd told her... *No, I'll keep this to myself for now.*

He held her close and considered how much easier his life had been with the Gentrys. Sure, his parents had died in the war with the Ru'Edan when the scout ship attacked the planet where they lived, but being sent to live with the Gentrys, his parents' friends, had given him a buffer and a family. They may not have been his birth parents, but in every way that counted, they were his real family.

He barely remembered his birth parents. Their frequent absence on research missions kept them from home, though he had a nanny and grandmother who had doted on him. His grandmother's fatal heart attack when she'd heard the news of his parents' death had changed his life forever.

The Gentrys had welcomed him into their small family, ensuring he felt valued and loved. It was their support that had made him who he was.

Mellissa though, she'd managed on her own, and his heart bled for the lonely little girl she must have been. The only other person she had felt a connection to would soon be dead, unless they could save her and bring her forward in time.

She stirred in his arms, and he thought she might try to break free. He held her closer, needing the connection as much as he was sure she did. Mellissa lifted her head. "Thank you," she whispered, reaching up and touching his lips.

"What for?"

"For being here. For holding me. For caring."

Each simple word filled him with warmth and strong emotion. She levered herself up in his arms and touched her lips to his. They still tasted of the saltiness of her tears. Her soft lips moved against his. He held himself still, letting her set the pace, even though the clawing need he'd banked during the day gnawed at him.

Slowly, her hands reached up to his face, cradling it between them. "I need to be held," she said.

He looped his hands around her waist. He damned himself even as he let her deepen the kiss. He was already aroused, making him feel sick. *Barsha!* She needed support, and he wanted nothing more than to sink inside her body.

She let her lips whisper across his cheek toward his ear. "I need to be loved by you. Help me keep the emptiness at bay, Duvall." She whispered the words, her breath dancing over his skin, setting licking tongues of fire alight along his nerves. He held himself still. "I need to love you," she said finally, looking directly into his eyes.

Her eyes glittered with emotion, holding his gaze. Her hands dropped to his shirt, slipped the first button out. She kissed her way down to the cleft in his chin. Her hands continued their unhurried path down his shirt, releasing each button slowly. She lavished him with open-mouthed kisses at his throat and over the chest she'd bared.

He tried to hold himself still, but he wanted to grab her, strip her bare, and sink within her soft, molten body. He let her continue, holding on to his control, though it was tenuous at best. His chest heaved with the effort of staying still, letting her set the pace. He kept telling himself this was for her, gripping the arms of the chair.

She continued the torture, eyes closed as she found his waistband. She couldn't get any purchase between them. The touch of her mouth sent currents of electricity coursing through his veins. Wherever she touched him, burned.

She stood and he opened eyes he hadn't realized he'd closed. She held out a hand, and he gripped it like a drowning man. He stood up with a jerk, and he was sure all his hard-won composure would crack.

She smiled at him and stripped off her shirt, then took his hand before she led him to the cabin. He knew instinctively that she needed to be in control this time. When she reached toward him and pushed the shirt off his shoulders, twining her hands behind his head and reaching up to kiss him, his mind exploded.

Her mouth closed over his. His control slipped just a little, and Duvall fisted his hands, seeking more.

"I need to touch you," she said, and reached again for his waistband, drawing his belt from the loops and unfastering his ship suit pants, pushing them down.

He stood in his boots and briefs with his pants puddled at his feet. She sighed with feminine exultation, her lips full and promising, skin glowing pink from arousal.

"Touch me," she commanded him.

He reached out and slowly, ever so slowly, peeled away her shirt. He wanted to touch her, love her. Duvall outlined lush breasts hidden only by a plain white bra. He unfastened the clips, his fingers fumbling before it gave, then he pushed it off her shoulders. The air was heavy with passion, the musky scent all around them, and her eyes shined with emotion. He kneaded her breasts, savoring the silky feel of her skin. Her nipples puckered, and he just had to lean forward, closer. He blew softly on them. She moaned as they tightened further, peaking below his mouth as if they ached for his touch, and so he leaned forward a little more, and the ripe berry tips filled his mouth as he suckled.

She placed her hands on the band of his briefs and pulled them down, watching as his engorged penis finally sprang free of the confining material. She lifted her eyes to his. They were hooded and smoky, and she burned, turned on by the need she read on his face.

Her heart skipped a beat when he surrendered the control to her. Slowly, she traced one hand up his body and tangled her fingers in his hair. His head lowered, then mouth met mouth in another scorching-hot kiss, their breath mixed, and they both panted. Her heart rate thrummed and heat grew. The scent of arousal filled the air.

His hands moved faster now. They slid over her waistband, unfastened the remainder of her clothes, and Duvall gently pushed them away. When their mouths parted, he bent down and removed his boots. The whole time, his eyes bored into hers, demanding all her attention.

Emotions, hard and savage, played over his face. Here he was, her own tender warrior. Letting him go would be like surrendering part of her own body and soul.

"You're mine now." His words mirrored her thoughts.

He stood back up to take her in his arms. "Mine," he growled against her mouth. Then he opened his to meet hers almost savagely as he plundered hers. He picked her up and carried her to the bed. "I need to be with you too." The words shook her with the possessiveness.

Placing her on the bed, he stripped off her boots and grasped her foot in his hand. She breathed deeply as he placed a quick kiss on her ankle, not stopping but butterflying kisses up her legs until reaching the juncture of her thighs, which he opened wide. Placing his mouth on her delicate flesh, he flicked at her. She jerked up in response. He touched her again with his tongue.

She was molten. Her arousal ran deep, demanding more while he caressed and teased. Her chest heaved before he devoured like a starving man.

He stopped, and she whimpered at the loss of his touch, heard him breathe deeply as he touched her with one finger, circling her core, then dipping the finger within her body. She shuddered, so close to climax, muscles rippling under his touch. Her body vibrated with passion, and she cried out. Her heart beat in overdrive now, and she sweated, panting, wanting to give him all the love in her heart. She writhed in his arms, fingers digging into the mattress as she moaned once more, beyond coherent thought.

He opened his mouth over her and sucked gently, laving her with his tongue.

She nearly splintered in his arms as he lifted his head. His eyes burned with passion. "I'm going to take everything you have to give," he growled, and she bucked beneath him as the light breath from his words played over her moist and swollen flesh.

He started to move up her body as she extended her hand and pushed against his chest. Hard. He rolled back as she moved over him, his chest bellowing, his muscles sheened with sweat. She opened her mouth on his nipple and flicked her tongue. He jerked. Her hand trailed down his body and found his erection.

She squeezed, then with a gentle touch pumped once, twice.

He shuddered and closed his eyes. "Stop," he wheezed.

Her hands stilled. He shuddered yet again as Mellissa licked the saltiness from his skin, whispering over his body. He grabbed her and stilled her movements, his hands like steel bands as they pulled her higher for his kiss.

Slowly, so very achingly slowly, he penetrated her, pulling her down on his cock as each delicious inch slowly joined with her. The slide so deliciously erotic, she trembled once more in his arms. She wrapped herself around him, glorying in how tightly he held on to control and wanted it to shatter.

"Duvall!"

He thrust into her harder and faster. She met his thrust, parrying with him. Together, they moved in tune with each other. Their mouths met and fused until finally her head flung back as she climaxed. He plunged one final time, holding himself within her, then exploded into the starlight with her.

✪  ✪  ✪  ✪  ✪

They lay together for some time afterward. "I meant it," he said, his words soft.

"Meant what?" Mellissa turned her head on the pillow to look at him. She seemed puzzled by his words.

"You. Forever." He took a deep breath, plunging into the most important conversation of his adult life. "Since the night you spent in the cabin away from me, I've been thinking. I know you had no choices with the time thing, but I want you with me. Forever." The skin of his cheeks burned as he waited for her reaction. He felt so unsure of himself. "I don't think I could ever let you go now." He stared into her shocked eyes.

"I love you," she said simply.

He felt humbled. After everything they had been through, she could say that with such certainty.

"I know," he said. "And I love you too." The words that

had him tied in knots came tumbling out. Once said though, he felt his chest lighten. "I know this has been quick, but we can take it slowly…you know. Take our time…" His voice trailed off. "*Barsha!*" he growled, rolling onto his side and holding her close. "I've made a mess of this." He ran his fingers through his hair. He felt like a fool. He couldn't even make a declaration of love to the woman in his arms without sounding like some sort of ape.

Mellissa smiled at him as if he had just given her the moon and stars. She reached out, her fingers touching each side of his face, and kissed him soundly. "That is the best, most amazing thing you could ever have said to me." Then she burst into tears.

He held her helplessly, a lump lodged once more in his chest. *Now what have I done?* He racked his brain, but all he could think was she hadn't wanted him to say the words.

"By *Eshra*, Mellissa, I'm sorry."

"No!" she wailed. "It was just right! I love you too." She pulled away, looked up, and smiled through her tears. "These…" She sniffled and crawled closer. "These are happy tears."

Confusion warred with love while his heart melted again. He pulled her close, and they remained that way for some time, entwined and quiet.

When they finally emerged to lunch hand in hand, they sat with Elara and Grayson. Elara lifted an eyebrow, and Mellissa nodded silently. She wants an update, Mellissa thought with a small smile.

The meal was companionable, and at the end they went their separate ways. Grayson and Duvall headed to the bridge, Elara to the SurgiTech suite, and Mellissa had a meeting with Chowd. He'd promised to show her some more basic self-defense techniques and the latest weaponry.

She joined him in the holographic station, where he stood in lightweight pants and a skin- tight shirt. She'd also dressed as he'd suggested. Entering the deck, she saw he waited on a thickly padded mat.

Duvall had agreed that even though Mellissa wouldn't have any involvement in any combat situations, she needed a way to protect herself until help came. So Chowd focused on the easy moves that required very little body strength.

"Like this." Chowd's voice cut through the silence in the room as he wedged a foot behind her knee and she fell to the mat.

"It's easy when you know how," Mellissa groused, pushing her hair behind her ear as she got up.

"You try." He pointed to her then gave her the come-on movement of his hands. She tried to wedge her foot behind his leg, but he danced away from her. She moved forward, and he feinted again. "Stay still."

"No bad guy is going to stay still for you to get him. You need to be quick and smart." He smiled at her as she growled her displeasure.

Her body ached and she reached for her rear, where she'd landed several times already. "Okay, that's enough of that for today. We have a bit of time to sort this out."

He led her over to a table where an array of weapons were displayed. He named each for her, encouraging her to lift each and feel its weight. She picked up a small blue pistol, the smallest there.

"Good choice." He stood behind her. "That's a laser pistol. It's deadly and accurate, with enhanced targeting. Tomorrow I'll show you how to use it. For now, go have a hot shower. That'll help relieve any sore muscles."

She hadn't managed to even pull Chowd down, let alone anything else. She sighed heavily as she made her way to the cabin, taking off her clothes once inside and crawling into the shower. The need to get clean overrode her anger at herself. "It's probably just as well I'm only ever going to be a researcher."

Briskly washing herself, she mused over what had happened and pulled a face. Sure, like she could really protect herself or help Jem. She shook her head slowly with a sigh, turning off the shower, drying herself, then locating fresh clothes. She looked forward to catching up with Elara, who had left a comm message of "When you're done for the day, head up to SurgiTech for a coffee."

Right about now, a coffee was the minimum she needed. She comb-dried her hair as she made her way to Elara's office.

Palming the door, she wandered into the suite. She made to enter Elara's office when she realized Grayson and Elara were wrapped in a serious clinch. Mellissa blushed and backed out awkwardly. Elara giggled, and Grayson lifted his head with a growl before he saw who was there. He cleared his throat, muttered something about leaving them to it, and left to Elara's rising laughter.

Mellissa stammered an apology, but Elara quickly put her at ease. "Oh, don't worry." She laughed. "He just popped in to update me on some news, and...well, things just ran away from us." She grinned, her eyes twinkling. "But you know all about that now, don't you?" her new friend teased playfully.

"Umm, he loves me?" Mellissa squeaked, looking both embarrassed and overcome. She looked at her friend.

"Yes!" Elara almost punched the air exultantly as she danced around the room. "I knew it. And you love him too." Elara wrapped her arms around Mellissa. "I'm so happy for you!"

"Oh, I'm happy too, but what happens next?"

Elara looked at her, a small smile on her lips. "He's so like Grayson in some ways, yet different too. You need to talk to him, find out what you are both happy to give and take, and find a compromise that works for you. Just like Grayson and I did. You know, it's not easy, or simple, but it's very, very rewarding." Elara smiled like the cat that got the cream.

"I guess," said Mellissa doubtfully, looking at her friend. She felt confident that Duvall had meant what he had said. He'd promised never to lie to her, and she believed that implicitly. It wasn't in him to make such a declaration lightly.

"I'm your friend, and if you ever need to talk, my door is open," Elara said. It was the one thing Mellissa needed to hear.

Then Elara changed the subject and they sat down to discuss their day, companionably chatting as they drank the coffeepot dry. Checking the time, Elara declared that they should meet at the mess hall in an hour.

Mellissa stood to leave, heading to the door, but she quickly doubled back, giving Elara a quick, fierce hug. "Thanks for being my friend."

Just before she was out of the room, she heard Elara say, "You'll do just right, hun. You'll do."

Mellissa smiled and kept walking.

As they hurtled through the slipstream, every member of the crew worked to prepare for the mission. Mellissa researched in the morning and worked with Chowd every afternoon, attempting to learn how the laser worked. Her aim improved, and Chowd nodded his encouragement, but when it came to the basic self-defense course he had created for her... Well, it never seemed to improve. She had yet to block a move or to throw him. Chowd shook his head, and she knew he shared the results with Duvall.

Mellissa felt more confident of her relationship with Duvall. The frequent touches, the way he kissed her, included her on the bridge, and encouraged her to participate in the briefings told her that their relationship had a permanence she craved. There was even a steamy kiss on the stairs, where he backed her up, grabbing her mouth for a hot, soul-stealing kiss that left both of them breathless.

She fretted endlessly about Jem though. How could she intervene to ensure her safety? The question ran around in her head ominously. The morning they were due to exit the slipstream just beyond Eris, she sat in her seat on the bridge.

Duvall was curiously quiet. The bridge stood empty, as they had headed up before any command staff and those on duty had been dismissed. Mellissa sat in her chair, concerned and watching Duvall.

"What's wrong, Duvall?" She watched a ruddy blush steal over his face.

He looked surprised, then sheepish. "Ahh…" he started, then grinned. "Well, there are a couple of things on my mind. The first," he said, sobering, "is that when you're back in your own time, you may not want to return with me." He looked uncomfortable at this admission.

Mellissa sat stunned. "Duvall, I love you. Let me tell you now, you're not going anywhere without me, and I'm certainly not staying there without you." It had never occurred to her that he could be uncertain of their relationship. "And what else?" she asked, encouraging him to continue.

"The other…well, when this is done, I want to talk to you. About us."

Her heart stopped. "What? What do you mean?"

His smile was strangely not reassuring, but he'd claimed to love her. Confusion once more raised its head, but she beat it back. *I trust him.*

"Nothing bad," he assured her. Grabbing her hand, he said, "We need to talk about how to make this more…" For a second he seemed lost for words. "…permanent." He glanced at her.

He said the last word gruffly, but joy filled her. Her heart rate settled down and she breathed deeply. Mellissa grabbed his face for a quick, hard kiss. They didn't have time for anything more, as members of the crew made their way onto the bridge in preparation for exit. Some looked at them with rampant curiosity, but no one said a word.

Strapping into her seat beside Duvall, she watched as he started running preparation checks. Elara entered and took her seat near Mellissa, and they waited for the exit chimes to sound. With a silent move, they exited the gate, waiting for Duvall's command to exit back into real-time space once more.

Mellissa felt that the magic of transfer through the port would never grow old for her. Duvall's gaze settled on her like a palpable thing, and she smiled. They both had work to complete, but later... A whisper of excitement fizzed in her veins. She had to finalize her research and create a report for the briefing that would take place later.

It was imperative they had all the information to plan dealing with Jem, tracking down Andurs, and find the infiltrator they were chasing. Her desk screen waited in the alcove and Mellissa hurried in its direction. Once settled in her seat, she tapped at the keyboard.

Once more seated in Duvall's office much later that evening for a dinner conference, Mellissa felt she finally had something to add. She made her report to the crew, who raised concern with the sparseness of the information she'd gleaned concerning Andurs.

"Are there any further obituaries that mention him?"

Mellissa shook her head at Duvall's query. "No. I've tried everything I can, right down to speeding and parking fines. There's just... There's nothing to find. It's like he barely exists." She glanced at those assembled. "That brings me to my next thing. Maybe he doesn't actually exists. I mean, we know his name is Andurs Feinstein, right? But how can we be sure? Maybe Andurs doesn't exist and he's someone else with an assumed identity."

"How would we track him then?" Chowd asked.

All Mellissa could do was shrug.

Around the table, everyone understood the impact of her words. Shoulders drooped, and more than one hand was dragged through hair.

Glancing at Duvall, it was clear he was unhappy with her suggestion. His mouth was pinched white at the edges, and his eyes narrowed. "All right then. We'll move on."

"Captain, I believe that we need to put in place some contingency plans," Elara said. Mellissa looked at her friend, and as Duvall gave her permission, she continued. "We need to fit the three of you with dermal transmitters. That way, should we need to track your movements, we'll be able to do so."

Mellissa could see Duvall thinking this over, and when he answered, "I believe that would be a wise decision," she felt his hand move to her knee. He needed almost as much reassurance as she did, she realized.

"We've also finalized the coordinates for the entry to your office, Mellissa." He turned to look at her. "In fact, we've timed the mission to the minute. There's a window of exactly twelve hours and thirty-six minutes to get in, complete the mission, and get out." He looked around the table. "Chowd, Grayson, and I believe that within this timeframe we can carry out the mission undetected by the current military satellites and detection systems."

"Your shop layout was most detailed, Mellissa. It gives us an accurate view of your location at the time Duvall transmitted you to the ship, so I've worked with Raven. We will transmit you back to that same spot within a half-hour." Chowd spoke slowly as if weighing every word.

"Well, that's great. But I have a small problem. Do you two intend to go in dressed as you are?" She waited and when they both nodded she closed her eyes. "You've got to be kidding me. Okay, you're going to stand out." Mellissa sighed.

From the arrested look on their faces, they hadn't considered their wardrobe options.

Duvall looked at her.

"Duvall and Chowd, we need to find you an alternative to your uniforms. Elara, are my original clothes still around?" she asked.

"Yes, they're in the ST suite. I can arrange to return them to you later today."

"Good. Is there any way of replicating them, but bigger?"

Chowd smiled. "I believe there is."

"Good. I also think we should grab my car and head straight to Jem's flat. It's not too far away, but if I phone first we may have a chance of getting her by herself. If you get her with Andurs…well, I doubt you'll get much sense out of her."

"I'm not sure that would be advisable. What if Feinstein is there with her when you make contact? He could communicate your plans to Crick Sur Banden," Chowd replied, quickly tapping information into his desk screen.

"Oh God, that never occurred to me." She sat back, horrified. With all eyes on her she closed her eyes, thinking about options. "The coffee shop. That would be a safe location and he'd have to see us or be there to… You know. Get the information to Crick Sur Banden."

"Even so, should we decide on that, we'll require the location of her housing complex," Chowd said, breaking through her self-recriminations.

"I have the GPS…umm…global positioning satellite coordinates and I've mud-mapped out her house."

Chowd looked up, lost. "Mud-mapped?"

"Oh right, a dirtsider term. It means I quickly drew one up on a piece of paper." She looked over at him. Duvall grunted, obviously accepting what she had said.

"Okay, so once we transmit, we are to all intents and purposes out of radio contact. The only communications acceptable are emergencies only, including withdrawal transmissions and the like. Grayson will equip us with tracking icons though, so anything we need transmitted— animate or inanimate—can auto-transmit using those. Anything else will likely put the mission in jeopardy," Duvall stated.

"I agree, Captain. But I would like, once more on record, to state that you should remain on the ship and I should take Mellissa dirtside with Chowd," pointed out Grayson. A swift look at Elara made it clear he had discussed this with her and she did not agree with his assessment.

"I accept that on the record, however, given the situation, I am overruling the same," Duvall said mildly. "When we get down there, we'll investigate the best option for making contact with Jemma. That decision will be based on the sit-rep."

"Sit-rep?" Mellissa blinked, hoping one of them would elaborate.

"Situation report," Elara clarified.

"Oh."

The meeting continued, with the final details being tied up. The fitting of dermal tracking devices was set for the morning in the SurgiTech suite. Raven would replicate the clothing for Chowd and Duvall in engineering. Grayson gave an estimate of their arrival on the dark side of the moon, where the ship would hide out of sight of satellites. Plans now firmed, the meeting broke up.

Finally alone, Mellissa walked into Duvall's arms, and together they retreated to their cabin.

# Chapter 13

Morning came too soon for both Mellissa and Duvall. Snuggled in his arms under the covers, her hands running over the body she loved and now knew almost as well as her own, his hand rubbing the downy curls that hid her secret recesses, they lay together. The touch was comforting and intimate, their bodies now in tune with each other. They both knew that soon reality would intrude. The only sound that broke through the silence was their breathing.

"Mellissa…" Duvall rolled over to face her, framing one side of her face with his hand. "Promise you won't take any chances." His eyes seared her with intensity.

This was a question that she could answer honestly. *Just don't let him ask me about Jem.*

"I promise," she whispered.

She knew he worried about her safety, but while the mission would be fraught with danger and possibly grief at once more leaving everything behind, it was clear her future lay here, with this man. She smiled lightly. He moved in toward her, placing a soft kiss on her lips, then resting his head against hers.

"I love you," she said.

They continued to lie there for another few minutes, skin to skin, offering a reassurance to each other. A buzz heralded the time to rise and dress. He took great care helping her into the clothes he had first seen her in, jeans and t-shirt, complete with the pink fuzzy slippers she had worn. It seemed so long ago now. She helped him with his jeans and t-shirt while she laughed at the heavy fabric and watched him team them with his own hefty black boots.

They had both agreed on an acceptable cover story that

she had met Duvall, a security officer, and they, with his friend Chowd, were hoping to catch up for coffee and maybe a meal. The three agreed it was better to keep it as simple as possible. Quickly, they made their way along the corridor and onto the bridge with Chowd. He dressed similarly to Duvall, and she nodded encouragement in answer to the question of his raised eyebrow.

She took one look at Chowd's finely chiseled face, patrician nose, and slicked-back hair and grinned. Good thing she had Duvall, otherwise he might be in trouble, she thought with a snicker.

Duvall settled into his command seat, and the crew took position while waiting for the *Elector* to come into orbit behind the moon, then he handed command over to Grayson.

They swiftly moved to the transmission room. They were slightly behind their timetable, so Elara had elected to meet them there with the dermal trackers. Elara held the applicator, while on the side lay the insert tubes, each containing a single tracker. "Just give me your arm, then you're good to go."

Mellissa held out her arm, and Elara place the applicator against the skin then depressed the button. Mellissa lifted her arm, examining it, but could see no wound, and nothing hurt; just a small amount of discomfort in the site of the tracker.

"All systems are ready?" questioned Duvall, and Grayson nodded.

Chowd quickly scanned them over with alert eyes and a single word. "Ready."

Elara swooped in for a last minute hug, Grayson checked the coordinates on a hand screen, then Mellissa grabbed Duvall's hand.

Duvall stated, "Three to transmit," and the world blurred and turned black.

When she opened her eyes, she held on to Duvall, and the three of them stood in her small, cramped living room. After so long away, it seemed almost alien to her. Duvall kept her in one place while Chowd checked to ensure the security of the area. Once he determined it was clear, Duvall let go of her.

"Check to make sure everything is as it was," he whispered to her.

She glanced around at the utilitarian furniture, and wandering quietly, trailed by both Duvall and Chowd, she checked throughout the flat. She nodded, signaling that everything looked the same.

Chowd indicated that they should retreat to the lounge then headed down the stairs as silently as possible in his heavy boots. The story she had seen showed that the break and enter had not been discovered until that evening when she was due to meet with Jem. That gave them roughly twelve hours to finalize everything and get out of there before the mission was compromised. Chowd stayed several steps ahead of both of them, and she noticed he seemed to glide in silence. Once down the stairs, he scanned the area and ushered them toward the corner.

She could see where the Ru'Edan infiltrators had tried for entry. The door swung on its hinges. "Shouldn't we fix that so no one can see in?" Mellissa whispered only to be met with a headshake from Duvall indicating no. Not happy, she nonetheless acceded to this.

He ushered her quickly into the office area where they had first met. She sucked in a deep breath once they pushed the door shut.

She pulled out a tiny information transference device she'd received from the comm officer and started to check information and sample data, just in case they'd missed anything to do with Andurs. It scanned for a connection to the internet, using a hidden IP and containing a self-extracting hack-key. She looked up and nodded to Duvall. Yes, it worked.

She tried government data, department of transport, and

even births, deaths, and marriages. Nothing.

"Chowd, I need you to check for signs of devices, including listeners." Duvall's voice cut through the silence as he scanned.

She opened her mouth, and he raised a hand to cut her off. Chowd watched the small box in his hand. While nothing seemed materially different, they needed to ensure it was safe before setting it up as their field base.

"Mellissa, I need you to check that nothing is out of the ordinary in here or has changed since we were last here."

Again she cast about quickly to check for any sign. Nothing was out of place and her computer had been humming when she'd entered. Her story of George and Eliza continued to fill the screen. She looked at it and frowned.

The woman who'd sat down eons ago at this computer had a totally different outlook on life. One glance at her story highlighted it. Now she knew her words and dialogue were flat and lacking the knowledge of slipstream technology and the future. Her grasp of the concepts was so sparse she wanted to laugh. She reached over to turn it off when she noted something with the slightest tinge of gray spread on it. She motioned to Duvall, who in turn motioned for Chowd. He scanned the item on the button, his face grim.

Duvall ushered her out of the office quickly before he said, "That is a Ru'Edan track system. Once you touch it, they have your DNA sequence transmitted remotely to their data banks. They usually also pack a series of micro-transmitters into it, making you trackable anywhere within the galaxy." He looked at her. "Did you touch it?" He growled the question, and she mutely shook her head.

Thankful that she had seen it before making contact, she swallowed hard. She still had so much to learn.

Duvall released a pent-up breath, his agitation clear. "I can see they entered this area looking for you and the handbook. We need to get started, but before we do, Chowd, update the clock." He looked over at Chowd.

"Captain, we have eleven hours and fifty-five minutes." With a brief nod, they returned to the stairs, and Duvall urged her up them.

"Mellissa, anything that you need that is urgent or of great personal value, pack it quickly. You have twenty minutes to get it in place." With a small push, he hurried her toward the bedroom.

She looked at him, surprised, then understanding lit and filled her, and she smiled. He meant that she should have the few important things from her previous life and had built the time for that into their schedule. She turned quickly and gave him a kiss, quick and hard against his lips, a wordless *thank you*. She pulled him with her as she headed for the bedroom.

Packing her life took no time. She had little of value, underwear and clothing, her few photos, and the items from her time at the orphanage. The files she had accessed thinking she might one day seek her parents, intending to ask why? The answers she had sought were contained inside the file, so she'd held onto the documents.

She shoved it into a box with other photos and documents, added a few books, and closed it. Then she threw clothing into several bags, knowing that they would be checked once they arrived on the *Elector* for trackers. She headed back to the living room after giving Duvall quick and careful directions and grabbed a few more books and knick-knacks she wanted to take with her.

Looking at the pile on the floor at the end, she realized that the majority of her belongings held no importance to her. The three bags and five small boxes didn't seem like much.

Each item received a transmission tag from Duvall, before he pressed the remote, and they disappeared. Chowd, who had appeared briefly, retreated once more to the stairs, giving them a moment of privacy.

"Why did you do that?" she asked him.

He grinned sheepishly. "Elara suggested it. Grayson, Chowd, and I had arranged for you to have some of your things once we were here so that you'd feel more settled. I just arranged for time. Elara assured me you'd manage to pack light, but most women I've met would need a lot more than that."

"So I surprised you again, did I?"

He grinned. "All I had to do was activate the function, and they'd transfer to the *Elector*, so long as the tag is securely attached." He cleared his throat. "I told you I wouldn't let you go, but Elara was right. You needed your items around you."

Her eyes burned with welling tears at the friends who thought about her needs.

Chowd came stomping back into the room. "Time to move, Captain."

Duvall looked at Mellissa. "Contact Jemma and find out where she is and with whom."

She nodded and reached for the telephone.

He grabbed her hand. "Keep it simple. Don't tell her where you are. Try to set up a meeting in a busy area, that way they are less likely to try anything if Feinstein is with her." His mouth thinned.

Mellissa nodded and picked up the handset. As soon as she heard a dial tone, she dialed Jem's number.

"Hey, Jem here." The bouncy voice filtered down the line.

Mellissa took a deep breath. "Hey Jem, it's Liss. What are you doing right now?"

She kept her voice as neutral as possible, watching Duvall's face. He tensed beside her, watching her and ready to transmit if he thought a threat existed.

"Hey, girl! I'm here at home on my own. Andurs and I had a fight last night, and he wandered out. He's supposed to get back here...oh, about six-ish. We'd planned to go to the movies, but his boss called him in to work." She sounded pissed still, and Mellissa tightened her grasp on the receiver, her gaze flicking between the phone and Duvall.

"How about I head on over to Coffee Pop and we can catch up? I have a new friend I want you to meet." Duvall had told her that *friend to meet* was the code for all clear. He subsided a little, and she watched him.

"Sure, can you give me like fifteen minutes though?"

"Yeah, that works for me."

They hung up without a goodbye, as if they had only been talking yesterday, which to Jem they had.

Mellissa took a deep breath as she replaced the receiver in the cradle. "Okay, we're on. The Coffee Pop is down the road a little way. We can walk there."

She picked up her bag as Duvall's hand shot out.

She knew he was concerned, and leaned in. "We'll be in broad daylight, on the street, and it is literally just down the road. It would look really weird for me to pull the car out to drive a couple of blocks."

He opened his mouth to disagree.

"Look, I know this place well. I go there a lot. People around here are used to seeing me walk. If I drove, that would raise the questions you're hoping to avoid."

His frown told her of his warring concerns. Her safety versus the questions and scrutiny.

"I understand, Duvall, but you told me how important it is to continue to operate within normal behavior. Plus, I've got you and Chowd here. What about if I promise to stay between you?"

He thought for a moment before consenting. "If I say to do something, you do it," he said, stroking her face with one hand.

"Okay," she acquiesced. She accepted that he was worried, and while she wanted to help him, she knew anything other than what she'd proposed could jeopardize everything they'd done so far.

The three of them walked back downstairs, and when she headed to the back door, he stopped her, indicating Chowd should go first. They watched as Chowd peered around the door outside and disappeared through the doorway, one hand on the pocket with the laser concealed beneath his shirt. They waited silently until finally he ducked his head in. "All clear."

Careful not to touch anything, they made their way out the door, which led to a hidden driveway. They walked past her little blue car. Chowd took point, and his gaze darted here and there, checking for any sign of a tail or threat. Duvall held her hand and kept her close as they exited the driveway and turned right into a small street. Several steps took them to a corner, and they turned to the left on her direction, the crunch of their boots on the pavement sounding over the traffic noise from nearby streets.

They moved briskly, and soon the Coffee Pop came into view. They stopped, and she nodded at the vibrant orange façade of the building. Chowd once more at the front, Duvall slipped in behind her as they entered.

The coffee house was popular, and they had to squeeze in to join the line for coffee. Chowd wasn't impressed with so many people; every line of his body tensed, but she knew that the location was as public as they could get.

Duvall instructed her to order so that they fit in, whispering it in her ear so that they looked like two lovers. Neither had experienced a mocha latte, though they both liked chocolate.

At the counter she greeted the cashier. "Hey, Snyder, can I get three mocha lattes for here, and Jemma's going to want a macchiato."

The staff at the Coffee Pop knew of Jemma's partiality for the strong drink, and Snyder looked around, clearly expecting her friend to appear at any second.

"She's on her way," Mellissa said.

The cashier nodded. "Nineteen dollars, please."

Mellissa paid and made her way to the table Chowd had chosen, with the metal order number stand. Chowd had likely picked the table because of its defensive location, she thought.

Subtle, low music filled the air, in direct contrast to the loud blue and yellow décor, which had always pepped her up. It made Coffee Pop the perfect meeting place under normal circumstances. Today, though, it just seemed overwhelming after the grays and blues she had become used to on board the *Elector*. She looked forward to the end of the mission when she could go home. With Duvall.

Snyder delivered their coffees as Jem entered alone, breathless and dressed in a loud red outfit that screamed *I don't care what you think*. Teetering on high-heeled boots, her black hair swept up to reveal the long line of her throat. Seeing Mellissa's wave, Jem wriggled her way toward the table. Duvall crowded Mellissa into the corner before they turned to meet Jem.

"Hey, girl!" she cooed, all the while checking out the two men flanking Mellissa, running her gaze up and down both Duvall and Chowd like something tasty on the menu. Mellissa fought down a possessive need to grab her and say Duvall is taken, but he held her hand as she introduced Jem, moving closer. She smiled privately to herself.

"Hey, Jem. Glad you could make it. I want you to meet Duvall and Stuart." She indicated to Duvall and Chowd in turn. Jem noted Duvall's closeness to Mellissa and smiled a broad grin, her eyes lighting up.

"Girl, you have some mighty good taste." Mellissa blushed at Jemma's grin.

"So…Stuart." Jemma swung toward him. "Come here often?"

He looked like a rabbit in the headlights, thought Mellissa, nearly coughing on her coffee.

"Err, no," he answered truthfully, blushing beet red. Mellissa nearly laughed seeing the rough-and-tough security officer intimidated by a bundle of energy.

Mellissa grinned. "Stuart is a security analyst." She nodded to Duvall. "And he's here with Duvall on business. I wondered if you felt like hanging out for a while? You know, maybe lunch?"

They had decided they shouldn't look too obvious in gathering the information from Jem, so they'd take whatever time they needed to do the job right. To ask straight-out increased the risk, and Mellissa agreed that minimisation was the right option, especially where Jem was concerned.

She sighed inwardly. Maybe the obituary was wrong, but she knew Duvall wanted to take every chance to leave the timeline intact.

She'd hoped to talk Duvall into taking Jem back with them, but so far she hadn't had time. Besides which, she'd prefer to give Jemma an opportunity to agree, but she doubted the headstrong woman would even believe her. After all, it was a pretty far-fetched situation.

"So, what have you been up to? How are George and Eliza getting on?"

Mellissa watched her friend take a sip of her steaming beverage while she thought rapidly. *Where was I up to?* "Oh well, you know. It's slow at the moment."

Jemma laughed. "I'll bet." A wink accompanied the words and Mellissa blushed. "But you need to hurry up and get it finished so I can see how they get together."

She knew Duvall kept half an ear on the conversation. His gaze flicked around the coffee shop as he kept a watch out with Chowd; she knew he'd protect her.

Time passed while Mellissa and Jemma talked about the latest goings-on before she finally asked casually, "Where did you say Andurs was?" She waited with her head down for the answer.

"Oh, he had to work a run for his boss last night, then he got called in again this morning. He doesn't expect to be back until later tonight." She made no attempt to hide her dissatisfaction.

"Who does he deliver for?" asked Duvall, and it sounded like polite conversation.

"Uh, he works for Roo Edan Industries. Always reminds me of jumping critters eating cheese." She laughed. "They're reasonably new in town, and only have a couple of staff at the moment. He does pickups from the airport and delivers all over the place." She turned to Mellissa. "Remember? That's how I met him. He came into the shop after a delivery, looking for an audio book. I thought he showed interest in you, but you didn't seem all that interested, so he asked me out."

Duvall stirred uneasily beside her. She remembered the first time Andurs had asked her for coffee. She'd brushed him off, and he'd accepted it with good graces. Now she was pleased she'd done that, but worried about Jem.

Mellissa felt Duvall touch her hand, reminding her of the passing time. The clock continued to wind down, and they needed to get done here.

"Are you planning on catching up with him today?" burst through Mellissa's lips. "Err, so we can do dinner. You know." She smiled weakly at Jem, who paid little attention, her eyes on Chowd. Mellissa could see she had picked her next target.

"What? Oh yeah, dinner sounds great," she answered as her cellphone rang, the *tsst tsst tsst* of her ringtone loud and the phone vibrating all over the table. Mellissa almost had to grab Duvall and Chowd as they reached for their pockets. They caught her look though and settled back to watch and wait

Mellissa sweated profusely as she considered the business of spying on friends. It was harder than she'd ever imagined, and she closed her eyes, breathing deeply. Duvall squeezed her hand under the table, giving her the support to keep going. She opened her eyes, listening to Jem's side of the conversation.

"No, I'm not hanging around waiting for you. You can come to my place at twelve-thirty or not at all. And if it's not at all, don't bother coming back." She flipped the top of the phone down, obviously angry, and Mellissa surmised Andurs Feinstein was the recipient of the outburst.

Jem's face glowed red, and she pushed the long strands of hair that had escaped the tie out of the way in a fast, angry move. "Gah! Whatever possessed me to think he was worth the effort?" she muttered to herself. She plunked the phone down on the table and took a swallow of the strong brew.

"Ahh, don't tell me that was Andurs breaking off your date?"

"No, not exactly. He wants me to join you at the shop and pick us both up for dinner," she replied. "But he was supposed to check that leaking tap, and then I was going to make lunch before he went back to work. Lately, he does that sort of thing all the time—we make a date and something comes up." She pursed her lips. Looking at Chowd, she asked, "Don't suppose you are any good with taps?"

Before Chowd could answer, Mellissa replied, "Yeah, he's fantastic. Let's go now."

Duvall scowled at the sudden decision, and Chowd opened his mouth.

With a shake of her head at Chowd, she leaned over to kiss Duvall on the cheek. "Trust me," she whispered. "I have an idea about a safe way to grab him." She gripped his arm. She could tell the plan change upset him, but she had bought them the entry they needed.

Jem rose, getting out of her seat and smiling at Chowd in a way that made Mellissa think of a hot dinner or ice cream and hungry mouths. They moved out of the Coffee Pop, Mellissa calling her *thank you* to the staff as they left, just as she had always done, trying to look like there was nothing unusual taking place.

They found themselves on the street, and Mellissa quickly suggested they grab her car and drive to the flat where Jem lived, about ten minutes away. Thankfully, Jem had chosen not to ride her bike and had instead opted for a taxi. It made it so much easier. They made their way, moving quickly. As before, Chowd moved to the front and Jemma kept pace. A couple of times Jemma craned her neck and Mellissa nearly laughed when she realized it was so she could view his backside.

Perhaps she could… No. When the mission was complete, they would leave here. She would never see Jem again, unless she could talk Duvall into letting her go with them. And if she could get Jem to agree, that was. That stopped her in her tracks. Duvall pulled up, looking and scanning. She gulped. Oh God! That hadn't really hit her until now. She looked at Duvall, who looked grim as well as concerned.

He pushed her to the side of the building, crowding her with his body. That was how it looked, she realized; in actuality though, he used his body to shield her. From the road it would look like he kissed her neck as he asked, "What did you see?"

"No." The word escaped, broken, and a tear trickled down her face. "Jemma? Will I ever get to see her again?" Her eyes burned once more.

"Mellissa…" he started, as Jem chose that minute to look back.

"Oh, come on! You can do that later!" The good-natured comment broke the moment.

Duvall pulled away from her and, gripping her tightly, promised, "We can discuss this after." He pulled her toward the building.

# Chapter 14

Jem opened the door to her little apartment. Strangely, Duvall had expected something loud, in tune with the tough attitude that Jem radiated. Instead, he walked into a tastefully furnished flat, decorated in shades of blue and gray that harmonized, the furniture obviously older but chosen with care and neat. Every piece was functional but soothing.

Mellissa dropped her bag on the lounge and set to work looking in the fridge and making drinks, obviously very at home there, Duvall thought with a pang. They were just about to sit down when a knocking started at the door.

Chowd moved swiftly, out of sight, and Duvall grabbed Mellissa, placing her behind him, out of the line of fire. Jem looked shocked as she opened the door until she saw the man about to enter. Andurs Feinstein had arrived, and Duvall had only a moment to see the shock on his face before Chowd moved in, grabbing him in a headlock.

Feinstein hadn't expected it, but his surprise was only momentary before he began struggling. Jem screamed, and Duvall let go of Mellissa, moving toward Chowd to help hold him. The captive twisted and turned, but Duvall grabbed him, pulling him to the floor.

"Let me go!" Andurs spoke in short bites of sound. He fought to free his hands, but Duvall held on grimly.

Mellissa grabbed Jem and tried to calm her. Jem looked at her with horror in her eyes. "What are you doing?" she yelled, trying to twist out of Mellissa's arms.

"Jem, hang on and I'll explain," she said, desperately, and he could see her attempts to settle Jemma were failing. Her eyes entreated Jemma to listen, but she was almost hysterical now, crying and twisting in Mellissa's arms.

Quick steps sounded outside the door, and a voice from outside called, "Jemma, are you okay? Do I need to call the police?"

Feinstein took advantage of the momentary distraction. With one almighty heave, he wrenched free of Chowd and Duvall and headed for the door. He ran out before they could grab him again. Chowd made to give chase, but Duvall stopped him.

"No. Did you fit the tracker?" he asked. Chowd shook his head. Duvall scowled. "Damn, then we need the information from Jemma about how to find him, his address, and place of work." He turned and looked at Mellissa.

"Mellissa, what in God's name are you doing? How could you let that happen?" Jem screeched.

"Jemma, do I need to call the cops?" the voice outside asked.

Mellissa called out, "No, Jem's fine. She just got a fright. Thanks, Mr. Stelling." She looked at Jem as if daring her to contradict her. "Come on, I'll fill you in on what I can, but you need to sit down and listen." She pulled the young woman toward the seat, but Jem twisted in Mellissa's arms.

As Duvall started to step forward, Chowd grabbed his arm. "Let her do this."

Mellissa tried to talk to Jem, but she wouldn't listen. "What do you think you are doing?" she demanded.

Mellissa looked at her friend and with a grimace said, "Promise to hear me out? It's going to sound... It'll sound weird, so listen all the way through."

She settled down onto a seat, and Duvall watched, as always fascinated with Mellissa's thought processes. It was clear she was deciding how to tell as much of the truth as she possibly could. She sucked in a deep breath, and he wondered exactly how much she would tell. Anxiety chewed at him, and he saw the twin emotion on Mellissa's face as well.

"Well, you see, Duvall and Stuart are really rather more

than just security experts. Their job is to track Andurs. They have been for some time. He has information about a…well, a major terrorist-type threat."

She glanced at Duvall, and he let the tension wash off. He listened intently but continued watching Chowd, who prowled. His friend wanted to go after Andurs, but waited because it was their best option.

"Anyway," Mellissa continued, "they believe that Andurs has been in contact with some really dangerous people and have to track them down before it can go too much further."

Jem looked disbelievingly at her. "Girl, if you believe that, you have read far too many romances. Real life isn't like that. You know it. I know it. F-A-C-T. Fact!" A cynical look spread over her face. "You're always so quick to believe, but you need to come into the real world."

Duvall stood up, ready to protect Mellissa. He purposely made his movements menacing. Mellissa held up her hand, stopping him and looking Jem in the face.

"No, Jem. He's exactly what he has told me. We need to track down Andurs, and quickly. That is what Stuart—dammit, I'm not going to use that stupid name. That's what Chowd is doing right now. Using the information we have to find him. I know this seems really far-fetched, but there is still so much left to do and very little time."

Duvall watched Mellissa's face; she looked at her friend with pity in her eyes.

"I know this sounds unbelievable. Really, I do. But I wouldn't put you in this position if it wasn't for a good reason." She bit her lip. "Jem, I need his home and work addresses."

Jem laughed and stood up. "Yeah, right, Liss." She looked brave, but underneath the bravado, there was hurt in her eyes. Moving slowly, she grabbed her bag, taking out a slim, black diary and turning to the last pages. She flicked through, obviously searching for an entry, then headed for the notepad and pen beside the phone, writing down two addresses. She thrust them to Mellissa. "There, now you have it. So go. Oh, and you know what? Don't bother coming back." She turned and pointed to the door.

Tears welled up in Mellissa's throat. She reached for Jem, but she turned away from the outstretched hand. Mellissa looked at Jem, her hand hanging for what felt like moments, then her shoulders slumped and she spun away, Jem's cold dismissal bringing tears to her eyes.

She knew Duvall watched what happened, but she tried to turn away, and he cursed. Duvall gave Chowd a pointed look then, with a nod, placed a small device on Jem. Chowd pressed the button on the little black box in his hands, and Jemma disappeared from sight.

Mellissa started forward, glanced to Duvall then Chowd. "What did you do?" she demanded hoarsely. "Where is she?" Her hands fisted, eyes narrowed.

"On the *Elector*. I had Elara on standby, ready for her. I planned to bring her back with us after what you found, but… There hasn't been time. You said she has no family, except you. She'll be fine," Duvall soothed. He reached for Mellissa and ran his hands up and down her arms. "Come on, we have to get going."

She was ready to rip through him, but time ticked away. They had only hours to find Feinstein and his contact. "Hang on then, before we go anywhere, I am guessing she won't have a chance to come back, will she?"

"No, Mellissa, she can't," he said, his tone gentle, and she felt her heart squeeze.

"Well, you can't take her without at least allowing her to have something. It's cruel. I can tell you, there is nothing worse than having nothing of your own. Being totally reliant on what is given to you. You said even Elara said the same thing with me. Jemma needs the same courtesy. Please? I just need a couple of minutes to grab her clothes and her important items."

Duvall looked at Chowd. "Do we have a couple of minutes?"

"Captain, I believe time is of the essence. However, perhaps ten minutes is acceptable," Chowd concluded with a sigh.

Duvall stared at Mellissa. "Ten minutes is all I can give you. Tell me what you want and I will start on her clothes."

With a quick, tight smile, Mellissa instructed him where to find bags, having helped Jem move in. She sent him in the direction of the bedroom. Chowd started emptying the shelves of photos. For herself, she headed to the single cabinet where she knew Jem kept the mementos from her childhood, the small battered box that contained the blanket, photo, and letter that she had from her parents. Within minutes, a small bundle of bags and boxes sat at their feet.

"Thank you," whispered Mellissa.

Duvall turned to her and simply asked, "Done?"

She nodded, and Chowd tagged the bags and box with the small tracking bugs, then clicked the button to transport them, just like they'd done with her things.

"Thank you." She reached up and placed a soft kiss on his mouth, then settled back on her feet, her eyes shining with love while her chest swelled once more. "Let's go."

❂ ❂ ❂ ❂ ❂

They barreled down the stairs of the flats, the sound of their boots tapping on the steps as they went in a staccato pattern. Mellissa felt pleased she had changed into her running shoes before they headed to the Coffee Pop. The slippers would have been worn thin by now, and their day still had hours of running before them. Her emotions turbulent after the scene in Jem's apartment, her head spun, and her stomach tightened. It could be hunger or nerves, she supposed, but she'd lay a bet on the latter. The thought occurred without any humor. She would need to explain what had happened to Jem once this mission was done, but she didn't look forward to the task.

They piled into her little blue car. Funny, the day she had bought it, it seemed so snug for just her, but now, she felt no pleasure in ownership as they squeezed into the tight seats. She turned the key, and the engine sparked, the motor purred, and she smoothly pulled out from the curb.

Chowd held the palm unit she had received from the comm officer in his hands, cursing at it when it did not cooperate. Having a vague idea of the location of the address Jem had given them, she drove across the bridge and in the general direction, looking for somewhere to pull over as Chowd continued to growl at the small machine in his hands. Spying a spot, she pulled off the road.

Duvall looked at her, but she held her hand out to Chowd wordlessly, who placed the unit in her palm. She entered her information and with a beep the unit started giving audible directions. Looking carefully at the road, she pulled back into the traffic, following the instructions to a nondescript building in a run-down area.

The building was quiet and creepy. Three stories high, dirty brown stucco, chipped with broken windows, it ominously blocked out the sun. A shiver ran through Mellissa as she undid her seatbelt and climbed out of the car. She clicked the car alarm, watching as once more Chowd placed himself in front of her. Duvall behind, then they made their way up the rickety stairs toward the door of the unit. They knocked, but the echo from within told them that it was probably too late.

Chowd took a small pen-like item from his pocket, laid it against the door, and hit the button. Nothing happened. He tried again. Mellissa reached a hand forward and tried the handle of the door, rattling and pushing it. It gave under the pressure of her push. Before she could enter, Chowd had pushed himself once more in front of her, his gaze darting back and forth, laser pistol in hand. Duvall kept watch from the rear, one hand around

Mellissa, the other on the laser she knew he had secreted in his pocket, ensuring no surprises from below or the doors either side.

"Clear," came Chowd's voice. They moved in, but the patterns of dust on the floor told them the apartment had sat empty for a long time. The elaborate phone system that sat on an empty bench gave them pause. Chowd pointed to the unit. "That was how they relayed the phone calls from Jemma to Andurs, I believe."

Duvall let out a long sigh. "Another dead end."

He shook his head and indicated that Chowd should at least take a look around in case something else would give them further clues.

"*Barsha!*" erupted from Duvall, and Mellissa watched him run fingers through his hair in frustration. "Just when we think we're getting closer, something else seems to slip away."

The sound of Chowd's footsteps echoed as he moved from room to room. "Captain, you need to see this." Chowd popped his head around the corner of a doorway.

Duvall, holding Mellissa's hand, stepped quickly in the direction, and they entered the room. In the corner stood an elaborate machine with lights winking and flashing in the gloom of the dusty room. She looked at Duvall. His face looked even more grim.

"It's a transmission system. Crude but effective," he said, letting go of her and inspecting it without touching. "It also has a holographic facility," he murmured to Chowd.

"I think it has long-range capability though," Chowd muttered, crouching down to inspect something on the unit. "See the way this is rigged?" He indicated a setting to Duvall, who bent down to look. "I would hazard a guess that it was built here and is the main point of transmission out of here to wherever they have a ship hiding, but if I were them, there would be a secondary unit somewhere nearby to act as backup in case it failed or was located."

"Can you get a fix on it?"

"Yeah, just give me a minute and I'll run a diagnostic on it." Chowd held up his small handheld palm screen and tapped in a command. It flashed for a minute or two, then a low beep told them he had downloaded the information they required. "Okay. Got it." Chowd looked at Duvall. "Do you want me to disable it?"

"I think that would be best, and maybe set a self-destruct on it so that there will be nothing left afterward, perhaps something remote," said Duvall. "But initially we need to disable it so it no longer works. That'll only slow them down though. We need to find the other unit in order to stop them."

Chowd nodded and pulled the device from his pocket again. Putting it to parts of the machine, he pressed the button. A series of pops and a puff of smoke later, the lights stopped whirring.

"I have set a self-destruct tag on it. Once I give the code the unit will effectively destroy any working systems and chips." He looked at Duvall, who nodded.

"We need to get out of here now," Duvall said, pulling Mellissa forward. "If they get wind, we're sitting ducks."

Mellissa watched as Chowd quickly checked the area, once more pushing to the front, checking around before ushering them out the door, down the stairs that quivered under their weight, and into the vehicle.

Time now running short, they still had to find Feinstein, work out the specifics of Crick Sur Banden's plan, and get out of there before detection. In her heart, Mellissa knew their chances of successfully completing the mission had just got more remote.

"If you had a plant in the past, at this particular time, Chowd, what would you think is the main reason?" Mellissa could almost hear his mind turning over the known facts.

"I would say it has something to do with the agreement that will be signed in the next few weeks by the varied governments of Earth. They agree to focus their military budgets to interstellar travel and colonization at the foreign leader's convention." Chowd's voice was thoughtful.

"I think that could be what this is all about. The timing, the location. It all points to that. They'll possibly have a mole close to the delegates." Duvall spoke quietly. "How else would they get in, but through their ability to supply goods to the various delegates? Swap the staff and they have access to the people they need to influence and replace." Duvall sat back with his eyes closed, head resting on the seat. "We have to succeed, or the past, present, and future will be changed." He turned to look out the window as they sped along toward the location of Roo Edan Industries.

✪ ✪ ✪ ✪ ✪

The small blue car sat outside an old warehouse, hidden in shadows as the sun started to dip in the sky.

"Why can't we just contact the leaders? It's not like you don't have the ability to do so." Mellissa huddled down in her seat.

"If we made contact, they probably wouldn't believe us, and it would mean making a material change to the timeline. It would also give them access to technology they don't have and shouldn't have for another couple of hundred years. When we do that, it causes a ripple in the future. We have to avoid that at all costs," Duvall said, his voice quiet in the growing gloom.

"But what about Jem? Aren't you going to change the timeline by removing her?" She watched as he closed his eyes in discomfort.

"Sometimes, when we make decisions that affect the timeline, because they are minor players in the big picture, we can minimize the damage. In Jemma's case, she is really more of a...minor casualty of the skirmish."

*Minor casualty? Jem was a minor casualty? Then what am I?* "What about me then? Am I a minor casualty too?" She felt horrified at the description of their lives. He reached for her, and she pulled away in disgust.

"That isn't quite what I meant. What I meant is that Jem will be dead within days, so the effect to the continuum is minor. It won't cause a ripple in the future, like your death would. We already know that you belong there, your books become important in our timeline. Besides which, I did it because you need each other." He looked her in the eyes. "As it is, I'll have to make a report on why I moved her and that's going to be problematical for everyone. I'm doing this because of you of how it will affect you if we leave her behind. Nothing about you, Mellissa, could ever be minor to me."

Mellissa nodded.

He dipped his head forward and placed a brief kiss on her lips. "Not much longer now," he whispered in assurance, putting both hands on her shoulders.

They'd been here for well over an hour and detected no movement, even though an older white van stood at the end of the alleyway, its rusted appearance making it fit in with the old buildings in similar states of disrepair.

"You stay here, out of sight," whispered Duvall. "Chowd and I are going to investigate. See what we can find out." Duvall cracked the car door open and climbed out, then both men silently melted into the night.

Chowd had been watching the front of the warehouse, hidden in the deepening shadows, and as Duvall moved closer Chowd nodded an all clear.

Exhaustion pulled at her, making her eyes seem heavy and gritty. She changed positions in the seat. "Duvall needs my help, because the infiltrator could be anyone."

Mellissa slunk down low in the seat, head against the open window, waiting for them to come back, waiting to see the door open. Waiting for something. Anything.

A rattling truck slowly pulled up, and Andurs Feinstein

jumped out. He headed directly to a doorway, which shut quickly with a thud behind him, then he came back out and motioned the driver in. They watched his furtive movements, waiting for the sounds of voices and feet to die away.

In the shadows, Duvall motioned to Chowd and watched as he moved to the left. He always took the right. For a second he looked back, over his shoulder, checking the location of the car. He didn't like leaving Mellissa alone; she was out of sight, he told himself.

They reached the door, listened carefully, and scanned the area. Everything was quiet.

They chanced an entry, slipping through the well-oiled door into what looked like a corridor, dimly lit with no doorways. He looked for spots where they could hide should they require it, but he found little to give them cover.

They inched forward, brushing against the surprisingly clean walls, stepping quietly as they listened to the creak and groan of the building. Raised voices came from the door at the end of the corridor.

"What do you mean they found you? Fuck! It was your job to pump the bitch for information—where the stories came from, how she knew so much. But no," the voice mocked, "*she won't have anything to do with me, but the young assistant will do just as well*." The voice rose, the pitch of anger evident. "Now you're telling me there are two men with the woman, but you don't know who they are? And they grabbed you?" Frustration bled from the raised voice. "How do you know they didn't track you?"

"They tried, but I fought when they had me on the floor, and they couldn't attach a tracker, besides which I stopped and checked my clothing before I came here." The note of self- congratulation in the answer nearly choked Duvall. Self-congratulation always indicated a sloppy operator. He waited for an opening or the information they needed.

"So of course they couldn't find you," came a third voice, more menacing, and one Duvall knew very well from his previous dealings. He cast a look at Chowd. How in hell did Crick Sur Banden get here undetected, and how would they deal with this now? It would take quick thinking on their parts to get out of this one.

Horror filled him at his own stupidity. It squeezed his chest and constricted his breathing.

Mellissa waited in the car by herself. Unprotected. *Barsha!* He hadn't expected Crick Sur Banden to take the chance of appearing himself. He damned himself, but they couldn't leave now. His face tightened.

He listened to the information Feinstein shared. "There is no way they could have found me. I haven't even brought the girl here," he said, his tone exultant.

Duvall inhaled and looked at Chowd, who watched him with cold, angry eyes.

It seemed like forever had passed, though Mellissa knew it hadn't been long since she'd closed her eyes. Minutes, surely? The dusk had closed in, shrouding her in darkness. Her stomach continued the impressions of knots. The air had cooled, and she shivered, pushing a stray strand of hair off her face. She heard a click behind her and turned her head, catching a glimpse of something bright. Before she could get a good look though, it felt like her head exploded, then nothing.

# Chapter 15

Duvall thought fast as the sound of a cold chuckle filled the air. *Crick Sur Banden.* "We've been found. They must be made to pay well for this mistake."

Duvall and Chowd pushed their way through the door, straightening with their lasers ready, but too late. Andurs Feinstein slumped to the floor, the dying whine of a laser sounding in the air. The stench of burned flesh filled the air, and the dribble of blood oozing from the center of Feinstein's forehead told the rest of the story, a surprised look on his face even as death settled.

The lanky man standing in the corner saw them at the same time as they caught sight of him. He ran for the door, ready to plunge through, when an image of Crick Sur Banden began to laugh.

"Duvall, such a pleasure to see you again. But once more, you are too late. You see my associate? His helpers have a friend of yours." The holograph of the Ru'Edan rebel smiled evilly. "What a shame I can't be there to see the fun in person." The image faded away as the message sank home.

He knew in an instant that they'd taken Mellissa. His heart stuttered in his chest. "Don't you hurt her!" But the holographic Crick was gone. Duvall damned himself a million times for leaving her unprotected. It hit like a punch to the chest squeezing out any oxygen.

If they touched so much as one hair on her head, he would crush them. That was unforgivable. His rage spewed over his face. The man backed up through the door, trying to get out. Chowd beat him to the man, leaping upon him, flattening him and holding him down. Duvall reached for the man, and Chowd rose, moving back.

Duvall grabbed a handful of shirt, knowing his eyes glittered with the dark rage that filled him. "Where. Is. She?" he said, his voice forceful.

The man looked at him, mute, terror pouring off him in waves.

"I. Said. Where. Is. She? And by *Eshra*, you better not have harmed her." His voice sounded menacing enough, but he exerted pressure on the man's throat, reinforcing the rage that ballooned within his chest. The man under him wheezed for breath. He pulled the man forward and with a single downward jerk made a connection of head to floor with a crack. The man jerked, looked dazed, and tried to speak. A gurgle erupted from his throat.

Chowd placed a hand on his shoulders, but nothing sliced through the rage. "Duvall? Duvall?" The cloud of rage filled his mind, and he pushed the hand away. "Duvall? Captain? You're going to kill him, then we won't find her or the information. We need to find out where they have her."

*Chowd.* The name seeped into his mind. The hand returned to his shoulder. It urgently cut through the fog settling over him. He raised his head, nostrils flaring, and clawed back some control. His fury with himself swamped him, stripping away the layers of civilization. He should have sent her back or at least sent for another security officer to protect her. His fury boiled over. The men would pay for using her.

*It. Was. Unacceptable.*

He took a breath, calming his rage. Pulled another into his aching lungs. He settled back, but didn't release the man in his grasp. "Where would they have taken her?" he demanded, his anger banked while he needed the assistance to find her.

"T-to…to the transmission and examination point," the man whimpered, and the smell of urine filled the air; in his terror, his body had reacted.

Duvall pulled him closer. "Where would I find that?"

"At…at the flat…"

Duvall pulled the shirt closer, tighter, cutting off his air again. "We've already been there."

"D-downstairs. Another one."

"Take. Us." The words pushed past gritted teeth. The man shook and quavered. He nodded furiously, and Duvall thrust him away, across the doorway into the room. The man clawed at his shirt. He was obviously some sort of courier for Crick Sur Banden, but an expendable one, he knew. Just like Andurs Feinstein.

Chowd took over, grabbing the courier and marching him through the doorway and into the night. For Duvall though, at the back of his mind, the memories of how they'd found Elara seared his brain, making him swallow with fear. If they found out how much Mellissa meant to him... By *Eshra*... Her danger would be more acute than before. Fear knotted his stomach. Closing his eyes, his stomach roiled as greasy waves attacked his gut. He breathed deep, fighting to control himself. He'd do anything to have her safe in his arms again.

He headed to the vehicle.

✪ ✪ ✪ ✪ ✪

Mellissa opened her eyes to find herself in the dark, rolling around to some sort of sway, pitching like a yacht, but the vibration below her and the whine filling the air told her it was a vehicle of some sort. A van?

Trussed like a turkey, she thought in disgust, struggling against the ropes that wound around her body. She took a mental evaluation. Her head hurt, as if it had been split with an axe. Both arms screamed with pain, but she attributed it to the way she was tied rather than any other injury. Her feet were loose though, so they obviously expected her to walk somewhere. That's fine, when the opportunity came, she'd run.

Her chest tightened. She couldn't account for why, but each breath cut like a knife. She struggled to remember, tamping down on the fear. She had been waiting in the car. God! Where was Duvall? Chowd? She sucked in a breath.

"Awake now, are you?" a voice echoed from the front of the vehicle.

She tried to lift her head but failed, lying on her stomach as the vehicle pitched again. The pain came again, stealing her breath. Nausea swept through her, and she felt like throwing up.

"Not long now and you can join our merry band of friends," he said, the last word menacing.

She knew though just what he meant. She had seen Elara's scarring, knew exactly how it had happened. A shiver of fear worked through her, and again she concentrated on her breathing, ignoring the nausea that warned her that if she weren't careful, the contents of her stomach would be expelled.

One final pitch of the vehicle, married with a bump, then it stopped, jolting her, sending another crushing wave of pain radiating through her body. She feared she had cracked a couple of ribs and hoped that was all. The engine stopped.

She could hear doors opening, and she braced herself for any opportunity to escape. The doors at the back of the van slid open, and she felt herself grasped by the ankle and pulled toward the rear. Her bare feet hit the ground, jarring her side. Her legs collapsed beneath her, the ground rushing up and scraping her face.

The man nearby chuckled. "Didn't expect that, did you? I do hope you're looking forward to your experience."

He hauled her up, and she waited until he was off-balance to give an almighty heave against him. Taken by surprise, he jerked, letting go briefly.

Once released, she pushed off and sprinted as fast as she could in the direction she was sure the van had come. The time in the vehicle, the blow to the head, and the aching side put her at a disadvantage. She had gone barely a few feet when he threw himself against her, knocking her back to the ground, thudding to the pavement and screaming as she fell to the ground.

Once more the evil chuckle sounded. "So much spirit.

Yes, you'll be fun."

He grabbed her up and jerked her toward the building. The building that had held the flat they had visited earlier. As the edges of her sight grayed, he pushed her inside into the dark.

✪ ✪ ✪ ✪ ✪

The car swooped around a corner at full speed. Duvall was beside himself with fear, but knew he needed to remain in control. He wanted to tell the man to drive faster, to arrive sooner, but they needed to get there in one piece and not attract any more attention. If stopped, it would take more time. He didn't think she'd have a lot.

He fired questions at their captive. "Who are you working for?" His face hurt with the pressure of holding his anger in.

"Man, I just get my orders, usually from a guy. Every now and again I have to front up to the place you found us. I'm just a courier. I don't make decisions. I just do what I'm told." He tried to shrink into the driver's seat as the stink of his accident filled the confines of the vehicle.

"Who do you answer to?"

"Man, oh man…you don't understand," the driver whined. "He'll kill me. Slowly. Not like Feinstein…"

"I don't much care how you die. I need an answer! Now!" Duvall bellowed. Chowd looked at him but wisely kept his silence. He kept his grip on the laser though.

"Oh God, oh God, oh God…Senator Elleston hired me. But then he disappeared a few days ago and I was told by the guy whose pic was talking…" He jerked his head around abruptly, showing terrified eyes. "The one who disappeared. You know? He took over then."

A name, finally. Chowd looked at Duvall and nodded. It was worse than they thought. Now to get Mellissa out and they could find out where Elleston came into the plan. His hand tensed. Time was precious, and Mellissa's danger increased.

They had attempted to hail the *Elector* while they drove, but the trace had stopped working, Grayson told him. They would have to find her the old-fashioned way. Duvall held onto his temper, but the thread frayed more with each passing moment.

They pulled up at the building they'd visited previously. Duvall's face crumbled in despair. They'd found nothing except the empty flat, the disabled transmitter, and the elaborate phone system before. Where could she be?

Frustration screamed through him, until he noticed the old white van. He remembered seeing the van parked near the warehouse earlier, and he didn't recall seeing it when they left.

Chowd reached forward to tag the man who claimed to be a courier. They would need him, and if he talked, the damage he could wreak would be too dangerous. He watched Chowd depress the button, and the man disappeared.

They clambered out of the vehicle, Duvall turning his attention back to the van. The smashed tail light, the rust in the body, confirmed their suspicions that they'd located the same vehicle. It looked old and down at heel, slumping on the pavement. Most people would just pass it by without another look. He was sure it had transported Mellissa here. Duvall took a step forward as a gut-wrenching scream rent the air.

Duvall started toward the building at a run. He was heading up the stairs when the sound came again. His heart pounding, he reversed back down the stairs and looked for a door. There at the end of the building, a door sat behind a tatty old sign. Chowd raced after him as he reached for the door. He tried the handle.

"It's stuck. Help me." No time he thought, backing up, and shoulder-charged. It didn't quite give, but he had certainly damaged it. He backed up again, and this time Chowd joined him; they ran at the door together, and with a surge, it gave, splintering the handle and locks.

Duvall pushed it aside and launched into the interior. Sobbing filled the air. He headed in that direction, laser drawn, ready to rip and shred anyone who got in his way. At the end of the hall, another closed door waited. Chowd beat him through.

Two men appeared, lasers in hands, and as they whined, he ducked, noting the splintering noise above his head. He didn't slow down. Mellissa was here somewhere, and he had to find her.

He raised a hand and fired. Missed the bastards. Ducked again and dove into the corner away from the fire. Another scream. His heart thudded wildly in his chest. Sweating, he fired again and noticed Chowd had made his way into the middle of the room.

Duvall's rage was a living thing, nearly ripping through his skin, muscles bunched and tightened. He launched himself at one of the men. Duvall aimed and fired, hitting the man in the middle of his chest. Watching as he went down, Duvall moved forward, throwing the tag onto the wounded man's clothing. He saw Chowd working quickly to secure the other man, his face streaming blood. Tagging him, Chowd pressed the button, and both disappeared.

At the end of the room he could see a window, and looking through his heart nearly stopped. Mellissa lay on an Ru'Edan exam table, fastened at wrist and ankle, her eyes closed as if dead. One of their scientists bent over her with a sonic scalpel in his hand, ready to begin his investigation of this new human specimen. The gray of his skin was evident under the white coat, and Duvall knew what he was.

Without thought, he wrenched the door to the left and hurled himself at the scientist. The Ru'Edanian heard him and turned, slowly, hand still clutching the scalpel. Duvall launched himself at him, landing on top with an *oomph*.

His eyes filtered with a red haze, and he hit the creature, one fist, then the other. The brutal blows seemed to explode from within him. He wanted to tear him apart for touching Mellissa. He kept going, even though the creature beneath his hands now lay compliant.

Hands pulled at him. Chowd grabbed him roughly, and

Duvall struggled against the hold, wanting to throw him off. The only thing that entered his consciousness in the end was Chowd's voice. "She's alive, but hurt. She needs you. *Now*."

Chowd once more the voice of reason. Duvall rose unsteadily and looked up at the table to see her eyes still closed. He drew in an unsteady breath.

"She's alive?" He reached out an unsteady hand and took an ungainly step toward her. Touched her skin to satisfy himself she lived still. She breathed, the movement of her naked body jerky, her skin clammy to the touch. The cuts and bruises marring her skin horrified him.

The slices he could see oozed blood onto the table, collecting into the corners. He looked around then finally saw the sonic scalpel on the floor. He stopped, pulling off his shirt and covering her, then he reached for the scalpel and picked it up.

With unsteady hands, he used it to cut through the bindings, then he gathered her into his arms. He was dizzy, but he gripped her tight to his chest and wrapped his shirt around her body.

He looked at Chowd. "Find any other survivors and set them free." He swallowed, knowing it wasn't normal to leave anyone behind alive. "Arrange transport for that," he said, his voice thick with emotion as he motioned grimly to the scientist. Then touching his commbadge, he merely said, "Two to transmit." He watched as the world faded away.

Duvall returned to Chowd later. His rage continued to burn, but it was tempered with the knowledge that Mellissa would make a full recovery. He hadn't wanted to leave her, but Elara had shooed him out of her way to let her work. He had transmitted back to the bookstore, where he knew Chowd waited.

He waited in Mellissa's office, having briefly transmitted to the ship long enough to bring the last of their prisoners aboard, then made his way back one final time to clean up any technology markers left behind. By agreement, they used the bookstore as the place to conclude their work on Earth before returning to the *Elector* and leaving forever.

Chowd sat in Mellissa's chair, a number of books in his hands, obviously intrigued with them.

"How is she?"

"She'll make a full recovery thanks to the quick efforts of Elara." Duvall ran angry strokes of his hand through his hair. "*Barsha!* I still feel like killing something when I think about it."

"We need them. So you can't," his security officer reminded him.

"Easy for you to say…" Before he could say any more, he took one look at Chowd's face and stopped, regretting his words. "Chowd…"

Chowd held up a hand. "You don't need to apologize, Duvall. I understand."

With a sigh, Duvall rubbed a tired hand over his face. "What information did you get from the prisoner?"

"Not a lot. Only that Crick Sur Banden had tried to worm his way into the assembly. Elleston is the only one he managed to replicate. Mellissa was his target, had been all along, because of the connections she makes between our present and our past."

"And the set up with Feinstein?"

"It was exactly that. The apartment was in Feinstein's name, but he didn't actually exist. He was a human, but disaffected with society. Crick had promised them all the same thing—a place in the new order when he finally took control of the Ru'Edan Empire."

"And the prisoners?" Duvall asked.

"Captain, at the end of the day, it's your decision." Chowd peered at him and Duvall stood and paced the length of the office.

"I believe it's in our best interests to transport them with us. The Admiralty will want to interrogate them further. We can fill in some of the gaps on the way back through the slipstream. Then the Admiralty can decide what to do with them."

"Yes, Captain." Chowd bent his head. "After you transmitted, I had a quick look around the building. I believe the location was the one we were looking for. There were no other survivors." He looked steadily at Duvall, then continued. "The location was likely chosen for the unsavory name it has. I headed back here immediately after transferring the prisoner. I believe, though, that this site has been compromised since we left as well."

Duvall turned to look at Chowd. "What do you mean?"

"Ahh yes, I knew that would grab your attention. When I got back here, this was sitting on the desk." Chowd held up a single desk print for Duvall to see. "It is in Eleric Script, and simply says 'You may have taken this round, but I will meet you again soon'."

Duvall moved to grab the missive.

"He's already gone. If we complete an ionic trail scan, you'll find that his craft has already left this area and slipped through a port." Chowd said.

"Do you think he would be brazen enough to use the one beyond Eris?"

"Captain, I wouldn't be surprised to learn he's used the port at Sienna, or even outside Rubicon VII. They have always been the most insecure of them all. That distance to the outpost of the Empire always meant it would be harder to police."

Duvall nodded. He touched his commbadge and requested an ionic trail scan, waiting for the answer that showed positive for the movement of the craft they sought.

"We need to make sure we cover our presence."

"I agree."

They quickly conducted one last look around the bookstore in case he'd missed something, ensuring their presence remained undetected. Chowd scanned for devices, finding only those on the computer screen. By wordless agreement, he tugged several newspapers out from under the desk, scrunched them, and touched the pile with a fire-initiator.

The crackle caught on immediately, and a glow filled the office.

Duvall reached for his commbadge one last time. "Two to transmit."

# Chapter 16

Duvall returned to Mellissa's bedside once he transmitted back to the *Elector*.

Elara had already examined her, declared that she would make a full recovery physically, and once she regained consciousness, she could assess any long-term emotional damage. He should be on the bridge. Yet, he could not leave until she opened her eyes. Grayson continued to act in the role of captain, allowing Duvall the freedom to stay with her.

Arriving back on the ship, he'd uttered one command to Grayson. "Get us out of here." Grayson had nodded and retreated to the bridge.

Elara worked quickly. "There won't be any scarring. At least on the outside."

Duvall hovered, listening to Elara speaking in calm tones as she worked on her patient. His concern growing the longer she remained unconscious.

"It is just her body, working to help her heal. She'll be back with you soon, but I'll keep her here until I'm satisfied."

Chowd had also reported to him, sitting beside him in the ST suite. "I made an anonymous tip concerning the five bodies we located, Duvall. We need to leave it to Earth's authorities to deal with that." Chowd glanced at Mellissa, still unconscious. "Mellissa was lucky. Most of the injuries were superficial according to Elara."

"Yeah." He nodded absently, holding her hand and watching.

Chowd left quietly as Duvall took a weary breath, resting his head on Mellissa's bed. He should be on the bridge, where he'd be busy, but the thought of her waking without him, tore him in two. He pulled out a palm screen and checked their current status and how the ship was coping. They'd exceeded the maximum payload, but the *Elector* was handling the extra weight without missing a beat. The thought brought with it a hint of a smile.

He started work on his report, adding in the information they'd gleaned, monitoring the ionic trails and the final outcome, showing Crick Sur Banden had abandoned his plan and run again.

He stopped and glanced at Mellissa. "I'm so sorry. I didn't expect they'd target you."

He should have brought more security with him, protected her better. He'd known the risks and accepted them, but even with the attempts to minimize it, things had still gone wrong. *Barsha!* He deserved to wear this mistake, both professionally and personally. "Hey you."

The weak voice caught his attention, and he closed his eyes in a silent *thank you*. Never before had he received such a magical gift. When he opened them it was to see her beautiful eyes, open and clear, watching him. Her slim hand reached for him, and he clasped it. He welcomed the slight pressure of her fingers.

"By *Eshra*," he said brokenly, "I thought I'd lost you."

He gathered her into his arms gently, like the most precious piece of porcelain. Tears rolled down their cheeks as they accepted the welcome support and held onto each other for a moment, anchors in a sea of overwhelming emotion, knowing that whatever came next they would see it through together.

"No, Duvall. I knew you would save me."

Elara bustled in. "Well, my sensors are working optimally," she stated, giving them a moment to swipe away the tear tracks. "They told me not only was my patient awake but also moving." She turned toward the work area, collecting items, then turned back to them. Tapping Duvall on the shoulder, she said, "I need you to let go of her so I can give her a final check over. If I'm happy…" She said it again, emphasizing her words.

"If I'm happy with her results, I will release her to you on the understanding that she rests quietly in your cabin." Elara stopped moving and looked at him. "Captain, you need to leave."

He started to stand up and move away, under duress.

"No! I want him here…please?" The look in Mellissa's eye made him grimace. Elara stopped, and he sat back down beside her, holding her hand tight. His Mellissa knew what she wanted, and that was exactly what she'd get.

"Okay, he can stay. But out of my way." She moved to his side of the bed. "All right, sit forward please."

Swiftly, Elara checked her over, clucking at the bruises and scrapes. He sucked in a breath when she checked Mellissa's ribs, the purple-bluish bruising blooming over her skin. Elara had already set a regen strap on her chest to deal with the broken ribs found during her initial evaluation.

"You're very lucky. Several broken ribs, a lot of bruising, concussion. You've been unconscious for several hours, and Duvall has barely left your side. They were just getting started with you when Duvall found you." Elara relayed the information in a matter-of-fact way.

Elara applied salves to the cuts and applied an antibiotic treatment.

"You are well enough to leave here, but you need to rest. Go slow. I'll see you in the morning for a check over." Elara grinned and shooed Duvall out of the room to help Mellissa dress. "I'll come to you."

He heard them moving around in the room, talking. He closed his eyes once more as he waited.

Later that evening, Duvall gave the order for them to enter the portal. They'd made good speed to the port, pushing the drives hard, Raven having given them the information that he felt the *Elector* could easily make faster time than they had previously thought possible.

Lying on the lounge chair in the captain's ready room, Mellissa listened to their discussions. They'd clearly obtained information from the prisoners that filled out the plan. The information they received pointed to a much deeper game.

"The scientist started talking. They'd been creating clones of the human species. Elleston was their first success, but he had problems with accessing the full suite of memories. Just imagine if they'd broken that aspect of the mind. They would have created drones utilizing each individual's unique DNA sequence and harvested memories, crafted to suit their needs of course to replace the senators who'd be voting." Chowd looked at Duvall, and she felt horror at what he was sharing. "One of the bodies found was Senator Elleston, a senior cabinet member. We believe their aim was to put in place clones of the people that would work for the Earth Empire in the next fifty years or so. Each member of the Summit had already been chosen and their replacements were being grown in maturational tubes at the back of the building."

Mellissa wanted to gag, listening to the plan being laid out. "But what could they hope to gain?"

"The intergovernmental alliance wouldn't happen, and space exploration would cease. That would limit any space travel and stop Earth's alliances which will protect them in the future, particularly against the Ru'Edan." Duvall concluded the report, shaking his head. "I need to complete my report while in slipstream so I can submit it as soon as we clear into real space."

"Yes, now that the plan has been uncovered, I doubt they'll continue down this road. We know what to look for, and given they have had little success and they don't have the resources to start again I think this plot is done." Chowd frowned into his Arturian wine. "However, this set back won't stop their biological testing—the scientists will continue seeking ways to break the humans."

Mellissa frowned at the caustic emotion in his words. "Chowd, is everything okay?"

He looked at her and smiled. "Yeah, it is. Thanks for caring."

His odd words surprised her.

Duvall tugged her tighter against himself. "And the Ionic signature?"

"It was Crick Sur Banden."

Meredith nodded. "After the warehouse was infiltrated, Crick Sur Banden sent an encoded message of retreat to his drones."

"None of the prisoners have further significant information, but I agree, best to hand them over to the Admiralty." Chowd nodded at Grayson's quietly spoken comment. Now that the mission had successfully concluded, they needed to get back to the Admiralty as quickly as possible.

During dinner that night, Jem sat sullenly at the end of the table, watching them. Mellissa knew she struggled with every bit of information being shared. She understood it was hard to comprehend, but she also knew if they had stayed, they would both have died.

"Jem?"

"What do you want? To send me somewhere else?"

Mellissa frowned at the anger in her voice. "We just want to help you." She reached out a hand and Jemma flinched.

"I don't want your help. I just want…" She blinked furiously and ran from the room.

Mellissa rose but Elara patted her hand.

"Leave her be. She has to come to terms with it. And right now, she's too angry to listen."

Mellissa hadn't missed the interested looks Raven had sent in Jemma's direction, but he didn't make any moves toward her. It was a tangle and her head had begun the drumbeat ache again.

"You're beat and supposed to rest. How about I clear everyone out?" Duvall's words filled her with warmth.

"That would be great, but I need to talk to Jem. Show her what would have happened. I can't stand to see her so upset."

Duvall wrapped his arms around her, and she rested against him. "I know, but to make a full recovery, you need to rest. I can talk to Jemma if you want me to."

"No, it should be me, and besides, she doesn't trust you after the incident in her apartment. It's just hard, knowing that not once but twice in your life everything is taken from you, and that it happened because of me." She looked up into Duvall's eyes. "It's even harder when it's someone you know and trust. When someone who knows what you have experienced does it to you." Her eyes filled with tears.

✪ ✪ ✪ ✪ ✪

Long after Duvall had talked Mellissa into going to bed, he watched her sleep. Memories of the fear slammed into him again—that she could be hurt again, or even worse dead, almost unmanned him. Tears burned in his eyes, and the weight in his chest seemed to grow bigger and more constricting by the moment. Elara had warned him she might have flashbacks and dreams, so he waited, ready to soothe her.

When she woke, he held her in his arms tenderly.

She traced his face with her hand, the bruises hidden in the dim light, and she smiled at him. When he would have increased the brightness, she stayed him, kissing him on the lips, increasing the pressure.

"I need to hold you, love you, and remind myself that I'm alive and well." Her warm hands slipped over his shoulders and down his back, tracing the muscles. "I love you," she told him tenderly.

"And I love you," he said, touching her like the finest glass, tracing her face with his fingertips.

His heart swelled. He kissed her eyes, then moved onto her cheeks, her chin, and her neck. She stretched up to grant him access to the zones that made her shiver. Dropping light kisses on his shoulders, her tongue barely glancing his skin, made him shiver.

"Touching your body is like touching the hardest metal under a velvet cover."

He laughed, glorying in the wonderful woman in his arms. "Oh, my love, I could say you are like the petals of a rose, but it's too cliché." He snickered, then sobered. "No rose could ever be as beautiful as you."

Their mouths met once more, this time hot and urgent. He moved her body up against his, holding her so close that her breath whispered over him. They clung to each other.

Gently, he worked his hand down her body, touching her breasts, holding one in his hand, feeling the warm weight, before flicking his thumb against her nipple. It grew engorged and tight. He dipped his head and opened his mouth. She jerked when he blew gently, then tugged lightly with his teeth. She arched and cried out. He soothed it with lapping kisses then long, drugging pulls with his mouth. Then he took the other.

He suckled at her breast, while her restless hands roamed in light touches over his body, finding skin to knead, running her fingers back up to cup his neck. His hand moved down her flat belly toward her core, found it warm and wet, and slid a finger in. He rubbed the sensitive nub, winding her tighter and higher. Her hips moved. Her breathing labored. She cried out in the night, and he swallowed the sound.

She rubbed her thumb over his erection and squeezed down gently. His hips jerked. He slipped a second finger into her, pumping slowly in and out.

"I want to be inside you," he growled. "I want to be with you forever. To come home to you, even if home is just this cabin." Her hips jerked. "I want you with me until the end of my days. Tell me you want that too, my love." His voice was hoarse, and his chest heaved.

"I do, I do," she crooned.

He pulled his hands from her, opened her thighs wider, and settled between them, guiding the head of his erection to her opening and slipping slowly, oh so slowly, inside her. He burned, so hot, knowing she felt the same. Yet he wanted to do this slowly and gently. He reined in his excitement. This was for her, he reminded himself grimly, hanging on for dear life.

"Now!" she demanded. "Fill me now!"

Her head thrashed, and he embedded himself to the hilt inside her scalding heat. He nudged once, and she sucked in a breath. His heart beat harder and faster than he ever thought possible. He nudged again, and she gripped him, winding her legs around his waist. She bucked against him, and he met her thrust, again and again.

Faster and harder they moved, pushing toward climax, in perfect harmony. He gripped her waist while she held on to his shoulders. Her eyes widened as with a final thrust he felt her contractions begin deep within her body as she tensed in his arms. She let out a soul-deep cry. He couldn't stop, thrusting again and again. *Eshra* help him, it pushed him over the edge. He pounded into her, joining her, feeling the powerful jetting as he finally achieved his release.

They lay together in the aftermath. He held her close as their heartbeats slowed. "Stay with me always. Travel the stars with me, and I will show you worlds you couldn't even imagine." He smiled as he waited for her response.

She smiled as he cast a look at her. Her quiet "I will" filled the night.

# Epilogue

F ar into space, a blip of information was sent and quickly received. Crick Sur Banden tsked to himself in anger, his gray
skin mottled as he reached for his drink. So the Earth Empire
thought they had him beat, did they? That Duvall McCord and
his arrogant crew had another thing coming though.

Something quite stunning. His wide mouth stretched
over yellowed teeth as he reminded himself of what he had to
look forward to.

He rubbed his hands together with glee. "Oh yes, McCord
and crew of the *Elector*, the worst is yet to come." He clicked on
his comm with his bony fingers. "Make haste for Rubicon VII.
Anyone who gets in our way, shoot them out of the galaxy." His
long, gray face took on a feral look, and his eyes sparkled with
a light of madness.

They might have thought they had won the skirmish,
but they certainly hadn't won the war. The Earth Empire would
develop—a shame, for it would be much easier if they hadn't,
but no doubt he'd find another way to remove them.

He looked forward to the high cost they would pay for
this defeat. There would be distrust in the ranks. His sigh of
satisfaction echoed throughout his uncluttered cabin, bouncing
off walls of burnished metal, as he contemplated his next move.

Duvall McCord was a happy man. His beautiful bride,
Mellissa Davis, smiled at him as she moved down the aisle.
He'd given in to her need for a traditional wedding, just as she

had agreed to his request for a Communing ceremony. She wore her markings with pride, as did he. It was a compromise that they'd both felt would meet their shared and individual needs.

He grinned as she stopped beside him, and he reached for her hand. He'd researched the archaic ceremony, and his reward? Her face shined as they recited their vows before a beaming Admiral Elphin. He looked at her in the white gown his mother had made for her. Elara and Grayson had agreed to act as witnesses to this special event.

He knew Mellissa was disappointed that Jem had chosen not to attend. It had hurt her deeply, and even more so that Jem had refused to answer any contact that Mellissa had instigated since her placement at the academy.

Raven had agreed to keep an eye on her while she was there. Maybe in time they could bridge the hurt she felt. He hated that he couldn't reassure Mellissa, but he could and would put her mind at rest about her safety and security. Between himself and Raven, they had pulled every string they could to get her a private room under the surveillance of the best of the tutors. He knew Raven had also asked his parents, both professors, to keep an eye on her. For now, that was the best he could offer.

He turned his mind back to the special woman who made him complete and the day where they officially became one. When they made their pledges of Communing, he glanced at their entwined hands. The bands of love they had previously given each other during the wedding sealed their commitment to each other. He caught sight of their markings. Instead of the current trend for teardrops, they'd chosen stars, marking the place they felt most at home together.

While they celebrated with their friends, carousing well into the wee hours with the crew of the *Elector* and those who had become near and dear to them, they thanked them for witnessing both ceremonies.

Finally, the time came for them to slip away to the well wishing of friends, both new and old.

Within the cabin that had become their haven, he held

her close.

"I love you, Mellissa." His chest nearly burst with pride. "Since you came into my life, everything has changed. It's become richer, and I can't even imagine a day passing without you by my side."

She beamed and framed his face. "I love you too."

They kissed and in time, to the tune of the song of their bodies, they became one, slowly in the unhurried way of true love, with fingers entwined.

One last thought arrowed into his mind. Truly, they could have it all.

# THE STAR

## OF

# ISHTAR

# Chapter 1

**"I** finally made it." Elara Sudonne watched as the hull of the *Star of Ishtar* loomed in the inky darkness. She clutched her hands tightly together as the shuttle approached the hulking battleship.

This would be her new home and first combat ST placement for the Earth Empire. She quaked inwardly with nerves but fought to keep her serene exterior. Previously her deployments had consisted solely of on-planet expeditions and in rehabilitation and dirtside facilities. When the chance had arisen to move to the battleship, she'd grabbed it with both hands.

The frigid air chilled her bones as she sat in her shuttle seat, but a trickle of sweat inched its way down her back under the fresh gray wool flight uniform. Little puffs of vapor escaped her mouth as she rubbed her arms. Nerves stretched tight, she looked through the small portal at the front of the vessel. She wanted to tug at the collar that somehow seemed to have grown tighter as the ship loomed ahead, but instead she firmed her mouth, straightened her spine, and concentrated on the future.

"So damned long." She'd been working toward this outcome since the day Grayson Myatt and Duvall McCord had saved her from her Ru'Edan captors. She was lucky, she'd survived the 'experimentation' of the Ru'Edan leader Crick Sur Banden's scientists. "And all I have to remind me are my scars." She didn't grin at her own joke.

The person seated behind her jostled but she ignored it, lost in her memories. On that day, so very long ago, the young Elara, fresh-faced and with idealistic views of the empire, was taken from the mall where she'd been shopping with friends, thrust into the back of a transport vehicle, and given to the Ru'Edan scientists to experiment on.

For days they'd worked on her and others, seeking an average pain threshold of humans, slicing her skin then noting reactions and how long it took to heal. They'd cut her arms, body, and even her face, and now she carried the extensive scarring of the exercise as a reminder to herself and others of what they were fighting for. Freedom. The freedom of Earth and its allied planets.

She'd never relinquished hope, it had been her constant companion as she fought against the all-consuming terror. Then they'd found her in that dirty, disused warehouse. They'd found others too, in various states of death and decay. The smells of despair had filled the air with a fetid ripeness that she'd never been able to forget.

Since that day she'd promised herself that she would pay the Ru'Edan back for what they'd done to her. What they'd taken from her. Over the years, she tempered and honed the rage while remaining adamant that she would see the final act played out. She couldn't physically fight, but she had learned about trauma, knew it and understood how it affected a person, and used it as a weapon.

The iron will forged through her experiences had fed her determination, and she'd applied herself to study, finishing in the top ten percent of her class. She entered the medical program at the academy, working hard to excel. Her family remained supportive if perplexed as to why she had chosen to keep reminding herself of what had happened.

The maw of the *Star of Ishtar* loomed closer, opening its cavernous mouth as she watched through the portal. She could hear the voices of the shuttle crew signaling their intention to enter and land, the tinny confirmation coming swiftly. She watched avidly while the shuttle maneuvered, imagining the invisible shields dropping to allow it entry.

Her hands twisted with fear and anger, but she tamped down her emotions. Anger never helped anyone. Staying strong, knowing your history, and ensuring it couldn't be repeated, they were the answers, she told herself firmly, pulling herself from the grip of a dark past so horrific she still saw it in her dreams. She pushed it away to the recesses of her mind and focused on what she was about to do.

A squark overhead, the usual mechanical sound that alerted all on board to a transmission by the captain, caught her attention. "Attention all passengers. We are entering the shuttle bay. Please ensure when you disembark you remove all personal items. Move beyond the white line and wait for your designation."

The lights of the bay flashed as they entered, and once again Elara marveled at how far humanity had moved since they had first walked the Earth. She saw the opening of the structure as the shuttle moved into the bay, inching forward slowly until it stopped its ponderous motion and began its descent to the floor. Something deep inside warmed even as the shuttle's environmental systems began to synchronize with the cooler temperature of the *Star of Ishtar*, and she felt a smile crawl its way over her face.

Elara breathed in deeply, inhaling the metallic-tasting, recycled air and welcoming the calmness that settled on her body. Her eyes closed as she filled her lungs. "I'm here." There was more than a little satisfaction in her tone, and she smiled. She slowly exhaled, finding that center of peace she relied on.

A loud thud and clank echoed as the deep drone split the air. The engines were powering down, and there she was, on one of the Earth Empire's Emeritus class battleships. She sat in her seat, waiting for the all clear from the captain, and once it sounded through the cabin, she rose, tugging at the webbing belt and disengaging it.

The small backpack beside her was all she carried as she made her way to the exit, not needing to duck as so many others did. She stepped through the door, her hands gripping the rail of the cold, metal stairs which connected to the side of the gray shuttle.

She clambered down them slowly, savoring the experience. The sting of the cold on her hands from the stairs, frigid from even their brief exposure to the blackness of space, made her flinch inwardly. The shuttle journey from the Admiralty's strategic base at Aenna to their current position had taken just over an hour, but the whole time it felt like her heart had been in her throat. Her mouth was dry as she followed the new recruits from the ship into the landing bay. She stopped, silently noting the slight mustiness of the air, the recycled quality easily recognizable. Everything, including the oxygen, needed recycling in space.

All around her people swarmed, either around the ships or into the dogleg line that now formed ahead of her. Someone had opened the baggage locker of the shuttle, and the sound of dropping bags hitting the plascrete floor echoed in the air. Another crewmember guided trolleys to the other side of the shuttle, pulling out boxes with important day-to-day items for the ship, including vaccines and plants. She watched briefly, all the while listening to the alien cacophony. Voices called in welcome to old crewmembers, while new ones watched, many goggle-eyed in the fresh uniforms of newly minted officers and crewmembers.

Her gaze flicked around quickly, taking in the sights, sounds, and smells, pungent with oils and grease; burning smells from the scorched plascrete and the press of sweaty or nervous bodies. She joined the line silently, tacking onto the end, and stayed at parade rest, knowing the welcoming voice would cut through the air soon enough. She felt somehow disconnected from the main throng. Perhaps the knowledge that this was the outcome she had worked for years to achieve set her apart. However, still, she felt so...distant from everything around her. She smiled secretly at the bout of whimsy.

"Attention!" The voice boomed out over the plascrete of the docking bay, and she snapped her body into position, noting the commander who had bellowed the words. Technically, she outranked most members aboard the *Star of Ishtar*, except for the command and leadership staff, but she knew all newcomers had to join the welcoming parade, regardless of rank.

Fleet Captain Elphin came into view, his tired features topped by salt-and-pepper gray hair, which highlighted his cool blue eyes. Elara also recognized a body prone to a little middle-aged thickness. Following behind him was his second-in-command, Duvall McCord. A young up-and-coming officer, his status as a fast-tracking officer heading toward his own command, with Elphin both his mentor and captain, had become almost legendary at the academy.

She looked closely at McCord, noting the dynamic drive of his actions and movements. Soon he would achieve a promotion to captain, and she rejoiced for her friend. She'd followed his career with interest and had to tamp down a smile as his eyes betrayed the shock of seeing her before settling into their flat command persona. So he hadn't been apprised of her deployment, she noted, and she had to restrain the tiny feeling of surprise and satisfaction. She filed that snippet of information away.

She caught sight of the man standing behind Duvall. Grayson Myatt. He'd made her heart beat faster for years. Tall and blond with a muscular build and a sexy, tight, little butt, he had pools of deep-blue eyes that had always made her think of forever. He had a growth of stubble on his chiseled jaw, and her fingers itched to touch his perfect lips. Yes, since the day he'd found her in that nasty warehouse tied down like a ragged animal, she'd worshipped him from afar.

Now she had her opportunity to tangle with him, hopefully much closer than any chance that had ever come her way before. With a sigh, she pulled her gaze back to the captain and forced herself to concentrate on his words. She couldn't afford to have her commanding officer angry due to her being distracted.

"Welcome to the *Star of Ishtar*. Most academy recruits want to join us because of what we represent, but on this ship, we only take the best of the best. So, if you made it here, you're the ones we wanted to take a look at. Getting here is only the first step. Staying here is harder to achieve. Our people are the best. Earn your place, and in return, we'll make you one of our crew—a member of the *Star of Ishtar*. Only the best and the brightest wear our uniform and badge. You'll be expected to perform to your absolute limit then give some more. We don't tolerate people who don't pull their weight. Do us proud and wear your uniform with pride." The captain looked out over the new members of his crew. His voice had echoed during his speech, and now it died away.

He scanned the faces before him, and she could almost read his thoughts. There were new security officers and a smattering of other crew. Some of them were young and impressionable, and she knew a few wouldn't make the cut as crewmembers. Others would carve out their place on the *Star of Ishtar* and move to better positions and placements, like she would: the new SurgiTech, a younger female, experienced but untried on board a ship. She smiled at that thought.

Some of those who stood with her would be replaced as they failed the exacting standards the captain set. She'd heard that he was a firm captain, fair but demanding. He'd have to be to command this ship. The Ishtar had well over five hundred at full capacity, and the captain could select their placements as his command staff saw fit from the many who applied to join the crew. She sensed his satisfaction with the choices in the relaxation of his body.

Abruptly, he turned to Duvall, breaking her study of him. "Get them to where they need to present themselves." His words echoed as he walked away. He had a purposeful stride. Quick but unhurried, like he knew where he was going and how to get there. A man who knew how to get what he wanted. Someone to respect and admire.

"My name is Commander Duvall McCord. I am your second-in-command, and my direct subordinate is Commander Grayson Myatt. While you are aboard the *Star of Ishtar* you will be required to fulfill your duties efficiently. As Captain Elphin said, do your job right and you will be one of ours, with all the benefits that come with being a crewmember of the *Star of Ishtar*."

He paused and eyeballed each of the newer recruits, those fresh from the academy. Many of them paled under his gaze, and she smiled inwardly. Even the older people in the line seemed to quake beneath his scowl. He'd always had that air of innate authority, even when barely out of the academy himself. She knew his methods and watched him make full use of the carefully practiced tone of presence.

"Each of you has been assigned. You will present yourselves to the chief of your section. Those details will be found in your orders. Commander Myatt has organized a team to escort you to your cabins. You will have approximately one hour to prepare. We've arranged for crewmembers to escort you to your superiors. Be ready to present for duty. Any issues, you will, of course, take up with your section commander. Should there be need to take any further action, you will see Commander Myatt. You should only see me if you are a command crewmember or as a point of discipline. I am not one for small talk, so if you present to me, have a very good reason."

He delivered the words slowly and deliberately, and Elara restrained a small smile on hearing at least one gulp from those in the line nearest her.

"We run a tight ship here. Discipline and commitment are the two key factors we look for beyond loyalty in our crew. You will from henceforth represent our ship everywhere, and we do not tolerate anything less than the best." He looked around once more, the stern demeanor he wore so well reinforcing the message. If she hadn't known him for so long, she too might have missed the hint of humor glinting in his eyes, the one many took for coldness.

Her legs ached, and she wanted to move and relieve the pressure on them, but she held herself still, waiting for the command to dismiss. She wouldn't let herself or him down now. Not after she'd worked so long to achieve this position.

As the new ST, she had no previous experience on ships.

She had vast experience in the field, but Elara was aware that would count for little in the eyes of most of the crew. She didn't intend to signal a weakness to anyone and least of all on her first day aboard the *Star of Ishtar*. That thought held her still and controlled.

She had big shoes to fill after her predecessor, Jamieson, had retired, even though she knew she could fill the void he'd left behind. As a long-term member of the crew—over twenty years—his tenure on the *Star of Ishtar* had placed him aboard since its launch. Due to his experience in the heat of battle with the Ru'Edan he had made a name for himself as the coldest of cold in the hottest of situations. She hoped to emulate that herself and carve out her own place aboard the Ishtar, as its crew lovingly knew her.

Duvall and Grayson knew how much she wanted to prove herself. They just wouldn't have expected it here, on the Ishtar.

She watched Duvall study her, then, quickly turning on his heel, call to those assembled, "Dismissed."

Once they started to move away, she softened her stance, preparing to turn when the call came.

"Sudonne! A moment if you please."

Elara turned to face Duvall. "Commander?"

"Welcome to the *Star of Ishtar*, Elara. While I am surprised you're the new ST, Grayson and I are pleased you could join us. But how did you manage to pull it off? Keeping it quiet that you were the new ST?" he asked, his voice deep enough to make most women shiver with anticipation.

She smiled, thinking it was a shame she didn't have any feelings for him except sisterly attachment, but then again, given his lack of deep commitment to women, maybe it wasn't such a shame after all.

She understood what drove him. He wanted his own ship and to captain his own future. They'd spent many nights over wine or ale discussing his beliefs that commitment grounded a person. Inwardly, she shrugged. He'd make those calls for himself, though she was sure that one day he would come across someone who would make him consider his choices a little more thoroughly.

"I'm pleased to be here, Duvall. Having an uncle who happens to be an admiral, he was able to let Captain Elphin know that I wanted to surprise you. It's a small world in the Admiralty. Elphin already knew of me, so he okayed my placement. Once the powers knew there was no impediments to me joining the crew, it was fairly simple from there." She felt a small smile creep onto her face, then let it drop away. "What do you think Grayson thinks?"

"Ah, still chasing him, are you?" He grinned, his eyes twinkling. "I think he'll be pleased you're finally old enough and you're here." He looked her straight in the eye. "But you may just need to remind him of that particular fact." He motioned for her to go before him, barking out a deep laugh. "Come on, I'll show you to your cabin."

Elara took a quick look around her SurgiTech Suite and felt a glow in her chest. "It's surprisingly well stocked and resourced." Her voice echoed in the large room stocked with the latest in diagnostic equipment.

The highly trained staff was moving quietly around the suite beyond her office, talking in muted tones. The walls were painted white with light-blue accents, a far cry from the gunmetal gray that covered the rest of the ship, and she grinned, knowing that the tones were chosen to soothe even the most badly injured crewmember.

Her office continued the scheme, which promoted healing and harmony. The floors, she noted, had been sealed with noise-barrier skins, meaning nothing would startle patients, least of all the doors, fitted with the latest sound-limiting devices. She breathed in the clean air. No recycled atmosphere here for recovering patients, she thought, satisfied that no expense had been spared in the equipping of the SurgiTech suite along with the rest of the battleship.

"And it's my office and my Surgi-Tech." A glow of happiness warmed her insides. She was finally there, not just on board the *Star of Ishtar*, but on the same ship as

Grayson. The years of hard work and study fell away as she drank in the excitement of her achievement. Elara knew she had proven herself repeatedly in her drive to achieve this placement. She took a deep breath and centered herself once more.

A beep at the door alerted her to a visitor outside her office, where she sat reviewing her day from waking on Aenna to her quick rounds of the suite. She tabbed on the comm, leaning forward in her chair. "Yes?" She kept her voice low and calm. Controlled.

"Commander Myatt here. May I enter?"

A frisson of excitement shimmered through her system at his voice. "Of course, Commander."

She gave the order for the door to open and stood, then walked to the other side of the desk, a smile on her face, with her hands outstretched as the door closed behind him with a *whoosh*. She moved silently forward into his open arms, taking in his grin. He looked so good in his formal uniform.

The hug was enveloping but not nearly enough. She wasn't some green girl to be pacified with a single caress. She breathed in his musky scent and nestled against his firm chest. She'd waited a long time and worked hard for this chance. She needed to act her age and role if she hoped to make him see her as much more than the girl he had rescued so many years ago. After all these years, she was done hoping he would work it out by himself. After all, he'd done a poor job of seeing what was there, waiting for him.

"Damn, it's good to see you, Elara. *Barsha!* Here you are as the ST of the Ishtar! Well done, little girl."

His triumphant grin didn't stop the sting of his words. Calling her *little girl* with that sexy-sounding voice of his cut through her once more, just as it had always done in the past when he had called her *his little girl*. She gritted her teeth. The time had come to let him know she was a woman, she reminded herself firmly.

He kept talking, and she watched his hands as they moved, keeping track of his words and actions. "But you surprised me. Why did you keep your transfer here so quiet?" His tone sounded good-natured enough, but she couldn't answer the question with words. She needed him to understand why she had transferred for himself.

"It's good to see you too, Grayson."

She reached up onto her toes, grabbed his broad, muscular shoulders, and kissed him softly on the cheek. Lingeringly. Elara allowed her lips to hover just longer than normal. She waited a heartbeat more so Grayson would recognize the implied invitation. He reared back in surprise, eyes wide open in shock as it registered. His face flushed as she stepped back from him, and inwardly she sighed, conceding she had her work cut out for her.

"Right." He backed away emotionally even as he spoke that simple word. The quick way he looked away from her face told her he was uncomfortable with the new Elara. He glanced down at her uniform. "You obviously got the memo about dress standards. We need to head directly to the captain's dining room. He was most insistent that you should join the leadership team tonight, as it is your first meal aboard the Ishtar."

He motioned with a short movement of his hand for her to precede him out the door, which opened automatically, then closed behind them. They stopped for her to give the voice command for the doors to lock her office and only open for herself and the three most senior officers of the Ishtar. Once Elara was satisfied that everything was in order, they made their way along the drab gray decking toward the elevators at the end of the corridor.

# Chapter 2

**A**s Elara walked in front of Grayson he watched her gait. No longer was it the coltish scramble he remembered from years ago, but a womanly, flowing movement as she moved along the deck, her dress shoes silent with each step.

She might be small, but time had filled out her body, giving her the graceful curves that he had caught glimpses of that first time he saw her, naked and tied to the examining table. The curves he'd watched for years had changed and filled out. His hands itched to touch them. Her hips swayed as she moved, and he felt the low curl of lust deep in his gut. Heat spread through his body, the clothing he wore was suddenly too tight, and a trickle of sweat burrowed down his collar and back; the same way he always felt after a close encounter with her.

The woman-child he remembered from years ago was gone, and in her place stood a sensual, composed woman, comfortable in herself. One who had learned the lure of the siren, causing the tightness in his chest that hadn't eased at all since that kiss on the cheek. That hadn't been a sisterly peck, not with her lips warm and supple against his face, the whisper of her breath fanning his skin.

For an instant he had to close his eyes to banish the burning thoughts that rose in his mind of her naked and writhing in his arms. When he opened them, he still saw her, her body clothed in her black formal uniform, which revealed her curves, each glorious one accentuated in a way he had never expected. These uniforms, he knew, were designed with gender balancing in mind, but somehow she obviously benefitted from the utilitarian fabric and cut. For years, he'd tried successfully to control his reaction to her, but now he failed, and the dark uniform conspired against him. His hands fisted as he walked along the corridor, his nails digging into his palms, but the pain offered no surcease to his arousal.

"Which way?"

He stopped and glanced at her face. "What?"

She grinned. "Which way do we go?"

He gestured to the lift doors and she paled. "Do we have to?"

"It's the only way, Elara."

He watched as she tried to control a shudder. He knew she didn't cope well in enclosed spaces, due to her experience in that warehouse, and he felt a bubble of pride grow in his chest at the way she controlled herself and her fear, standing firm even as he knew it buffeted her. He watched her closely and saw that beautiful jawline firm and the pink lips tighten as she controlled her reaction while they waited for the elevator. It arrived and they stepped inside the small cubicle.

"It's the command elevator, keyed to only certain staff." He swiped his personnel card and depressed the button. The light shined, showing the command had been accepted, and the doors closed silently, enclosing them within the confined space.

"Well, at least it'll be quick." She spoke quickly, as if forcing the words from her mouth. He heard the sound of her swallowing and silently applauded the way she held herself together.

Suddenly a clank filled the air and the lights went out in the elevator. It shuddered to a stop, pushing them both slightly off-balance for a second. Her rapid intake of breath rasped in the elevator car, and her breathing grew faster as, he was sure, the memories crowded in. He moved toward her instinctively. The need to wrap his arms around her urged him forward. He felt the tension in her body making her stiff and silent in his arms. She grabbed his waist, clutching him tightly.

"It's okay. We've been having a few problems with this particular elevator over the last few days." He murmured the words in her ear, hoping they would help her fears, give her some relief from the demons that rode her hard, but he mentally chastised himself for choosing this elevator. *Barsha!* He'd known they were having issues. He should have used one of the others. He could feel the thudding of her heart through the material of her uniform.

He groped in the pocket of his formal ship suit for the small personal communicator he kept on hand, hoping it would work in this elevator shaft. It was military issue and refurbished to give it maximum connectivity, but that didn't give him any reassurance that it would work in the reinforced well. Grayson pulled it out and flicked it open, watching as it lit up the interior of the elevator, casting shadows into the corners. His jaw ached as it remained clenched, and a nerve pulsed in his cheek as he held his anger at himself in check. He hit the commbutton and waited for the signal to connect. And waited as it searched for a connection before finally confirming and hailing the recipient.

"Gray? I don't like this." She shuddered in his arms and he hauled her closer, tight against his chest. He only sought to settle her nerves, but his body reacted. He sucked in a breath, the sound loud to his hearing.

A grainy-sounding noise came through the speaker. *Barsha.* Duvall hadn't answered his communit, and the message recall service activated. He decided to leave a message, knowing Duvall checked it regularly. "Duvall, I'm in the command elevator, and it's seized again. Elara is with me." His friend would decode the unspoken message.

Elara released a sound, a cross between a moan and hiccup.

He angled his head so that his lips whispered against her soft hair. "Shh, Lara. Duvall will sort this out quickly," he reassured her, hoping Duvall would pick up his message sooner rather than later.

Her small hands gripped his waist as he closed the communicator with a snap against his leg. "I hate this," she whispered, her breath brushing against his skin.

"I know."

She shuddered slightly, and he kissed the top of her head.

Her scent rose toward him, filling him with its heady exoticness, and his body ached in response. He rubbed his hands up and down her back as he marveled at the restraint she showed, feeling her soft curves under his hands.

Given the circumstances, he wouldn't have been surprised if she had started screaming by now, but she continued to hold herself together with a strength greater than most women he had ever met. He could feel the tension in her body, knew she fought herself fiercely. He closed his eyes, hating the need that rose in him even as he sought to find a way to soothe her. The burning warmth of her body invaded the coldness of the silent elevator shaft.

His communicator buzzed in his hand. He flipped it open. "Grayson," he said, his voice now harsh with restrained emotion. On the other end, he could hear Duvall through the static.

"...working on...done...soon...hang tight." The crackle and pop of the interference of the metal in the elevator made it hard to understand, but he got the general gist of the message. Duvall knew the situation and was dealing with it. He would have them out as soon as possible; all Grayson had to do was keep Elara from losing it.

"That was Duvall. He's working on it, and he'll have us out of here as soon as he can." She nodded against his chest as he moved her toward the wall of the elevator and encouraged her to sit, feeling her slide down the wall. The interior of the elevator was dark and silent with no light shining from its blank panels. He lowered himself beside her, the roundness of her backside touching his thighs.

Since the screen of his communicator shined, he kept it open, letting it illuminate their prison. He knew that the pale green glow provided small comfort for her.

*She's probably remembering her days as a prisoner.* The warehouse had been dark, except for the experimentation rooms. He remembered that horrible room well. It was where he and Duvall had found her. He knew a little of some of her experiences. That she'd spent a lot of time in darkness listening to the screams and moans of the other victims. They'd kept the prisoners in cages no bigger than cupboards. Elara had suffered from claustrophobia ever since then.

Elara pulled away slightly, her hand gripping his. Her grip squeezed his fingers hard, nails digging into his skin, but he ignored it. "I hate places like this. It reminds me of that building. Those days they had me there." Her voice trembled, and the broken tones shattered him.

He squeezed the hand he kept safe in his. She returned it, her hand soft but strong, as if she drew strength from the connection. As it always did, a rage welled within him, black, greasy, and threatening to drown him.

"I know," he said, "But I won't let anything happen to you. You know that, don't you?" A sound like a wet hiccup escaped from her. Reaching over, he pulled her forward once more. Wetness seeped through the shoulder of his uniform and he knew what it was. *Barsha! She's crying.* He hated when she cried. Elara was so strong, but sometimes even she couldn't keep the tears at bay. Anger at himself rose again. She'd cried more tears than anyone should have to, and now he blamed himself for reminding her once more of the terror and pain.

"We got the bastards who held you prisoner, Elara. And they stood trial. They paid. If I could lay my hands on Crick Sur Banden though, I'd squeeze him until he was dead." He knew his voice sounded cold, and she shuddered again. He needed to give her something to hang on to, he reasoned. Had to make it better for her, somehow, no matter the cost to himself.

"I know that, but I still see them at night in my dreams. I can't ever escape the memories."

The broken whisper of her voice nearly killed him. He pulled her onto his lap, and she reached her arms up around his neck. He could only see dimly in the green light from the communicator, but the tear tracks on her damaged face shined bright in the watery light. He groaned and pulled her closer to his chest.

He needed to comfort her, and with no thought other than showing her he understood and cared, he pulled her face up to his, placing his hand on the silken skin of her chin, and kissed her. It was merely as a comfort, he told himself. The shock of her soft lips on his kick-started something within him. *Hard.* His body reacted, and he deepened the kiss. Her hands gripped his shoulders, and her mouth opened to his, accepting his touch even as her tongue slid against his own.

The commlink beeped and he froze, shoulders tensing. "McCord here. You two still okay?"

Grayson realized what he'd done as she pulled back, looking at him. *Barsha!* She was hurting and there he was taking advantage of the situation! He mentally chastised himself. Her eyes opened wide, shining in the light. He closed himself against the shock he guessed he would see in her face at his ill-timed and ill-considered move. How could he? The words echoed through his brain. How could he take advantage?

A noise intruded into the dark elevator, and suddenly the lights on the command pad started to flash back to life. One by one, the lighting strips flickered on, off, then back on. He grabbed his communicator and stood, pulling Elara upright as the last of the lights came back on.

Duvall's voice filtered through the communicator. "Are you both okay?"

"Yeah, we're fine," Grayson said tersely, his chest now unbearably tight as anger roiled within him. That stupid maneuver with Elara had cost him. He'd already been wound tight, his emotions in turmoil, just like every other time he'd been in her presence. But somehow this time seemed worse than his previous experiences.

He shook his head mentally. He'd have to watch his step. Otherwise, he could be facing a harassment charge, and more importantly he'd lose the brief contact he had with her. It wouldn't be Elara who'd bring the charges though. He knew that. She'd never damage their friendship like that. Unlike him and his ill thought-out ideas. No, someone else would do it, and he'd likely deserve it unless he reined himself and his emotions in.

Elara had figured in so many of his fantasies for so long, he had stepped over the line without really thinking about it. *Barsha!* She was swiping tears away with shaking fingers, and he handed her the handkerchief he kept in his pocket, watching silently as she tidied herself. The elevator began to whirr back into action as she handed back the soft cloth. He turned away.

Within minutes, they stood outside the captain's dining room, waiting for the door to open. They waited in silence as Duvall joined them. She glanced at Grayson several times, as if she wanted to say something. He thanked the stars she didn't.

✪ ✪ ✪ ✪ ✪

The memory of what had happened in the elevator played on a loop in Elara's mind, dragging her attention away from the dinner she now pushed around her plate. She had been shocked at finally feeling Grayson's lips on hers. When she'd pulled back so she could see his face in the gloom, he'd once more withdrawn from her, probably thinking she didn't want his touch.

*Damned idiot woman. You've wanted this for so darn long, and you finally get the chance and you blow it.* She'd made a huge mistake in pulling away because she'd needed to gauge his response to the passion that flared between them.

She hated confined spaces, as they reminded her of times she wanted to forget, and yet this time her lust for Grayson had overshadowed that completely. That was a totally new experience.

She'd felt his mouth move, while the taste of him had drugged her with its dark-yet-sweet essence. She lifted a finger to her lips, reliving the feeling of his mouth on hers, and she smiled. Then she sighed as she recalled where she was.

One step forward and three steps back. He'd be on his

guard now, she mused, all the while inwardly kicking herself. She should have known he would react like that. The big brother syndrome raised its head every time she thought to move this relationship forward into new territory, and this time she had let those emotions loose, albeit unwittingly.

"Are you enjoying the meal?" Duvall asked, interrupting her introspection.

"Honestly?" she asked.

He quirked an eyebrow, and she frowned and leaned forward.

"Not really. I keep thinking about... Well, let's just say, if he runs any further, he'd probably be back on Earth." Her whispered words were echoed in the slump of her shoulders.

"Oh."

"Yeah." She turned back to her plate and speared the food on it with her fork. She didn't really want it. In fact, she'd rather be back in her cabin, nursing the jagged hole that had opened in her heart. She knew others enjoyed the food with its lovely presentation, but she might as well have eaten nutrient bars for all the enjoyment she felt.

Grayson kept glancing at her, and she tried to figure out a way to let him know she hadn't found his kiss unwelcome. The only thing that came to mind was actually saying the words aloud. But she couldn't do that in the present company, no matter how urgently she felt the need to clear the air. Her fingers tightened on the fork she held. Her mind tumbled around the possibilities, but nothing helped her.

She sighed inwardly, before moving restlessly in her seat as she tried to work through her options in her mind. She knew that the longer the words remained unsaid, the harder it would be to say them.

Then she had to pull herself back to the discussion at hand, turning to answer a question from a fellow officer about her experiences in the Admiralty.

Once the meal ended, the captain excused her on grounds of her experience in the elevator, and she wasn't surprised when

Duvall chose to accompany her back to the cabin.

"So, he dodged it, huh?" Duvall said as they left the dining room. Elara shrugged. "You knew he would."

They walked silently down the deck, making their way toward a set of stairs. No way would she do the elevator thing again tonight, and she felt an absurd pleasure that Duvall had intuited that. When they reached the bottom of the stairs Elara stopped abruptly, turning toward Duvall.

She inhaled sharply. "I messed up again with him, you know." Her smile wavered, and she felt tears gathering behind her stinging eyes.

"I got that impression." He smiled, laying a hand on her shoulder. "I don't think I've seen him back off quite so quickly before." His expression softened, and he gave her a quick, hard hug. When he pulled away, his eyes were full of understanding.

"I kissed him. In the elevator. Well, technically he kissed me." She dropped her gaze. "I wanted it as much as he did, but then he backed off." She shrugged.

"By *Eshra*! You didn't. Did you?" He looked at her intently, a hint of a smile ghosting around his lips.

"Yeah. I think it scared him because I backed away to see his face and he probably thought I didn't want it." She shook her head. "Dumb, wasn't it? *Barsha.* I've wanted this for years. Now I get the chance, and I blow it." Her heart weighed heavy, feeling like a rock in her chest at the thought she'd wasted her chance. Her eyes closed against the welling of tears.

"The stupid thing..." He stopped the words, and she looked at him, waiting, "Well...it's not really for me to say." A sigh erupted, and for a second she saw the weariness in his features. It hurt to know she had added to her friend's worries. "Elara, you really need to get it together.For both your sakes. Either you're in or out. I mean, it's bad for the ship, but it's worse for you." Duvall shook his head as if unable to comprehend their stalemate. With a twist of his lips, he shrugged his shoulders, then continued walking.

She watched him, one step, and another.

"Duvall?"

He stopped and turned back.

"Does he want me? Really?" The words erupted before she could stop them.

He looked surprised, his dark eyes wide with shock, then a smile moved over his face. "That's a question you need to ask him."

His eyes, which had just twinkled, now filled with compassion, and she bit her lip and nodded. She shouldn't have put Duvall in that position. She thanked him silently for not answering. As much as she might need the answer, this wasn't right. Putting Duvall in the middle was cowardly, and she refused to allow herself to take that option.

Elara sighed glumly. "You're right, of course. I need to take this by the horns." She firmed her shoulders. "What shift is he on tomorrow?"

"He's on early. Same as you." He backed off at a million miles an hour, and she smiled. Something in his eyes betrayed his fear of commitment and being anywhere near someone looking for one. He always said watching one couple go down with the commitment bug gave other people ideas. This sexy, handsome, and well-built friend of hers didn't want anything to do with long-term and commitment.

She focused her mind on the task ahead. So Grayson had the early shift tomorrow, just like she did? Duvall had a serious problem with commitment, but maybe, just maybe, she could use his fear of commitment to her advantage. After all, Grayson knew his stand on relationships and wouldn't expect Duvall to be in on her plan. It would lull him into a false sense of security. Right now, any advantage would be welcome.

Poor Duvall, he really did have issues with women and commitment. Her assessing glance at Duvall died away as she thought of her friend facing a similar situation sometime in the future. His turn would come, and she looked forward to seeing it happen. But first, she needed to get her man.

"Right then, time for a direct plan of action, I think." Elara watched a frown form between his eyes as the kernel of a plan grew in her mind. It was time to bring out the whole arsenal, and now was her opportunity. She had let this continue for years, and it was time to take control and beat the situation into submission. She followed Duvall to her door. "So, what happens for entertainment around here?"

He looked at her, the change of topic clearly surprising him, and she grinned.

"You see, I heard of this thing they used to do centuries back, and it seems like a great idea." Quickly, she outlined her plan, and he nodded.

"We need some new ideas, and that sounds like fun. I'll see what we can do about it."

"How about tomorrow?" She spoke the words softly, and he looked at her, nodded, then turned. She watched him walk away. Yes, she was definitely on a roll.

# Chapter 3

Elara stretched at her desk. The first full day in the seat had mainly required her to overview the files of the previous ST. Unsurprisingly, she found them concise, including follow-up details where required.

"Well, that could have been a lot harder." She spoke quietly while she cleared her desk, her loose hair bobbing around her shoulders. The previous ST could be described as ruthlessly organized, and that made for an easier transition for everyone.

She glanced at the time on the corner of her desk screen. She would pack up in a few minutes and head back to her cabin to freshen up and change into something a little more comfortable and definitely more interesting.

She made a final notation on the desk screen about the files she had perused. Among the current makeup of the crew, she found no significant and ongoing conditions, the situation quite different from her previous experience. The long-term health center now lay empty, with any serious injuries cases transferred to the main medical facility on Aenna upon arrival at their dock.

Only one minor incident had occurred since boarding: a broken arm that had been immediately set and a bone regenerator employed. She had discharged the unlucky recipient to his cabin, and the suite had regained its calm silence.

She checked the time again. Nineteen hundred hours. She supposed she should make her way to the cabin then the officer's mess. She'd just stood up when the chimes on her door sounded.

"Yes?"

"Grayson here. Can we talk?"

She gave the command for the door to open, and he stepped inside. The door closed behind him. He looked uncomfortable, and she smiled. Time to implement the first step of her plan—surprise him with her talents and abilities.

His blond hair looked disheveled, as if he'd had a long and stressful day. Her imagination hit overdrive as she looked at him, imagining her hands spearing through his hair. She wanted to grab him and kiss those luscious lips and taste him once more. The urge to wind her arms around his muscular neck and trace her fingers over his strong, supple body called to her, but she held herself still.

*You're a senior officer aboard the Ishtar and this is work time.* Besides, she couldn't afford to spook him further. But the wild thumping in her heart as desire sparked once more told her she could only hold onto restraint for so long. She worked to contain it and herself.

"Have a seat." She indicated the seat opposite her with a hand and sat back down behind her desk. She would control herself, she reminded her body savagely.

"Thanks, Elara. Look, about yesterday..." His words trailed off. A red tide of embarrassment rose over his cheeks, and he squirmed in his seat. She reined in the urge to soothe his feelings.

"Yeah, yesterday, that was wild." She nodded sagely. Maybe she could allow a little latitude given he'd opened the topic. "Do you know you're a great kisser?"

He blinked and tilted his head to the side.

Elara silently congratulated herself on seeing the surprise on his face. She needed him to see that she was willing to deepen their relationship. Maybe she could also upset his equilibrium just a little?

"What?" he said.

She smiled. Yes, this was definitely the right tack. "Well, I thought you'd like to know that you're an exceptional kisser."

He squirmed again in the seat, his blue eyes staring at her.

"Oh, don't get me wrong, the elevator incident reminded me of what has happened, but life goes on regardless of our experiences." She scooted to the edge of her seat. "I also know you need to make the most of the opportunities you have." She stilled. Up until now, her voice had lilted, but the time had come to spear him with the truth. "I want to experience those same opportunities. With you." Her tone changed and became calm and controlled. "I believe yesterday illustrated the fact that we have chemistry that should be investigated."

There. She'd hit him between the eyes with her calm and scientific delivery. *Let him argue that!*

He looked at her, his mouth gaping. Obviously, no one had ever tried this approach with him before, and she felt a surging thrill of possessiveness.

Standing slowly, Elara smoothed her uniform over her body, knowing it emphasized her feminine curves to his hungry eyes. She watched as his gaze roamed over her frame. Elara casually sauntered over to him and dropped into the seat beside him, reaching out a hand to his knee and touching him gently.

She gave him her best come-hither smile before speaking again. "So, how should we go about this?"

He went red and almost choked. She squelched the sigh and eye roll as he bolted straight up in his chair.

"That's okay, we can take it as slow as you need," she cooed, hoping to soothe him. His fingers gripped the chair arms in alarm, his eyes wide and staring at her. He looked so startled, as if he didn't know how to respond. Oh yes, now she had him ensnared, she could see his mind whirling as it had never done before. She was on target, and by *Eshra* she would make the most of it.

"I need to go," he said in a strangled voice, and without a backward glance, he stood and all but fled from her office.

She waited for the door to close behind him before allowing herself a brief chuckle of triumph. Round one to Elara, she thought, remembering with fascination his surprise at her behavior. Then she stood up and moved through the door to the corridor. Round two would begin after dinner. She had a partner in crime to line up first.

Grayson walked the hall, assuring himself he wasn't running away. Somehow, he'd made it through the meal in his cabin. Being alone hadn't helped to find his equilibrium.

"I'm not so sure anything will." The sight of her smoothing down her uniform... His gut tightened as did his groin. She'd blindsided him, true.

He felt unable to ignore his feelings for her. Something had changed, because, dammit, he'd had them for a long time, and before now, it had never been so difficult to ignore those hungry emotions.

His groan filled the air. It went against everything he'd ever believed—that her attachment to him was purely because he'd saved her. In his mind, the question he'd ignored for years arose. If she felt this so-called attraction to him, then why didn't she react the same way to Duvall?

Somehow, trying to bring the little girl he remembered into focus was impossible. All he could see now revolved around a riot of curly red hair, luscious lips, and twinkling eyes. Not to mention a body that put the ancient Venus to shame. Elara had curves in all the right places and a wit and gaiety that called to him on so many levels. He ached to hold her close and make her his.

He shook himself mentally. He had to see Elara as the little sister he never had, he reminded himself. But there was no conviction in his thoughts.

The memory of the kiss in the elevator scorched him. He'd nearly died and gone to heaven when his lips had touched hers and when she opened her mouth. Dear *Eshra*! How could he fight against that?

"I won't take advantage." The words sounded thin and forced. No, it was better not to open that Pandora's box. His best bet was to keep her a friend rather than to lose her for good when she woke up to what she really wanted and found it wasn't him. His stomach clenched and churned at the loss, but he accepted that she couldn't be part of his future.

His commbadge buzzed, and almost afraid, he answered. "Grayson." He held himself still until he knew who waited on the other end.

"Hey, man. Where are you? I'm waiting in the mess for you. You coming soon?" "I...ah...sure. Be there in about ten." He really didn't feel in the mood for socializing, but if he didn't turn up, it would cause more questions; the sort of questions he knew were better avoided.

He backtracked past Elara's office door, flicking a quick look at it, but the red of the palm plate told him the direct door to her office was locked.

Thankfully, the elevator was empty, and he tried to clear his mind. He needed a clear head when he reached the mess, because his defenses were weak and ineffectual on any other level. It was all he had left. Duvall would know if something was up.

The door opened with a *whoosh*. It never occurred to him that Elara would join them, would be waiting with his best friend. *With Duvall.* She talked, wine glass in hand, smiling and laughing at his words, her eyes shining just the way Grayson wanted them to shine at him, and a tearing pain struck him. Those smiles she should only share with him.

She had obviously had time to change, and her attire included long, flowing pants and some kind of strappy light top, which more than hinted at the curves of breasts just below the surface. It skimmed her skin, baring her midriff, her skin glowing under the lighting, her hair flowing down her back, curls rioting and kissing skin he desperately wanted to touch. His fingers itched to reach out and slide within the glorious silk cloud.

The pain in his chest confirmed his fears that he suffered from terminal jealousy. It grabbed him and choked the air from his body, and his throat burned at his petty behavior. He couldn't have her, but he couldn't and shouldn't stop her from experiencing a relationship with someone else. He felt no consolation right now. The new and negative emotion was caustic, stripping away his carefully built walls.

"*Barsha.*" The quiet word didn't dispel the *unpleasant* sensation.

His fingers curled as he fought the need to grab Elara, pull her to him, and brand her with a scorching kiss so no one would doubt she was his. He held himself still while wrestling with his demons. Others passed by, keeping a wide berth as they noted the scowl on his face.

Once he was sure he'd controlled his reactions, he stalked toward them, and both Duvall and Elara turned in his direction. Duvall nodded, something glittering in his eyes. Elara smiled at him, an intimate, just-for-you smile, and he felt it like a body blow. His body heated once more, and his restraint nearly crumbled. He took a deep breath, but instead of calming him, the scent of her perfume filled his senses with promises of luscious curves, the heady and rich tones seducing him further.

"Drink, Grayson?"

Her throaty words curled around him. It took effort for him to answer normally. "Yeah. Something red."

Duvall headed to the bar, returning with a deep ruby wine.

Grayson inhaled, hoping to lose himself in the bouquet. When that didn't work, he took a sip. He watched as the halo of red hair shined under the lights, and her beautiful green eyes sparkled in the changing lights of the room. He allowed himself to look at her, see the subtle metallic thread in her top catching the lights and making her sparkle even more, and noted that her nipples stood erect before his gaze. He pulled in a ragged breath before dragging his gaze back up. Her expression softened as if she knew how hard he fought against himself.

He balled his free hand. He couldn't. He wouldn't. Giving in could never be an option for him. He took another sip of wine, then glanced down at the red liquid in the glass he held. He gathered his wits, looking up to see Duvall watching him with a frown.

"Come on, Gray," Elara said. "Tonight there's something completely different planned." She indicated an empty round table, and the three headed toward it.

He grabbed a seat, Elara sitting on his left. His hand itched to hold hers, but he fought the urge. The young ensign working duty took their orders and returned with another round of drinks. Duvall and Elara keyed in dinner options, and finally Grayson let his mind rest as the other two sat quietly, each probably lost in their own private thoughts.

"So, what's tonight's program?" Grayson kept his voice neutral.

Duvall grinned. "We found this ancient concept called a karaoke. It involves everyone getting up and singing a song." He laughed. "Apparently it makes for a fun evening. And as you know I've scoured everywhere for some great ideas to increase the camaraderie, especially with the newest recruits to fold into the crew. Everyone picks their own song and sings it."

Grayson frowned. "So not everyone sings the same song?"

"Oh no! The words are displayed on the screen so everyone can see whether they get them right or wrong. Of course no one is exempted if they are here." Elara chuckled. "Start thinking about your song."

Duvall clapped Grayson on the back, the warmth of the friendship giving him a subtle lift.

"What a fantastic idea." He forced the words out, but privately he wasn't so sure about the concept.

He watched as final meals were served to latecomers and the young ensign moved around with plates clutched in his hands. The room filled with the sound of laughter, the chinking of glasses on tables, and the rumble of conversation. Finally, Duvall pushed his drink aside, standing up and moving to the front of the mess.

"Welcome everyone. Tonight we have a treat for you. My good friend, our new ST here, has come up with a new idea. Well, we believe it's actually a really old one from before our interstellar travel days." He followed with the explanation of the concept of the karaoke. The crowd laughed, and Grayson could tell the idea went down well with those gathered in the room. Duvall reminded everyone that as the Master of Ceremonies for the evening, he alone could exercise his exemption, and a bubble of laughter enveloped the room once more.

Duvall called Elara forward first, and she grinned broadly as she stood, making her way toward the front, obviously primed as she'd already picked a song and was waiting for the beginning beats to play.

The first sounds rang through the air, and he remembered the song from her academy graduation, which he had attended with Duvall so long ago. She danced and gyrated with the song as she sang along, her eyes shining and her hair swinging, her body enticing him further with every movement. Her eyes never left his, and they shined brightly with an invitation his body clamored for him to accept. Dimly, he noted she had a melodic voice. Something inside him broke open, his restraint shattering as she undulated in time with the beat, and the promise of passion shimmered in the air between them.

He started to sweat, and his arousal soared to a feverish pitch. Watching those lips move and remembering the taste of her became unbearable. Unable to contain himself any further, he stood, pushing away from the table in jerky movements. His gaze narrowed as Elara made her way back toward the table, obviously having finished while he'd been lost in the struggle to control his body.

She watched him, her gaze hungry and a slight flush pinking her skin. She was clearly oblivious to those who glanced at them.

Grayson turned and started to move, heading out the door of the mess, when her small hand grabbed his.

"Elara..." Longing filled his voice.

"Please, Grayson."

He couldn't contain himself any further. Need sang through him. He surged through the door, dragging her behind him and to the side, roughly pushing her back to the wall.

A victorious groan rose as he plastered himself to her, his body screaming with the lust and passion he had fought for so long. Arousal roared through his system as he pushed up against her, savoring the touch of her body against his.

Opening his mouth and kissing her with every bit of pent-up lust inside him, years of longing poured out of him. The kiss, rocket hot, scorched everything in its path, and he felt it all the way to his groin. His erection strained against his pants.

Her lips parted under his, and he felt the touch of her tongue against his. She grabbed him and pulled him closer. She groaned into his mouth, and he pushed himself closer still, as close as he could get fully clothed and in the corridor of a battleship without completely forgetting himself.

She gave back just as hot. Her touch ignited him as her hands roamed over his body. If possible, his core heated further, demanding release from the torture. *Barsha!* How he wanted her. He raised his head. He knew she wasn't unaffected. Her face was flushed, her eyes glittering, and her chest heaved. He swung back to lean against the wall next to her, gasping for breath while his fingers groped for hers.

"So, what now?" she whispered to him. She turned in his direction, and their gazes collided. Her eyes held an invitation he could no longer deny.

He pulled away from the wall and towed her along the corridor toward his cabin. Thank *Eshra* his cabin was on the main level. She followed him, her hand fluttering in his grasp.

When he stopped outside his door, the last shred of sanity returned, brittle beneath the raging feelings. "If you don't want this, tell me now. Once I start, I don't think I can stop." His voice was graveled and tight, just like his body, and he felt amazed he could even get the words out. His chest shuddered with the effort of stopping himself from throwing her through the door and onto the floor, taking her right there on the carpet.

He watched her, waiting and holding his breath, praying she would accept, yet something in the darker recesses of his brain cried out *what will I do if she turns away now?*

"I've never wanted anything more, Grayson." Her eyes softened, and her hand, so dear to him and yet so scarred, reached up and pushed away a lock of his hair, brushing against his face. "I want what we can have." Then she smiled.

He palmed the door, and they entered together.

# Chapter 4

Elara's heart thudded and thumped in her chest. He'd accepted it, this passion she'd carried for him for so many years. She was exulted.

When they entered his cabin together, he turned and she reached out with a shaking hand. Grayson moved closer while she caressed his back with her thumbs. He pulled her toward him, their lips meeting and clinging.

The kiss deepened. Heat seared her, while their mouths opened, and tongues danced. He grabbed her shoulders and pulled her against his body. She could feel his strength, and she shivered with anticipation. Her body tightened as his hands traveled down her back, toward her butt, pulling her even tighter so there was no doubt of his body's reaction.

"Oh, Grayson!" She couldn't help it, as she exhaled the words, the feeling of his erection through his flight suit, so hard against the softness of her body had her straining for more.

Her back arched and his lips skimmed from her mouth across to her cheek and down her throat, scorching her; everywhere they touched, her skin burned.

Grayson's hand slid up her body and around to grasp her breast underneath the light top, kneading and firming. The ache inside her intensified, and she cried out. She squirmed, trying to reach him, the sensations coursing through her body, firing her at his touch.

"Perfect. So damned perfect," he muttered, and the secret recesses in her body melted. "By *Eshra*! I've wanted you for so long, Elara. Let me see you. Touch you. I need you."

His words were guttural now, and she looked up. His beautiful blue eyes glittered with the light of need.

She felt so womanly, something she'd never before thought she could feel. Her scars had turned off so many men, but Grayson... He'd always looked beyond them to see her. He alone saw the person within, and finally, the woman with needs and desires. She let the thought skitter away as he once more touched her, no longer tentative, his blunt fingers exploring slowly.

Her answer was to simply help him peel her top over her head. To begin undoing her loose pants, slipping the buttons through their loops slowly while watching his face as his hands traveled her body. She only got two undone before he pushed her fingers aside and completed the task.

It was as if his whole being focused on watching her. Slowly, oh so slowly, he brushed the open sides further apart, his features hard with need.

She reached for his suit, and he allowed her to slip the buttons through. "You are so beautiful," she said, her voice husky as inch after glorious inch of his magnificent chest appeared. No hair, she noted, just beautiful chest shining in the half-light of the cabin and waiting for her hands and her mouth.

"No, that's you, Elara. You're beautiful inside and out."

Then there was no room to talk as their mouths fused. His mouth held hers captive, his tongue dancing with hers in a rhythm that aroused as Grayson pushed her gently down to the bed. His hands shook as he peeled away her pale pink bra and slid the panties from her body. The ones she'd chosen to wear for him.

She reached for his underwear and pushed it down. *Finally!* He was hers. Her body shivered with anticipation. She gloried in his hot looks, the long, drugging kisses, and the scorching touch of his hands.

His fingers trailed up and down her body, arousing her to a fever pitch, touching her breasts. He bent forward to dot tiny kisses on her nipples, blowing, then opening wide to suck her nipples inside his mouth.

She writhed beneath him, clutching his body closer to hers, burning hot with a passionate fever only he could quench.

Coherent thought fled as she moved beneath practiced hands, heaving each breath and glorying in his touch. "Please!" Her entreaty was breathless, but his hands still moved slowly, finding their way down her body to the juncture of her thighs.

He carefully pushed them apart before brushing over her most intimate skin and laying the head of his cock against her empty core. As he slid within, she arched again, needing the connection of skin to skin.

Elara cried out as her orgasm rippled through her. "Grayson!"

He moved slowly, letting her settle, and she gripped him tightly as his thighs trembled, her brain once more consumed with need. She shuddered as she touched him, running her hands down his body to grasp his erection. She rubbed him and told him with quiet words how much she wanted him.

"I've wanted to touch you for so long." She looked into his eyes.

He moved inside her faster once more, and he murmured incoherently as she twined her legs around his hips, his words of love spilling from him as she arched, orgasming once more with a cry. He rubbed over her while she regained herself, heart thudding in her chest, but he didn't release the sensual tension fully.

His mouth found her collarbone, and she shivered as he laved it. When he pulled away, she was mindless as sensation after sensation washed over her, lapping at her beleaguered mind.

"I'm going to make you want only me. My cock, buried deep inside you."

She moaned low in her throat.

One of his hands gripped her breast, fingers finding her sensitive nipple and flicking gently while the other gripped a buttock, Grayson's hand silently urging her to slide up and down his length. Then he kissed her, wild and dark. She angled upward, wrenching her mouth from his, and watched his face.

He stilled his actions and reversed their positions so she

splayed over his supine body. "I love you, Grayson. I always have, and I always will." She moved around him, undulating over his body. He pushed upward into her, and suddenly the fire took them. He pushed and pulled, and she met every thrust with her own. Her legs gripped his hips.

Her hands twining in his hair, she rode him furiously. Finally, when they both thought they couldn't go any further, with one tremendous burst, they both found heaven.

✪ ✪ ✪ ✪ ✪

Resting in his arms afterward, Elara turned to him. "I do, you know. I love you. I always have." Her eyes burned with tears and her chest swelled.

For so long he'd denied them both. She needed to make sure he understood both the depth of her emotions and the relationship she wanted with him. It would take time to grow a secure relationship, but if they were committed to making it happen... She smiled.

"I love you too, Elara. I really want this to work." His words took her by surprise, warmth filling her.

She rubbed her hand over his chest. "If that's the case, then why did you run?" He grunted. "It's hard..."

"No, it isn't. You've already done the hard bit." He blushed and she almost choked on a chuckle. "I don't mean that!"

"I was afraid." He paused and she waited, knowing he had to say the words to understand his fears fully. "I thought... I thought it was because I was there, you know. On the day you were found."

She sighed, appreciating just how much the words hurt him. It only increased her tenderness. "I can understand that. From a purely psychological perspective, I can tell you that if that were the case, I'd probably feel the same for Duvall."

He stiffened beneath her gentle touch. "I don't. You do

understand that, right?"

For a moment her breath stuck while she waited, her whole body tense. How would he respond? Her breath escaped on a sigh when he nodded. "I do."

"Good. Then that's one thing out of the way. So let me be clear, I know you've worried that my feelings came because you were the one that saved me all those years ago. It's more and bigger than that. It's... Every time I saw you, I needed to be with you. Not all the time, because I know that's not healthy. But the connection between us, the friendship, it was never enough. It didn't fill the hunger inside me."

His face took on a surprised look, and she thought it was time to take pity on him. "Besides, if that's all it was, I think it would have worn off by now with all the chasing I've had to do." Her voice was tender but filled with a soft humor. "Only my love has pushed me through the years to get to here. Where I need to be. With you." She lifted a hand and slowly, carefully, brushed a strand of hair away from his face.

He held her tightly in his arms, and she knew he was finally ready. The man of her dreams had accepted everything she held in her heart.

✪　✪　✪　✪　✪

Elara rested beside Grayson while he lay there thinking over all the things she'd said. How she loved him and had waited, even when he'd stubbornly refused to accept the truth.

"I should have done this sooner," he said.

"Yes, you should have." She gave a snicker and rolled over, drawing a path along his chest. Tiny flickers of fire followed the trail.

"I need to think." He groaned at her muffled laugh. "Tomorrow, we sit down and work out what we'll do. How to make sure we stay together."

"Or we could talk now."

"We could. But right now I have other plans." With a lightning quick roll he surged above her, her gasp of surprise filling the cabin. "Elara, through my stupidity I nearly lost a treasure I didn't know was mine. Stay with me. Share my forever." "Yes." She reached up and tugged him closer.

He sealed her answer with a kiss.

# About Imogene Nix

Imogene is published in a range of romance genres including paranormal, science fiction, and contemporary. She is mainly published in the UK and USA due to the nature of her tales.

In 2011, Imogene Nix was born at the Bondi ARRA (Australian Romance Readers Association) Conference. Returning from the conference enthused, Imogene sat down and worked tirelessly for three months culminating in the book *Starline*. This book became the first in the Warriors of the Elector series. In fact, she has completed six entire series. Imogene has successfully been contracted for twenty-five titles and self-published three others under this pseudonym. She has also completed another three and is, like many of her contemporaries, seeking homes for these books—with at least one likely to be self-published once ready.

Imogene is a member of a range of professional organizations, including Romance Writers of Australia (where she holds a committee position as the Public Relations). She is also a member of Romance Writers of America, FFP (Fantasy, Futuristic, and Paranormal) Chapter of RWA (US), Australian Romance Readers Association (ARRA), Science Fiction Romance Brigade (SFRB), Dark Siders Down Under (the Australian Paranormal, Fantasy, and Futuristic Chapter of RWA), Erotic Writers of Australia, and Queensland Writers Centre and most recently Romance Writers of New Zealand.

Imogene's Website: www.imogenenix.net
Reader eMail: imogene@imogenenix.net
Newsletter: eepurl.com/cp-bZD

# Books by Imogene Nix